THE SHAMAN'S GAME

Books by James D. Doss

The Shaman Sings
The Shaman Laughs
The Shaman's Bones
The Shaman's Game

THE SHAMAN'S GAME

A MYSTERY

James D. Doss

AVON BOOKS, INC.
1350 Avenue of the Americas
New York, New York 10019

Copyright © 1998 by James D. Doss
Interior design by Kellan Peck
Visit our website at **http://www.AvonBooks.com/Twilight**
ISBN: 0-380-97425-8

Library of Congress Cataloging in Publication Data:
Doss, James D.
   The Shaman's game : a mystery / James D. Doss.—1st ed.
      p.   cm.
   1. Moon, Charlie (Fictitious character)—Fiction. 2. Police chiefs—Colorado—
Fiction. 3. Ute Indians—Colorado—Fiction. 4. Ute Indians—Colorado—Folklore—Fiction.
5. Colorado—Fiction.
   I. Title.
PS3554.O75S5   1998
813'.54—dc21   98-4494
                                                                                CIP

First Avon Twilight Printing: September 1998

AVON TWILIGHT TRADEMARK REG. U.S. PAT. OFF. AND IN OTHER COUNTRIES, MARCA REGISTRADA,
HECHO EN U.S.A.

Printed in the U.S.A.

FIRST EDITION

QPM   10   9   8   7   6   5   4   3   2   1

For Jeremy Katz and Susan Ginsburg

And all my days are trances,
And all my nightly dreams
Are where thy gray eye glances,
And where thy footstep gleams—
In what ethereal dances,
By what eternal streams.

—Edgar Allen Poe,
From *To One in Paradise*

"It is not known how many days the dance will last.
. . . It is like an angel comes and stands by his bed while
he is sleeping and tells him he should be Sun Dance
Chief, and tells him how he should run the dance, and
how long it should be."

—Anne M. Smith,
Ethnography of the Northern Utes

THE SHAMAN'S GAME

CHAPTER 1

It is the final day.

Almost the eleventh hour.

Far overhead . . . unseen by mortal eye . . . the hawk circles slowly. And waits.

On the parched plain below, encircled in a dry embrace of willow bones, is the annual ritual . . . the acceptance of pain.

Here are men with numb, heavy legs . . . blistered, bleeding feet padding on sun-baked earth . . . swollen tongues whisper prayers for healing . . . for the flesh . . . for the soul.

In this place . . . men launch quests for visions.

Some . . . make fatal decisions.

It is the Sun Dance.

In the center of the enchanted circle stands the sacred tree.

1

With patient monotony, the Cheyenne drummers thump the taut rawhide.

The crippled Paiute singer wails his tales of times when animals walked and talked like men.

On the first day, there were sixteen enthusiastic dancers. Now, a trio of weary men shuffle their feet and sweat . . . and bleed.

Joseph Mark—his brothers of the Blue Corn Clan call him the Sparrow—is the last Shoshone still able to stand before the consecrated tree.

Only these dancers remain with the Sparrow: the hatchet-faced Sioux and the skinny white man.

The other Shoshones have spent all the strength that was in them . . . and then borrowed. Their debt is a heavy one.

And others have given it up. A glum Blackfoot reclines on a blue cotton blanket, his knees drawn close to his chest as if he would withdraw into the womb of the earth. A dusky Bannock sits in the dust, a hollow look in his yellowed eye . . . muttering incoherently . . . shivering as if he were cold. Even the brash young Ute from the land beyond the southern mountains is finally too exhausted to stand in the sun. Though his head is unbowed, he is now a spectator . . . though of a more exalted rank than the scattering of visitors who sit along the north wall of the brush corral.

But the lone Shoshone has not retreated from his quest.

The Sparrow's coarse black braids are streaked with gray; his eyes are like slits cut in leather. The Shoshone dancer wears a single garment—soft deerskin breeches decorated with a shimmering fringe of porcupine quills. His lean body is unadorned except for this: from wrist to shoulder, his arms are painted a garish blue. A cord of braided horsehair is looped around his neck; suspended from this is a whistle fashioned from the hollow bone of an eagle's leg. Fixed to the whistle with twists of dried sinew are two small plumes from the same bird.

His parched lips are cracked like the bed of a dry pond, his swollen tongue might be a lump of sandstone in his mouth. The soles of the dancer's feet are padded with stinging blisters; a doughy mixture of blood and dust is caked between his toes. The insatiable sun has roasted his lean body . . . and basted him in a salty broth of tears and sweat. Now he feels hungry tongues of fire lick at his face . . . and his fingers . . . the flames taste him. Will he be swallowed up?

A part of the Sparrow's mind whispers urgently to him: *Withdraw now . . . you have played the man . . . take your rest . . .*

But he is a stubborn pilgrim.

And so close to his heart's desire.

The lone hawk leans into the wind . . . and circles lower. And watches.

A spectator winds the coiled steel spring in a cherished pocket watch. Tiny segments of time . . . links in an infinite cosmic chain . . . are pulled along by minuscule toothed wheels. As the tiny gears' teeth bite and swallow the seconds, thin metallic hands rotate on the ivory face of the timepiece. They can only revolve clockwise, of course—toward the future. Minutes thus digested can never be tasted again. Not in Middle World.

Like all genuine revelations, it comes suddenly . . . without warning. Without expectation.

The blue-armed dancer's agony is set aside—into some remote partition of himself. The Shoshone has almost ceased to exist in this exhausted body . . . even in this world. Now the Sparrow dances in *another* world. It is a place of astonishing, unnamed colors. There are fleeting shapes of shaggy horned beast and rumbling cloud-spirit, rolling streams of crystalline waters. Voices of ancestors and spirit winds sing together among the peaks of snowy mountains.

In Middle World, the spectators, the other dancers . . . these mortals hear only the incessant thumping on the rawhide drums and the monotone, nasal voice of the aged Paiute singer. It is a familiar song called Flathead Woman Who Took Grizzly Bear for a Husband.

But for the isolated dancer, perceptions are of another kind. Though the pain has remained in Middle World with his physical body, all his senses—shaped and honed by the suffering of the vision quest—are exquisitely sharp. And oddly inverted. Except for the sacred tree—and this symbol stands ever before him—the familiar landscape of Middle World is reversed. All is backward. Upside down. Inside out. The midday sky is a shimmering orange pool beneath his feet, the crude brush corral an enormous golden wreath floating above his head like a victor's crown. The frigid black sunlight makes his skin glisten with intricate patterns of frost. The other dancers, the drummers, the spectators . . . are naked, transparent . . . he can see their articulated bones and stretched tendons . . . all of their innermost parts.

The Sparrow must strain to hear the drum's hollow call. The old man's comic song about Flathead Woman's children by Grizzly Bear comes from impossibly far away . . . from another world. But in this new place, the smallest sounds are easy to hear. In his altered state of consciousness, the drone of a distant horsefly is a humming whirlwind in his head . . . he hears the labored breath of another dancer . . . even the pop-snap as the eyelids of a spectator close and open.

And he hears his heart pumping the blood of life.

Thu—whump. Thu—whump. Thu—whump.

And now . . . now he hears many hearts beating . . . many hollow drums drumming.

One heart drums much faster than the others.

The anomaly shrieks at him—but this warning he does not hear.

The Paiute elder ends his song.

The Shoshone puts the eagle-bone whistle to his raw lips; he blows one long, shrill note, then another. He dances forward—just three halting steps. He reaches forth with the tip of his finger. To *touch* the sacred tree!

The white man, who understands that the blue-armed Shoshone is reaching a climactic point, dances backward to the edge of the corral. He squats and leans his bare back against the rough weave of willow branches that make a coarse wall behind him. The weary Sioux dancer, also sensing the approach of the Power, retreats respectfully toward the rim of the circular enclosure and dances in place. He watches the visionary . . . and attempts to swallow the lump of envy that is lodged in his throat. Aside from the Shoshone, the Sioux, and the white man, a dozen exhausted dancers are gathered around the inner wall of the makeshift corral. Some are huddled in dusty blankets. A few sleep fitfully, feverishly—they dream of cool water to drink. Now, one man nudges another; some are awakened from their uneasy slumbers. There is an urgent whispering in the brush corral, a perceptible gathering of tension. The drummers, at a nod from the Sun Dance chief, cease their drumming and lay aside the leather-padded sticks. The chief of the dance nods again at the Cheyenne drummers. The eldest of the trio begins . . . in a slow rhythm . . . to drop the palm of his hand upon the taut rawhide. It is like the muffled boom of distant thunder. Participants and spectators alike lean forward in anticipation; they squint at the solitary dancer.

The Sparrow raises his arms before the tree, which has neither leaf nor limb, bark nor root. It is, to the eye of the uninformed, little more than a twelve-foot post with a fork at the top. It is decorated with painted stripes and satin ribbons whose significance is obscure to the scattering of curious tourists who have come to spend an hour gawking at the Sun-Dancers.

The supplicant's lips move. In silent prayer, perhaps. Even he does not understand these words he utters, this archaic language he speaks.

Someone flips open the golden cover on an antique timepiece. The black hands sweep across its eyeless, ivory face. And the little clock ticks . . . and ticks . . . and ticks.

The blue-armed warrior has passed through the nested circles of fire . . . that shimmering tunnel between worlds. Now, the Sparrow stands before the Tree. Not the imitation, not the symbolic version that has been ceremonially "shot" by a flint-tipped arrow. Not the cottonwood post that has been "planted" by Shoshone elders in the center of the crude brush corral that stands within sight of Crowheart Butte.

No.

He stands before the eternal Tree. Even as he watches, its emerald branches bloom with flowers of scarlet, indigo, and gold. The blossoms are alive, and each flower has an eye—and can see into the spirit of the man. And through their eyes, he also sees himself. Transparent, he is . . . a man not of flesh, but of a bluish-white fluid. Like molten glass. His heart is a flickering flame, his brain a burning ember, his bones like the supple shafts of the red willow. He marvels at the zigzag line connecting his head to his heart.

A sweet, resonant voice tells him this:

> Before time was, this path was made by the Creator.
> He is about to glimpse . . . the infinite mysteries of Wakantanka.
> If he will only ask, he will be healed of his afflictions.

He strains to hear the voice of his Beloved. It is a whisper . . . it fades away . . .

But his ears hear something else. Something back in Middle World.

> The timepiece ticks.
> Once. Twice. Three times.
> And then, it is the eleventh hour. Too late, it is.

In the Shoshone's ear, each tick of the chronometer is the sharp crack of a bullwhip. And now there is an odor . . . the dancer pauses and sniffs the air. This is a very bad thing . . . it should not be in this sacred place. The Sparrow tells himself that this smell is only his imagination. It is not real. He wants to believe this. But he knows. Something that should not be . . . is here. In this sacred lodge of the sun.

For a few heartbeats, a suffocating fear covers the dancer—but this must be overcome. Deny the fear or the Power will vanish like smoke in the wind. Even his life may be taken away. He raises the whistle to his lips . . . and blows a shrill, wavering note to frighten the demon away.

It is not enough.

Now the sun's rays are sharp . . . many small blades cutting his flesh. The drumbeat is louder now; it synchronizes with his faltering pulse and throbs in his head. The world is no longer upside down. The familiar yellow dust is under his bleeding feet, the pale blue sky far above his head. And he cannot swallow . . . his thirst is almost unbearable.

Even the tourists can see that something has gone wrong . . . they murmur uneasily among themselves. An aged Shoshone woman sits at the entrance to the Sun Dance Lodge; she vigorously shakes a willow branch to encourage the faltering dancer. "Shu-shu," she calls, "shu-shu . . . "

He lifts his head to the tree. Yes . . . yes . . . the Power is surely not far away. With dogged determination, the blue-armed Shoshone accepts the pain. He resumes the dance and waits longingly for that somber voice from the mountains.

It is not to be.

Once again, he smells the dreadful odor. He would run, but where can a man hide from such evil as this? The blue-armed warrior makes his decision. He must face this assault. He opens his eyes.

And sees.

Another face stares back at the dancer. These eyes are at once eager . . . hungry . . . desperate . . . almost pleading. The hands . . .

the fingers . . . they move just so on the *thing* . . . the gesture is an unspeakable obscenity.

Surely, this is also an illusion.

The Shoshone turns his back on this dreadful abomination, his head swimming. No, such a thing cannot happen. It is like the bad smell . . . a thing in his mind . . . not real.

But his fears overwhelm him. The sickness comes suddenly, like a rumble of thunder in his belly. He bends at his waist . . . clenches his fists . . . and shudders like a man suffering the final chills of a deadly fever.

The blue-armed warrior has but one hope . . . that the end will come soon.

The Sparrow hears the whuff-whuff of great wings cutting the air . . . and the mournful call of that solitary spirit who nests in the darkness of Lower World and feeds among the deep shadows of Middle World.

Now, it calls to him.

By his very name, it summons him.

And then . . . he feels the sting of death in his flesh.

From the deep pit, with the stink of death upon his wings, cometh the ravenous owl.

To devour the wandering soul.

From heaven's light, the hawk's feathers gleam like burnished brass. He folds his crimson-tipped wings . . . and falls to earth.

His eye is on the sparrow.

One Week Later

It was a long walk to this place; his journey began while there were stars in the sky. Now it was hot enough to keep the blue-tail lizards content.

Only a few thousand years ago, this had been a lush land

of knee-high grasses and small lakes lined with reedy marshes. There had been mammoth and giant bison in this place, even camels and pygmy horses. And men with short spears and throwing sticks. All were gone. Now this was a sun-baked desert. Dotted with forlorn clumps of mesquite, greasewood, and tumbleweeds that rolled before the winds. And the occasional stunted piñon or juniper, like deformed children cast out from their tribe.

He paused from his labors and straightened his back, grateful for the late afternoon shade under the anvil-shaped sandstone overhang. He blinked at the crude sketches etched into the stone over his head. A meandering snake with a diamond-shaped head. Twin zigzags of lightning. Nested circles that were the shaman's tunnel to other worlds. Stick-figures of dancing men and four-legged animals that might have represented deer. The thirsty laborer took a long drink of tepid water from an aluminum canteen. He opened a small can and speared Vienna Sausage with the blade of his pocket knife. As he enjoyed his modest meal, he thought about how it was good to live on the earth. He also thought about his prospects. All day he'd dug in the rocky soil. And what did he have to show for it? Nothing. But it was here.

He could *feel* it. In the tingling of his fingers.

After a short respite, he was on his knees again. Prying at slabs of reddish-brown sandstone, scooping up handfuls of grainy soil. He did not move the earth with pick or shovel. His tool was an archaic one—a sturdy oak staff, its sharpened end hardened in the hot ashes of a campfire. He worked slowly. Deliberately. With the patient determination of one who knows what he wants. Many drops of perspiration fell from his face into the oblong hole.

Wait . . . here was something.

He removed a glossy sliver of stone and held it up to the light, turning it over this way and that. He rubbed off the dust of ages with his thumb. A thin flake of gray flint. It had been carried to this place; it showed signs of having been worked by the hand of man. There was delicate chipping along one edge.

Probably used for skinning rabbits, he thought. Nothing to brag about. But still, it was a sign. He dropped it into his shirt pocket.

Only minutes later, under a broad slab of stone, he found the earthenware jar. The ceramic vessel was resting on its side. It had a long neck and was painted in bold black and white stripes. He removed the artifact and inspected it with some interest. Yes. This was pretty old stuff. Anasazi. Inside, there might be remnants of an offering. Corn pollen to be returned to the Thunder Gods. Or food for that long journey into the land of shadows. He placed the artifact on a heap of rubble near the small excavation.

Using his folding knife, he began a careful excavation around the place where he'd unearthed the ceramic vessel.

It was as he expected—the bones were beneath the place where he'd found the long-necked jar. The skeleton was an adult, knees pulled up near the chest. The skull rested on its side, the lower jaw separated in a garish grin. Half of the teeth were missing, the others worn to the dentine by consumption of flinty blue corn ground into gritty meal on granite metates. The ribs were soft, the pelvis crumbling. The finger-bones were in pretty good shape. The feet, which had been intercepted by the hole of a burrowing rodent, were little more than splintered flakes. The long bones, though yellowed with age, were in excellent condition. He tapped a femur with his knuckle. Hard as rock.

A large oyster shell lay beneath the jawbone on a section of vertebrae. This ornament had a pair of holes drilled in it. He marveled . . . this had been brought all the way from the Gulf of Mexico . . . or the Pacific coast. Either way, a long walk. The shell pendant reminded him that these were the remains of a person who had lived and breathed . . . and died. He spoke to the Old One. "Who were you, Grandfather . . . what was your name?"

As if in answer, a hesitant stutter of thunder spilled over the barren wastelands. He paused from his work, raising his head to squint at the source of the sound. A half-dozen miles to the northwest, there was a heavy cloud. Attempting to speak . . . to water the earth . . . but this precious moisture would evaporate before reaching the ground. Long, pointed gray wisps hung from the broad chin of the thunderhead.

"Cloud Whiskers," he muttered with a glance at the yellowed skeleton. "So that was what you were called. Yes . . . a good name."

There were flashes of blue-white light—so intense that he instinctively raised his hands to shield his eyes. Now the storm seemed to be a living thing. For a moment, the approaching cloud stood on trembling legs of lightning . . . shuddering like an old gray horse about to collapse. And then it bellowed thunder . . . terrible, elemental sounds . . . like great mountains tumbling down.

The intruder had no doubt that this was the protesting spirit of the Old One whose rest he had disturbed. It was a natural thing that Cloud Whiskers wanted him to go away, leave these bones in peace. But the trespasser would not depart from this sacred place. *Could* not until he had accomplished his grim task. He set his jaw and turned once more to his work.

It was almost dark when he turned his back on the ancient burial site and trudged away toward that place where a faint smudge of scarlet stained the western horizon. This man who had worked so hard had taken nothing to sell to those wealthy collectors of ancient artifacts. He had returned the valuable ceramic water jar to its resting place in the dust of ages. The remarkable shell gorget remained upon the crumbling vertebrae of the Old One. After carefully refilling the hole, he had brushed a juniper branch over the ground to disguise any remaining evidence of his diggings.

Weary from his labors . . . and satisfied . . . he longed for home. But his work had only begun.

The Following Summer
Yellow Jacket Canyon, Colorado
The Tree

It was barely past dawn in the rugged country. Aside from Poker Martinez—the Ute Mountain Sun Dance chief—there were about thirty men in the crew. Because of the sacred nature of their duty, all were either Sun-Dancers or men approved by the chief. Stone Pipe, the hard-eyed Sioux, was here. Even the white Sun-Dancer, the thin *matukach* who calls himself Steele, had been permitted to participate. The chief couldn't remember the pale man's first name. Didn't matter. All white men's names sounded much alike. Aside from a half-dozen "Southerns" from Ignacio who were trusted relatives, the rest of the crew were men of the Ute Mountain tribe. Most of these lived within ten miles of tribal headquarters at Towaoc.

Many of the men were leaning against dusty four-wheel-drive pickup trucks and battered jeeps. They talked quietly about how bad this pitiful excuse for a road was, about what the Denver Broncos might accomplish next season, about tribal politics. And, of course, about women. Most drank steaming coffee from vacuum bottles or plastic cups. The younger men munched on bologna or cheese sandwiches. For dessert they had little store-bought cakes with chocolate icing and white cream filling. The older men gnawed on beef jerky seasoned with black pepper and red chili, or they smoked cigarettes. All tried not to breathe the alkali dust whipped up by the capricious winds of early July.

The Sun Dance chief noticed that the white man munched a granola bar and drank distilled water from a plastic bottle. He was peculiar—like all the *matukach*. But not a bad sort.

Larry Sands—a Southern Ute—approached Poker Martinez. This fellow, nicknamed Sandman by his peers, showed no outward indication of disrespect to the Sun Dance chief. But neither was there the least sign of deference.

In clipped, matter-of-fact speech, Sands pointed out a few relevant facts to the tribal elder, who (he assumed) apparently didn't have any notion where he'd led the small caravan of vehicles. For one thing, the Sandman informed the old man, they had crossed the tribal boundary some miles back, where the jeep trail turned north at Moccasin Ditch. For another, they were on BLM land. Government land. He waited for a response.

The blank expression on the chief's face did not change. But inside, the old man burned. This smart-assed boy (who rarely spoke in the Ute tongue) had himself a framed piece of paper from a college. Worse still, there were nasty rumors that he planned to go away to some uppity university and study the white man's medicine. Eventually, he'd leave the reservation for good.

The young man waited, though not patiently. This old duffer apparently did not understand. Larry Sands resumed his polite report, but in a more urgent tone. It would not be lawful to remove a tree from this place—not without a federal permit. It wasn't a smart thing to do. Getting these tree-hugging Feds on your case was like having a cross-eyed bulldog bite your ass. They didn't let go till they got their chunk of flesh.

There were reasons that the Sun Dance chief did not care to hear about such things. For one thing, he had a toothache that had been throbbing since midnight. For another, his wife had presented him with cold cereal for breakfast. Little donut-shaped things floating in skim milk. The cold milk made his tooth hurt all the more. Absorbed in his miseries, he did not give a damn about white men's boundaries or rules. Without looking at the young man, the chief spat into the yellow dust. This was his answer. The Sandman retreated and said no more. Let the stubborn old bastard do as he wished. He smiled. Maybe the tree would fall on him. Hammer his hard head, drive him into the earth like an iron spike.

Poker Martinez growled to himself. Being Sun Dance chief

was a significant honor, it was true. But it was also a sharp pain in the ass—dealing with these young know-it-alls. And it was not like he had a choice about where to get the tree. He'd had two dreams. In the first dream, he had walked along the rocky banks of the Yellow Jacket, following the narrow deer path that led up the small branch called Burro Canyon. And he had seen the tree that must be taken. Just below an outcropping of dark sandstone, its thirsty roots fed by a trickle of a spring. The cottonwood would have a nice straight trunk, with a symmetrical crotch about sixteen feet above the ground. If it wasn't on Ute Mountain land, well that was just too bad.

In the second dream . . . well he had seen something even more important. The memory of that promise filled him with anticipation.

The old man folded his arms and surveyed his little band of Saturday warriors. He figured he had maybe ten good men, and most of these had seen at least fifty winters. The young fellows seemed to think this was a weekend picnic. Like going out to cut a Christmas tree. When these chubby town Indians had finished their sandwiches and sugar cakes and sweetened coffee, maybe they could manage to walk a mile or so to the place where the tree waited. He opened the door of his aged Dodge pickup and reached behind the seat for a parcel rolled up in an old bed sheet. He unwrapped a Brazilian lemonwood bow and a single arrow. The bow was store-bought and fancy; the arrow was not. The shaft was made of serviceberry wood; split magpie feathers served as fletching. Fixed to the business end was a pink quartz arrowhead his granddaughter had found down in the New Mexico desert, in the long shadow of Shiprock. With this arrow, the Sun Dance chief would shoot the tree he'd seen in his dream. Then, the older dancers would take turns putting ax to trunk. Novice dancers would have the honor of stripping off the bark and branches, and loading the post into Poker Martinez's battered old pickup. This afternoon they would drive up to the mountain, to the sacred Sun Dance corral, and dig the hole. Other Indians, even a few whites, could help with that. Tomorrow, right after the sun came up, the tree would be ceremonially "planted." Dead center in the brush corral. This would be followed by some drumming and singing. And praying. Before the sun had gone to rest behind the mountains, the Sun Dance chief would apply the paint and the banners to the sacred tree. It would be a good day.

And next week *taku-nikai*—"thirsty dance" would begin. Yes, everything would go well. It would be a fine dance.

This is what he thought.

CHAPTER 2

Ignacio, Colorado
The Play

All day, every minute, Myra Cornstone had been thinking about the man. In the mists of her imagination, she saw Charlie Moon. His tall frame, broad shoulders. His shy smile, quiet ways . . . his hands.

In an hour or so, she'd hear the rumble of his pickup truck coming up the lane.

And everything was just perfect! She'd driven all the way to Pagosa for her new dress, and it fit like the skin on a peach. Especially around the hips. Cute pleated skirt that fell just below her knees. Little white buttons down the front. She'd read in a magazine that buttons (especially down the front) were sexy. Gave men ideas. She intended to give Charlie Moon an idea or two.

The baby-sitter was early. Mrs. Martinez, the matronly woman from Ignacio, was already cuddling the baby in her arms and singing a sweet Hispanic lullaby. Chigger Bug was almost over his cold, and would behave. Most likely. And Myra's blind grandfather was listening to KSUT on his old radio. Maybe Walks Sleeping would also behave. With any luck, he'd soon nod off to sleep. When she got home, she'd pay the baby-sitter and put Chigger Bug in his crib. She'd feed the old man his nightly ration of fat-free ice cream, then lead him to the four-poster bed he'd been born in about a hundred years ago. Walks Sleeping refused to eat or go to bed when Mrs. Martinez was in his house. He swore that "the Mexican woman" would lace his beans with hot chile peppers and—after suffering great agony—he'd surely die from it. He also believed that "the confounded young woman" liked to watch him undress. Mrs. Martinez, who was past sixty, giggled about this. Said the old man had ugly knees . . . like an ostrich she'd seen at the Albuquerque Zoo.

Myra heard a heavy knock and glanced at her wristwatch. He was early. She smiled to herself. Maybe Charlie Moon was eager. She padded barefooted down the hall, buttoning her new red dress with both hands. Leaving the top button undone, she opened the door. There he was. All six and a half feet of him. Grinning sheepishly.

"Hello Charlie." She tried to sound like finding the big Ute policeman at her door was no big deal. Like she had lots of boyfriends dropping by. But Myra Cornstone's heart was thumping hard under her ribs. Affecting a casual movement, she pushed her long black hair back behind her ears. So Charlie could see the new rhinestone earrings.

He took his black Stetson off and ran his hand through his coarse hair. "Hi." Hmmm. She'd bought a new dress. Looked nice in it, too.

"Come in." She noticed his glance at her bare feet. "I've got to finish getting dressed." She thought he looked worried. "You're early."

"Well," he said, "we've got to pick up somebody before we go to Durango."

Myra's face froze. He was in his pickup, so surely this wasn't police business. "Who?"

He shot a sideways glance over his shoulder. Toward the desolate canyon country. Where a cranky old woman lived by herself. Unless you counted the dwarf . . . "Aunt Daisy."

"Oh." Her dark eyes went flat with disappointment. Daisy was a very traditional woman. And didn't approve of a Ute girl whose baby was fathered by a *matukach*. Especially when the Ute girl hadn't married the white man.

Moon turned the stiff hat brim in his hands. "She wants to go see the church play. I figured we could drop her off at Saint Ignatius and then head on up to Durango for dinner. And pick her up on the way back."

Myra smiled. That wasn't so bad. It would still turn out to be a great evening.

This is what she thought.

The priest pulled back an embroidered cotton curtain and peeked out the window.

They were already showing up. The graveled parking lot in front of St. Ignatius Catholic Church was occupied with all varieties of pickup trucks, shiny little Fords, Chevrolet coupes, a sprinkling of Toyotas, Isuzus, and Volkswagens. This turnout should have pleased the priest. But Father Raes Delfino was not altogether happy. It was not that he was *unhappy*, but the little shepherd felt stung to see this proof that his flock of Hispanics, Utes, and Anglos would turn out in far greater numbers for entertainment than for worship. The Jesuit, who was a scholar, had never wished to be a pastor. He'd wanted to teach, do research, write scholarly papers. But here he was. "God's will be done," he whispered.

The drive from her remote trailer home to Ignacio had been unusually silent.

Daisy Perika generally looked forward to these rides with her nephew. It was a fine opportunity to lecture the big policeman about his driving, how he should find a better job and make something of himself—and how he should get himself a wife. Maybe a woman from the reservation over in Utah. Get yourself a woman from Bottle Hollow, she liked to say. He never said anything in reply, just grunted.

Charlie Moon, as usual, drove about five miles over the speed limit and (the old woman thought) didn't miss hardly a single pothole in the road.

But one thing wasn't as usual.

The slender Ute woman who sat between them, that's what. The young woman who'd taken up with a worthless *matukach* cowboy and had his baby boy. The little boy was funny-looking. He had bright red skin. Like a sunburned white child.

Some of the old women had told Myra Cornstone that her son had a rash; maybe Daisy Perika could mix up a poultice for him. Myra, who thought it was funny, ignored them. She called her precious little red child 'Chigger-Bug' and was devoted to him.

Daisy Perika had heard the whole story. The freckled white man hadn't even been in town when his son was born. He'd come back from his so-called construction job when the baby was about two weeks old. He'd taken one long look at the drooling berry-red child, downed a half-pint of Tennessee whiskey, and left in his pickup truck for Las Vegas or someplace. After he was gone eight months without a word, his woman decided maybe he wasn't coming back. So Myra had started fishin' around for a man to share her bed—and help raise her son. Daisy Perika knew that this was all true because it was common tribal gossip. And, of course, the cause of a few lewd remarks and much chuckling.

Last year (so the gossips said), Myra had wiggled her skinny little hips at Scott Parris, Charlie Moon's best friend. Another white man, of course—wouldn't you know it? Daisy was of the opinion that Scott was an uncommonly good man—especially for a *matukach*. On top of this, he never did get drunk and he had a steady job as Chief of Police up at Granite Creek. Yes, even if he was almost twice Myra's age, he would've been a good catch. But in the end, he'd slipped off the hook and gone back to that pretty strawberry-haired woman who wrote stories for the newspaper up in Granite Creek.

So now (everybody was talking about it) Myra had cast her line for Charlie Moon.

It should have been okay with the old woman, both of them being Utes. But Daisy Perika—for reasons she wasn't quite sure of—didn't much like this match. Maybe it was because Myra'd taken up with the pitiful white cowboy rather than get herself a good Ute man in the first place. Maybe it was because Myra Cornstone had that sly, hungry look. Like a coyote bitch in heat. In the darkness of the pickup, she'd pressed her knee against Charlie's leg, and him tryin' hard to drive a straight line down route 151. And thought an old woman wouldn't notice.

Myra attempted to strike up a conversation with the tribal elder. "It's a nice night. Warm."

"Gmmph," Daisy replied, her reply barely audible over the rumbling drone of the big V-8 engine.

Myra was relieved to hear a sound from the old woman. "So you're going to the play at the church?"

"Sure," the old woman said in a pious tone, "I go to church every time I can." *Unless I got something else I want to do.*

Moon grinned to himself. At Father Raes Delfino's request, he'd cajoled his aunt into seeing the play. She'd relented, he thought, for two reasons. First, her friend Louise-Marie LaForte was an actor in the piece. Second—and most important—Daisy's TV set was in the shop for repairs.

"Well," Myra said brightly, "I bet you'll enjoy yourself."

Daisy wondered if they were really going to a restaurant up at Durango. *Probably you want Charlie to park down by the Rio*

Pinos . . . and you'll make your own little play. Maybe Myra wanted herself another baby. This one by Charlie Moon. These two needed looking after. She smiled sweetly at the Cornstone girl. "Why don't you two come and see the play with me?"

Myra hesitated. What she wanted was to be rid of this grumpy old biddy for a while. And have a nice, quite dinner with Charlie. They'd have little enough time. By ten that evening, Charlie had to be back in Ignacio. So he could pick up his aunt at the church. And haul her back to her trailer out in the wilderness south of Chimney Rock. Where she did whatever she did out there all by herself. Liking talking to a dwarf that was supposed to live in a badger hole in *Cañon del Espiritu*. What foolishness.

No, she didn't want to go to the play.

On the other hand . . .

Myra considered the fact that Daisy was an influential woman in the tribe—and she seemed to have some sway over her nephew. It wouldn't hurt to be on her good side. She swallowed hard and forced the words out. "Well . . . maybe Charlie and me could see the play"—she glanced uncertainly at the big policeman—"and *then* we could go to dinner. All three of us."

Daisy Perika smiled. This was a smart girl. Maybe she wasn't so bad for Charlie after all. He needed a clever woman to give him direction in his life.

Myra grinned up the big Ute. Like she'd done him a big favor.

The thought of delaying his dinner didn't particularly please Moon. His stomach growled in protest. He shrugged amiably. "Whatever you want." He wondered whether he had enough cash in his wallet for an extra mouth at dinner. When someone else was paying for her food, Aunt Daisy ate like a starved hog loose in a cornfield. Well, there was always the American Express card he hardly ever used.

Daisy, soothed by this victory, relaxed. "Charlie, you shouldn't drive so fast, you bein' a policeman and all. And try not to hit

so many of them holes in the road. It makes my backbone jangle."
She rubbed at the small of her back and managed a pitiful groan.

"Hmmph," Moon said. But he slowed down. It was a puzzle.
On the way to Aunt Daisy's trailer, Myra'd said she was famished
because she hadn't had a bite to eat since breakfast. But now she
wanted to see the church play *before* they went to dinner. And
she'd also said it would be nice for them to have some time alone.
And now she'd invited Aunt Daisy to go to Durango with them.
Women. They were sure hard to figure.

Fifteen minutes later, he turned into the parking lot at St.
Ignatius.

Old Popeye Woman

The small children in Ignacio were afraid of Stella Antelope.
They feared her because she was . . . different. It was not only
that she always wore coal-black dresses and a shawl that was just
as dark. Her shoes (one of which was custom-made by a German
craftsman in Denver) and stockings were also black. And it was
not only the children who turned their faces away from Stella.
There was, even the adults admitted, something about the aged
Ute woman that made them uncomfortable. If they had been
asked why, these citizens would have offered a variety of
explanations.

"I dunno. Somethin' kinda funny about her . . . don't you
think?"

"Well she's just . . . just peculiar, that's all. Gives me the
shivers."

"A damned *bruja*—that's what she is. Every time she walks
by my house somethin' weird happens. The milk goes sour or a
lightbulb pops or I get a prickly feelin'. Know what I mean?"

Stella Antelope's unfortunate combination of disabilities only
added to this sense of peculiarity. There was the deformed foot
that she dragged along at an odd angle. She had been born with

this burden. There was another disfigurement, and this frightened the children far more than the clubfoot. Stella's left eye protruded from its socket. This gave her a sly, sinister appearance—much like those evil witches in illustrated storybooks. It was because of this mild deformity that an unkind soul had once referred to her as "Old Popeye Woman." The name, sad to say, had stuck. And now, as a complication of untreated diabetes, the old woman was blind.

There were even a few adults—particularly among the Utes—who were certain that she *could* see, especially out of the left eye, that her blindness was a sham. The bulging orb, they insisted, was an *evil* eye . . . a mere glance from Old Popeye Woman could cause bad luck, sickness . . . perhaps even death. Why, anyone could see that.

But her friends knew that Stella Antelope was an uncommonly good soul. When someone died, Stella was always there for the family with offerings of food . . . and prayers. She gave ten percent of her meager income to St. Ignatius Catholic church. Father Raes Delfino, though moved by the poor widow's generosity, always found obscure ways to see that her tithe was more than returned. Her recompense would be a box of groceries left mysteriously on her doorstep, a druggist's bill paid anonymously, and other such kindly schemes. Stella had never seen through the good priest's subterfuges; these blessings remained a sweet mystery to her . . . perhaps the act of an angel . . . a messenger of God.

Who would deny it?

On this evening, from across the darkening street, it might appear that Old Popeye Woman was tied to the little boy who walked in front of her. The hank of clothesline rope was, in fact, fastened securely around the boy's slim waist. A knotted end of the rope was wrapped around her left hand; her cane was in her right. The boy led his grandmother at a slow pace that suited her creaking knee joints.

Stella's oak cane was painted with a gay double helix of broad red and white stripes, like a barber's pole or a Christmas peppermint. The walking stick made its rhythmic tap . . . tap . . . tap . . . as the odd pair marched slowly down the concrete sidewalk. Occasionally, the blind woman spoke to her guide child. As they crossed a narrow side street, she encouraged him about this evening's outing: "The church play will be very nice," she croaked, "You'll like it. Just you wait and see."

The little boy nodded, as if the blind woman could see him through the bulging eye, but he did not speak. Billy Antelope was a remarkably silent child. And a dreamer of dreams. He still had this one really bad dream. Daddy would come home yelling; he'd hit Mommy with his fist. In these dreams, Daddy would stand there frowning down at Mommy, like she ought to get up. Then, Daddy would go sit on the bed and cry for a long time. The dream always ended the same way. Daddy would wink at him, like this was a big joke. "You're a good boy, aren't you, son? Go outside now . . . run along to the neighbor's house." Then, Daddy would reach under a pillow for something. In this bad dream, Billy would leave the house like Daddy said, but he'd always turn around to look inside . . . to see if Mommy was going to get up off the floor. This was when he'd see Daddy put something long and dark into his mouth; like when he smoked one of his big black cigars.

And there would be this big booming noise . . . and he'd wake up screaming.

There, there, Gramma Stella would say. Hold on to my hand Billy. I'll sit here with you till you go back to sleep. Now, now, don't you cry . . . it was only a dream.

And he guessed it was. He couldn't remember anything about what had actually happened to Mommy and Daddy. Except that some people had taken Mommy to that pretty place down by the pond with the big goldfish, the place with bunches of big trees and yellow flowers. About four or five people came to see her pretty box put into the ground. One of the big kids at school told Billy that his old man was in the county graveyard where they buried poor folks and criminals. In a big Styrofoam box like a hamburger.

Grandma Antelope had come down to Arizona with Uncle Reuben, and they'd taken him back to Ignacio. Now he lived in her little apartment. Life was good. And the Ignacio community had bestowed a gift upon him. Like his grandmother, Billy had a descriptive, though less imaginative, nickname. He was Little Rope Boy.

The priest watched the audience assemble, and sighed. It was much like Sunday morning worship service; the citizens of Ignacio gravitated toward the seats in the rear.

But not the old Ute shaman. At Daisy Perika's insistence (she was determined to have a close look at Louise-Marie's performance), Moon led the women to the empty front row.

A hundred citizens of Ignacio were seated on a variety of folding wooden and metal chairs. The makeshift auditorium echoed with the unintelligible murmurs of many voices, impatient grunting from the elderly, whines from small children. There were suppressed giggles from girls in pretty print dresses who sneaked saucy looks at the boys in faded jeans and tee-shirts. Some of the younger members of the audience leaned against the paneled walls. A half dozen surly teenaged fellows stood in the rear, under the red Exit sign. The leader of the pack had a cigarette tucked behind his left ear, another chewed on a mint-flavored toothpick from Angel's Diner. They had lowered their voices at the appearance of the big Ute policeman. Last week Charlie Moon had caught two of them in the Sky Ute Casino. Their sins were multiple.

They were underage and drinking beer.

Harassing the honest gamblers.

They had not left when he'd asked them kindly.

This had been a mistake.

He'd carried the pair of them out by the seats of their britches, like they were sacks of small potatoes. And deposited them head-first in cans meant for trash. This was a great event that had caused much amusement among the Utes and townsfolk alike, so the toughs would not speak of this humiliation. They pretended, in fact, not to notice Moon's presence. If this damn silly play turned out to be as dull as they expected, they were outta here man. Some inhaled the corrosive fumes of filtered cigarettes. Others whispered vulgar jokes, snickered inanely, and winked suggestively at any girl who looked their way.

A few girls found all of this most appealing; most made a point of pretending that these nauseating, immature creatures did not exist.

All muttering ceased when the little boy entered, leading the old woman by the usual hank of rope looped around his waist. The blind woman grasped the knotted end of the cord; the red-and-white cane tapped tentatively on the scuffed hardwood as they moved down the center aisle. Such a contrast they were. Little Rope Boy was barely six years old; a perfect picture of tender youth. His grandmother, Old Popeye Woman, was filled with years beyond reckoning. Like a few of the oldest Utes, Stella had no birth certificate or other proof of her age. Some said she was over a hundred years old, but she insisted that she had just turned eighty-nine. She had insisted upon this age for at least a decade. They moved as one. The child was the eyes, she the voice. Together, some had observed, they were like a single person. Or a little engine pulling a ramshackle caboose.

Most of the crowd was hushed, absorbed in the small spectacle.

Daisy Perika heard the sudden quiet. She turned her head to see the pair. "Billy," she shouted hoarsely, "bring your grandma over here by me. I saved some seats for you."

A faint smile touched the child's lips; he led the old woman to the front row. She tapped along, seeming to stare through the bulging eye.

Daisy reached out and touched the wrinkled hand that gripped the gaudy barber-pole cane. With Daisy's help, the boy guided his blind grandmother into one of the uncomfortable folding chairs.

Old Popeye Woman sighed with relief as she sat down; the chair creaked under her slight weight.

Daisy Perika patted her friend's hand. "Hello Stella . . . how you been?"

Old Popeye Woman raised a brow over the singular eye. "I been better—about sixty years ago."

Daisy chuckled and reached to pull at the boy's ear. "Charlie's here with me," she said to the blind woman. "And," she added as an afterthought, "Myra Cornstone's here too. You know—Walks Sleeping's granddaughter." *The one who bedded down with a no-account white man and had herself a child who looks like a plump strawberry.*

"Ahhh," Old Popeye Woman said, "that's nice."

Myra smiled. "Good evening, Mrs. Antelope." She nodded at the blind woman's little escort.

Billy Antelope hung his head shyly. That big policeman sure had himself a pretty girl. *Maybe when I'm growed up, I'll be a policeman. Just like Charlie Moon. And have myself a pretty girl to go places with.*

Charlie Moon squatted in front of Stella. The Ute policeman murmured a greeting to the blind woman. She reached out to touch his face. He smiled and patted the boy on the shoulder. "Hello, Billy."

The child looked up with enormous brown eyes; he wiggled the fingers on one hand to acknowledge the greeting. He hoped everybody had noticed that Charlie Moon had spoken to him.

It was about to begin . . .

The priest parted the brown curtains and stood before the crowd. Unwelcome cigarettes were hastily concealed by the young toughs; smoke was swallowed with muffled coughing. Girlish giggles were choked up inside. The older parishioners, already weary of sitting in the hard little chairs, sighed with open relief. The sooner this thing got started, the sooner it'd be over.

Father Raes Delfino folded his hands prayerfully, smiled, and cleared his throat. "It is good to see so many of my friends . . . whose faces have become almost unfamiliar to me." There was nervous laughter from a few Hispanics and Anglo Catholics who had not been to church since Easter. The truant Utes offered him stony glares. The priest continued. "I am happy to welcome the Pauline Players, a group of traveling thespians from Denver. I think I can promise you a delightful evening." He clapped his hands lightly, and was joined by polite applause from the Hispanic and Anglo members of his audience.

The Utes, though an amiable bunch, did not applaud. A logical folk by nature, they could see no sense in being thankful for a mere promise. Talk was cheap stuff. When the thing was delivered, then they would judge its worth.

The priest continued, his voice tinged with genuine enthusiasm. "It is traditional that the Pauline Players use local talent whenever possible. We are particularly honored that one of our own will be an honorary member of the cast for tonight's performance."

Most of the audience already knew about Louise-Marie's part—it had been the subject of a feature story in the *Ute Drum*—so this got a murmur of approval.

"Louise-Marie LaForte," the cleric said, "is a faithful member of Saint Ignatius Catholic Church—a sheep of His fold—who attends services at least twice each week." Here he frowned meaningfully at the scattering of Catholic goats in the audience. "Louise-Marie will play the part of Tabitha." He turned and smiled at the invisible bustling in progress behind the curtains. "In her youth, Louise-Marie had professional experience in theater."

This was not an exaggeration. Her father, before he died in the War to End All Wars, was an itinerant magician. They had toured the small towns of Quebec, even the remote logging camps of the northern forests. The girl was routinely sawed in half, levitated over sharpened stakes, and made to disappear from cleverly devised wooden boxes. When Louise-Marie was a winsome thirteen, a grizzled farmer had stayed after the show to meet the players. After looking her up and down, and pulling on his beard, he offered to trade a half-dozen prime goats for the magician's slim daughter. The offer was gently refused by her amused father, who politely explained the importance of his daughter to the magic act. The goatherd hesitated, eyed the pretty child, then upped the offer by a dozen guinea fowl to boot. The father, who had a peculiar sense of humor, pretended to consider the offer. He rubbed his chin thoughtfully, then asked to inspect the livestock.

Much to the embarrassment of both men, Louise-Marie had burst into tears.

The goat-man had given it up as a bad deal and stalked away to his mule-drawn wagon.

"In addition to Louise-Marie," Father Raes added, "we have what I might call . . . " His voice trailed off, as if he could not find the words. Members of the audience leaned forward, the better to hear him.

Not unfamiliar with the effective use of drama, the little priest assumed a thoughtful expression and cocked his head. "We have, shall I say . . . a mystery guest. One of Ignacio's own has returned from afar to participate in this drama. But I will not tell you her name . . . " Now he smiled roguishly, "see if you are able to recognize her."

This brought raised eyebrows, much whispering and nudging and speculation. Whoever could it be?

The curtains parted. The darkened stage was populated by a scattering of simple furniture and a few still figures who tarried like ghosts in the shadows. A murmur of expectant whispers rippled through the audience. The women were nervous for Louise-Marie. Poor old thing, they whispered to their husbands and boyfriends, she would probably muff her lines. Maybe even trip over the furniture and fall down. Yes, the menfolk agreed—this might be a pretty good show after all.

All thoughts of Louise-Marie faded when a lovely blond lady stepped to center stage. The curtains closed behind her. No bigger than a girl, she wore an ankle-length white dress with a bright red sash—and tiny silver sandals. Her golden hair—such a divine contrast to her olive skin—was done up in a long braid; this was arranged artfully over her bare left shoulder.

Charlie Moon's eyes were fixed on the angel.

Little Rope Boy stared without blinking.

Even the punks leaning against the rear wall were entranced by the purity of her beauty. This must be the good fairy who'd left dimes under their pillows in exchange for bloody little teeth. But as the evening progressed, even they would understand . . . this was an angel from heaven.

Myra Cornstone glanced at her date. To her, it seemed that Charlie Moon's mouth was hanging open; his eyes popping. What big dummies these men were.

Moon leaned forward and stared. He surely had seen this woman somewhere before; but wouldn't he have remembered the gorgeous golden hair?

"It's just a blond wig," Myra whispered, as if she could read his mind. She could.

Moon barely heard Myra's voice. His mind was occupied with the slim but shapely figure . . . and those enormous dark eyes. Yes, there was something familiar about those eyes.

And then the angel spoke, and the voice was from his childhood. It was, in fact, a child's voice. Now he knew who it was. But when she'd left Ignacio to go off to college—was it three years ago, or more?—she'd been a pudgy little girl with long black hair.

"Dear brothers and sisters," the angel said with a sweet curtsy, "we are here to present a drama." She turned slightly and, with a wave of her delicate hand, indicated the actors hidden in shadows on the small stage. "Tonight, for your pleasure and edification, we will re-create a series of stories from the Acts of the Apostles."

The angel paused. For a moment, not a soul in the audience breathed.

The boy leaned close to his blind grandmother; he put his hand on hers.

Old Popeye Woman smiled; Billy was such a good boy.

"You," the angel made a gesture at those seated in the little hard chairs, "will see the Holy Spirit come as a mighty, rushing wind . . . and, like tongues of fire, rest on the followers of our Lord."

All eyes rested upon this lovely creature.

"At the gate of the temple called Beautiful, you will see a lame man healed."

Whispers, nods of approval. This'd be good.

Old Popeye Woman felt a slight tingle from her club foot. Wouldn't it be nice to be able to walk like a normal person, without dragging her foot behind her . . .

"You will see Stephen the deacon martyred . . . killed by stoning."

The softhearted sighed their sorrows; tears formed in three-score eyes.

"On the road to Damascus, you will see Saul blinded by God's light, and hear the mighty voice from heaven. And you will see his sight restored."

Yes! The audience was delighted. Even the teenage toughs were open-mouthed with awe.

Old Popeye Woman swallowed hard; she wished she could see . . . anything. Even a little speck of light from heaven.

The golden-haired angel paused, raised her arms to the crowd. "In Joppa, you will see Tabitha restored to life!"

There were whispers and speculation amongst the townsfolk. The Anglos wondered how they'd manage the special effects to make tongues of fire. The Hispanics—eager to see these staged miracles—waited with great anticipation. The Utes were ominously silent—this talk of raising people from the dead was dangerous. It could bring bad luck to visit. Ghosts might come calling. And spirits of the dead could bring sickness.

"And now . . . I invite you to enjoy that which has been prepared for you." The good fairy smiled and raised her hand in a gesture of heavenly delicacy. The house lights were dimmed.

Little Billy Antelope clapped with great enthusiasm, and this triggered immediate applause from the crowd.

Daisy Perika had been struggling with her memory to place that face . . . that voice. The light dawned. She nudged her nephew with a sharp elbow. "Charlie—I know who that is . . . that's Delly Sands. Larry Sands' little sister. Smartest girl ever to come from this tribe. And now she's lost her baby fat."

Moon nodded. "She sure has."

Myra repeated her earlier observation. "That's not her real hair. It's a wig."

"She used to be kind of heavy," Moon whispered in wonder at the ability of nature and time to transform a child into a woman, "and now she's so . . . so . . . "

"Thin as a rail," Myra said bitingly. "She must have been sick. Probably caught something up there in Denver." *Probably something contagious—like a venereal disease,* she almost said, then bit her lip.

Charlie Moon thought about that. It didn't make sense. Myra was as slender as Delly, and she hadn't been sick. "Delly looks well enough to me," the policeman said reasonably.

Myra wanted to hit him. Hard.

Daisy was delighted to see the little Sands girl, even if she was wearing yellow hair and dressed up kind of peculiar. She'd been off to college, so you had to make allowances.

Moon grinned. Sure was a lucky thing Myra had wanted to see the play.

Myra Cornstone wished she'd had better sense than to suggest coming to this dumb church play. She could have been alone with Charlie. It was all Daisy Perika's fault. If she hadn't been trying to please the old woman . . .

The angel bowed and disappeared behind the curtains.

Soon it would begin.

It began. And the little angel was the narrator.

The holy tongues of fire touched the apostles, who were

thereby enabled to speak in languages of the gentiles—and thus to their kinsmen who had lived for generations among the goyim.

An old Anglo man, crippled and bent with arthritis, wept at the healing of the beggar at the gate called Beautiful. *When will someone pray for me . . . when will I be healed?*

Stephen gave his moving speech about the history of God and Israel—and saw the portals of heaven open. Women wept openly as Stephen was stoned to death by the outraged mob; a few hard-muscled men also wiped at their eyes.

Saul, on his way to Damascus with legal documents that would empower him to arrest those who followed the Way, was blinded by the light from heaven. The voice of the crucified rumbled like August thunder and rattled the pine rafters. "Saul . . . Saul . . . Saul . . . " the voice called. It was terrifying. Small children hid their faces under mommy's arm; adults trembled in delicious fear. And yet the voice had a sad sweetness: "Saul . . . Saul . . . it is hard to kick against the cactus pricks . . . why do you persecute me?"

The Baptist minister from Bayfield was entranced, but he secretly wished they'd kept closer to the actual script in the Book.

But it was the finale that truly gripped the crowd. It began, as the other scenes had, with the stage darkened. The spotlight was on the narrator with golden hair, who stood primly at stage right.

"At Joppa," the angel called out in her sweet little-girl voice, "there was a certain disciple named Tabitha, which is translated Dorcas, which means deer, or antelope."

Stella Antelope nodded her approval and hugged her grandson.

"Now this woman was full of good works and charitable deeds which she did. But it happened in those days that she became sick . . . and died."

A few weary old women—those who felt the nearness of death—groaned inwardly.

"When they had washed her, they laid her in an upper room." A spotlight sent a beam onto a simple cot. The golden-haired angel turned to behold the figure of Louise-Marie, pale as a ghost, who lay under a thin blanket. She was very still.

There was a sympathetic murmur from the audience; a little Hispanic girl who knew and loved the old French-Canadian woman—Louise-Marie certainly *looked* dead—wept and hugged her mamma.

The angel smiled serenely and continued her narration. "Now since Lydda was near Joppa, and the disciples had heard that Peter was there, they went to him, imploring him not to delay in coming to them. Then Peter arose and went with them. When he had come, they brought him to the upper room."

A tall, bearded man appeared onstage. He was followed by several women dressed in dark robes.

The angel opened her little mouth and almost sang the words: "And all the widows stood by him weeping, showing the tunics and garments which Dorcas had made while she was with them. Peter sent them away; he knelt down and prayed."

The women departed, stage left. The bearded man kneeled by the cot. And he clasped his hands and prayed—silently.

Louise-Marie, the very image of a good corpse, did not stir.

His prayer finished, Peter turned to the body and said softly: "Tabitha, arise."

But she lay there—pale as a ghost—like a great sack of flour.

The women in the audience were in agony. What if Louise-Marie didn't respond . . . maybe the old woman'd had a stroke . . . perhaps she *was* dead . . . Oh, she'd make such fools of them all. Several of the men chuckled.

But Louise-Marie LaForte was not dead. Her chest heaved with a breath. And then . . . and then . . . she snored.

The audience was deathly silent.

"Wake *up* Louise," a little Anglo girl piped out. She was hushed by her mortified mother; there was a titter of nervous laughter from the audience.

Little Rope Boy smiled; this was great fun.

Old Popeye Woman, who could perceive the silent stage with

her mind's eye, sighed. That old woman was so vain about memories of her childhood "acting" career . . . Louise-Marie might die of embarrassment if this didn't come off well. Stella Antelope prayed for Louise-Marie. "God, please help her to wake up."

"Peter" was a trouper who'd played a thousand nights in a thousand little makeshift theaters. This actor was not ruffled; indeed, he was cool as ice. He slapped the cot with his palm and called out loudly: "Arise, Tabitha!"

Louise-Marie shuddered. She opened her eyes, blinked at the blinding spotlight focused on her pale, wrinkled face. She sat up, wondering why she'd left the bedroom light on and why was it so bright? She turned and drew a sharp breath . . . who was this nasty-looking bearded fellow wrapped in a bedspread . . . and why was he glaring at her? And what was he doing in her bedroom? She reached for the big revolver she kept under her pillow, but it wasn't there. And this didn't even look like her bedroom. Maybe it was a bad dream. Her chin trembled; she opened her mouth, as if to scream.

"God help us," Peter muttered under his breath. It was a most sincere prayer.

Old Popeye Woman intensified her own prayers.

And God answers such appeals in unexpected ways.

Daisy Perika, who was not three yards from the actors, cupped her hand beside her mouth: "It's all right, Louise-Marie. It's just a play. You settle down, now."

The old actress heard the Ute woman's calming words, and immediately it came back to her. Yes . . . this was the Acts of the Apostles play. The bearded fellow who looked so stern, he was the Apostle Peter. She smiled and blinked at the dark vault where the audience held its collective breath. She reached out to take Peter's hand. With heartfelt gratitude, he kissed her on the forehead. This was not in the script.

As one, the audience heaved a communal sigh of relief—many of the Catholics and Anglicans crossed themselves. The

Baptist minister thought the Apostolic kiss a good touch. Might've happened just that way . . .

Except for the spotlight on the blond angel, the small stage darkened.

The narrator's sweet voice floated like incense over the audience: "Then Peter gave Tabitha his hand and lifted her up, and when he had called the saints and widows, he presented her alive. And it became known throughout all Joppa, and many believed on the Lord."

Most of the congregation were inspired to their marrow.

Except for one among their number, the Utes shuddered at the thought of a dead body rising. Daisy Perika, the old shaman, was frowning at the stage. She was pondering what she'd seen. The Ute woman had known since she was a child that Jesus had raised that Lazarus fellow from the dead, but she'd never known that an ordinary fisherman like Peter had been given such powers by The Great Mysterious One. Yes . . . this was something to think about.

The curtains were closed.

The audience was transported back from the dim and miraculous past to the earthly present. From Joppa, in ancient Israel. To Ignacio, in Colorado. The applause was a sudden thunder that rattled every pane in the mullioned windows.

The curtains parted; the house lights were on. The entire party of players came on stage to bow and smile and wave. A little boy dressed in a crisp blue suit brought an armful of small bouquets and distributed them to the actors. The angel-narrator was taking her third bow when she recognized Charlie Moon. And smiled her angel smile at the big Ute policeman. Delly Sands blew a kiss; a dozen men and boys in the audience fantasized: *this kiss is meant for me alone.*

Little Rope Boy blushed; his heart pounded.

But the kiss was only for Charlie Moon.

Now Charlie did not know this . . . not for sure.

Myra Cornstone knew. For sure. And ground her teeth.

The curtains closed, for the final time.

Father Raes breathed a sigh of relief. And offered a prayer of thanks to God.

In the days that followed, a more cynical soul than the priest may have thought this expression of gratitude to be . . . somewhat premature.

The hall was almost empty. Billy Antelope had led his sightless grandmother away, one wrinkled hand gripping the hank of rope around his waist, the other grasping the red-and-white striped cane.

Daisy Perika had pulled her woolen shawl over her shoulders. The old woman stood patiently by Myra Cornstone, who tapped the toe of her shoe on the hardwood floor. Both women were watching Charlie Moon. Waiting for him to make up his mind to leave. Daisy was hungry for the promised free supper. Myra had lost her appetite.

The big Ute policeman seemed barely aware of their presence. Black Stetson in hand, he stood before center stage, directly in front of the part in the curtains. He thought maybe she'd be back. Hoped she would. He remembered Larry Sands' little sister from years ago, in the school yard. The plump little girl with the big eyes . . . years younger than him . . . following him around at recess. She was very shy . . . never speaking to him. Except with her enormous eyes. She had been a little sickly in those days. Something with her lungs . . . asthma, he thought. But she looked fine now.

It happened suddenly. The golden-haired angel fairly burst through the brown curtains. Even as she stood on the stage, Delly Sands had to look up at the policeman. "Charlie Moon," she said, and there were tears in her brown eyes.

He held his arms out and she leaped into his bearlike embrace; her sandaled feet hung barely below his knees. "Charlie, Charlie Moon," she said, "Oh Charlie . . . "

Moon held the little angel like a child hugs a favorite doll;

she was so small . . . and soft. He felt her warm breath against his neck.

Daisy Perika felt tears forming. She found an old red handkerchief in her purse and dabbed under her steel-rimmed spectacles at her eyes. Delly had always been such a sweet child. And everyone knew she'd always loved Charlie Moon. Everyone except Charlie.

Moon's date folded her arms and looked at the paneled ceiling. "This is sickening," she muttered.

After what seemed an age to Myra, Moon lowered the little angel ever so gently . . . so that Delly's feet touched the floor.

Myra watched the pair with a bitter, twisted smile. If she'd driven her pickup to town, she could leave now . . . but she'd rode in with Charlie. And a good girl always left with him who brung her. So she'd have to ride out the same way. Dammit.

There was a murmur of conversation between the tall man and the elfin woman. Delly wiped happy tears from her eyes, and laughed at some joke Moon made about how he didn't recognize her under all that makeup . . . had she bleached her hair?"

She giggled. "It's not my hair, Charlie, see?" She removed the blond wig and shook her black hair . . . it fell barely under her ears.

Moon pretended to be surprised that the yellow mop was a wig. Her hair used to be long. All the way down to her waist.

She patted at her head, replied that short hair was the latest style—didn't he think it was just too cute?

He said sure it was too cute and then something about his own hair being right in style if he got about three inches lopped off. And they laughed some more.

"She's such a sweet child," Daisy murmured to Myra.

"Yeah. Sweet." Myra choked back a surge of nausea. Maybe she could still catch a ride with someone. Get home early and save some of her hard-earned money on the baby-sitter's bill. She'd fix some ice cream for Grandpa, who'd be grateful . . . and she'd get a hug from her baby boy. Chigger Bug was always glad to hug her. And neither he nor Grandpa cared much for other women.

Moon, with the angel's tiny hand in his big paw, approached the women who waited. "You remember Delly . . . Delly Sands."

Myra tried to answer, but her throat was dry. She croaked incoherently, then nodded dumbly.

Delly Sands hugged Daisy Perika, then Myra Cornstone—who stood stiff as a post. Little Delly's enthusiasm was obviously genuine as she glanced from one face to another. But she saved her longest looks—her adoring looks—for Charlie Moon. "I'm so *terribly* happy to be back in Ignacio . . . spent some time studying drama at the university before I switched over to journalism . . . don't have all that much talent but . . . when I heard about the Pauline Players coming to my hometown . . . well I called and just *begged* to be given a part . . . any little part . . . " And she went on and on. Delly was apparently unaware that she'd been the star of the piece.

Myra's forced smile hurt her face. *This little girl is so pretty. Just like a real angel. So sweet. So pure. So precious. So full of grace. God help me . . . I'd like to choke her to death . . .*

Myra was shocked out of her daze when she heard the angel's voice chattering on: "But we must all go out to dinner . . . so much to talk about . . . unless you've already made plans . . . "

Moon glanced doubtfully at his date. "Well . . . I'm taking Myra and Aunt Daisy to the Strater . . . "

"Oh," Delly said, "I had no idea you two were—I mean if you have other plans we can . . . "

Myra heard her own voice speaking. It was flat. Disconnected from her body and will, like a recorded response on a telephone answering machine. "Oh no, that'll be fine. The four of us."

Delly closed her eyes and sighed. "Oh, it'll be so wonderful . . . I can't remember the last time I ate at the Strater."

But Myra remembered *her* last time. It had been when the handsome cowboy proposed to her. Which is to say, made his proposition. Not that they should marry, of course. His notion was that they should live together in the same apartment. Sleep in the same bed. Her apartment, of course. Her bed. And she would support them by waiting tables while he was "in-between" his infrequent jobs. It was a bitter memory.

Now Moon was leaning over her. "Myra . . . you sure it's okay?"

She shrugged gamely. "Why not?" A fitting end to a perfect evening.

Delly clapped her hands. "It'll be so much fun!"

"If I don't throw up," Myra whispered.

Moon had his heavy arm around her thin shoulders. "What?"

"Nothing," she said. And that about summed it up.

The service at the Strater was prompt, the silverware spotless, the china immaculate, the food delicious.

Delly nibbled at the remains of a pasta salad. The little angel was very deferential to Myra Cornstone, who was very quiet.

Daisy squinted through the bottom of her bifocals at the dessert menu. The waiter appeared at her elbow. He was young, pale, and very thin.

Almost imperceptibly, he bowed. "May I be of any help?"

She blinked owlishly at him and pointed at the menu. "What's silk pie?"

"A delicious dessert, ma'am." He closed his eyes and assumed a dreamy expression. "Luscious chocolate filling, lightly spiced with nutmeg. Topped with real whipped cream."

She frowned at the menu. "Whipped?"

The waiter curled his lip in a snarl. "Viciously."

Daisy made a fist and tapped her chest. "I've got too much gas to eat any more now. But I'll take a chunk home with me." Charlie was buying; it was an opportunity not to be missed.

The waiter winked. "Certainly, ma'am. I'll prepare it for you."

Charlie Moon couldn't figure out what was wrong. Delly hadn't smiled since they left Ignacio. Myra Cornstone had a funny, distant look like she was worried about something. It had been kinda crowded in the pickup, maybe that was it. The policeman started to speak to Myra, but she was frowning at her spaghetti like it was a plateful of bleached night crawlers. Taking the safer bet, he turned to Delly. "So when do you head back to the university?"

"I'm . . . kind of between semesters. Sort of burned-out with school. I needed a break, and when I heard about the play—and the opportunity to visit Ignacio—it seemed like just the medicine I needed. And I'll get to spend some time with my brother."

Moon nodded. Larry Sands had been his buddy when they were in high school. And the Sandman's little sister had followed him around the playground, making a general nuisance of herself. "I had breakfast with Larry last week. Understand he's gonna be in the Sun Dance over at Sleeping Ute Mountain."

Delly rolled her eyes. "He says it's just a warm-up for the Southern Ute dance." Larry was such a show-off.

Charlie Moon wasn't surprised. This ambitious schedule was typical of Larry Sands, who hadn't exactly been shortchanged in the self-confidence department. The Sandman had earned a night-school degree in chemistry while he worked for the Southern Ute natural gas operation. Then, he'd joined the army and gotten himself a handful of shiny medals. Everything from Sharpshooter to Distinguished Service. He'd been discharged over a year ago, and had spent a year taking anthropology courses at Rocky Mountain Polytechnic in Granite Creek. Now, according to what he'd told Moon during their breakfast at Angel's Cafe, Larry was looking at medical schools. He already had an offer of a full scholarship from Tulane. The young man had his life planned out in some detail; after he got his M.D., Larry was going to train to be some kind of specialist. And Delly's older brother had already picked out the mountain town where he'd practice—Granite Creek. Because, the Sandman explained, it was an upscale university town. Not big enough to have a city's problems, not too small to have all the things a professional man wanted. Granite Creek had a growing list of "clean" industries moving in and the median income was among the highest in Colorado. Moon, who had a subscription to the *Wall Street Journal* and dabbled in obscure stocks, appreciated Larry's sensible notions about money. Being rich didn't solve all your problems. But being poor sure didn't solve any problems at all. Except dealing with income taxes.

"Well," Moon said, "that don't give him much time to rest between dances."

"Oh, Larry will be all right," Delly said with a dismissive little wave. "He had two Sun Dances last year. And they were just six days apart."

Moon sipped at his lukewarm coffee; that hadn't come up during their breakfast. But the Sandman was one busy fellow. "Where did he dance last year?"

Delly shrugged. "Somewhere up north." She glanced uncertainly toward Myra and Daisy then returned her big-eyed gaze at Moon. "I guess I'll have to go and watch Larry dance. Any of you intend to come to the Ute Mountain dance?"

"I'd like to go," Daisy Perika said with a meaningful look at her nephew. "If somebody'd give me a ride over to Towaoc. I could stay with the Sweetwater bunch; they'll be takin' their little camper trailer that has a nice bathroom."

"As it happens," Moon said, "I'm on traffic patrol for the Ute Mountain dance, so I've gotta be there for the whole thing." He grinned at the old woman. "I'll take you over to stay with your Sweetwater kinfolk." He turned to his date. "And maybe you'll get a chance . . . "

Myra Cornstone looked up from her plate. "I don't know— I'll have to see if I can get off work for a couple of days." She had no interest in Sun Dances. And couldn't afford a baby-sitter for that long. But Myra also couldn't afford to leave Charlie Moon alone with this oh-so-perfect little Sands girl. Almost to herself, she said: "I might have to bring my Chigger Bug."

Delly Sands's pretty face was a question mark. It sounded like some kind of little car. "Chigger bug? What's a—"

"My baby boy."

"Oh." Delly raised an eyebrow at Moon, then looked back at Myra. "I've been away a long time. I didn't know you two were . . . you know."

"We're not . . . at least he's not," Myra said woodenly. "I am. Or was. Or maybe I wasn't, actually." She looked through moist eyes at Charlie Moon. "I'm awfully tired."

"I'll take you home," he said.

Daisy looked around for the waiter; she hoped that the young man had remembered to put her rag pie in a box.

Moon left with the check, calculating how many Angel's Diner cheeseburgers he'd have to skip to make up for this meal. A good-sized pile, that's how many.

Delly watched the big man's retreating form, then reached across the table to pat Myra's hand. "I'm sorry. I guess my mouth was working and my brain wasn't."

Myra blinked at the pretty little girl. "It's all right. I'm tired. I just need to go home and lie down." *And die.*

Daisy Perika, who had watched this little drama unfold, sighed. These young people had such complicated lives. But everything would work out all right.

This is what she thought.

CHAPTER 3

Home of the Mountain People

In the village of Towaoc—the center of life on the Ute Mountain reservation—are a variety of neat, modest homes with well-kept yards. Under cottonwood and elm that provide a welcome bit of shade from the July sun, children play with dogs. There are a scattering of small Christian mission churches. At the center of things, there is a fire department. And a police station, with a jail yard surrounded by an eight-foot fence topped with glistening concertina wire. A trio of prisoners outfitted in electric-orange jumpsuits wander to and fro. Town Drunk is an optimist and friend to all; he calls to a passerby: "Hey, bro—you got anything to drink?" Horse Thief is an innovator and a risk taker; he rolls toilet paper around a wad of pulverized leaves of various weeds that grow around the fence. All this to construct a small cigar. Before the night comes, he will be deathly ill. Wife Beater is a brutish man with bloodstained hands; he mutters darkly about the injustice of his incarceration. He is certain she will not press charges; he'll be home before week's end. It is true. But before the winds of winter moan around the eaves, he will be a murderer.

Through the ages . . . mystics and sages . . . surveyors and episcopate . . . purveyors of real estate . . . all have understood the importance of *place* in human affairs.

The little village Towaoc—the isolated home of the Mountain Utes—is nestled in the arid Montezuma valley. Were it not for a noisy roadside casino, this place would go unnoticed by the passing tourist. But the home of the Mountain Ute tribe—in a way not generally appreciated—is in the very center of things. To understand this, one must stand in this isolated place, and consider the four cardinal directions.

Where Cosmic Fires Are Rekindled . . .

A long day's walk to the north of Towaoc is the brooding rubble of a small village that has never felt the sting of the archaeologist's pick. There are a scattering of pottery shards, a few flakes of obsidian. This appears to be such an ordinary ruin. The fallen walls of a half-dozen houses. The dimple of a small kiva, half-filled with sand and rubble. A pile of hand-hewn rocks that had once been a tower of stone. The obscure ruins are an outlying suburb of a major community that was—in times long forgotten—called the Stone Tower People. In this particular small settlement lived less than three-score souls. Most worked the stony soil or hunted deer to support a half-dozen men who belonged to a peculiar, secret organization—the Duck Foot Clan. These priests performed no ordinary toil, and they slept during the day. They were not lazy—quite the contrary. Slumber during the time of light was a necessity. From sunset until shortly after dawn, their members held rituals that were hidden from those not privy to the clan's deep secrets. But there were rumors. It was whispered that the Duck Foot rituals were cosmic in their intent—and affected the fate of the entire world. Without this nocturnal priesthood, life on earth would have been impossible.

It had begun in this manner, on a fine autumn day almost nine hundred years before the Spanish invaders arrived. In that faraway time, a band of sturdy traders had come to the Stone Tower community to trade rainbow-colored seashell ornaments and hard cakes of fine white salt. In exchange, they received nuggets of turquoise and thin blades of blue-gray obsidian. One of these travelers spoke the language of a tribe that lived in a nearby desert and made fine baskets, and some among the Stone Tower People understood this tongue. So they talked. The Shell People had come—so the traveler said—from a very far land situated at the very edge of the world. These travelers claimed—not without some pride—that a man could walk no further than the lands of their people, because this was the very end of the world itself!

The people of the Stone Tower villages were no fools and had entertained their share of braggarts and brigands. How can this be, the wily highland people asked? Would a man fall off the edge of the world if he walked past your village? And where would he fall to?

Through their interpreter, the Shell People traders provided an answer that stunned the highland dwellers: What we have said is true. There is a great body of water at the edge of the earth, which tastes of salt and has huge fish that can swallow a man. These waters have no boundaries—they go on forever like the sky itself. As a measure of proof, it was from these waters that the large shells were taken, and from the tidal ponds that the cakes of salt were processed.

Through the interpreter's words, the tedious language of hand signs, and pictures drawn in dust with callused fingertip, the highland people heard a most disturbing report: During the hours of darkness—when ghosts walk upon the earth—the sun falls into that bottomless pool. The cold waters extinguish this heavenly fire that—by making the grasses grow—sustains all life on the earth. It was from these shell traders that the Stone Tower People learned this astonishing fact: the sacred fires of the sun must be rekindled by nightly song-prayers . . . and by the burning of a continuous fire on a mountain by the great waters. And—upon occasions dictated by the heavens—by the sacrifice of blood. All this was accomplished by the sages among the wise and prosperous Shell People, so not to worry.

But the highlanders did worry.

After the traders departed for their homes by the great pool of water, the shaman and wizards among the highland people gathered to take counsel among themselves. They had also been told that in the land of these Shell People, the earth sometimes moved and whole villages were swallowed up. What if—by some such great calamity—the priests among the Shell People all died, and there was no one among the peoples of the earth who continued to replenish the fires of the sun? The conclusion was all too obvious—darkness would envelop the land forever . . . all life would perish.

This could not be allowed to happen.

So in that same year, a clan called Duck Foot was born among the Stone Tower People. From the edge of their inhabited lands, they made a three-day's walk toward the place where the sun returns at dawn, and founded an outlying village for their new society. In the center of this village, they built themselves a tower that reached the height of seven men. At the top of the tower was a black basalt slab that served as an altar . . . and a place of fire. The determined priesthood took their sleep only after the sun had risen. Each night—after the orb of fire had been extinguished in those unseen waters so far away—they offered gifts of maize and pollen and turquoise to the fire that burned continuously at the top of the tower. Whenever the moon was a thin scythe of ice cutting stars from the sky, they spilled the blood of captives to replenish the life of the sun. If no captive was available, the priests spilled their own blood by drawing a sliver of obsidian along their tongues. This was very painful, but their work was very important.

Soon after this work began, a most peculiar thing happened. In an ordinary town, where the Duck Foot Clan was almost unknown—a small child fell into a trance. Her sleep continued for three days. Her mother wept—surely her daughter was to be taken from her. But the little girl did not die. When she awakened, she asked for two things. For a drink of cool water. And to see the chief priest of the Duck Foot Clan. Her parents were astonished, but her father walked for days to reach the village of the Clan who had built the tower with fire at the top. With bowed head, he told the chief priest that his little daughter wished to speak to him.

Bemused at such a brazen request, the aging wizard came.

The child did speak to him. And told him an astonishing tale. When she had fallen into her long sleep, she had visited a very far place in a land where the sun never sets. She had been shown many wonderful things, told many secrets. And she made this startling statement: No sacrifice from the Duck Foot People is required to cause the sun to come up and go down. It is the Great Mysterious One who causes all the heavenly lights to move over the face of the earth . . . not only the great lights of mother sun and sister moon, but also those distant lights that are like the sparks from campfires—and those wandering lights that foretell the births and deaths of whole peoples. The priest of the Duck Foot clan, the child explained, need not worry about the comings and goings of the sun.

Then, as proof of the authority of her words, the child told him his secret name. And gave him orders from the ruler of that faraway place.

This I say—No longer will you sacrifice slaves on the basalt altar.

This I say—No longer will you slit your tongues for blood.

This I say—The blood of my own soul has already been spilled to keep the darkness at bay, and it is sufficient for all purposes.

Henceforth, the priests should labor during the day to earn their food. And take their sleep at night, like all the Stone Tower People.

The head of the Duck Foot Clan was astonished to learn that this child knew of the secret purpose of his organization. Almost, the wizard was convinced. But his heart was filled with pride— was he not among the wisest of men? Would a little child lead him with babbling from a dream? Certainly not.

After his long trek home, he called together the priesthood of the Duck Foot Clan. He told them the tale, leaving out only the three commands, because these were obnoxious to him. The opinion was unanimous: the child's body had been occupied by an evil spirit. What should be done? A decision was made . . . to call upon the spirits from Lower World.

Three times the bones were cast by the wizard.

Three times, the bones spoke.

The girl must die.

Her mother was warned of this danger in a dream. The parents immediately slipped away with their child and dwelt for a time among the basket makers of a far desert. Years later, when the commotion had subsided, they returned to their home village.

With unshakable stubbornness, the chief priest and his clan brothers continued in their sacred duties. The breasts of slaves were ripped open with obsidian knives. When no captives were available, tongues of priests were slit open. Much blood was spilled on the basalt altar.

Gradually, the purposes and activities of the Duck Foot Clan became known among all the people. Six generations after the incident with the child, a successor to the original chief priest was honored by a visit from a high chief who ruled a wonderful city that would someday be called Chaco. This ruler thought it too prideful for any clan to claim that they made the sun move through the sky, and said so.

This is what the toothless chief priest said to the youthful administrator of the great city: "Though some may scoff at the

Duck Foot Clan—our rituals have never failed. Travelers tell us that the Shell People and their priests have long since vanished from this earth. But every morning, the sun rises."

The mayor of Chaco had no answer for this logic.

Where the Serpent Slithers . . .

To the east of Towaoc, one finds both old and new. The boundary of the ancient is the rugged battlement of West Rim. Beyond the towering cliffs of this stark mesa are various places with names like Pulpit Rock, Eagle Eye, and Wickiup. Winding along the base of West Rim is the new, the intruder. It is a long, meandering snake of asphalt. Some say its tail lies at Shiprock, its head at Cortez, but this interpretation is parochial and not to be confused with geography. A casual inspection of a road map reveals that the route actually stretches from Gallup in New Mexico to Monticello in Utah. Those who count themselves wise insist that this is only an ordinary two-lane highway, with a long stripe of yellow on its back. But others mutter: "Count the number of those who die where this serpent's belly crawls. And count the number of the Beast . . . it is six hundred and sixty . . . and six."

The reptile rubs its scaly side against the casino—where the faithful come, the blind . . . the crippled . . . the poor. And those soon to be poor. These pilgrims arrive in twos and threes in shiny cars and dusty pickup trucks. They come as families, and bring their children. They are hauled in by the dozens in gleaming buses. The solemn Navajo, the taciturn people of the scattered Pueblos, the mystical Hopi, the cheerful Ute—all these travel to this noisy cathedral and join with the hopeful congregation of Anglo and Hispanic. Seated together, these supplicants stain to hear the resonant Voice of Promises over the loudspeaker—to *commune* with this beneficent source of unspeakable riches. But to draw bounty from this deep well of treasure one must, of course . . . prime the pump.

It is a matter of faith.

In case there is some heretic tendency, the flock is frequently reminded: this is not gambling—this is *gaming*.

The disembodied voice speaks the truth. Too little is left to chance to call it gambling.

But it is an empty game. The Voice of Promises tempts the hopeful with the lure of quick riches in return for an unquestioning obedience . . . subverts the mind that recognizes not the harsh laws of probability . . . or believes that such laws can—if only for a moment—be held in suspension. Almost without exception, these communicants offer up a continuous collection of paper greenbacks to the felt-covered altars . . . of silver-plated copper coins to feed the insatiable appetite of the beastly little machines. The dice are tossed, the cards shuffled, the lever pulled. And the sun sets and the sun rises.

Where the Woman Waits . . .

A day's walk to the south of Towaoc—almost on the horizon—stands a towering figure of stone wearing a cone of pleated skirts. Though this formation is called chimney rock by those government scribes who make official maps, it is not to be confused with another monolith of the same name on the neighboring Southern Ute reservation. One elder (who prefers to remain unnamed) insists that the stone monolith is actually Standing Woman Who Waits—a maiden who abides until her bridegroom cometh. This is not to be confused with geology. Or theology.

Where the Warrior Sleeps . . .

Look to the west of Towaoc, far from the noisy din of the casino. A long, rugged ridge of granite reclines on a crumpled bed of layered stone. This mountain is called the Sleeping Ute. Once the suggestion is made, the mind easily perceives the oblong head, the arm flung over the chest, the bent knees, the feet.

An aged Ute woman has another view, and she shares this insight with a visitor. This is not a sleeping Ute. No—it is Sleeping Man, a being who has been dreaming since the creation of the world. But his day is coming. And on *that day*, she says with a warning wag of her finger, Sleeping Man will awaken. And stand. And walk south to join Standing Woman Who Waits . . . and on *that day*, the whole world will tremble. Entire cities will be swallowed up by the earth; mountains on the coastlines will tumble into the deep and the seas will boil and the rivers will run dry. The moon will turn red like blood, the sun and stars will not be seen. And a great stone will fall upon the Beast whose number is six hundred, three-score . . . and six. And after the old serpent is thus dispatched, Sleeping Man will join hands with his bride, Standing Woman Who Waits. There will be a new earth, she says with unshakable confidence. And a new heaven. "Amen and amen," she whispers.

But as a scholarly priest later tells the visitor, such romantic expectations are not to be confused with prophesy.

On the Mountain

Much as a medieval monastery perches on its lofty crag overlooking a sleepy Italian hamlet, the Ute Mountain Sun Dance Lodge hangs in the clouds above Towaoc. But this sanctuary is not made of hewn limestone; it is a wreath of wooden limbs. This sacred place is connected to Towaoc by a winding road of sun-baked yellow earth and flinty stones. And, of course, dust.

As the time for a Sun Dance approaches, the Mountain Utes work hard to smooth the bumps in the road, to fill the potholes. They even water down the dust. Still, it is a dry, bone-jarring ride to this nest of thirsting eagles.

The site, nestled among the sparse groves of bushy piñon and pink-barked ponderosa, was selected by an elder of these people. The old man dreamed that the sacred circle should not be placed in the broad Montezuma valley. No, it must be nestled in the bosom of the great mountain called the Sleeping Ute. The circular structure is, some elders say, the bellybutton of the reclining figure. The umbilical cord of the sleeping man meanders beneath the sacred place . . . to be nourished by springs that are in turn fed by those great rivers flowing beneath the world.

The rough dark pebbles that pepper the ground have been swept from inside the brush corral. This is necessary, because the dancers' feet will be bare. It is enough to expect of a man—to "dance thirsty" for three or four days while his body is slowly baked well-done by the sun. The Ute are willing to suffer for a good purpose, but they are also a practical people. A sensible man should not be expected to dance on sharp stones. There is no glory in that.

In the Shadow of the Mountain

The final meeting was in the backyard of the Sun Dance chief's home. The host was tending a small piñon-wood fire that was encircled by a boundary of smooth river stones. The guests, who sat facing the flames, were sandwiched between a dozen thirsty rows of stunted blue corn and a healthy patch of yellow summer squash. The day was almost spent; they were submerged in the shadow cast by the raised elbow of Sleeping Ute Mountain.

For most of these men, it was a time of camaraderie. After the chief's instructions, they would eat supper. Poker Martinez's wife (who was of the Uintah people) was preparing fried yellow squash, sweet corn seasoned with black pepper and green chile, boiled new potatoes, roast mutton (the final taste of meat before the arduous dance), and bread pudding. There would be gallons of sweetened iced tea.

The dancers sat patiently in a semicircle, on blankets spread over the warm, sandy soil. Most were Ute Mountain men, but there were several kinsmen from the neighboring Southern Ute reservation. And there was Stone Pipe, the hard-eyed Sioux. And the white man, of course. Year after year, this odd pair tended to participate in the same dances. But one rarely acknowledged the presence of the other—Stone Pipe didn't much care for whites. Especially this particular yellow-haired, blue-eyed dancer.

It was no secret that a clique of Sioux and Cheyenne activists wanted non-Indians excluded from the Sun Dance. A few, like Stone Pipe, argued that whites should not even be allowed to participate as spectators. Because—he pointed out—the Sun Dance is a Native American tradition. And these blue-eyed devils are descendants of the hated invaders who'd brought disease that had decimated the indigenous peoples of America. And stolen our lands. And broken countless treaties. And brought slavery to these sacred soils.

Stone Pipe's sister—who had a master's degree in American history from Southern Methodist University—had reminded her angry brother that Native Americans had almost certainly infected the invaders with syphilis, and this new disease had been the scourge of Europe for a century. Moreover, the Sioux and Crow and Blackfoot had been stealing land from each other for hundreds of years, and conducting genocidal warfare. And used captives as slaves and for blood-sacrifice.

Whether or not such things had happened, the young man responded to his sister, was beside the point. That was family business. The European invaders were a special case. He didn't want to hear any more excuses for the *Wasichu* devils. He was ashamed for his sister. But what could you expect from a Sioux who got her education at the white man's school?

Poker Martinez, who was feeding dry branches to the small fire, frowned thoughtfully at the Sioux and the white man. There was, the Sun Dance chief knew, another more personal reason for Stone Pipe's hatred of Winston Steele. This particular white man was tough as shoe leather and full of endurance. For the past ten

years Steele participated in three or four dances every summer—
in North Dakota, Wyoming, Utah, and Colorado.

There was one man here who would not dance. This was
Red Heel, an elderly Shoshone from the Wind River country in
Wyoming. This guest sat in an aluminum lawn chair with his legs
crossed at the ankles; he held an unfiltered cigarette between his
finger and thumb, occasionally taking a short puff. The old man
seemed lost in his thoughts until a glint of silver appeared in the
east, slipping over the chocolate-brown rim of the mesa. Red Heel
quizzically inspected the face of his antique Hamilton pocket
watch, then looked up to frown at the massive satellite. As if it
was a guest who had arrived early.

A first-time Ute dancer nudged his older cousin. "Look," he
whispered, "the old Shoshone . . . you think he can set that old
clock by the moon's rising?"

The cousin shook his head. "Red Heel would set the heavens
to move according to the timepiece. If he could, he'd make the
moon come and go according to the ticking of his old pocket
watch."

The youth thought this was a fine joke. The notion that any
man—even a Shoshone wizard—could influence the course of the
moon was silly. He appreciated the witticism and wanted to smile.
But he could not. Red Heel was staring at him, down that hooked
beak of a nose. Like a soaring red-tailed hawk eyes a fat chipmunk.

The chief of the upcoming Ute Mountain event, who had
been squatting by the fire, pushed himself erect. Poker Martinez
stood before this gathering of men, his hands clasped firmly behind his back. The small bonfire behind him crackled and
snapped; it cast a yellow, flickering light on the dancers' faces.
His face was masked in darkness. The old man knew a thing or
two about effective theater.

The Sun Dance chief studied the faces of the men. He read
what was in their eyes. Fear. Bravado. Uncertainty. Eagerness to
get on with it. All of these things mixed together. He took stock
of the material he had to work with. It was too bad that the

finest Ute Mountain dancers were unavailable this summer. His best Sun Dancer had broken his leg when a tractor rolled over on him. Another longtime dancer was sick with the stomach flu, still another had gone to his sister's funeral in Las Cruces. Aside from himself—the chief always participated in the dance—there were only four men in this group who could be considered seasoned dancers. Those didn't need his final instructions. The Sioux and the skinny white man danced several times each summer. And two of the Southern Utes would make a good showing. Old Hooper Antelope knew how to pace himself. Though his hair was getting white around his ears, he would do all right. And of course, the arrogant fellow the youngsters called Sandman. Larry Sands had the endurance of youth. But these two Utes were long shots to finish the dance. On the last day it was likely that only the white man and the Sioux would be standing. The Sun Dance chief reminded himself that dancing thirsty was not a contest. No, there should be no competition in the sacred corral. Each man was, quite independently of his comrades, on his private vision-quest. And the success of one visionary would enrich all.

That was supposed to be how it was . . . but still, he'd like to see a Ute give the grumpy Sioux and the cocksure *matukach* a run for their money.

But he knew it was not to be. Not this year. So, taking his comfort where he could, the chief rationalized that it was good that his Ute Mountain men would be outdone by the outsiders. It'd teach them a hard lesson. Give some of the chubby ones an incentive to stop eating all those little sugar cakes. Yes, if they'd shed those rolls of fat and learn how to walk for a day or two in the sun without water . . . then maybe they'd be truly ready for dancing thirsty.

Poker Martinez stood immobile, shrouded in his silence, gazing over their heads. He might as well get it over with. He spoke English because it was the only language common to them all.

"Some of you have danced before. You know pretty much what to expect."

Except for a prideful smirk on the Sandman's face, there was no response from the seasoned dancers.

"Some of you young men have never danced thirsty. So listen to what I say. You must think good thoughts. Don't think about any bad things. Be pure in your heart. Remember that this is a sacred thing we do."

There were eager nods and grins from the hopeful youth.

"First, I will tell you the rules."

Rules. The grins disappeared.

"No water, except a little just after the sun goes down. Just enough to wash out your mouth. You can't swallow it. When it's good dark, then you can eat. Fresh fruit is best. Oranges. Pears. Canned peaches are good, too. And . . . after the sun is at rest . . . you can drink a little fruit juice. Maybe a pint—no more."

This brought a sigh of relief from the newcomers.

Poker Martinez continued like a stern teacher, with a wave of his finger. "Stay away from meat. Let the tourists eat the hamburgers."

There were shrugs. It was only for four days. Kind of like Lent. No big thing.

"No alcohol." He began to walk back and forth, and scowled at the dancers. "No drugs. Not even an aspirin. And," he hesitated, "don't think about sleeping with women. Don't even think about women at all . . . that will make you weak."

There was a muffled snicker from a young man who'd just married himself a plump Navajo woman from down at Many Farms. He already felt weak.

The Sun Dance chief paused in front of the youth and leaned forward. His voice was menacingly gentle: "Something you wanted to say?"

The newlywed shook his head quickly, coughed, and assumed an innocent expression. What they said was true—this old fellow was a sure-enough hardnose.

"Now," the Sun Dance chief continued, "remember the goals

of dancing thirsty. First, and most important," he held one finger up, "is to finish. With honor."

There were no smiles now. Everyone, especially the old-timers, knew that it was not easy to finish.

"Second," the chief said, "there may be a healing that comes from your dancing. It can be for you," he glanced at a Towaoc dancer who suffered from terrible headaches, "or for someone else." One of the old men from Ignacio was dancing because his wife had cancer of the liver. White man's medicine had given up when it spread to her bones. She'd had the Catholic priest pray for her, of course. That would help too; Father Raes Delfino had strong medicine.

"Finally," Poker said, "the Sun Dance is a vision-quest."

The atmosphere was suddenly electric. Deep in their hearts, whether they needed a healing or not, this was what they all hoped for. What they dreamed of. The vision. A direct connection to the Power.

The chief held his arms out, as if blessing his small congregation. "I know this: at least one of you . . . will have his vision." He looked at their upturned, expectant faces.

Every eye was on the Sun Dance chief; they all hung on his words.

"I had a dream last week. The same night I dreamed where the sacred tree would be found up by Yellow Jacket Canyon."

The unanswered question was on every face.

Poker Martinez shrugged. "I don't know who it will be. But it will happen . . . I have dreamed it. It will happen."

Not a soul among them doubted the truth of his words.

The Sandman had lost his knowing smirk.

The Sioux shifted uneasily on his blanket. *It will be me. This is my summer . . .*

Though the white man's face was without expression, his blue eyes sparkled in the firelight.

The Sun Dance chief knew that it could be any one of them. Even one who did not finish the dance. A man might have his vision on the first day, and then collapse in utter exhaustion. It had been known to happen. Poker Martinez did not tell them about the particulars of this dream. There had been strange sounds . . . a peculiar humming. Like a bumblebee. He turned to the old Shoshone who sat in the lawn chair near the back door of the house. "Red Heel, when you were a younger man, you danced thirsty many times. We have heard that you had many visions . . . gained much power. This summer, you have come to see the Ute Mountain Sun Dance. Do you have anything to say to these men?"

All faces turned expectantly to the Shoshone elder.

Red Heel inhaled deeply, then took the remainder of the cigarette out of his mouth. "Yes," he said. He dropped the butt to the sand and ground it under his boot sole. "I'm about ready for supper."

The dancers laughed amiably; the tension was eased.

Even the Ute Sun Dance chief smiled. This would be a fine dance. One to remember . . .

That is what he thought.

He was half-right.

Sleeping Ute Mountain
The First Day

The Ute Mountain people were, of course, close at hand. They drove up the winding mountain road to the sacred place among the pines from Towaoc, and from the great valley of Montezuma. Utes from the neighboring Southern tribe came from Ignacio, Redmesa, and Bondad. Uintah people had journeyed down from Utah, through the lands of sculptured stones. From Fort Duchesne, Bottle Hollow, and Altonah. Shoshone and Arapaho were here from the Wind River country of Wyoming. From Fort Washakie and Crowheart. There were Cheyenne and Sioux from the Dakotas. They came from Iron Lightning, Thunder Butte and

Firesteel . . . Pine Ridge and Oglala and Wounded Knee. They arrived in old pickup trucks, in overloaded vans, in overheated flatlander station wagons.

There was a smattering of tourists, both serious and recreational. Professors of anthropology and ethnology. Writers of fact and other fiction. A family from Wisconsin, pausing on their long, sacred pilgrimage to The Land of Disney.

This varied assembly slept in snug campers on foam-rubber mattresses. Under patched canvas tents on wool blankets. And under distant stars . . . snuggled upon the lap of the mountain.

They broiled ribeye steaks in shining butane ovens. They boiled lamb stew on blackened burners of green Coleman camp stoves. They roasted strips of dry venison over cherry-red piñon embers.

Very early on the first morning of the first day, before first light, the Sun Dance chief sat alone in his camp on the mountain. He pulled a cotton blanket around his shoulders, and watched the sparks rise from a small fire. It was not like the sparks had a choice. They always moved upward in the hot air. Cold waves of an old memory washed over the distant shores of his mind, and caused him to shiver. It had been many years since he had sat at his mother's feet and listened to her voice. He could not recall every word she'd read from the Book. But this is what he remembered . . . this is what he whispered to himself:

For affliction does not come from the dust . . .
nor does trouble spring from the ground . . .
Yet man is born unto trouble . . . even as the sparks fly upward.

Charlie Moon had arrived the night before and deposited his Aunt Daisy with the Sweetwater clan. They had—much to Daisy's relief—brought the camping trailer with the little bathroom. And they had pitched three army surplus tents in the shade of a stand of spruce. They were eating watermelon when he left them, and telling lies about how well all the children and grandchildren were doing. And gossiping about those relatives who were not present.

The Ute policeman took his rest by the SUPD Blazer, whose cramped quarters were not nearly big enough for him to sleep in. Moon rolled his frame into an eighty-inch-long wool blanket a Truchas weaver had custom-made for him.

Now, the sun was lightening the eastern horizon.

He got to his feet, stretched, and rolled up the blanket. After he'd brewed a small pot of coffee—and drank it down to the grounds—Charlie Moon headed for the Sun Dance Lodge.

The Taos Pueblo drummers were first on the schedule; they warmed up on a pair of cowhide drums.

The Sun Dance chief grumbled about the drumming, as he did every year. Poker Martinez—who was a perfectionist—always managed to find fault with one thing or another. The cowhide on the drums was stretched either too tight or not quite tight enough. The drummers' tempo was either too fast or it lagged behind the singer, or the trio of drummers weren't quite together on the beat.

Poker Martinez scowled at the old Paiute singer—a fixture at a half-dozen Sun Dances every year. The man was very old now, with hardly any meat on his bones, and lame. The Paiute leaned on a heavy staff of varnished bamboo, and began to wail one of his favorite songs. Some foolishness about a Flathead girl who took a bear for a husband. Poker was of the firm opinion that this story had nothing to do with the theme of a sacred Sun Dance, but what could you do with these stubborn old men, so hidebound in their ways? "Hah," the Sun Dance chief snorted so the Paiute elder could hear, "I wish he'd learn some better songs."

The Paiute singer, who had grown accustomed to complaints from ignorant men, simply ignored this troublesome Ute. Sun Dance chiefs were much alike—a bunch of would-be big shots.

And under the watchful eye of the chief, the dancers danced. Even the first-timers had seen enough Sun Dances to know the drill. They stood with their backs to the brush corral, facing the sacred tree. Then, one by one—sometimes in pairs—they approached the cottonwood post, blowing a long shrill warble on their eagle leg-bone whistles. Each of the seasoned dancers had developed his own style. Some took short, quick steps toward the symbolic tree. Stone Pipe performed an odd, stomping two-step that the Utes assumed must be characteristic of the Sioux Sun Dance. The white man, with his blond head bobbing, moved toward the tree slowly. He carried a long gray feather in his right hand. Sometimes, as he approached the decorated post, this pale *matukach* would gesture toward the tree with the feather, then make a sign over his chest . . . like a Catholic crossing himself.

Charlie Moon found the spectators as interesting as the dancers. Most, he knew. There was a bearded professor from Fort Lewis College, a couple of dancers' wives, two or three girlfriends. But there was one he hadn't seen before. Near the entrance to the Sun Dance Lodge, a blond woman outfitted in a white cotton pantsuit sat cross-legged on a colorful Mexican blanket. She shaded her fair skin under a pink parasol. It was an expensive accessory, mounted on a lacquered cane shaft inlaid with mother-of-pearl. Even sitting down, it looked like she'd be tall for a woman. Five-eleven, maybe six feet. She rarely took her gaze off the white dancer. Her smiles and eager nods were intended to encourage the pale man; sometimes she seemed almost ready to applaud as he sweated stoically in the oppressive heat.

The Ute policeman turned his attention to the men who'd come to dance thirsty. The youngest dancers rested little; they stumbled about with great energy and showed little originality of style. Most attempted to imitate one of the seasoned dancers—particularly the Sioux; Stone Pipe was a favorite. The young men (except for the Sandman, who was quite content to be like himself) attempted to emulate this bronzed warrior from the Dakotas. Primarily because he was rumored to have taken much Power from his Sun Dance visions. And also because women generally considered Stone Pipe to be a mysterious, romantic figure. Several young Ute women came to watch the muscular stranger who danced in a breechcloth tucked under a beaded doeskin belt. They watched the cotton cloth flapping as the hard-eyed, muscular man danced. They watched the sweat form on his copper skin. The boldest girls whispered among themselves—speculating about whether Stone Pipe wore anything under the foot-wide breechcloth. Sometimes, with their hands over their mouths, they giggled until the Sun Dance chief scowled at them.

The Sun Dance chief shared his complaints with the Shoshone elder who was his guest of honor. There was, Poker Martinez grumbled, no spirituality in the dancing of these youths—they were merely performing. And not for the Great Mysterious One; in their vanity, they danced for their wives and children and relatives—or for their silly girlfriends who watched with undisguised pride.

Red Heel nodded his solemn agreement. But, he reminded his host—since time began, was this not always the way of young men? Did not he and his Ute brother, as youths, behave in much the same manner?

Poker Martinez smiled grudgingly, and nodded. Yes, what his Shoshone friend said was true. All young men were much the same. It was good to keep a balanced view. Poker wondered about his guest. This old man was a typical Shoshone who loved the land Chief Washakie had won for his people when he fought Big Robber, chief of the Crow nation. Red Heel rarely left the Wind River country in Wyoming. So why had he traveled all the way to Towaoc to watch the Ute Mountain Sun Dance? Red Heel had claimed that this was a courtesy call—he was merely returning visits that several Utes had made to Shoshone Sun Dances. Maybe that was the truth. Or maybe the man's shrewish wife had been fussing at him, and he needed to get away for a while. Or maybe some troublesome in-laws were visiting. Whatever his reason was, it didn't matter. Poker Martinez was pleased that Red Heel was here.

The chief watched the dancers.

The seasoned Sun Dancers seemed to pay no attention to the spectators. Stone Pipe, the white man, Hooper Antelope—even the youthful Sandman—were quietly aloof from such distractions. And they paced themselves, even as the ordeal began, by resting often. By tomorrow, the first-timers would be exhausted and dehydrated—sitting on their blankets, cursing themselves for having little enough sense to get involved in this old-fashioned foolishness. By the third morning, the first-timers would hardly be on their feet at all. By the evening of the third day, one, maybe two would have given up. It would be too great a humiliation to actually leave the corral, so they'd sit on their blankets and doze. And solemnly pray for an end to this torture.

The experienced men would be dancing for only one or two of every ten minutes—still pacing themselves . . . blowing their eagle-plumed bone whistles with great exultation . . . approaching ever closer to the sacred tree. And there would certainly be a vision; Poker's dreams never lied to him. When the vision came—and it didn't happen in every dance—then all present were blessed, even the spectators. But one of these men would penetrate the shadows . . . touch the Truth. And be healed. Perhaps even empowered.

The Sun Dance chief was presiding over this congregation, musing about what great things might happen in this dance, when he heard the voice . . . it came from some sacred place . . . from some holy dwelling. These words were whispered in his ear:

Let us run with endurance the race that is set before us.

Inspired by this unexpected blessing, Poker Martinez immediately placed the polished bone whistle between his dry lips . . . and danced a few steps in place, in rhythm with the monotonous thumping of the big drums. All eyes were upon the Ute elder as he made a short, running approach toward the tree, stopping two yards short of the skinned cottonwood post. He raised his wrinkled hands to the heavens . . . flames from the sun licked at his face. The Sun Dance chief blew a long, wailing note through the hollow leg bone of the eagle . . . the plumes on the tip of the bone cylinder levitated in a light breeze that cooled his face.

Ahhh . . . it was good.

Charlie Moon saw little of the sacred dance. Mostly, the policeman helped his Ute Mountain kinsmen direct traffic, helped people set up their camps, breathed alkali dust, and answered visitors' endless questions about where are the latrines and how long does this thing last and is it okay to wear earrings inside the Sun Dance Lodge? He found the lost parents of a tiny Arapaho girl. He visited the Sweetwater camp to make sure Aunt Daisy was as content as one of her nature could hope to be. On one occasion, this routine was broken by an enthusiastic drunk who needed arresting. Such action was rarely necessary. First, because the presence of alcohol in the Sun Dance grounds was a serious breach of etiquette. Second, because the mere sight of Charlie Moon's tall, wide-shouldered frame was sufficient to calm the most boisterous among those who celebrated in the old-fashioned way.

There was another, more welcome diversion.

At noon on the first day, Delly Sands showed up in her old Toyota sedan. She waved gaily at Charlie Moon and demanded his personal attention. The Ute policeman found the young woman a parking spot that was partially shaded by a bushy juniper. The Sandman's sister was wearing a white cotton blouse with a little black ribbon at her throat. And cornflower-blue pants. Being a trained observer, the policeman noticed minor details. Like how none of her clothes looked new. And how snug the pants were.

With all his attentions given to the young woman, Charlie Moon was unavailable to help his Ute Mountain comrades with minor matters such as directing traffic. He brought her cool water in a paper cup; they sat in the shade and talked of many things.

Of the old days that were really not so long ago. Of mutual friends dead and gone. Of the future. About how she needed a job.

Then, when the sun was low and the mountain's hue turned from a soft grayish-green to a lustrous hue of lilac, they went for a walk. Delly put on her pert little sunglasses and a broad-brimmed straw hat with a gray feather in the band.

Moon was entranced. At school, she'd been such a pest, always following him around. Now he was following her.

She was attracted by his shy manner. The Utes who liked to brag on their big policeman offered the opinion that Charlie Moon wasn't afraid of anything. But, Delly realized, they were wrong. He was a little bit afraid of women. Or maybe . . . just *particular* women. And this revelation more than pleased her. She put her hand into his; this seemed to startle him. After a few steps, he relaxed.

They strolled among the scattered encampments, exploring the settlement of pickup trucks and canvas tents, the few tepees that had been set up by traditional plains Indians. Whether Ute or Navajo, Hispanic or *matukach*, Cheyenne, Shoshone, Apache, or Pueblo folk—Charlie Moon was a stranger to no one. Even those few who had been arrested by the Southern Ute policeman greeted Moon cordially and offered him and his "little lady" a strip of beef jerky, a frosted donut, or iced lemonade.

Their stroll eventually took them to the edge of the encampment. Aside from the soft song of the wind in the branches of the pines, it was very quiet.

He touched the drooping brim of her straw hat, which gave her an oddly comical appearance. "You steal that big sombrero from Pancho Villa?"

"It protects my face from the sun, Charlie . . . keeps my skin soft." Delly guided his big hand and touched it to her cheek. "See?"

Jimminy, it *was* soft. Just like a baby's behind.

Under a Ponderosa whose bark was pink with age, Moon found a black-and-white magpie feather. Without a word, he offered it to his companion. She gave him a shy smile in exchange for this gift, and removed her straw hat to insert the feather under the band.

Moon observed that the magpie feather was a good deal larger than the gray one. Maybe, he suggested, it'd look best all by itself . . . on the other side of her hat.

She gave him a sly sideways look. No. These feathers looked just right together . . . they made a fine pair. So Delly placed the big feather very close to the small one. And squeezed Moon's hand.

And so, hand in hand, they wandered a mile away from the campgrounds. To a place where they could gaze upon the broad plain of Montezuma. To the northeast, they could see the blue finger of the river Dolores . . . and the reservoir lake called McPhee. To the southeast was the eternal spire of rock . . . Standing Woman Who Waits. And farther away to the south . . . shrouded in waves of mist, the great prow of Shiprock. And beyond this was Beautiful Mountain . . . the people of Sanostee . . . the Chuska range . . . and the inhabitants of Lukachukai. Though some of it was too far away to see with eyes, this is what they saw. Though it was much nearer, they did not notice the slithering asphalt snake whose number is 666.

The Ute policeman felt free. Unencumbered. Hand-in-hand, they strolled along—without the need for words. Presently, Moon spread his denim jacket in the shade of a great melon-shaped boulder; Delly Sands sat beside him. She opened her purse. He watched in quiet amusement as she searched through a merry disorder of hankies, keys, aspirins, coins—the usual paraphernalia of women's purses. She produced a foil package.

And offered him a peppermint.

He accepted.

After a few minutes, she leaned her head lightly against his shoulder.

There was a stillness in this place that may be encountered only in the wilderness. It was made deeper still by the occasional harsh call of the raven or the whispering wings of a red-tailed hawk. On the breath of the soft breeze, they could barely hear the distant, hollow thump of drums in the Sun Dance Lodge.

Delly waited for Moon to break the silence. A long time, she waited.

He didn't.

"Charlie," she said.

He snapped a dry twig between his fingers. "Yeah?"

"Is there . . . anything serious . . . between you and Myra Cornstone?"

Moon considered her question. Rolled it around in his head. For a long time.

Delly Sands rubbed her fingertips on his wrist and sighed. "Charlie . . . did you hear me?"

"Yeah," he said.

"Yes, you heard me, or yes, there's something serious . . . with Myra?"

"Yeah."

The sun is balanced precariously on the West Knee of Sleeping Ute Mountain. A little later . . . so the old people say . . . the gigantic sleeper will yawn and pull his woolen blanket over his chin. At that moment, the swift swallows and darting bats will take wing. Later still, the sleeper will stretch his stiff legs just a bit . . . this will cause his earthen bed to creak and rumble . . . that great sphere of fire will slip off the sleeper's knee. The sun will roll down the west side of the mountain into that bottomless cavern called Here I Sleep . . . into the soothing pool of blue waters called Here I Forget. Then the moon, that shy sister of the brazen day . . . that twilight spirit of sweet relief . . . will sail across the rolling sea of night. Her arrival will bring the coolness of a sea breeze to the sandy shore of this high desert. Following in her foamy wake are the silver stars . . . those distant suns . . . these ghostly sons . . . that shadowy band of spirit hunters. Nightly, they urge their dusky horses westward . . . on that eternal quest through the infinite. The relentless riders, it is said, search for three things. These hunters would find the herds of buffalo who have departed from this earth and gone to graze in the endless pastures of that place beyond the beyond. These wanderers also seek their father's home. And finally, these souls long for rest eternal.

But the sun has not yet rolled off the knee of Sleeping Ute Mountain. Nor has the pale spirit of the twilight come to spread her cool, moist garment over this parched, arid land. The ghostly warriors have not yet begun their nightly ride across the sinuous trails of the sky, though the thunder of their restless steeds' hooves can be heard just beyond the eastern horizon.

In the Sun Dance Lodge, the drummers are still going strong. The crippled Paiute elder is singing some of his songs for the third and fourth time. Most of the dancers are resting from their labors . . . a few sturdy ones are blowing shrill notes on their whistles, occasionally approaching the tree in hope of a blessing.

Delly Sands was furious with herself. After their lovely walk among the pines, Charlie Moon had brought her back to the campground. He'd made some lame excuse about needing to check on his Aunt Daisy, tipped his hat, and wandered off. Delly silently cursed herself for having mentioned Myra Cornstone. It had been such a dumb thing to do.

Now she waited patiently by the entrance to the Sun Dance Lodge. Finally, a parched tourist gave up his spectator's spot in the corral and retired to his camper in search of liquid refreshment. The young woman immediately claimed the territory, about twelve feet from the entrance. She seated herself on a tattered blanket she'd brought for the purpose, and placed her purse beside her to save a spot for Charlie Moon. Maybe he'd show up later. When the apricot moon was high and the drums had fallen quiet. And the dancers rested from their labors.

He didn't.

So Delly Sands spent her evening watching the dancers. One of them, especially.

The Second Day

Moon got up from his bedroll, stretched himself, and groaned.

He had two cups of black coffee with some of Daniel Bignight's relatives from Taos Pueblo.

The Ute policeman wandered around the encampment, looking for any signs of trouble. A white man was drinking beer awfully early in the morning, and alcoholic beverages were strictly forbidden on the Sun Dance grounds. Moon paused, chatted with the man about weather, politics, and the stock market. Even offered the fellow a tip on the effect an early frost would likely have on the citrus crop in Florida and how this would affect the value of California orange juice stocks. When the man was completely relaxed, the Ute policeman gently reminded him about the rules on alcohol. The offender put away the bottle and promised ("on my mother's grave") not to have another drop. Moon thanked him and moved on. It'd taken almost a half hour, but the problem had been solved with no fuss. And more important, with no hard feelings.

Moon returned to his camp and pumped up the fuel tank on his Coleman stove. He heated a quart of beef stew over the blue flames and ate it directly from the saucepan. It was good. Very good.

His appetite sated, the policeman continued his patrol of the sprawling encampment. Last night, he'd noticed that Delly had moved her old Toyota near a Uintah campsite. She'd told him she was staying with some relatives. One of her uncles from Utah had set up a couple of big canvas tepees. One for the women and children, another for the men. Delly had been a town Indian for some years now. Moon smiled at the thought of this college girl sleeping in a tepee.

He headed toward the narrow mountain road and helped his Ute Mountain brethren unsnarl a minor traffic jam caused by a jeep with a flat tire. He performed some additional police duty by breaking up a heated argument between a couple of snarling teenagers who were ready to fight over a pretty girl in shorts. She stood off to the side, pretending to be innocent of the whole affair. She had full, red lips, and a silk rose in her shining black hair. He confiscated a wicked pair of folding knives and sent the overheated youths off in different directions. And tipped his black Stetson to the pretty girl. She hesitated, then flashed a flirting smile before turning on her heel. And looked back over her shoulder. It was obvious that she wanted this grown man to follow her. She was maybe seventeen years old, Moon estimated. And about ninety-five pounds of dynamite. No doubt about it, there would be more knives drawn over this one; blood would flow. But if he could help it, not on Ute property.

Moon headed for the Sun Dance Lodge. There was a new set of drummers this morning. It was the group from Isleta Pueblo, and the singer was a young man with a red bandanna tied around his head. He had an acceptable voice and a fine sense of how to sing, but Moon did not understand any of the Pueblo languages. He paused at the corral entrance. An aged Ute—they called him "Sheriff Pete" behind his back—was firmly reminding tourists (Indian and *matukach* alike) that the opening into the brush corral must be kept clear at all times . . . they must not bring any metal objects into the Sun Dance Lodge . . . women must be dressed in a respectful manner, because this was no different than being in a church . . . that meant no shorts or halters . . . no food or drink whatsoever could be brought near the corral . . . children could not be allowed to run around the outside of the corral and whoop and holler like damned little bandits . . . and so on. As he made this final admonition, Sheriff Pete was almost tripped by two small Hopi boys who galloped by, one astride a pine-branch horse.

Moon leaned forward and looked into the brush corral. The blonde was in her usual spot, near the entrance. Her eyes were on the white man, whose name Moon had learned. Winston Steele. That's all he'd found out, except that this *matukach* danced at least two or three times every year. Rumor was, this man had visions. It was said that he had gained much power from the dance. But the policeman didn't remember seeing Steele at a Ute Sun Dance.

Stone Pipe, the Sioux, was matching the *matukach*. Step for step. Moon grinned. These fellows took this suffering business pretty seriously. Campfire talk speculated that the Sioux and the white man—who didn't exactly exchange Christmas presents— might have a go at one another before the dance was finished. The gossip was partially inspired by the fact that Stone Pipe— though he hated whites in general and this one in particular— had seated himself near Steele. They were on the west side of the corral. It was a favorite place for seasoned dancers . . . where the first rays of the rising sun would touch their faces. But, Moon thought, it didn't seem like a good notion to have these particular fellows so close to each other.

Though Moon didn't know it, the Sun Dance Chief shared his view. Although fights in a Sun Dance Lodge—particularly among dancers—were unheard of, there could always be a first time. So Poker Martinez had asked Hooper Antelope to go sit between them. Hooper was an older, even-tempered man. If sparks flew between the hard-muscled *matukach* and the hot-tempered Sioux, Hooper would likely keep a fire from starting.

Delly's brother danced for a few steps and sat down. Moon thought the Sandman looked like he was doing okay. Saving his strength for the long stretch. His sister was in the section with other spectators. Delly Sands was sitting on a blanket, hugging her legs, her chin resting on her knees. Much of her face was hidden by the drooping brim of her oversized straw hat. Moon noticed that the large and the small feather were still in the leather band. Side by side. She looked fresh and cool in a yellow dress and seemed to be watching the dancers—Stone Pipe and Winston Steele—through her plastic-framed sunglasses.

After waiting for the song to end, the Ute policeman made his way into the corral, nodding respectfully at the Sun Dance chief.

Delly Sands saw him coming, and patted the blanket beside

her. He sat down with a grunt. She smiled up at him, and reached out to touch his hand. Moon held her hand in his. Until he noticed the Sun Dance chief glowering across the corral at him. There was a long list of things a man didn't do in the Sun Dance Lodge. Like hold hands with a pretty girl. Moon pulled his hand from her grasp and solemnly turned his face toward the dancers.

Delly giggled.

Like a little girl, he thought. But then Moon remembered another pretty little girl; the one with the silk flower in her hair. The young lady who'd recently inspired a knife fight. No. Neither one of them could rightly be described as "little girls."

"I'm glad you came, Charlie."

He cleared his throat. "How's your brother doing? Holding up okay?"

She ignored this evasion. "It gets lonely here all by myself. You intend to sit with me for a while?"

"A few minutes. Then I got to get back to work."

A few minutes passed. From the corner of his eye, Moon saw a slim young woman arrive at the entrance to the Sun Dance Lodge. A pretty woman. Arms folded, her little foot tapping the sun-baked earth. Myra Cornstone. Looking straight at him. She wasn't smiling. As soon as she caught his eye, she turned and, with a flounce of her skirt, departed.

Oh boy.

"I guess," Moon said, "I better go and be about some . . . ahhh . . . police business."

Delly had noticed neither Myra's arrival nor her departure. "Oh poo," she pouted. "You're no fun at all, Charlie Moon."

He walked along beside Myra. "How's your kid?"

"Chigger Bug's fine. I hired a sitter." *And it'll cost me a day's wages.*

He glanced at her face. She looked tired.

"So, how's it going, Charlie?" *As if I should care.*

"Oh, I've been pretty busy."

"I noticed."

He ignored this. "Stopped a fight between a couple of boys. It was over a girl. Just a kid."

She kicked at a pebble. "Delly Sands is just a kid."

"Yeah. She's . . . uh . . . sleeping with her uncle's family." *Why did I say* sleeping? He'd meant to say she was *staying* with the Uintah clan.

Myra allowed herself a bittersweet smile. "Where are *you* sleeping, Charlie?"

Moon nodded glumly toward a distant clump of piñon, where his SUPD Blazer was parked. "Over there." He winked at the slim, attractive woman. Myra looked like she could bite the head off a brass rat. "You want to see?"

"See what?" she snapped.

"Where I'm sleeping. On the hard ground . . . lots of sharp little rocks. Use pine branches to cover me up. Got a big chunk of rock for a pillow. And it's awful cold after the sun goes down. Big hairy centipedes come out at night and run across my face. Woke up this morning with a scorpion in my shirt pocket."

In spite of her annoyance with this big brute, she laughed. "Find me something to drink, big fella."

He put his hand on the small of her back. "What's in it for me, little woman?"

"Lean over, and I'll tell you."

He leaned.

She whispered in his ear.

"Well now," he said, "that sounds fair enough."

Myra wrapped her slender arms around his neck. And kissed him on the mouth. Charlie Moon, startled at the suddenness of her advance, stood up straight. She didn't let go. She hung there, her little red shoes dangling beneath his knees.

Hmmm. Wouldn't be a good thing if she slipped loose. So he put his arms around her.

Just to keep her from falling . . .

Ignacio
Old Popeye Woman's Bedroom

The aged woman lay on her side, her thin legs covered by a blue cotton sheet. She had already said her evening prayers. Now, she waited for sleep to come and take her away. But Stella Antelope's singular experience began before her nightly journey into that world of unknowing.

Because it was July, the pair of tall windows near her bed were open, to invite the entry of any breeze that happened by. Metal screens kept the fluttering moths at bay. But on this night, another presence approached her bedroom. Uninvited.

Stella thought she heard rustling sounds near the rosebush. It could be a neighborhood dog rummaging around out there. Or one of them fat raccoons snuffing around for something to eat. But it was not. She listened with shortened breaths at the scratching sounds on the outside wall . . . as small hands pushed the window screen aside. Stella knew that she should call out to her grandson, who slept on a couch in the small parlor. Billy could run for help—get a neighbor to call the police. But there was something so very peculiar about this . . . she did not make a sound. And then the blind woman understood that this was not a burglar. Not an ordinary intruder.

The fear departed from her . . . and took the darkness with it.

As if this were a dream, the blind woman could see her visitor plainly.

For a moment, he stood by her bed, the top of his head barely visible, his yellowish eyes blinking. He hesitated, then climbed into a straight-backed chair and squatted there. His left hand scratched at his scrawny neck.

He wore short breeches, old-style ankle-high moccasins, a wrinkled shirt that was far too big for him, and a funny little black hat with a narrow brim. She almost laughed at the hat, but her natural good manners limited the old woman to a wry smile. She had never seen him up close before, but like all Utes, Stella

Antelope had heard many tales of the *pitukupf*. This bowlegged dwarf who—so it was said—spoke only to the People.

And speak he did.

The gruff little visitor addressed her in a version of the People's tongue so archaic that the Ute Elder could barely understand him. He told her of things past. And things to come. After the Ute Mountain Sun Dance had run its course, the little man confided, Stella and her son Hooper would each make a journey.

Would they travel together, she asked?

No. Theirs would be different journeys.

Well, she thought, Hooper liked to travel and was always going someplace. So that was no surprise. But Old Popeye Woman received the news about her own trip with some misgivings. "Where will I go?"

The dwarf pointed a bent finger toward those far lands where the snows are made.

So. She would go to the north. To Fort Collins, most likely. Stella loved to visit her cousin who lived there, but for the past few years she was always too tired to make the trip. "Will somebody drive me? Or do I have to go on a bus?"

She had listened in open-mouthed astonishment to his reply, and shuddered. "I'm kind of nervous about being in high places."

The apparition had assured the aged woman that hers would be a short journey. Her son's trip would be a long one.

Not too long, she hoped. Hooper tired easily these days.

At his journey's end, Stella was informed by the elfin messenger, her son would enjoy the rest he so needed.

That was good, the weary woman had said. But when would she have her rest?

There was no answer. Even as she asked this question, the *pitukupf* departed from the blind woman's night vision.

Though this encounter had the queer flavor of a dream, Stella was certain that she was awake. She heard the dwarf slip over the windowsill, heard him mutter as he got tangled up in her favorite rosebush. She chuckled.

A dog barked nearby . . . then howled.

And then the *pitukupf* was gone. The blind woman was, once more, covered in darkness. Stella Antelope lay in her bed, considering the strange message brought by the uninvited guest. The more she thought about it, the more unlikely it seemed—that she would travel through the sky. She assumed, of course, that the dwarf meant she would take a trip in an airplane. She could not afford the price of a ticket and they sure didn't give those things away. And now that she thought about it—Billy would need a ticket too. She could go nowhere without the boy . . . the child was her eyes. Tomorrow, some neighbors would take her and little Billy over to Sleeping Ute Mountain where her son was dancing. Maybe she'd tell Hooper about the *pitukupf's* visit. Or maybe not . . . he'd think she was so old she was getting silly in the head.

These were unsettling thoughts.

But though she was cursed with many physical infirmities, Stella Antelope enjoyed this singular blessing: she was not given to pointless worrying. Neither about those things already done, nor of things to come. After a few minutes, Old Popeye Woman drifted off into the childlike slumber of innocents, and dreamed her sweet dreams. She saw an old man whose face was familiar. He led two fine young horses on a narrow path through a shady forest of pine and spruce.

Her son Hooper was riding one of the ponies.

The Third Day of the Dance

It was the prerogative of the chief of the affair to determine how many days the men would dance thirsty. Poker Martinez had planned a four-day dance. The third day began without any hint of what was to come.

Myra had gone home late on the night before, but Charlie Moon hadn't stopped thinking about her. Her flashing brown eyes. Shining hair that fell to a slender waist. Tiny feet in little red shoes. The perfume she wore. Smelled like something good—apple cider?

Moon directed traffic until shortly after lunch, then made the rounds of the encampment. There were no fights. No use of alcohol. Most of the casual spectators had departed. The midday sun was searing and tourists soon found the Sun Dance monotonous. Those few who remained in the campground were an agreeable bunch; there were smiles on most everyone's face as they drank chilled soft drinks and gossiped and strolled from camp to camp.

There was a smile on Moon's face.

He was thinking about what it would be like to come home after work every evening to Myra. And to spend all his nights with the young woman. She did have the baby boy, of course, and a child was a big responsibility. But Chigger Bug seemed to be a pretty good kid. Myra said he usually slept all night without stirring. And he was talking a bit now, too. Sure. It might be fun, having a kid around his house. When he got bigger, playing on the rocky banks of the shallow Pinos. Of course, Myra was also responsible for her blind grandfather. And Walks Sleeping would never think of leaving his house and coming to live with Charlie Moon. Maybe they could make arrangements for someone to take care of him.

The Ute policeman wandered in the general direction of the Sun Dance Lodge. As he approached, he could feel the sound of the drums reverberate in his chest. These Cheyenne drummers were . . . well, they were *loud*.

The big Ute stood at the entrance to the sacred corral. He wasn't particularly interested in what was happening. But it was Charlie Moon's burden that he could not evade the habitual behavior of all policemen. Unconsciously, he absorbed every detail.

The old Paiute singer was sitting in sullen silence near the drummers, his bamboo walking staff cradled in his lap. He would not sing today. The Sun Dance chief had bestowed the honor on a younger man: a fat Cheyenne who was his wife's second cousin.

Two of the young dancers were lying on their blankets. Looking like death warmed over. Right now, they were promising themselves that they'd never do anything this dumb again. But by next year, they'd think of themselves as seasoned dancers. They'd be back.

And there, across the corral from the entrance, stood Larry Sands. The Sandman was dancing slowly in place, like one of those battery-operated toys. He showed no sign of approaching the tree. Delly Sands was in her usual spot. But she was paying no attention to her brother. Over her sunglasses, which sat pertly on her little nose, Delly seemed to be watching the half-naked Sioux. Or maybe the white man?

Suddenly, Stone Pipe and Winston Steele were trotting toward the tree at the same time. For an instant, the simultaneous shrill call of their plumed bone whistles produced a warbling, dissonant note.

Moon watched the Sioux retreat slowly from the tree; he looked worn out. And plenty peeved at somebody. Somebody who had blue eyes and white skin and shouldn't even be in this sacred circle.

The slender white man was sweating buckets but seemed fit enough. The blond woman, protected from the sun by the shade of a pretty pink umbrella, nodded at her man, smiling, urging him on. Moon wondered about her. She was probably not his wife. Wives are practical creatures who look to the future. A spouse would be worried that her stupid husband would collapse from sunstroke. She wouldn't be urging him to even greater exertions, in hopes that he would leave the Sioux panting in the dust of his heels. Only a man's starstruck sweetheart would be entranced by this heroic display of brutish endurance. And sit in the sun for three or four days, just for the opportunity to urge him on.

Oh no. This was romance.

Moon had a long look at Delly Sands. Maybe she'd invite him to come and sit by her. There was plenty of room now, and he had nothing in particular to do. But the young woman didn't notice him; she seemed lost in the sweat-soaked drama of *dancing thirsty*.

The Sioux dancer sat down on a dusty blanket at the right hand of Hooper Antelope. The Sandman sat to Hooper's left, but there was a space between them for the white dancer. The pale *matukach* had not retreated from his parched quest. He moved forward; he reached out and barely touched the sacred tree with the tip of a gray feather. He raised his face and seemed to stare at the sun . . . he shuddered . . . his eyes rolled back. Now, his lips moved.

This brought a slight surge of tension in the onlookers. Was the dancer about to have his vision . . . receive his share of the Power? Steele stood there before the tree; he squinted through swollen lids at the ribbons tied to the crotch of the cottonwood post and muttered something. A prayer, no doubt. He backed away; the spectators sighed and relaxed.

The white man sat down at the left hand of Hooper Antelope.

The Sioux muttered something in his own tongue, then turned to stare holes in the blue-eyed devil.

The white man turned to return the brazen stare. He smiled, and for the first time, he spoke to the Sioux. "You look kinda pooped. I bet you'd like to have a nice cold drink of spring water."

Muscles tensed in the Sioux's legs; he was a panther ready to spring.

The white man's smile was now full of teeth. He whispered: "C'mon big guy . . . let's see what you got."

Hooper Antelope was bone-weary, but it was his task to keep the two young rams from butting heads. The old man turned first toward the surly Sioux, then he glanced at Winston Steele. "You fellows hear the one about the grasshopper?"

The white man wiped at his brow with the back of his hand. "Don't think so."

The Sioux grunted. Telling jokes in this sacred place was bad form. Worse still, this was part of the old Ute's continuing (and transparent) effort to get him and the white intruder on friendly terms. Hooper Antelope was a fool on a fool's errand.

Hooper cleared his throat and began. "Well, this grasshopper, he goes into a bar."

The *matukach*, his eyes still on the Sioux, helped the story along. "Which bar?"

"Ahhh . . . let me see now. If I don't disremember, it was the Mud Hen Bar, down in Aztec."

"Yeah. I know the place," Steele said. "So what happened?"

"Well, the bartender, he looks down at this grasshopper. 'You know something,' he says to the hopper, 'we got a drink named after you.' The grasshopper he says: 'Why would anybody name a drink *Winston?*'"

Winston Steele laughed.

This subtle comparison of the skinny white man to a grasshopper pleased Stone Pipe immensely. The Sioux wanted to laugh, but this was a sacred place. He struggled to prevent a grin from touching his lips. The effort hurt his face.

Hooper Antelope, enormously pleased with himself, sighed with contentment.

Blessed are the peacemakers . . . blessed . . . blessed.

Charlie Moon wondered what Hooper was saying to the Sioux and the white man. Suddenly, the *matukach* threw his head back and laughed; he slapped the old Ute dancer on the back. Moon guessed that Hooper had told them one of his awful jokes. Evidently, the Sioux didn't think it was all that funny. Moon wasn't surprised. The Utes and the *matukach* love a good laugh but these Sioux were a very serious people.

Moon's musings were interrupted by a bloodthirsty deerfly that buzzed around his face. He glared at the insect, and muttered a phrase in the choppy Ute tongue. Something about mashing the insect under his thumb. The fly hesitated momentarily, did a figure-eight, and departed.

*   *   *

The sun's relentless heat baked the ground. And seared the dancers' skin.

The Ute policeman scouted the grounds, then returned to the Sun Dance Lodge. He wished he had a glass of ice water. Or better yet, a root beer float.

For several minutes, there were no dancers on the blistering dust.

A few of the spectators wiped at their brows with handkerchiefs; others squinted through tinted glasses at the hated sun and dreamed of cold water. More than one considered retreating to his camp to get an ice-cold soft drink. But this hardy residue of onlookers had their pride; no one wanted to be first to leave.

Unexpectedly, Hooper Antelope got to his feet. He was old for a serious dancer. Pushing seventy, maybe passing it. His feet were like heavy stones as he danced slowly toward the sacred tree; there was a lilting trill to his eagle leg-bone whistle. Hooper carried a pair of bluish-white feathers in his right hand; he paused before the tree and closed his eyes. He removed the bone whistle from his mouth.

And stood for a long time. With his face tilted toward the sun. In utter silence. Like a dead man who didn't know how to fall down.

A few seated dancers watched with more than ordinary interest. And waited.

Three minutes passed.

Five.

Ten.

Still, Hooper Antelope stood before the tree. Occasionally, his lips seemed to move, but there was no discernible sound.

Delly Sands pulled her sunglasses down on her nose and peered over the plastic frame. Was this old fellow having some kind of mystical experience, or was he simply too tired to move? A wisp of cloud moved between earth and sun. A shadow passed over the sacred circle. The young woman removed her floppy straw hat and placed it in her lap.

Winston Steele's blond girlfriend was mesmerized by the old man who stood before the tree. The anthropologist folded her pink parasol and wrapped the flimsy material around the lacquered wooden shaft. Was this one about to have visions of another reality? Salina Timms reached into her purse. Her long, manicured fingers searched among many things. Keys. A compact. Lipstick. A nail polish bottle. A scented lace handkerchief.

Charlie Moon was as fascinated by the spectators as by the central figure in the phenomenon. Several of the younger dancers were gaping openmouthed at Hooper Antelope. Even the tourists whispered among themselves about this dancer's odd behavior.

The bearded professor—his bald dome protected under a Panama hat—scribbled furiously in a small notebook. A skinny young woman seated next to him—Moon took her to be the professor's assistant—gawked unblinkingly through thick spectacles at Hooper Antelope. She whispered a running commentary to the academic.

Among all the spectators, only Delly Sands seemed to have lost interest in the dancer. Greatly to the Ute policeman's amusement, the pretty young woman was absorbed in a delicate task that required all her attention . . . she was shaping her fingernails with a tiny file.

The white man's girlfriend seemed oblivious of everything except the drama being played out by Hooper Antelope. The statuesque blonde seemed to barely breathe as she slowly turned the folded umbrella in her hands.

Charlie Moon found all of this to be highly entertaining.

It was well known that the Ute Mountain Sun Dance chief strongly disapproved of unorthodox behavior at this most solemn assembly. And Hooper Antelope had always been a conservative, traditional dancer. Poker Martinez, mildly annoyed by his odd behavior, squinted oddly at Hooper, as if the man were some type of exotic creature. It would be troubling if the old man got sick right in front of everybody. But something about what he beheld was oddly familiar to Poker . . . as if he'd seen it all before. Finally, the Sun Dance chief got to his feet, as did Red Heel. Followed by his distinguished Shoshone guest, the Ute Mountain Sun Dance chief approached the dancer. Poker Martinez urged the elderly man to sit down. And rest. He had the Sun Dance chief's permission to leave the corral and drink some fruit juice. The Shoshone elder nodded his agreement with this sage advice.

But Hooper's countenance was blank; he did not reply. Indeed, he seemed barely aware of their presence.

The Shoshone joined in the effort at persuading the exhausted dancer to sit down and rest. Red Heel patted Hooper on the back. They cajoled. They reasoned. There were veiled threats of the dire medical consequences of heat stroke . . . blindness . . . going silly in the head . . . death. Even impotence.

The dancer seemed not to care.

Desperate, Poker Martinez played his trump card. If Hooper would rest, he would take him over to the Martinez camp. And he could drink a whole pitcher of lemonade.

Hooper Antelope was deaf to all entreaties.

Charlie Moon watched the curious spectacle. It was much like a baseball game. Hooper Antelope was the aging once-great pitcher who'd lost his best stuff. The wise old coaches, Poker Martinez and Red Heel, had "approached the mound" and were consulting with the weary player.

Moon grinned at the imagined conversation:

POKER MARTINEZ: Hooper my boy, you've thrown your looping curve, your low whizzer, even your spitball. And you've done good. But it's the bottom of the eighth. The game's tied. And the arm's gone, old man. It's time to give it a rest. Tell you what—I'll bring the Sandman in to pitch. Sure, the kid's green and kind of wild, but he's got a fast ball that'll knock their socks off.

HOOPER ANTELOPE: No way, Coach. I got me a few good pitches left. Just leave me in for one more inning. You'll see . . .

But Hooper Antelope said not one word.

And this wasn't a baseball game. This was *dancing thirsty*. The chief of the dance might remove a participant for unseemly behavior, but not because he was old or weary. Or about to drop from exhaustion. A dancer was supposed to be tired to the bone—that was the whole point. Dance thirsty till you fell on your face—or had your vision. So the two elders, the Ute Sun Dance chief and the Shoshone visitor, finally gave it up. They returned to their seats near the drummers.

A few of the spectators began to lose interest in the pathetic old man.

A weary tourist from Iowa fanned herself with a copy of *Newsweek*, and fantasized about a tall glass of iced tea. With a twist of lemon.

A little boy whined. When would they get to Disneyland? Shut up, his daddy advised.

Winston Steele watched Hooper Antelope through slitted lids. This old guy was on the verge of collapse. Or perhaps something entirely different . . .

The Sandman watched the pretty blonde. Wondered what it was she saw in this skinny *matukach*. Besides his good looks. And his brains. Well, there was his money, of course. Someday, Larry Sands promised himself, he would have money. Big piles of it.

Salina Timms felt Larry Sands' hungry eyes caressing her body. She found this mild assault terribly rude, but still it pleased her. The attractive woman found a small scarlet bottle in her purse. She unscrewed the ivory cap, and sniffed at the scarlet fluid. She began to paint her long nails with a small brush.

*   *   *

Somewhere, someone shuddered. And whispered these words . . . By *the pricking of my thumbs* . . .

The Sun Dance chief, his earnest pleas ignored, sat sullenly and glared at the foolish dancer.

Red Heel popped the cover on his antique pocket watch, and squinted at the thin black hands. With the methodical patience of an old man, the Shoshone elder began to wind the stem. Gradually . . . increasing the tension on the coiled spring.

Hooper Antelope stood before the sacred tree. He raised his face to the sky, and sniffed. Like an old wolf on a scent, Moon thought.

Not another dancer moved. They waited. And watched the Ute elder. To some, this was getting embarrassing. What was going on?

Of all people, a Sun Dance chief should have known.

A few dancers did know . . . or at least suspect.

Poker Martinez, his patience wearing thin, made a gesture at the singer.

At this direction from the Sun Dance chief, the plump Cheyenne got to his feet and began chanting a monotone song. Moon didn't understand the peculiar language, but it made good cadence with the booming pair of rawhide drums.

The singer sang.

The drummers drummed.

Hooper Antelope stood before the tree, like a make-believe man hewn from dry wood.

It happened suddenly, as if the dancer were answering a question. Hooper opened his mouth. And began to sing. Softly, at first. It was a humming, droning song without words. It had a stumbling kind of rhythm that did not kept pace with the drumming from the Cheyennes.

Poker Martinez leaned forward. Squinting at the dancer. Listening to the song. A faint memory began to stir in his soul. Yes . . . as if through a dim mist, it came back to him. This humming . . . almost like a honey bee, meandering among the fragrant blossoms . . . wasn't this the odd sound he'd heard in his dream? But was it possible? Hooper Antelope—could he be the man marked for a vision?

The Cheyenne singer also sensed that something was happening; he abruptly ended his song about three black wolves and sat down. At an almost imperceptible sign from the Sun Dance chief, the drummers slowed their tempo to a hollow, rhythmic beat.

As if on cue—as if this small drama had been staged—little things began to happen. Important little things . . .

Daisy Perika made her first appearance at the Sun Dance Lodge. She had a thick wand of willow branches in her hand. With an audible grunt, the old woman sat down on a wooden folding chair at the entrance to the brush corral. It had been abandoned by an earlier spectator who—for all of his remaining years—would bitterly regret leaving early on this sultry July day. To encourage Hooper Antelope, Daisy began to wave the willows. Under her breath—in the choppy Ute tongue—the shaman prayed to The Great Mysterious One. And whispered her blessings upon the dancer.

He would need them.

The old man's humming song continued.

Billy Antelope approached Daisy's chair. Around his waist—strung through the belt loops on his faded jeans—was the familiar hank of clothesline rope. Stella Antelope was, of course, close behind her grandson. Grasping the knotted end of the rope in talonlike fingers. Tapping at the parched earth with the gaudy barber-pole cane. Dragging her malformed foot in the dust. Old Popeye Woman had insisted on being present, at least for a little while, to encourage her son. Hooper Antelope, though a tribal elder, was still a child to his aged mother.

Daisy Perika pushed herself to her feet. She hugged Stella, gave her a share of the willow wands, then steered the blind woman into the wooden chair. Old Popeye Woman sat down with a nod of thanks, and leaned the striped cane against her knees.

With much puffing and grunting, Daisy seated herself on the ground beside the chair. She pulled Stella's grandchild onto her lap. The little boy was terribly embarrassed by this display of motherly attention. But out of respect for the elderly woman, Billy did not resist Daisy's embrace.

Stella Antelope waited patiently. Now far from her bed, with the welcome warmth of the sun on her shoulders, the night visit from the dwarf was all but forgotten. The blind woman listened to the few sounds in the corral, trying to imagine what was happening. There were the drums, of course . . . but beating so slowly. And muted conversations. She heard a clicking sound . . . a rustling of cloth. She tilted her head this way and that like a curious puppy.

A large yellow butterfly entered the Sun Dance Lodge. It fluttered around the dancer's head. Those who had heard tales of similar mysterious visitations held their breaths.

Daisy Perika nudged Stella Antelope's chair and whispered. "Something's come to visit Hooper."

Old Popeye Woman leaned toward her friend and grasped Daisy's shoulder. "Tell me . . . what is it?"

The shaman squinted at the dance of the golden creature. "I'm not sure. It's either a Power Spirit . . . or a butterfly."

Hooper Antelope was not aware of the butterfly. Or of the fact that his mother had arrived. The dancer swayed slightly, as if in some otherworldly ecstasy. He continued his strange, droning song.

Poker Martinez patted his bare foot to the rhythmic beat of the drums, and smiled. The presiding Sun Dance chief now had no doubt. This fulfilled his prophetic dream. Hooper Antelope was about to have his vision. The impact of this realization brought tears to the old man's face.

A few of the non-Indian spectators exchanged embarrassed glances. They wondered: Is the man drunk? Or has he gone mad from hours of exposure to the oppressive heat?

Old Popeye Woman titled her head quizzically and listened to the vision-song. The blind woman did not have to be told that this was her son's voice. To encourage Hooper, she waved the willow branches with her left hand. The short hank of rope—the physical link to her grandson—was tightly grasped in her right.

The boy, who had escaped Daisy's clutches, was now at his grandmother's elbow. He watched his uncle, who stood before the tree. In spite of the heat, Billy Antelope felt a coldness inside that he did not understand.

One man is so intent upon his business that he has not noticed the arrival of Daisy Perika. Neither is he aware of the blind woman who clings to the knotted cord, nor of her grandchild who anchors the rope. Like Hooper Antelope, he is in an exalted state of consciousness—each of his senses is elevated to an extraordinary level.

He moves his hand closer to the unlikely weapon wrapped in the folds of a cotton blanket. When the time comes, no one will notice. Except his victim. And then it will be too late.

He waits for that moment . . . his fingers tremble with anticipation.

Like the solitary man who waits, Hooper Antelope is unaware of the presence of his blind mother, of his little nephew. Moreover, the dancer is unaware of his own presence in this brush corral nestled in the bosom of Sleeping Ute Mountain. Hooper Antelope is not dead, of course—not in the traditional sense. But the dancer has departed from this world.

He stands in a lovely place . . . on the shore of a great sea, standing on swirls of orange and blue sand . . . before him stretch the great, endless waters . . . from the boiling pink clouds thunders the voice of the Father of Waters, who calls to him by his secret name. It is rapture. It seems to go on forever, this communion . . .

And then he has a connection to the limited, physical world.

The dancer can hear certain things. He can hear the drums. And other sounds, as well. He feels himself drifting back. To the heat . . . the dust . . . to Middle World.

Ahhhh . . . he no longer stands on the sandy beach, the fresh breeze does not wash his body. Nor does he smell the salty water. Or hear the deep voice calling from the pink clouds.

Now he is acutely aware of the crude brush corral . . . of the decorated cottonwood post that he helped fell in the wilderness . . . of the other dancers, all seated . . . of the drummers drumming . . . of the curious onlookers. Of his aged mother, her blind eyes fixed on the sky—and the child who stares in fascination at his uncle.

And of something else . . . his sense of smell is extraordinary. That foul scent keeps coming back . . . like pungent little waves in this shifting sea of dry air. He sniffs. And sweeps his gaze across the dusty floor of the Sun Dance Lodge.

What he sees with such terrible clarity is an unthinkable, unspeakable thing . . . something told in old tales . . . his soul freezes within him . . . now the dancer's vision fades. The darkness begins to enfold him.

One finger touches something . . . soft . . . and warm. There is immense anticipation.

Another finger touches something . . . hard . . . and cold. There is a dreadful trembling.

Hooper Antelope feels his tired heart racing; the dizziness almost overcomes him. He reels sideways like a drunken man, then rights himself. Now his eyesight is almost gone; the sun over his head is like a dim light on the ceiling of a darkened room. He raises his thin arms to the heavens. Pleading for deliverance, he turns in place . . . and wobbles . . . like a faulty gyroscope slowly spinning down. It is a piteous ballet. He hears an anxious whispering move around the edge of the brush corral. The dancers . . . the spectators . . . they murmur. Should someone go forward to assist this old man . . . or is it forbidden by the unwritten rules of the dance?

The heavy drumbeat is briefly interrupted, then, at a nod from the Sun Dance chief, resumes.

Now, his vision of Paradise is gone. Hooper Antelope cannot even see the sun, nor feel its fire on his skin. The old man, his arms uplifted, continues to turn—seeking aid from any direction whence it might come. Reality is salted with the deadly spice of imagination.

The drum thumps loudly . . . and so slowly, Hooper Antelope muses. Like the heart of some great beast that stalks him. But what beast can this be?

Now, the dreadful presence calls to him.

By his very name, it summons him.

He hears its approach and trembles.

Whuff . . . whuff . . . whuff . . . the feathered shadow wings slice the thin mountain air.

Almost simultaneously . . .

It is a small thing . . . almost hidden under the heavy thump of the rawhide drum.

Few hear the sound. It is a sharp cracking . . . a crisp snapping . . . like a dry bone breaking.

A muttered syllable . . . a virulent curse.

As the beat of the drum reverberates in his body, the dancer feels the sting of death in his flesh.

With a suddenness that startled the boy at her elbow, the blind woman leaned forward to point the willow wands toward the sacred tree. "My son . . . " she whispered, "No . . . do not harm my son."

Daisy Perika held her breath. The old shaman was certain. Somehow, through the blind eye that bulged hideously from its socket, Stella Antelope had perceived some unseen thing that moved among the darker shadows of this world.

Now, Old Popeye Woman dropped the willow wands and cried out; her mournful wail carried across the Sun Dance Lodge. Everyone heard the woman's dreadful moan.

Everyone except the dancer who reeled before the tree.

Daisy Perika shuddered with the awful realization . . . of the presence of evil. She grasped Stella's hand, but neither woman spoke. There was nothing to say. The boy hugged his grandmother; he made faint, whimpering sounds, like a small, injured animal.

Stella reached out with a trembling hand—toward her son . . . to keep him from falling.

Too late.

Hooper Antelope toppled. There was a certain cosmic inevitability about it . . . as if an old, rotted-out ponderosa had fallen on the rocky shoulders of Sleeping Ute Mountain. To return to the earth from whence it had come. To be consumed by the pine-scented soil. To sleep sweetly and deeply . . . nevermore to dream.

Everything happened at once.

Charlie Moon's eyes searched the Sun Dance grounds for a Ute Mountain police officer. They carried portable radio transceivers.

The Sun Dance chief did not move; he might have been a man chiseled from stone.

The Shoshone visitor was also still. Red Heel bowed his head, and closed his eyes.

The Cheyenne drummers shook their heads and murmured. This was a very bad thing. And this mountain was a bad place. Maybe they should go away and leave this troublesome business to the Utes.

Anxious spectators waited expectantly for someone to give an order . . . to go forward to help the fallen man. To *do* something.

The remaining dancers were now on their feet. Some gaped at the fallen man, whose body went into a spasm that caused the limbs to quiver. Others exchanged uncertain looks with their comrades.

Delly Sands stood up, her small fingers clutching at the brim of her straw hat. Her lips moved soundlessly. "Oh God . . . no . . ." She looked across the corral at her brother. And the white man. It was a pleading look.

Larry Sands shrugged hopelessly. The expression on the Sandman's face said it all. This man had been too old—too weak for dancing thirsty. So now he was dead. That's the way it was. Foolish actions have unfortunate consequences.

The blond woman looked smaller; almost fragile. Salina Timms used the parasol to hide her face from this unsavory scene.

Winston Steele knew what was expected of him; he did not hesitate. He trotted across the corral toward the man who had fallen on his face, the fingertips of his right hand touching the wood of the sacred tree. The white man, a veteran of many Sun Dances, kneeled by the stricken dancer. His face was unreadable, his manner brisk and businesslike. He touched the man's shoulder. The spasms had stopped. Skin was hot and dry. The man had exhibited other classic signs of heat stroke. Confusion . . . stupor . . . possible seizure. He took the wrist of the hand that touched the tree. No pulse. Steele rolled Hooper Antelope onto his back and pressed his ear to the man's chest. Nothing. And everybody was watching . . . expecting him to do something.

So he did.

He entwined the fingers of both hands to made a gristly club. He hammered Hooper Antelope's chest. Hard.

Once.

Delly Sands clasped her hands in prayer. "Please, God . . . please."

Twice.

"Nice try," Red Heel muttered to himself.

Three times.

The old man's belly expanded with each sharp blow to his chest.

Four times.

Poker Martinez flinched, as if he could feel the white man's intertwined fists. The fallen dancer's body should not be subjected to such violence—especially not in this sacred place. But the Sun Dance chief did not move, nor give any voice to his objection.

Five times.

With each hammer on the frail chest, the onlookers winced in empathetic pain.

The white man, who was breathing in short gasps, put his ear to Hooper Antelope's chest a second time. It was as he expected—still nothing from the pump.

Charlie Moon spotted a Ute Mountain police officer on the west side of the brush corral. The cop was engaged in an animated conversation with a shapely Hispanic woman who cuddled a white poodle in her arms. The Southern Ute policeman shouted and waved at his fellow officer, who grudgingly left the attractive lady behind. But he wasn't moving fast enough to suit Charlie Moon.

Moon waved again; the Ute Mountain officer understood that something was terribly wrong and broke into a trot.

Ignoring good manners, tribal protocol and jurisdictions—this was not the Southern Ute reservation—Charlie Moon muttered a terse instruction to the Ute Mountain policeman. The startled officer saw the fallen dancer. He jerked a radio transceiver from the canvas holster on his gun belt and made the emergency call in English: "Hey . . . Dispatch . . . you read me? This is Chula . . . Yeah . . . I'm up at the Sun Dance Lodge. A man is down. Repeat—a man is down. Medical emergency."

The dispatcher immediately relayed the alarm to the Cortez police department.

Cortez PD's response was calm and businesslike. A medivac helicopter would be in the air within three minutes. Yes, the pilot knew the general location of the Sun Dance Lodge, but it'd help to have some guidance from the mountaintop.

The Ute Mountain officer relayed instructions for the pilot.

Immediately to the south of Horse Mountain, there is a radio tower. The Sun Dance site is located downslope from the tower. A bonfire will be started near the landing area. A fire that'll make plenty of smoke. Won't be any trouble finding the place, not in broad daylight. And wind gusts are under five miles per hour.

Cortez PD rang up the company that owned the medivac copter.

Skyway Rescue Services agreed. The pilot would look for the tower and the smoke. ETA was thirty-five minutes max.

This confirmation was passed back to Towaoc PD, and relayed by the dispatcher to the Ute Mountain officer's portable transceiver. He headed off to gather wood for the bonfire.

Charlie Moon stalked across the dusty floor of the Sun Dance Lodge, toward the fallen man.

Winston Steele gritted his teeth, and wished he was somewhere else. This was little more than a performance for the hopeful spectators. The old man didn't have an ice cube's chance in a hot skillet. A long shadow was cast across the unconscious man. Steele looked up at the towering form of Charlie Moon. "You CPR qualified?" Most cops were.

"Sure." It was a requirement for employment with the SUPD. Even the dispatcher was trained in cardiopulmonary resuscitation.

"We'll double-team him, okay? I'll do mouth-to-mouth, you take care of the chest compressions. We'll go fifteen-plus-two."

Moon nodded. It was straight out of the manual. The rhythm would be fifteen chest compressions . . . then two long breaths. "Sounds like you've done this before."

Steele nodded grimly. "Couple of times."

The Ute policeman kneeled by the body. "Let's do it." He watched while the *matukach* tilted Hooper's head back and lifted his chin. This would move the tongue away from the throat and open the airway to the lungs.

Steele inhaled deeply, placed his mouth over the man's bluish lips, then exhaled. Within ten seconds, he'd pushed two long breaths into the lifeless lungs; Hooper Antelope's hairless chest heaved with each breath.

Now it was Moon's turn. He put the heel of his right hand over the breastbone, and fixed the palm of his left hand over the right.

The white man watched warily. This one would be written up as death by natural causes. Dehydration leading to exhaustion . . . leading to heat stroke . . . leading to heart failure. One way or another, almost everybody died of heart failure. When the postmortem was done, he didn't want any complications that'd need explaining to the medical examiner. Like unusual injuries on the body. This big Indian cop looked like he could crush cinder blocks with those mitts. "Easy does it, Officer. Wouldn't want to break his ribs."

Moon, who appreciated the sober reminder, nodded. He compressed the stilled heart fifteen times, then moved away so the white man could breathe more air into the dancer's lungs.

Again and again, they repeated this grim rhythm.

Old Popeye Woman listened stoically to Daisy Perika's somber explanation of what was happening. Tears rolled down Stella Antelope's face, but she did not speak.

The small boy clung to his grandmother like a fragile green vine on a dying tree. Uncle Hooper would be all right, he told himself.

The tears continued to move through the rivulets in her wrinkled face. Old Popeye Woman stared toward the sacred tree with her sightless, bulging eye. She turned her head, as if searching the corral for some unnamed source of evil. This was when she felt the first piercing ache in her chest . . . the dull pain rippling along her left arm.

Hooper Antelope is hardly aware of the flurry of activity on his behalf. He notices the discarded body not at all.

The Sun Dancer's whole attention is focused on the elder who approaches, leading two unshod horses. A fine pair of matched Pintos, with white blankets on their backs. The traveler drops the braided deerskin reins and the animals pause. One whinnies and paws impatiently at the dusty earth; the twin raises his head and sniffs at the scents in the dry mountain air.

Hooper watches the old man, who has paused to comfort the horses. The fact that this is a fellow who's supposed to be dead would normally have terrified the Ute dancer. But all fear has departed from him. Furthermore, he thirsts not . . . neither does he hunger.

But Hooper does wonder about his visitor. If you believe that Mexican woman who still lives in a crumbling adobe hut next to Nahum Yaciiti's pasture on the banks of the Animas, this old man died in a sudden windstorm that killed all his sheep. How long has it been? Four . . . five years ago? And that wasn't all the old woman told the Ute police. Armilda Esquibel claimed she'd seen holy angels come and carry Nahum's body away. It was a crazy tale, but the story stayed in circulation for one reason: though the carcasses of his sheep were scattered like broken toys, not the least trace of the old shepherd's body has ever been found.

For a while, a few of the People were of the opinion that Nahum was back on the bottle, a ragged derelict wandering the streets of some distant city. Other members of the tribe argued that Nahum's family had secretly buried his body in the badlands east of Bondad.

Whatever has really happened, Hooper thought, Nahum looks good now.

Indeed, the shepherd is strong of limb and clear of eye. He is outfitted in a fine deerskin robe, clean and white as newly fallen snow. The astonishing garment is decorated with a dozen trout made from thousands of beads sewn onto the soft leather. These jeweled fish are of many colors.

Glimmering emerald . . . the deep shade of cool forest paths.

Glistening sapphire . . . crystalline tears shed by mourning spirits.

Crimson drops . . . these are beyond cost . . . the blood of the Lamb.

Bright feathers fringe this garment. Hooper knows that such fine eagle plumes as these are reserved for those who have served well in hard-fought battles. And counted many coup . . .

Now, the old man approaches. Nahum looks into the dancer's soul. And offers his hand.

Hooper Antelope hesitates, then accepts the shepherd's hand. The Ute is relieved. This isn't a dead man's flesh . . . taut gristle and dry bone. It is warm with life.

Nahum gestures toward the faraway lands outside the Sun Dance Lodge and smiles. "It's time, Hooper."

"I know."

The shepherd looks toward the east. "We'd best be goin' on our way . . . while there's enough light."

The dancer takes a deep breath. "Is it a long trip?"

Nahum nods. "But we got good horses."

Moon and the white man worked hard at the CPR procedure. Steele breathed his breaths into Hooper's lungs. Moon pressed the heels of his hands against the dead man's chest.

It didn't help. But they couldn't stop.

Everyone was watching.

Expecting them to perform a miracle.

Finally, Winston Steele paused. The weary *matukach* turned his face toward the Ute Sun Dance chief.

Poker Martinez's eyes were pleading. Don't tell me this . . . no . . .

Steele shook his head slowly. All knew the verdict.

The dancer was dead.

Moon was enormously relieved to hear the staccato *phut-phut-phut* of the medical helicopter. It sat down in a whirling cloud of dust and bonfire smoke, thirty long strides from the corral.

Poker Martinez made the expected announcement. This summer's Sun Dance was terminated. The dancers were dismissed.

The Cortez paramedics were wheeling the lifeless body from the corral when someone noticed the frantic gestures of the little boy who had a rope dangling from his waist. This child was mumbling, trying to tell them something. They did not understand. It was Daisy Perika who realized that Stella Antelope was slumped in her folding chair. The blind woman's jaw was slack, her eyes closed as if she slept. But Old Popeye Woman did not sleep.

The paramedics immediately gave a pair of Ute Mountain policemen charge of the gurney bearing Hooper Antelope's lifeless body. The medical technicians began a systematic examination of the elderly Ute woman. The Hispanic man put his finger under her jaw and checked the carotid artery for a pulse. They checked for breathing. The woman pulled back the lid over the bulging eye, thus exposing it to sunlight, and watched for dilation of the pupil. After a frantic fifteen seconds, the heavyset young woman and her comrade exchanged brief smiles. This one was still alive.

The Ute policemen hurried toward the helicopter with Hooper's body. They did this not because they thought he might still be alive and in urgent need of medical attention. The Utes made haste because they knew that he was dead—and it was a bad thing to be so close to a fresh corpse. It was best to turn this grim burden over to the *matukach* technician who waited in the helicopter. There was a complication—to slide the gurney inside the aircraft, it was necessary to collapse the mechanism that held the eight-inch rubber wheels.

In their eagerness to rid themselves of this unwanted burden, the policemen made a bad job of it.

Dozens of onlookers watched in horror as the gurney tilted and the dancer's body flopped onto the stony ground. The policemen stood like statues . . . loath to touch the corpse. A pale tourist came forward; the burley man helped the helicopter pilot load Hooper's body back onto the gurney. The embarrassed Ute policemen stood at a safe distance, muttering dark curses at their bad luck. And wondered at the foolishness of these *matukach*, who thought nothing of touching a newly dead corpse—whose spirit still hung over it like a bad smell. Any civilized person should

100 JAMES D. DOSS

know to stay away from a dead body for at least a day. And then move them only after they were properly wrapped in a blanket. Maybe such ignorance was why the whites were always getting sick with unheard of diseases.

Within minutes Stella Antelope was installed in the aircraft next to her son's body. Then, as the night visitor had foretold, the mother went on a flight. The noisy bird ascended. It flew toward Cortez. To the north.

Her son, led by the shepherd, already approached the place where he would find his rest.

The blind, crippled woman, who had lost count of the hard winters of her life, was bone-weary. But Old Popeye Woman's rest would be delayed.

For a time . . . and a time . . . and a time.

They watched the helicopter rise into the pale blue emptiness over Sleeping Ute Mountain.

Moon surveyed the small crowd. Delly Sands was speaking to the blond woman, whose face was shaded by the pink parasol. Larry Sands, who seemed unaware of his sister, was standing with Winston Steele and a group of the younger dancers. Poker Martinez was there, as was the visiting Shoshone elder. Even the Sioux was counted among their number. All watched the aircraft turn into a black dot as it sped away toward Cortez.

Delly Sands appeared at Moon's elbow. She looked so small. So alone. Like a lost child. She leaned on him.

He put his arm around her shoulders.

"Charlie . . . Larry says that dancer . . . is he . . . "

He nodded.

"But why . . . how . . . ?"

Moon shrugged. "Who knows. Hooper was pretty old for dancing thirsty. I imagine his heart just gave out."

She shuddered. "And his mother?"

He hugged her tighter. "She'll be fine."

*   *   *

Moon gathered Daisy and the child into the SUPD Blazer. It was a slow, bumpy ride down the barren, rocky road that criss-crossed the slopes of the mountain. Within half an hour, they had left the village of Towaoc behind. Minutes later, Moon turned north by the casino onto route 666. The child was in the back seat, craning his neck in a vain attempt to see the aircraft that carried his grandmother and his uncle to the hospital.

Daisy Perika leaned close to her nephew; she spoke in a hoarse whisper so the child would not hear. "I don't like this."

Moon watched the speedometer needle jitter pass seventy. "I don't guess any of us do."

"Except," the old woman rasped, "the one who's responsible."

He frowned at the stretch of highway snaking along in front of him. "Responsible?"

She nodded vigorously. "Sure. For what happened to Hooper Antelope."

Moon started to speak, then kept his peace. Hooper was an old man playing a young man's game. That's why he'd collapsed. But there was no point in annoying Aunt Daisy. Once she got started . . .

She glared up at him. "You don't even know what I'm talking about, do you?"

He assumed an innocent expression. "Nope."

"Hmmph."

Well, she was in a bad mood already. To soothe his aunt, the Ute policeman pretended to hazard a guess. "You believe somebody . . . *caused* what happened to Hooper?"

Her eyes snapped at him; she jutted her chin toward the dusty dashboard. "I don't *believe*. I *know*."

The policeman shrugged in a fashion that was intended to be noncommittal.

The old shaman interpreted her nephew's gesture as dismissive. And arrogant. Well fine. Let the big smart aleck find out for himself.

It is a curious thing that children are often treated as if they neither hear nor understand. From the back seat of the police car Billy Antelope had listened intently to every word. Like the old woman—even more than the shaman—the quiet child had seen what he had seen.

And knew what he knew.

CHAPTER 4

Cortez
The Hospital

Gradually, they began to arrive in the visitor's lounge. All were acquainted with Hooper Antelope; most knew his mother. Hooper was dead, so they'd pay their respects to his ailing mother. And to her brother Reuben, who had been camped at the Sun Dance, but had missed all the excitement at the brush corral.

Poker Martinez arrived early, accompanied by Red Heel. The Ute Mountain Sun Dance chief and his Shoshone colleague nodded gravely to the assembly, then sat down on a vinyl-upholstered couch. The lame Paiute singer shuffled in, nodding amiably at one and all. Stone Pipe showed up. Looking, Moon thought, like an Indian who'd stepped right off one of them old nickels. The gloomy Sioux spoke briefly with Reuben Antelope about the death of his nephew in the Sun Dance Lodge, and inquired about the health of his sister.

Reuben informed the Sioux that Stella was still in the emergency room. Soon as they put her in a private room, then maybe she could have visitors. That was all he knew.

This formality completed, Stone Pipe had a hushed conversation with Red Heel, then seated himself cross-legged on the floor.

When the white dancer showed up with his blond girlfriend, the Sioux's face became stony; he got to his feet and moved to the farthest corner of the room. The white man introduced himself to Reuben Antelope as Winston Steele. From Denver, he said. The blond woman, who was dressed in a filmy white skirt and blue silk blouse, was Salina Timms. She sat on a chair in the corner and crossed her legs. Very long legs, they were, and well shaped.

Delly Sands arrived. Her large straw hat—suspended from a cord around her neck—bounced on her back. She nodded politely to Steele and his girlfriend, who nodded back and smiled sweetly. Delly patted Little Rope Boy on the head, hugged Reuben Antelope (who did not mind this attention from the pretty girl), embraced Daisy, then sat down on the couch by Charlie Moon.

Delly noticed Moon's occasional glances at Steele's statuesque blonde and whispered this in the policeman's ear. "Bleached. Or maybe a wig."

Moon allowed himself a smile. This was about what Myra Cornstone had said about Delly's locks at the church play. And, of course, Myra had been right. It had been a wig. Miss Timms might be bleached, but he'd give odds she wasn't wearing a wig. Funny thing, though. When a woman was homely, other women never questioned the authenticity of her hair color.

Delly scooted closer to Moon, so that her hip barely touched him. What was it men saw in bleached hair? "Winston Steele says Hooper Antelope died of heat exhaustion. Said he should never have been dancing . . . he was too old and too sickly."

Moon nodded. That about summed it up.

"Is Stella okay, Charlie?"

He looked at his clasped hands and shrugged. "Far as I know."

"Well," she said with forced cheerfulness, "I'm sure she'll be all right."

The Ute policeman grunted. Right now, he wasn't all that sure of anything.

Delly Sands desperately wanted to strike up a conversation with this silent man. Maybe some guy talk would do it. She nudged Moon gently with her elbow. "So how're the Denver Broncos doing?"

He looked down at this uncommonly pretty girl. "Guess we'll have to wait and see."

She raised her eyebrows. So innocently. "Wait for what, Charlie?"

"Well . . . for football season to start."

"Oh," she said. And bit her lip. And looked awfully embarrassed.

Charlie Moon immediately wished he'd kept his mouth shut. She'd only wanted to make conversation that'd interest a man but didn't know the first thing about football. Poor little kid. He put his arm around her shoulders.

Delly closed her enormous brown eyes and rested her head against the big man's chest. She smiled. In her purse was a Bronco season ticket. In her head was the name of every player on the team. And, of course, the regular season schedule that began on August 31 and ended on December 21.

Charlie Moon was a few yards down the hall from the waiting room, dropping dimes into a coffee machine. He held a brown plastic cup under the brown plastic dispenser and pushed a brown plastic button under the Coffee/WCrm/Wsug label. A spurt of muddy liquid filled the cup just enough to spill over the top and scald his fingertips. He sniffed at the steaming liquid. There was almost no aroma . . . the stuff was the color of greasy dishwater.

He took a sip. Yep. Dishwater all right.

The Ute policeman dumped the contents of the plastic cup down the drain and wished he hadn't wasted his forty cents.

Moon turned when he saw Larry Sands stomping down the hall.

The Sandman spotted the tall man and spoke first. "Charlie, you know where my sister is?"

Moon nodded toward the end of the hall, where Delly Sands and another two dozen people waited to see whether Stella Antelope would live or die.

Sands paused, noticing the empty plastic cup in Moon's hand. He glanced suspiciously at the coffee machine, and fumbled in his jeans for change. "That stuff any good?"

Moon frowned at this dispenser of foul liquid. "Well, I sure emptied *my* cup."

The newcomer began feeding coins into the slot.

The policeman leaned on the machine and watched the Sandman's face. "Maybe you could help me."

"How?" Sands punched the button that said BLACK.

"Tell me about some of the people at the Sun Dance."

The Sandman gave him a wary glance. "Which ones?"

"First of all, the *matukach* dancer."

The young Ute shrugged. "He's kind of a friend of mine. Winston Steele. Or I guess I should say *Doctor* Steele." There was a hint of envy in his tone.

Moon wondered—what kind of a friend? "What kind of a doc?"

"Oncologist."

"Oh. Cancer specialist, huh?" That wasn't a subject he cared to pursue. "What about the blond woman who watches him dance?"

The Sandman's face twisted into a leer. "Salina Timms. Or again, I guess I should say *Doctor* Timms."

"What kind of—"

"She's not *that* kind of doctor," Sands said quickly. "Salina's a Ph.D. A very successful anthropologist, as a matter of fact."

Moon was surprised at this revelation. She didn't *look* like an anthropologist. The Ute had met up with his share of these folk. Most of 'em were . . . well they weren't at all like *this* lady. Dr. Timms didn't look like someone who'd know a pickax from a trowel. But looks often fooled a man. "She do any fieldwork around here?"

"Salina's spending the summer over at Crow Canyon. I may just drop by and see her sometime." Now the leer threatened to twist his face off.

Moon chuckled. "So you gonna steal your doctor friend's gal away?"

The Sandman winked slyly and shifted to his supercilious college-boy tone. "You infer far too much from my remarks."

Moon shifted gears. "Who's that old man hangin' around with the Sun Dance chief?"

Sands' brow wrinkled in a thoughtful frown. "Oh . . . you must mean Red Heel. He's a Shoshone elder. Some kind of big shot Sun Dance expert." The young man paused and thought about it. "I've seen him somewhere before. Probably at a dance up in Wyoming." The Sandman took a drink of the greasy black liquid and immediately spat it onto the floor. He coughed and wiped his mouth with his shirtsleeve.

"Dammit, Charlie, I can't believe you actually drank this swill."

Moon grinned happily. "You infer far too much from my remarks."

They had put her in a private room, on a bed with starched sheets.

Stella Antelope, a pitiful lump of humanity under the faded lime-green cover, was suitably wired and plumbed. Electrocardiogram leads sensed minute electrical signals on her chest and displayed sharp spikes on a green cathode-ray tube. With each S-wave, an annoying beeper chirped. A catheter inserted into a hardened artery measured blood pressure. A transparent IV tube snaked from a yellow plastic bottle to a patch of adhesive tape on Old Popeye Woman's thin wrist. This assembly dripped a solution of saline, vitamin-enriched nutrients, and medications into her knotty vein.

One eye was almost closed; the bulging eye rotated this way and that. As if the blind woman were searching for something. Or someone.

A grim cluster of Utes stood in the hall, occasionally stealing quick glances through the sickroom door. Muttering dark commentary on the untimely death of Hooper Antelope. Exchanging dire opinions on how sick his mother was. And what Old Popeye Woman's chances were. If her brother had not been present, bets would have been made.

The boy stood by his grandmother's bed. The hank of rope was still looped around his waist. Billy placed the knotted end in Old Popeye Woman's hand. She grasped tenaciously at this lifeline to the world of the living.

Daisy Perika wiped at the old woman's forehead with a damp washcloth.

Charlie Moon stood just inside the door. The big man rocked back and forth, easing his weight from the heels to the toes of his boots. He rotated the wide brim of a black Stetson in his big hands. Stella was almost hidden under the sheet; he watched his aunt and the little boy attend to her. Too bad Hooper Antelope had cashed in his chips at the Sun Dance. Right in front of his mamma. Even though the blind woman couldn't see her son fall on the sacred tree, Hooper's death had been too much for Stella. The cardiologist said he'd found proteins in her blood that indicated a myocardial infarction. In layman's terms—heart attack. But Mrs. Antelope was too old and weak for surgery, so they'd do what they could with medication. Well, Moon thought, that's the way it goes. A policeman sees more than his share of folks die. And you never know when your own number will come up. As far as Stella's chances, he guessed it was a two-to-one shot against her lasting out the night. It was up to the doctors and the nurses now; there wasn't nothing much a policeman could do about something like this. He left the sickroom and joined the cluster of Utes who waited in the hall.

Stella's only surviving brother was a gaunt man bent forward like a broken reed. Reuben Antelope leaned on a heavy oak walking staff and stared through thick spectacles down the hall toward the busy nurses' station where women in white uniforms and rubber-soled shoes darted back and forth. This old man was uneasy in hospitals.

Reuben's son Horace stood at his side, his thumbs hooked under a beaded belt, chewing a wad of tobacco. And something of importance occupied Horace's brain. This is what it was: even though Aunt Stella had moved into town to that little bitty apartment, Daddy still kept her bedroom for her. Daddy always said his sister had slept in that same corner room when she was a little girl—and it was still hers. But Aunt Stella hardly ever used it, except sometimes on the Sunday night when Daddy brought her and Billy home after church. It wasn't fair. Horace leaned close to his father and muttered: "Daddy, if Aunt Stella dies, can I get her bedroom?"

"Hush up, boy." Reuben had once thrashed an Ignacio drunk who'd called Horace a half-wit. But the father knew his son. Horace would need some extra schoolin' if he wanted to learn to be a halfwit.

Horace, thus chastised, turned away. He moved close to the door of the small room where his aunt lay on the bed. Billy, Aunt Stella's favorite, was in there. With that damn rope. And Daisy Perika, that funny old woman, was also with Aunt Stella. He'd heard funny stories about what happened sometimes when someone died. Like that Mexican woman, who'd claimed she seen angels come to get Nahum Yaciiti right after the old shepherd died in that tornado. Aunt Stella looked almost dead already. Maybe somethin' would happen. Maybe angels would come for her. *Swing low, sweet chariot . . . comin' for to carry me home . . .* it'd sure be a fine thing, to see some angels. Would they have wings? Horace leaned on the door frame. And watched. And listened.

"Old folks like my sister," Reuben Antelope grumped to Moon, "don't get well in these places."

Moon patted the tribal elder on the back.

The old man nodded, agreeing with himself. No, this was just half a step to the grave. Poor Hooper, who'd pushed himself too hard in that Sun Dance, was dead as a stone. And Reuben had a sense of impending emptiness in his life . . . before the night was over, Stella would also leave him. And before too much longer, he would follow his sister. Last summer, the young wife he'd recently married had left in his pickup and found herself a man down at Aztec who had a prosperous business selling bottled gas. Didn't even bother to get a divorce. It had bothered Reuben enough that his fifty-six-year-old wife was bedding herself down with a new husband. But it made him furious to think of that wife-stealing bastard driving his fine Ford pickup truck, which was barely two years old. Not even broken in good. So he'd sent his son to steal the truck back. Horace wasn't none too smart about most things, but he was good at doing sneaky stuff. And with the spare pickup keys in his pocket, he'd had no trouble at all. The old man was determined that his unfaithful wife would never have the pickup again. Reuben thought maybe he'd have the F250 buried with him, like a warrior with his favorite horse. This thought brought the hint of a smile to his thin lips.

Reuben Antelope felt in the pocket of his bib overalls for the small cotton bag of Kentucky Black Leaf tobacco and the packet of tissue-thin papers. He thought about making himself a smoke. These nurses would fall on him like the plague if he rolled a cigarette. Well just let 'em try to tell *him* what to do. He waited until the nurse attending his sister had left, then turned his back on the nurse's station and removed the cotton sack from his bib pocket. He poured a generous helping of fragrant tobacco into the white rectangle, licked the edge of the paper, and sealed the twisted smoke. If them nurses don't like it, that's just tough. I ain't afraid of no women, so piss on 'em all. But, as he struck a match on his overall leg, Reuben trembled at the thought of being discovered.

Horace Antelope, who dared not enter the sickroom, watched the two women and the little boy. He strained to hear what was going on at Aunt Stella's bedside.

Billy Antelope watched his grandmother through unblinking eyes.

Daisy muttered comforting words to her friend. Occasionally, the old woman whispered a reply, and Daisy would lean forward to place her ear close to Stella's mouth.

Horace could not hear these words. Nor did he yet discern the approach of angels. But gradually, he began to feel it in the marrow of his bones . . . something important was about to happen.

Stella Antelope tugged on the rope; Billy responded by moving close to his grandmother's face. She whispered in his ear; the boy's eyes widened. After a few seconds, Old Popeye Woman waved her hand, indicating that she was finished talking to him. But even as he backed away, Stella held on tightly to her end of the hank of clothesline rope. Billy looked up expectantly at Daisy Perika.

Now Stella beckoned to the faithful woman who stood patiently at her bedside. She had something to say. Something important.

Daisy leaned over Stella's bed. "Yes?"

"Hooper . . . my son . . . he's . . . "

"Be still, now," the old woman said. "The doctor don't want you movin' around."

With an enormous effort, Stella raised herself on one elbow. "Hooper's . . . dead." It was not a question.

Daisy nodded, as if the blind woman could see her.

Old Popeye Woman didn't blink. The blind eye stared coldly at Daisy Perika. "It was . . . *uru-sawa-ci*."

The shaman nodded at the protruding eye. "I know it was a witch, Stella. But we don't know who—"

Stella Antelope raised a withered hand; it trembled. "I'll show you . . . I'll show you who . . . " Her head turned toward the window, then the door. Her small frame shuddered once, then again. Like an old, worn-out engine. About to stop running.

Daisy Perika waited for Old Popeye Woman to tell her who the witch was.

But Stella collapsed upon the rumpled pillow and began to breathe her rattling breaths.

Horace Antelope, who had overheard the conversation, moved to his father's side. "Aunt Stella just told Daisy Perika that it was a *witch* who killed Hooper."

Reuben frowned at his son. "It's bad luck to talk about witches. You keep quiet now, you hear me?"

But the Utes gathered in the hall had heard Horace's troubling report. This was followed by an uneasy silence . . . knowing nods. And by dark murmurs. Reuben's boy might not be overly smart, but he had other gifts to make up for his small brain. Yes, Horace could hear a grasshopper spit tobacco juice at twenty yards. So if he said he'd heard what them whispering women had said, why you could bank on it. So the story passed among them, then down the hall to another group of Utes who were just arriving. The story grew with each telling. Old Popeye Woman had told Daisy Perika that it was a witch who'd killed her son. Daisy Perika—you know what *that old woman* can do—she'll find out who the *uru-sawa-ci* is. And when the witch is exposed—Daisy'll know what to do with him. Why he's already as good as a dead man. Opinions varied on who the witch might be, but they were unanimous in their agreement that it could not be a Ute. It would be a Navajo, most likely. Or one of them peculiar Pueblo Indians from New Mexico. A few bets were made. The smart money was on an old Navajo man who'd driven up Sleeping Ute Mountain in a new Oldsmobile. The car had Texas plates and a bumper sticker that proclaimed: DONT BLAME ME—I VOTED GREEN. He'd hung around the Sun Dance grounds, smoking smelly cigars, winking at pretty girls, singing a Willie Nelson song about how Pancho wore his gun outside his pants. A wrong customer if ever there was one.

Horace returned to his post by the door. And waited. Like a vulture, Daisy Perika thought. The old woman got up from her chair by the bed. She closed the door in his face.

There was a stillness about the room.
It was time.
The shaman felt the dreaded *presence* coming near. It was dark . . . and chilly . . . like a steady rain at midnight, beating on the metal roof of her trailer home. Made you want to shiver and pull the covers over your face. Daisy looked uncertainly at Billy; the faithful boy stood by the bed, the rope linking him to his grandmother was taut between them. Should she send the little boy away on some errand? No. Though he was awfully young . . . this was his rightful place.
Stella Antelope also sensed the approach of the visitor. But what she sensed was neither dark nor dreadful. Death was overdue, and welcome.
One hand still clutched the rope. With her free hand, she reached out toward the boy and touched his face. "Be good," she said. Then, Old Popeye woman relaxed. And seemed . . . to sleep.

Daisy opened the door; she gave Charlie Moon a hard look and jerked her head to indicate the still form of Stella Antelope.
Reuben Antelope had lighted a twisted tube of tobacco just before he heard Moon's grunt. Reuben thought it was a warning. Certain that he'd been discovered by those hard-nosed nurses, the old man muttered a curse under his breath; he attempted to stub

the offending smoke out in his bib pocket. But the minor commotion had nothing to do with the nurses, nor with his home-rolled cigarette. Something else was wrong.

"Down here," Moon shouted, "we need some help." The big man's bass voice boomed along the hall like summer thunder. A half dozen nurses paused in midstride, two sprinted toward Stella's room. A thin, harried-looking R.N. took one look at the aged woman's still form, the blue tint of her lips. "Code Blue!," she shouted, "clear the room."

Moon and Daisy attempted to remove Billy from his grandmother's bedside. But the rope, tied securely around the boy's waist, was clutched tightly in Stella's hand. The nurse pried at Stella's bony fingers, but couldn't get the knotted cord loose from the death grip. Somewhat clumsily, she attempted to untie the knot at the boy's trouser loop, but could not. "Please," she said to the policeman, "we've got to clear the room for the cart."

Moon produced a bone-handled folding knife from his pocket. He cut the rope. This action seemed to remove a lifeline between the old woman and the boy. Stella's fingers relaxed; the hank of knotted rope fell to the floor. The boy made a dull, choking sound; his eyes rolled backward. Moon scooped the child up in his arms and was barely outside the room when a husky young man pushed a heavy cart through the doorway. The nurse shouted: "No respiration. Can't find a pulse." She was pressing on Stella's chest. "Prepare for defib. Move it!"

And then the door was closed.

The Utes stood in the hall, waiting helplessly.

They were joined by Winston Steele and his blond girlfriend. And Red Heel . . . and Stone Pipe . . . and the Paiute Singer.

A tall, stoop-shouldered man showed up with a gurney. He was careful not to make eye contact with any of the Utes who waited in the hall. The orderly pushed the wheeled cart into Stella's room. The door was closed again.

The boy in Moon's arms was stirring.

Daisy Perika stared glumly at the shut door. Seemed like all of her old friends were dying off; every month there were one or two funerals in Ignacio. And new graves in the cemetery on the banks of the Pinos.

Reuben Antelope's gaze moved back and forth between the closed door and the child cradled in the policeman's big arms. Stella was going away to that far place where no one returned from. Well, she was old as sin—and crippled and blind—so it was bound to happen someday. He'd have to get her properly buried, of course, because she had no other kin who could see to it. This reminded him of the child. Once Stella was gone, Billy would have to be taken care of. He'd have to take him in and raise him up to be a man. It'd been a long time since he'd had a child in his house. Horace had a child's mind, of course, but that was different.

Horace fidgeted. He told himself that he didn't really *want* her to die. But if Aunt Stella did die, he'd for sure get her cool corner bedroom. And go to sleep listening to the cottonwood leaves rustle on the rusted steel roof. As he thought of this, the door to his aunt's room opened. Horace watched two men hurry down the hall, one pushing the gurney, the other steering it from the front. Aunt Stella was on it.

A nurse came out of the room, pushing an IV stand. She paused and patted Reuben on the arm. "We're doing everything we can for your sister."

The resuscitation procedure continued in Intensive Care. With dogged determination, the physician pressed the stainless steel defibrillator paddles on her frail chest. Upon the first application of electric current, every fiber in the quivering, impotent muscles of Stella's fibrillating heart was shocked into complete immobility. Again and again she discharged the capacitor through Stella's pallid flesh. The theory behind this was that the heart muscles, once completely stopped, would restart themselves. And beat normally.

Most of the time, this is how it worked.

Not this time.

The grim-faced cardiologist found the assembly of Stella's friends in the waiting room. She said the usual things you say. We did our best . . . the patient was very weak . . . I'm so sorry.

Daisy wept openly at the news, as did Delly Sands. The blond woman dabbed at her eyes with a linen handkerchief.

A few men turned away and coughed. And wiped at their eyes.

The child did not weep. Billy went to the window and pushed his nose against the cold pane. He stared at the place where the sun had set; it was like a smear of blood in the sky. A wound that would not heal.

The Ute policeman went to stand by the boy. The cut rope still dangled from Billy's waist. Moon checked his jacket pocket for the knotted end of the cord. Funny thing . . . the hank of rope still felt warm. Like he'd just taken it from Old Popeye Woman's hand. He put his massive hand on the child's frail shoulder; Billy seemed not to notice this kind attention.

Reuben Antelope also came to stand by the boy. The bent man leaned on his oaken staff, and looked up at the big policeman. "So it's finished."

"Yeah," Moon nodded to Stella's brother, "it's over."

But it was not over. *It* had just begun.

Reuben Antelope—flanked by Daisy Perika and Charlie Moon—approached the room where Stella had died. The boy held on to Moon's thumb. Reuben, crunching his hat in his hands, leaned forward to look at the bed where his sister's body had lain. The bed was, of course, empty. A short, plump nurse's aide was struggling as she attempted to stretch a fresh sheet across the lumpy mattress. Reuben stared rudely at the woman's rump. And thought fondly of the wife who'd left him.

The nurse, as if feeling the old man's eyes on her behind,

turned to discover this odd group of visitors. "Yes?" She offered a motherly smile to the cute little boy, who responded by looking at the floor.

Moon decided to speak for the old man. "Ma'am . . . this is Reuben Antelope. Brother of Stella Antelope, the woman who . . ." the Ute policeman cleared his throat, "the deceased."

Daisy raised an eyebrow at her awkward nephew, then smiled at the aide, who appeared to be a bit slow on the uptake. "Stella was the old woman who was in that bed. She died. Her brother Reuben needs to make arrangements."

The nurse stared blankly. "Arrangements?"

Daisy pointed downward. "For burial."

The nurse's aide put her hand to her mouth in a sympathetic gesture. "Oh, I'm *so* sorry. I just came on shift and didn't know anything about—" She pointed. "Maybe you should check with the nurse's station down the hall."

The station was manned by a white-frocked woman with broad shoulders and the hint of a mustache on her lip. Reuben completely hid himself behind Charlie Moon, who took off his hat. "This," he said, "is Reuben Antelope. Brother of Stella Antelope."

The head nurse blinked at Daisy Perika, then raised her eyebrows. This sure didn't look like nobody's *brother*. She opened her mouth to comment, then shut it. She was a kind-hearted soul, who hardly knew how to address a man who looked and dressed exactly like a woman.

Daisy Perika chuckled. "Not me, honey. That's Stella's brother, behind Charlie." She nodded toward Reuben, who peeked uncertainly around the policeman's arm at the nurse.

"Oh," the nurse said. She addressed her words to the tall policeman. "And what can I do for you?"

Moon jerked his thumb toward Reuben. "Mr. Antelope's sister died a little while ago. He'll need to make some arrangements . . ."

"For her body," Daisy said.

This brought a look of puzzlement to the nurse's broad face.

She picked up a clipboard and blinked at the papers. She looked blankly at Moon, then at Daisy. "The body of the deceased . . . Mrs. Stella Antelope . . . was picked up about ten minutes ago."

"By who?" Daisy asked.

The nurse consulted the clipboard to make sure. "By the pickup man from Spaidman and Son's Funeral Home."

Moon frowned. "Who authorized removal of the body?"

The nurse shrugged. "I was coming on shift while they were taking her out. I naturally assumed that the next of kin had given the okay, but you know how it is when . . ." She ran out of words. Usually it was an honest mistake, but sometimes the pickup man got a little too eager and a body was carted off without proper authorization. Whatever had happened, it wouldn't do to get a bunch of Ute Indians all pissed off. No, this could get nasty. If these Indians raised a big fuss, the hospital administrator would chew on her like a hungry old dog with a fresh bone. "Maybe I'd better call up the funeral home and see how this happened."

"I'll go over there myself." Reuben sighed with the resignation of one who has endured many outrages." The old man looked up imploringly at Charlie Moon. "Would you come with me?"

Moon was about to make an excuse about needing to get back to Ignacio to take care of some police business, when Daisy cut in: "He'll be glad to go to the funeral home. And take me along." She elbowed her big nephew. "Won't you Charlie?"

The boy, still hanging on the policeman's fingers, looked up at him with enormous, hopeful eyes.

"Sure," Moon said woodenly.

It would not be long before he would regret this decision, forced upon him by his troublesome aunt. And the child.

The entrance to Spaidman & Sons was the portal to a large, oval room. This parlor, which served as a lobby of sorts, was carpeted in deep burgundy. An assortment of antique chairs and lamps were placed strategically around the papered wall. In the very center of the oval room was an immaculate oval table. In the center of the oval table was a white telephone. Behind the varnished table, seated prettily in an antique chair, was a small woman with a pretty oval face. She wore a custom-made pinstriped suit and horn-rimmed spectacles that gave her a mildly comic, owlish appearance. Her hair, the reddish-gold tint of clover honey, was done into an old-fashioned bun. Barely raising one perfectly formed eyebrow, she peered though the round spectacles at the Utes. Especially the tall one. A smile visited her lips.

Charlie Moon had a brief one-way conversation with the polite young woman, who nodded at appropriate intervals. When he had stated his business, she promptly lifted the telephone receiver off its cradle, and pressed two digits. To summon the director of Spaidman & Sons mortuary establishment.

The Utes waited in the sumptuous red-carpeted parlor.

Daisy Perika, who was oblivious of the stares from the bespectacled receptionist, wandered about. She touched each piece of furniture, turned lamps on and off, squinted critically at paintings of lush forest and meadow.

Reuben Antelope, hands thrust deep into his pockets, stood uneasily by a marble fireplace. He kept a wary eye on his son.

Horace Antelope was trying hard to convince himself that it was too bad the old woman had died. But his aunt had been awfully old—and clubfooted and blind to boot. Maybe even tonight—if Daddy didn't put up a big fuss—he'd put his pillows and blanket on her fine bed in the corner room.

Of them all, only Billy was completely content to be where he was. Little Rope Boy stared with wide-eyed fascination at a shimmering chandelier whose slender crystals played rainbow games with dancing rays of light.

The director of the funeral home entered the parlor without making a sound. His contact at the hospital had already informed him about the situation. My goodness, the old man was actually wearing *overalls*. He approached Reuben with a solemn countenance. "Mr. Antelope, I presume."

Reuben nodded.

"I understand that there was some . . . ahhh . . . confusion about the authorization for removing of your sister's body from the hospital. I want to assure you that I have had a stern talk with those of my staff who were responsible for this . . . this unfortunate misunderstanding."

Reuben's response was barely audible; the director leaned close to hear. "Stella . . . her body . . . she's got to be wrapped up in a blanket." The old man paused and blinked at the warm rays of light beaming through a west window. "Before the sun goes down," he added. The weary man turned to his son. "You and me, we'll go and buy a blanket."

Horace shrugged and made a sly half grin. Aunt Stella got herself a blanket, but he got a whole new bedroom.

The funeral home director, who expected such eccentricities of the Utes, nodded graciously at Reuben Antelope. "Quite," he said as if addressing himself. "The brother of the deceased will provide a blanket. We will use it . . . as directed. There are some other details to be worked out . . . such as selection of an appropriate coffin."

Reuben seemed to be looking far away. At nothing.

"The coffin decision can wait until tomorrow," Moon said. The words were uttered softly, but with unquestionable authority.

The gray-haired man nodded. It looked like he'd be dealing with the tall one. "We have some preliminary preparations to make. And then you may view the remains." She was already in the fridge. Embalming could wait until tomorrow morning.

The pastor of St. Ignatius Catholic church, alerted by tribal police of the untimely death of Hooper Antelope and the hospitalization of his mother, had immediately departed for Cortez. But Father Raes Delfino had arrived at the hospital too late to provide any comfort to Stella Antelope. Old Popeye Woman's bed—now covered with crisp new sheets—was occupied by a pale man who'd suffered a heart attack while mowing his lawn.

The priest crossed the threshold at Spaidman & Sons Funeral Home just as a thin young man with perpetually sad eyes brought this solemn news to the visitors: the remains are ready for viewing.

Billy Antelope remained in the lobby with the pretty receptionist, who sat him on the oval table. With admirable disregard for that valuable antique, she offered him a donut coated with powdered sugar. The gift was gratefully accepted.

The sad-eyed young man led the mourners down a wide hallway. The emerald carpet under their feet was like spongy moss along the path in a shady glade. The wallpaper, which had a pattern of tall ferns, enhanced the effect. At the end of this twilight corridor was a large arched doorway, painted in antique ivory. Looks like the Pearly Gates, Horace thought. This was, in fact, the entrance to the Golden Visitation Room, where, so it seemed, the abandoned cocoon of Stella's soul reclined.

In the silent chamber beyond the varnished arch were a half dozen ornately carved oak chairs. The soft amber lighting was indirect, the sources of illumination cunningly hidden in various crannies and crevices. The display coffin was centered on the far wall, resting on a carved support fashioned of stained walnut. Because the woman who had occupied the body was a Christian, a polished birch cross had been placed on the wall above the altar.

Charlie Moon, Reuben Antelope, and his son Horace paused in the broad archway that led to this inner sanctum. Reuben would not enter the Golden Visitation room because his sister had died so recently. For the next several hours, his sister's ghost would still be hovering near her body. And newly-born ghosts tended to be somewhat cranky; you could never tell what one of 'em might do.

Moon, who knew himself to be a man who was totally free

of superstitions, told himself that he stayed in the hallway because . . . well, because old Reuben needed the company.

Horace Antelope remained with his father. He busied himself with the close inspection of a marble statue. Hmmm. This was a mostly naked woman, with some kind of wrinkled cloth hanging over one shoulder. And a thick snake coiled around her extended arm.

The pastor of St. Ignatius Catholic Church—long accustomed to death and corpses—entered into this silent place with an easy familiarity. The floors, the walls, even the ceiling, were covered with tawny sound-absorbing carpet.

Father Raes was trailed by Daisy Perika. It was eerily quiet, she thought. Like if you opened your mouth to say something, the words wouldn't be able to get past your gums.

The priest approached the coffin; the lid was open. And there she was. Stella Antelope's arms were folded on her chest, her eyes closed in that final slumber. Father Raes crossed himself and knelt. He whispered a prayer for Stella Antelope's spirit.

He whispered . . . to God.

To the Lamb of God.

He appealed to the Blessed Mother for intercession.

And to the multitude of blessed Saints, for their prayers.

And then, for some minutes, he was silent.

Finally, the priest got to his feet and viewed the pitiful body. It seemed a waxen likeness of Stella Antelope. The old woman's small form was clothed in a black cotton dress. He sighed. A funeral home employee must have brought her clothing from the hospital. A river of memories flooded over him. Stella had—in gambler's parlance—been dealt a bum hand. Born with a deformed foot. Orphaned when she was not ten years old. Married to an alcoholic when she was fifteen. She'd had a daughter who died of measles. And much later in life she'd had two sons. Hooper had stayed on the reservation. William, the younger, had gone to Flagstaff and landed a job with the post office. He'd also married himself a good wife from Nevada who waited tables in a greasy spoon just off I-40.

Stella's husband had died of tuberculosis, and for many years she had lived alone. For a while, she'd stayed out in the country with her brother Reuben. Then, with financial assistance from the tribe, she'd moved into a small apartment in Ignacio. Her poor vision had gradually grown worse, making the old woman a virtual prisoner in her new home—except on those cloudless days when the sun was very bright. On such happy occasions, she would tap her way along the sidewalks with the striped cane, blinking at those solid things that had become mere shadows of themselves.

Only last year, it had fallen on Father Raes to take the dreadful news to the old woman. With Reuben Antelope's connivance, the priest had decided to keep a portion of the dreadful truth from this poor soul who had troubles more than sufficient for one lifetime.

There had been a very unfortunate incident, Father Raes had told Stella. Her son William and his wife Jillian were dead. Suspicious circumstances . . . there would be an investigation, of course. The priest, blushing at the half-truth, did not tell her that the Arizona authorities were certain it was a murder-suicide. The root cause was probably William's alcoholism.

Stella had not asked for details. Maybe the blind woman had seen it coming. Didn't want to know more than she had to.

Father Raes did inform her that Billy was about to become a temporary ward of the State of Arizona. The priest offered to use his influence to have the child assigned to a Catholic institution. Stella refused this kind offer. Despite her poverty, the elderly woman had immediately welcomed her orphaned grandchild into her small home. Billy had been a good boy. And though he rarely said more than two or three words, his presence had been a considerable blessing to the lonely old woman.

Father Raes Delfino knew that Stella had never complained about her troubles. Diabetes and heart disease had been, it seemed, the dual illnesses that would relieve her of the burden of living in this hard world. But the old woman had survived, only to suffer the terrible isolation of blindness. If it were not for the little boy who had led her around Ignacio on a rope . . . a tear coursed down the gentle man's face. Then another. The priest made the sign of the Cross over the forehead of the gracious lady the towns-folk knew as Old Popeye Woman, and said the ritual prayer . . . the solemn words from the book. This official act completed, he offered up his personal supplication.

> O merciful God . . . O Savior . . . Lover of my soul
> Shower her sweet spirit with the blessings of your love
> In that far land so fair . . .
> open her blind eyes to rainbows
> mend her feeble limbs
> heal her broken heart . . .

After a long silence, wherein he heard the soft whisper of the Spirit in his soul, the priest sighed. He blinked, almost as if he had forgotten where he was. Father Raes turned to Daisy and nodded toward the corpse resting in the box. "Do you have any last words . . . or . . . " He paused, helplessly. He'd been their pastor for almost a decade, and still didn't quite know how to deal with a Ute when one of them died. Most of these people had a horror of the dead. A ghost that hovered over a fresh corpse could bring sickness—even death. And if the dead were not prop-erly buried, their ghosts might come back and harm the living. So the priest was gratified when Daisy Perika nodded and came forward. She approached the casket slowly, and gave Father Raes Delfino a meaningful glance. He understood that she wanted to be alone with her old friend.

The priest was dismayed to see Horace peering through the doorway. Though he was in his forties, Reuben's son looked much like a child on his first trip to the zoo. Horace's jaw was working on a chaw of tobacco. In a far corner of the outer chamber,

Charlie Moon and Reuben Antelope were having a quiet conversation with the chief executive of the establishment, who had returned with a form to be filled out.

The priest hurried through the arch into the hallway, attempting to brush past Horace.

The young man blocked his way. Horace took off his tattered Caterpillar hat and grinned at the smaller man. "Hello, Father Raes."

The priest, feeling guilty about his discomfort in the presence of this slow-witted fellow, stopped and forced a thin smile. "Good afternoon, Horace. I was very sorry to learn of the passing of your—"

"Now that she's dead, I'll get Aunt Stella's bedroom." He paused, shifted the chaw to the other cheek, and lowered his bass voice to a conspiratorial tone. "They say it was a witch that killed Uncle Hooper." Horace screwed his broad forehead into a tortured frown. "Do you believe in witches?"

The most profound questions invariably came from little children. Or, as on this occasion, from children in grown-up bodies. "Well," the priest found himself treading on shaky ground, "not in the traditional sense, but there are certainly those who use evil means to achieve—"

Horace's mind had already shifted gear. "I know how to tell if a person's a witch."

This caught Father Raes off guard. "Ahhh . . . now is that a fact?"

Horace glanced quickly over his shoulder at his father and Charlie Moon. They were discussing something with the mortician, who had a large clipboard in his hand. Horace leaned close to the priest, who got a whiff of the sickeningly sweet odor of the tobacco. "Names," he said in a hoarse whisper.

"Names?" Now this was opaque, even from the mouth of Horace.

"Sure. People do all kinda stuff just because of their names." Horace jerked his shoulder to indicate the funeral director. "That guy over there in the suit, he buries people and whatnot, don't he?" He didn't wait for confirmation. "You know what his name is?"

The priest raised an eyebrow in the direction of the mortician. "I assume you refer to Mr. Spaidman."

Horace winked knowingly. He tapped a stubby finger on the priest's chest. "Sure. Spade-man. Same thing as Shovel-Man. So he can't help hisself; he's gotta go dig a buncha holes in the ground. Graves, see?"

Father Raes, who thought it best to remain silent, merely nodded. Gravely.

This apparent affirmation served only to encourage Reuben Antelope's peculiar son. "And not only that," Horace continued with increasing enthusiasm, "Joe Piper up in Bayfield, he's a plumber. And I had this teacher in Ignacio—Miz Lerner. She learned me how to read stuff like 'Mary Jane she went to the well with her bucket' . . . and I heard about this fireman in Durango . . . know what his name is?

The little Jesuit sighed and shook his head.

Horace punched him playfully on the shoulder. "Guess."

Father Raes did not care to be poked at. He rubbed at his shoulder. "I really don't think I could guess . . ." He gazed hopefully past Horace at Reuben Antelope. The priest's expression was pleading. Save me from your son.

"Go on, Father Raes—guess." Horace punched his shoulder again. Harder.

The smaller man recovered from a slight stagger and instinctively clenched his fists. It would be a distinct pleasure to fell this hollow tree with a quick left hook under the chin . . . to hear the back of his head thump onto the floor. But the good priest closed his eyes. Counted to five. Forgive me, Father . . . six . . . for I have entertained sinful thoughts . . . seven . . . this, too, is one of Your children . . . eight . . . Gradually, he relaxed. Unclenched his fists.

Horace had mistaken this silent interlude as one of intense concentration. "Well," he demanded, "have you guessed?"

The priest took a deep breath. "Well, let me see. Is the fireman . . . is he . . . Mr. Blaze?" The learned Jesuit blushed. This was an intolerably stupid conversation.

"Nope," Horace said—now loud enough to attract his father's attention—"but you're gettin' warm. His name's Buddy Ashe. Get it? His job is puttin' out house fires and his name's *ash*. Like I told you already, people does the things they do on account of what their *names* is."

"God," the sufferer murmured, "is there no end to my affliction . . . ?"

Reuben grabbed his son's arm. "Horace, you quit botherin' the priest."

The appearance of an angel from heaven could hardly have been more welcome. Father Raes Delfino muttered a fervent prayer of thanks for this deliverance and left the young man standing by the arched doorway.

Horace soon forgot about the priest. He had found a new way to entertain himself. With his dusty boots planted under the arched entrance into the forbidden chamber, he watched Daisy Perika with a mix of curiosity and childlike apprehension. Now what was that queer old woman up to, standing there by Aunt Stella's body? Maybe *she* was a witch. Hmmm. "Daisy" was a kinda flower. But what did "Perika" mean?

For a long time, Daisy Perika stood by the casket.

A few other Utes began to drift into the funeral home. Most were distant relatives of Stella Antelope. They gathered in the dimly lighted hallway, expressing their condolences to Reuben Antelope. A few nodded their greeting to the Christian priest, hoping not to hear their little pastor say he "hadn't seen them in church for a long time." One by one, they learned that Daisy Perika was *in there*. With Old Popeye Woman's body.

And they wondered why.

Occasionally, Daisy would lean close to the face of the corpse; she muttered words that Horace could barely hear. A few other visitors peered through the doorway. The Utes whispered among themselves. What was the old woman doing? Why was she talking to a person who was dead and couldn't hear thunder?

What the old shaman did was this:

In the Ute tongue—and taking the liberty to innovate just a little here and there—Daisy said the Lord's Prayer.

In English, she recited the Twenty-third Psalm. It was a flawless recitation. The Catholic priest would have been surprised that the old shaman had memorized the King James version of this song. But it was Father Raes' little secret that he had also memorized the hymn from the Anglican Bible. The Protestant version was so beautiful.

Her praying done, the elderly woman talked to Stella Antelope. About when they were children, making little mud people of blue clay from the banks of the Piedra. Arms and legs were twigs; clothing was made of willow leaves. Grass for hair. Acorn hulls for hats.

Finally, Daisy Perika was emptied of words.

She stood by the casket and gazed at the hollow shell of what had been her oldest friend. Now Old Popeye Woman was dead. And laid out in a wooden box. Soon, she'd be buried. For a while, most of the old ones among the People would be careful not to mention her name, lest it bring her ghost to haunt their dreams. And after a little while longer, hardly anyone would think about her. Or her son, who'd fallen down dead at the Ute Mountain Sun Dance. But inside, Daisy Perika fumed. No matter what Charlie Moon thought, Hooper Antelope had not died a natural death. Someone had killed him. And whoever had murdered Stella's son, had—even if indirectly—also killed Old Popeye Woman. It didn't matter whether they had meant to murder her or not—Stella was stone cold dead. And she'd died before she could say who'd witched her son.

Daisy leaned over the corpse. As if in a trance, she passed her hands over Old Popeye Woman's leathery face . . . and muttered her last words to her departed friend. "I guess you've got a long trip to make, Stella. But you'll find lots of good friends over there waitin' for you. And before too long, I'll be comin' too."

It was a minute past midnight when Charlie Moon turned the big Blazer off the blacktop of Highway 151 onto a rough gravel road that meandered into the arid canyon country. All the way from Cortez, not a dozen words had passed between him and his aunt. Moon knew that she was annoyed with him because he didn't believe a witch was responsible for Hooper Antelope's death. Funny old woman.

Minutes later, just a few hundred yards from the mouth of *Cañon del Espiritu*, the policeman turned off the rutted dirt road into the dusty lane that led to her trailer. He parked, shut off the V-8 engine, and went around to open her door.

Daisy Perika grunted as she leaned on her nephew's arm and got out of the big SUPD Blazer.

They stood there for a moment, the tall young man and the little old woman. The old and the new . . . symbols of the Ute tribe.

There was no moon hanging above Three Sisters Mesa. But the velvet cape of the heavens was embroidered with strings of white-hot diamonds.

Even summer nights were chilly in the high country. Daisy glanced anxiously toward her small trailer home; it would be warm inside. And she had a good bed to sleep in. But her nephew, the big shot policeman had something on his mind. And until he'd had his say . . .

"Thing is . . . " he began, and his voice trailed off.

She grinned in the darkness. Charlie Moon wanted to know something. And he didn't have the nerve to just up and ask her. So Charlie was working his way up to it. Well, if this big smart-aleck policeman wanted any help from her, first he'd have to admit to some things. Like how he'd been wrong in dismissing her suspicions of foul play at the Ute Mountain Sun Dance Lodge. Of course even if he did get up the courage to ask for advice, maybe she still wouldn't talk to him anyway. Because it wouldn't help none. Charlie Moon, though he was a Ute, was like so many of the young people—he didn't believe in the old ways. And if you didn't believe, you couldn't understand.

The Southern Ute policeman pondered the situation. Hooper Antelope's body had been sent up to Granite Creek for an autopsy, and that was bound to show he'd died a natural death. But no matter what the medical examiner said, a few Utes would suspect that a witch had been at work over at the Sleeping Ute Mountain Sun Dance. And Aunt Daisy was likely to add fuel to the fire. It wouldn't be all that hard to convince the older, more traditional Utes that the dancer had been murdered by some old-fashioned hocus-pocus. And if the rumors grew legs, even some of the younger people would get nervous about the upcoming Sun Dance on their own reservation. What if the witch shows up here? There would be pressure on the tribal government to do something. Maybe even call off the dance. But that would be a last resort. First, the tribal chairman would lean on the chief of police. *And Roy Severo, he'll pass the buck down to me.* Moon stared at the dark spot where his aunt's face should be. Except for a reflection of starlight from her bifocals, he saw only shadows under the shawl. "If people get the wrong idea about how Hooper died, it's gonna create a problem." He was certain there wasn't a crime involved. Almost certain.

Daisy Perika blinked at the dark form looming above her. "Well, I guess all of God's children has their problems." She faked a long yawn. To make the point that she was sleepy. And that she wasn't particularly interested in hearing about the policeman's worries.

Moon felt ashamed of himself. It'd been a long day; the poor old woman must be dog tired. But he had to ask. "I wondered whether . . . when you were with her over at the hospital . . . did Stella Antelope have anything to say?"

"About what?" *Big jughead, you'll have to come right out and ask.*

She wasn't going to make this easy. The policeman allowed himself a thin smile. "I wondered what she . . . ahhh . . . thought about her son's death."

"What does it matter what she thought?" Daisy's bitterness cut to the bone. "She was just an old woman, like me. Who didn't know nothin'. An was blind on top of that." Daisy pulled her wool shawl tightly around her shoulders and headed for the trailer. "It's too chilly to stand out here and talk foolishness with you."

Moon spoke to the back of her head. "It'll sure make my job harder if any rumors start floating around . . ." Rumors about witchcraft at the Sun Dance.

As she hobbled off toward the steps of the shaky wooden porch, the weary, ill-tempered woman dismissed her nephew with a rude wave of her hand. "Then don't you *start* any rumors."

Charlie Moon grinned amiably at her back. She was a contrary old soul.

One painful step at a time, Daisy began to climb the porch. She had enjoyed the brief exchange with her nephew. Mainly because she'd had the last word.

Long after Charlie Moon had departed, Daisy Perika lay on her small bed. The exhausted woman closed her eyes. And rolled onto her left side. And then her right. She tried to put aside the events of the tragic day. But sleep would not come, because the thing was unfinished. The old shaman wondered what she should do—what she *could* do.

Almost an hour later, a low cloud hung over the heads of the Three Sisters, who sat on the long sandstone mesa. Daisy could smell the soft scent of rain in the canyon long before it began to pelt the aluminum walls of her trailer home. Ahhh . . . rain. *This will help me drift off to sleep.*

Though she was barely conscious of it, somewhere deep inside her head a most peculiar train of thoughts had been coupled together. An enigmatic little engine—fired by the embers of her imagination—was getting up steam. On crooked little tracks, warped little wheels were spinning. And the peculiar assembly rattled through the dark glades of her mind.

A rumble of thunder stumbled drunkenly down the canyon—bouncing off the sandstone walls—muttering incoherent curses.

The shaman drifted off into an experience unlike any she'd ever had before. First, there were hoarse whispers coming from some impossibly distant place. The voice was Stella Antelope's. Daisy listened carefully to Old Popeye Woman's words. And heard a ghostly tale. About a witch who'd come to the Ute Mountain Sun Dance. And killed her son Hooper. But it wasn't over.

It had just begun.

This witch would pay a visit to the summer's last Sun Dance. And sit in darkness . . . in the sacred corral.

The final Sun Dance of the year was held on the Southern Ute reservation.

The second part of her experience was visual. The scene was, Daisy would later recall, like watching an old movie, in black and white. The shaman's spirit hovered over a large circle . . . a crackling wreath fashioned of the dry bones of dead trees. In the center was a small fire, fueled by twigs of piñon and juniper. The moon was high over the midnight-blue mountains. The dancers, wearied from their labors, rested and waited for the dawn.

Within the sacred Sun Dance Lodge, old songs were sung.

Firelight flickered.

Drums talked.

Someone whispered.

And *someone* walked . . .

The transcendent experience seemed to move in snail-like fashion, but this was merely time's illusion. When the thing was finished, the pictures faded.

The shaman sat up in her bed, heart thumping, breath coming

in short gasps. She thought about what she had seen . . . it was an incredible thing. But she knew that this was something Old Popeye Woman had wanted her to see. And a true vision always came with a purpose for the visionary.

Daisy entertained not the least doubt. She knew what was required of her.

And trembled.

It was just past eight o'clock the next morning. Charlie Moon was in his home on the banks of the Pinos. Asleep in his bed. Dreaming of someone. She was slim, wearing a filmy pink dress with a black belt; the skirt floated like twilight's mist around her ankles. Pretty ankles. The woman's hair was black and glistened; her long braids were done up in pink satin ribbons. For a moment, the face was Myra Cornstone's. But now she raised her arms, in the manner of a swanlike ballet dancer. She did a quick pirouette on the tips of her shiny red shoes, and showed the dreamer another face. Charlie Moon saw the smiling mouth, the large, luminous eyes of Delly Sands . . . she blew him a kiss and laughed. It was a fine dream. Too fine to last.

The telephone, the one he'd had installed only last month, jangled. Once. Twice. Three times . . .

The policeman rolled onto his side; he grabbed for the receiver and knocked the instrument to the hardwood floor. He found it, groaned, pressed the cold plastic to his ear. He didn't speak, but he heard the voice of Police Chief Roy Severo.

"Charlie . . . Charlie . . . you there?"

"No, I'm not. This is my answering machine. When you hear the tone, please leave a message." He attempted a beeping sound. It sounded more like a burp.

"Charlie Moon, don't you mess with me. We got us a problem."

Moon sat on the side of the bed and attempted to clear the muddle from his head. It was hard. Dreaming of a woman who was Myra Cornstone . . . and Delly Sands. And waking up to hear his boss yelling in his ear. "What kind of problem, Chief?"

The agonizing creak of Roy Severo's chair was audible over the telephone. "Something bad happened last night."

Moon was thinking about making some coffee. Strong, black coffee. Maybe a gallon. "Something bad? Where?"

Severo propped his scruffy bullhide boots on the scarred government-surplus desk. "Over at Cortez."

Cortez? Why was the chief of the Southern Ute Police Department waking him up about something that happened in Cortez? That was a long way from their jurisdiction. And then he remembered the hospital. And the funeral home. "Tell me about it."

"You know that Stella Antelope's body was took to Spaidman & Son's in Cortez? That's a mortuary."

"Sure. I was over there yesterday afternoon."

"Well, it ain't there now."

Moon rubbed at his eyes. Maybe the chief was sucking on the bourbon again. "The funeral home ain't there?"

"Her *body* ain't there, dammit."

He got off the bed; the springs creaked. "They lose Stella's body?"

" 'Course not, Charlie. Funeral homes do not lose bodies. And they're pretty upset about it bein' . . . ahhh . . . lost. Don't want the newspapers—not even their local cops—to get wind of it. It's embarrassing, see? Bad for their business, when stone-cold corpses just up and vanish."

"So how'd you find out so quick?"

"Seth Spaidman—the fellow who owns the funeral home—is an old buddy of mine, so he called me. He figured we could help him work this thing out. And," Roy Severo added, "keep things quiet."

"When did they find out the body was gone?"

"This morning. Some college kid who opens up early found Stella's slot in the cooler was empty. According to what they say, it was like the body just got up and walked off. They hadn't had time to inject her with any of that preservative stuff yet, so . . ." There was a pause. "So I wonder whether Old Popeye . . . whether Stella Antelope maybe wasn't actually dead or something."

Moon ran a hand through his coarse, tousled hair. "She was dead."

"If you say so, Charlie. But she's missing, and that's what matters. And we can't let this get out. I can't use but one policeperson on this one." He snickered. "My best policeperson." There was a pregnant pause. "So guess who's going to find the body and bring it back?" The chief of police laughed his braying, donkey laugh.

Moon groaned. "Roy, this is my day off."

The chief guffawed all the louder, like this was the funniest joke he'd heard all week long. "Get your ass in high gear, Charlie. I don't want to see your face until you've found the body." And then he hung up. He'd already told the receptionist at Spaidman & Sons that Officer Moon would arrive before noon. She'd seemed to know who Severo was talking about.

Moon dropped the telephone receiver into its cradle. And thought about it.

By the time he'd finished his first cup of coffee, the policeman had a pretty good notion of what'd happened at the funeral home. Nope, this little mystery of a missing body wasn't going to be hard to solve. A few hours, and he'd have it all wrapped up.

CHAPTER 5

Cortez, Colorado
The Funeral Home

Charlie Moon had interviewed the employee who'd discovered the body was missing. He wasn't much help. The kid was scared stiff. Like he'd lost the corpse himself and half-expected to lose his part-time job. Moon had checked every door and window on the premises. Even the ventilation system. There was no sign of forced entry.

Now the Ute policeman sat across the massive oak desk from the man with the silver hair. The director's office was, like the rest of this place, magnificent. And smelled like money. Seth Spaidman was nervously wiping his beautifully manicured hand along the side of his perfectly styled hair. "Officer Moon, isn't it?"

The Ute nodded. "That's me."

"I remember you, of course. You were here only yesterday—

with the family of the deceased." Hard to forget an Indian cop who was damn near seven feet tall.

"I remember you too." Hard to forget a fellow with hair that pretty.

"May I offer you some coffee?"

"Sounds good." Moon sniffed hopefully. "Is that sweet rolls I smell?"

Seth Spaidman pressed a button on his intercom. "I imagine those are a bit stale by now." The director relied heavily on first impressions. He was certain that Roy Severo, who did not throw praise around casually, had not exaggerated about Charlie Moon. Here was a solid, dependable police officer. A man who could be trusted with sensitive matters.

The efficient receptionist responded to her boss's electronic signal. "Yes?"

"Samantha? Coffee for our guest. No cream, but please bring the sugar."

The Ute policeman raised an eyebrow. This fellow had taken the trouble to ask Roy Severo how Charlie Moon drank his coffee. Now that was first class.

Seth Spaidman was pleased at the policeman's appreciative response to his homework. "And send someone over to the bakery. Get a selection of fresh pastries."

He switched off the intercom and the smile vanished. "You understand, of course, that this is a rather delicate matter."

Moon nodded.

Seth Spaidman paused, wondering how to begin.

The silence was interrupted by a tap at the door; the director said, "You may come in."

It was the receptionist. The small woman with the pretty oval face. But she looked quite a different woman today. Immediately after she'd learned that Officer Moon was returning to Spaidman & Sons, Samantha had made a quick trip to her apartment. She had abandoned the large spectacles. Today, her reddish-gold hair was not confined in a bun; it fell in soft waves over her shoulders. The receptionist had hung the pin-stripe suit in the closet; she wore a tight white skirt, a blue silk blouse with lace at the elbows, an expensive cameo at her throat. She carried a silver tray with a gleaming coffee dispenser, translucent china cups, and a crystal bowl filled with sugar cubes. Samantha smiled knowingly at the big policeman. She knew what he liked. "We'll have the pastries shortly."

Moon thanked her with a nod, and she was gone.

After the door was shut, he used small silver tongs to drop four white cubes into the cup, then took a sip of coffee. It was good. Very good. And Samantha was bound to be a highly paid employee. This funeral business must make a pile of money.

The director waited patiently for the policeman to savor the freshly ground Kona blend. Specially prepared for Seth Spaidman by a coffee vendor on the Big Island. "I expect you'll want to ask some questions."

"I've already had a talk with the young man."

"Albert," Spaidman said.

"Albert says he opened up this morning at five. Made his rounds, checking supplies, doing some paperwork, the usual drill. And when Albert went to check the thermostats, he noticed that a door on the cooler was open. And that Stella Antelope's body was missing."

Seth Spaidman winced at the directness of the policeman's observation. He closed his eyes and clasped his hands under his chin.

Like a monk in prayer, Moon thought. But aside from the usual things, what did a mortician pray for? Maybe for business to pick up a bit?

The silver-haired man opened the cold blue eyes and stared over his clasped hands at the Ute policeman. "You must understand, Officer Moon . . . this is most embarrassing. Spaidman & Sons is an integral part of the community. A respected institution. My great-grandfather started this business in the 1920s. We have never been touched by the least scandal."

"I know what you mean." Moon allowed himself a hint of a smile. "My people have been in these parts quite a while too. And we'd just as soon work this out without attracting a lot of attention." It would upset the Utes, having one of their dead unaccounted for. Maybe roaming around the neighborhood, scaring the little children. Making the dogs bark at night.

Seth relaxed and exhaled. This was a smart cop; he understood the need for discretion. Yes, Officer Moon was definitely the right man for the job.

Moon pushed his black Stetson back a notch. "Why don't you tell me what happened with the body after I left yesterday?" He thought he knew exactly what had happened, but these *matukach* folks felt better if a policeman asked 'em some questions.

"Shortly after the brother of the deceased—accompanied by his son, I believe—brought the new blanket, our . . . um . . . client . . . was wrapped in a traditional covering. Per Mr. Antelope's instructions."

Moon took a small notebook from his jacket pocket. "What'd the blanket look like?"

Spaidman closed his eyes to call up the memory. "Mostly dark blue. With large red stripes. Zigzag stripes as I recall." Kind of an inexpensive-looking item, he thought. If there was much call from the Indians for blankets to wrap their dead in, perhaps we should bring in a stock from Juarez.

Moon grunted as he wrote. Red zigzags on a dark blue background. Lightning in a midnight sky. "Then what happened to the body?"

"After Mr. Antelope and his son left, the remains of the deceased were placed in our state-of-the-art holding area."

Moon looked up. "Holding area?"

"A temperature-controlled environment, of course."

"Oh. You mean the icebox."

Seth smiled in a manner that was almost condescending. "In a manner of speaking. But I assure you that our holding facility is far more sophisticated than a common refrigeration unit."

"How?"

With a blank expression, the director repeated the word. "How?"

Moon raised his right palm and grinned. "How—that wasn't an Indian greeting. I meant *how* is your storage thingamajig different from a refrigerator?"

The mortician sniffed. Mainly, it was more expensive. And more . . . horizontal. "Well, for one thing, they're humidity controlled. Our environmental units are rather fully occupied right now, but if you would like to inspect them—"

The Ute shuddered inside. "Later, maybe. Do these . . . uh . . . environmental units . . . have a lock?"

Spaidman was genuinely shocked. "Certainly not. After all, who'd think anyone would want to steal a sti—a corpse? I mean if someone wants to burglarize this place, there's several hundred thousand dollars' worth of antique furniture and paintings to pick from."

"How about your outside doors?"

"They have Yale dead bolt locks. I closed the place up last evening, as is my common practice. The last thing I do before leaving is check every door. No one could get in without a key. Not unless they broke a lock . . . or a window."

"Interesting," the policeman said. Now, he measured his words carefully. "But could someone get *out* without breaking a lock?"

"Well, of course—there are fire safety regulations—but surely you're not suggesting that . . ." His voice trailed off. This was simply incredible.

Moon leaned back in the comfortable chair; he linked his fingers behind his neck. There was no mystery here; the facts fitted his theory like the skin on a peach. But he might as well have some fun with this fellow. "I understand you know Roy Severo. My boss."

Spaidman nodded. "We're good friends. Do some golfing together."

"When Roy called me this morning, he mentioned a theory he had."

"Theory?"

"Old Roy's pretty good with his theories." Moon leaned forward. "You hadn't injected the formaldehyde stuff into her veins yet. So Roy, he figures maybe the hospital had made a mistake. Maybe Stella wasn't one hundred percent dead. And sometime late last night, the poor old woman just woke up in your cooler, wonderin' where on earth she was. And she got out of your . . . environmental unit . . . snug in that new blanket her brother Reuben brought for you to wrap her in. And then, prob'ly, after she had a look around, Stella walked right outta your front door. Which wasn't locked so's it'd keep someone *inside*." Moon looked out the window at the swaying branches of a Russian olive. "Who knows where the poor old soul might be right now?"

The silver-haired man paled, and tugged at the tight collar of his silk shirt. He responded in a near whimper. "That's absurd. Utterly impossible."

"My very words to Roy Severo." Moon poured himself another cup of steaming coffee from the silver pot. "But after seeing how she just disappeared all by herself, I can't be altogether sure Roy's theory ain't right. With someone like Old Popeye Woman, you can never tell."

"Old Popeye—I don't understand."

The Ute counted out six sugar cubes; he watched them dissolve in the hot, black liquid. "That was Stella's nickname around Ignacio."

"Because of her . . . her slightly protruding eye, I suppose."

Moon looked thoughtful. "Partly that," he said. "But there are other things about Old—about Stella. Peculiar kinda things. But I guess a police officer shouldn't repeat that sorta talk." *Maybe when Roy Severo gets the report from his golfing buddy, he'll think twice about waking me up on my day off.* The big man took a sip that drained half the cup. This was first-rate Java.

Seth Spaidman seemed to have lost the power of speech.

"There's something you can do for me," Moon said. "I need some paperwork."

The director of Spaidman & Sons Funeral Home gave his guest a wary look, and cleared his throat. "What kind of paperwork?"

The policeman told him.

He thought about it. "Of course I can prepare such a document for you, but I don't see how it will help unless—"

There was a tap on the door.

Seth Spaidman recognized the tap. "Yes, Samantha?"

She entered, carrying an aromatic cardboard box. "The bakery provided us with quite a selection of fresh pastries." Her words were for Spaidman, her blue-green eyes for the big policeman. Samantha leaned close to Moon, barely brushing her hair against his face. "I hope you find something to suit your taste. They're still warm." Her breath was also warm and honeyed. "If there's anything else you'd like . . . please let me know."

Moon grinned at the warm box of donuts, then at the pretty woman. This lawman job didn't pay all that good. But if a fellow made an effort, he could learn to enjoy it.

As the Southern Ute policeman made his way up the crumbling talus slope on the north skirt of Three Sister's Mesa, he mused about his life. And his chosen profession.

In Charlie Moon's experience, there were mainly two kinds of police work.

There was the impossible. Like figuring out who poisoned the nervous dog that barked all night and kept a dozen neighbors awake—all who'd dearly love to see the beast dead. Even if you were pretty sure which one of 'em killed the animal, there would be neither witness nor confession. So you couldn't do much about it. You might have a stern talk with the old lady who'd just bought a box of rat poison at the local hardware store, but you generally had to give up on those kind of problems. And go on to something more productive.

And then there was the dead easy. Like Stella Antelope's missing body. Except for a couple of details—and those didn't matter that much—this was no puzzle at all. The silver-haired mortician hadn't figured it out because he was a *matukach*. All he knew about the local Native Americans was that they lived on a reservation and made pretty clay pots. The Utes, being hunters, had never made much pottery in the old days. They'd traded worked leather goods for cookware with the Pueblo Indians— especially the farmer folk down at Taos. Now, of course, there was the tourist trade, so they made some pottery.

Any Ute policeman would have figured it out. Roy Severo would have guessed what had happened if he'd known about how the funeral home removed the body from the hospital without permission from Stella's family. And about how Reuben Antelope had brought a special blanket for his sister to be buried in.

Moon topped the edge of the mesa and walked slowly along the surface of the weathered orange sandstone. He was headed almost northwest, toward the blue foothills of the San Juans. The junipers on the mesa were fragrant. A striped lizard darted across his path and skittered up a piñon snag. And stared at the human being with shiny, unblinking black eyes.

He could have driven right to the spot two hundred feet below in the canyon, but that wouldn't have been nearly so much fun. It was a long walk along the spine of the mesa before the policeman sat down and pulled the gray canvas pack off his back. He unzipped the thing, removed several items and laid them on a flat sandstone outcropping. Moon adjusted the navy surplus binoculars and searched the floor of the canyon. No fresh tracks in the sandy road. So they hadn't showed yet.

But they would.

The Ute eyed the position of the sun, guessed that it was about half past one. He checked his wristwatch. One-forty. He had a long drink of sweet black coffee from an insulated bottle, then unwrapped the aluminum foil from a sandwich. Heavy slices of sourdough bread enfolding a thick slab of ham. Mustard, of course.

Life was good.

Almost an hour slipped by before he heard the distant rattle of a pickup truck. Moon took the last swallow of coffee from the bottle, then pressed the powerful binoculars to his eyes. Within a couple of minutes, it chugged around the bend trailing a small cloud of yellow dust. He watched the approach of the truck along the canyon floor. "Uh-huh," he said to himself, "that's Reuben's Ford pickup." The one Horace had stolen from Reuben's second wife who'd taken up with the man down at Aztec. Horace was probably behind the wheel; his daddy didn't drive when someone else would do it for him. The truck turned off the dirt road almost directly beneath the policeman's position on the sheer cliff edge of the mesa. Moon couldn't get into the canyon from this place; it was a two-hundred-foot drop. Straight down, so you wouldn't even bounce off the wall. But from his eagle's-nest perch, the policeman could see everything he needed to see. Without being seen.

The first thing he saw was a still form in the back of the truck. Tightly wrapped in a new blanket. Just like the mortician had said. Dark blue with jagged red stripes.

Horace Antelope got out of the driver's side of the truck. Reuben took a bit longer to open the door and slide his old frame down from the high-riding F250 to the ground. He had his blind sister's red-and-white striped cane in his hand. And then Little Rope Boy climbed out.

Billy Antelope, who had a plastic bag in one hand, watched as the men went to the rear of the pickup. They unfastened the chain hooks and lowered the heavy tailgate. There was a brief conversation between Reuben and his son, then the old man trudged off, the striped cane in his right hand, little Billy hanging onto the left. They headed up a winding deer path—precisely where Moon had known they'd go—into the side canyon directly across from his position on Three Sisters Mesa. The older Utes called this place the Sand Bowl. It had been the secret burial place of the Antelope family for a century. It wasn't, of course, a well-kept secret.

Moon shifted the binoculars back to the pickup.

Horace pulled the blanket-wrapped corpse from the truck bed. On the second attempt, he managed to get the burden onto his right shoulder, like an infantryman might carry a mortar. Moon adjusted the binocular focus; the blanket had been wrapped in several places with cotton twine. So Stella's corpse wouldn't come loose and slip out. Horace followed his aged father and the small boy into the burial site. It was about fifty yards across, and oddly circular for this stark canyon of angular, irregular shapes. The almost vertical walls of the cylinder of layered sandstone were of various hues . . . like an enormous cake of varicolored chocolate. The winds swirled almost every day in this depression, disturbing a floor of sand that was a yard deep in spots. Moon watched the Antelope family leave their footprints in this trackless bowl. By tomorrow, the breeze would have wiped the tracks away. There would be no evidence that someone had buried a loved one here. Maybe that was why some practical ancestor of the Antelope clan had picked this place. That . . . and the caves.

The lowest layer of sandstone was soft and honeycombed with small caves and crevasses carved by the wind-driven sand. Rodents nested in some, coyotes or foxes might find temporary shelter in the larger ones. Reuben Antelope might pick any one that was large enough to hold the body of his sister. The party was heading to the left, to the west wall. To get a better view, Moon back-tracked a few yards down the rim of Three Sisters Mesa. Reuben was pointing at the wall, speaking to Horace, who was making slow progress with his gruesome burden. The Sand Bowl was a natural amphitheater, concentrating and echoing the sounds to Moon's position almost two hundred yards away. He caught most of Reuben's directions.

"Here. This is the place."

The younger man nodded obediently; he made his way across

the sand. As gently as possible, Horace placed the blanket-wrapped corpse in a narrow horizontal crevasse.

The child, at a nod from Reuben, removed something from his plastic bag. At more urging, the boy placed the object beside the blanket-wrapped corpse. It was a small clay pot. Filled with grains of blue and yellow corn, Moon guessed. Food for Stella to take to the Land of Shadows. Where the dead dwelled.

Reuben patted the boy on the head, and his words carried across the canyon. "You did good, Billy."

Horace, wearied from his labors, sat down to rest. The old man and the boy began to pick up chunks of sandstone and place them in the crevasse. The crunching sounds shot across the canyon to the policeman's elevated vantage point. It wouldn't take long until the opening of the tomb would be walled in. Reuben, who was a traditional Ute, would come back later and add wet clay to the cracks, to seal the rocks in place. Then, even the tiniest insect would not disturb the body of Old Popeye Woman. After the autopsy, when Reuben got custody of Hooper's remains, he'd be placed here too. The fallen Sun-Dancer would rest near his blind, lame mother.

With a suddenness that was astonishing, a bittersweet memory flowed over Moon—the reenactment of a lonely drama he'd seen long ago. When he was a boy. When *his* mother was buried, not so far from this spot. The policeman grunted to himself and attempted to dismiss the phantoms from his mind.

They would not depart from him.

Maybe he should go and check. Make sure all the rocks were still in place. Take some blue clay from the riverbank, mix in cold water from the Piedra. Seal up any cracks . . .

Moon was distracted from these thoughts. Another vehicle was winding its way up the canyon. The Ute policeman lay down on his belly and squinted through the binoculars. It was a black car. Familiar looking, too. Old Buick? No. Surely not . . .

But it was.

Father Raes Delfino parked his car on the road behind Reuben

Antelope's pickup. And then, another surprise. Daisy Perika got out of the passenger side of the priest's black automobile. She took Father Raes' arm and led him toward the Sand Bowl. Moon was holding his breath. Well, if this didn't beat all.

The priest paused at the entrance to this place Daisy called Sand Bowl. He looked up at the circular walls towering above him. Swallows darted here and there. Sunlight danced off polished stone surfaces. It was like . . . a cathedral. And so peaceful. He heard Reuben Antelope's greeting echo off the vaulted walls, and returned the old man's wave. Yes. This was a good thing to do. When Reuben had come to him with his astonishing proposal, he'd hesitated. But the little priest knew now, without the least doubt, that he'd made the right decision.

But God alone could help him if the bishop got wind of this.

Charlie Moon sat on the crag. And watched. And listened.

Reuben sang an old Ute song. About sacred smoke coming from the ground . . . about many blessed spirits who waited . . . about how death was a good thing for old people who were weary.

The Ute song finished, Father Raes Delfino stood before his tiny congregation and led them in another song. The hymn had been written by an English captain of slave ships. A wretched man, who had lived off the pain of other men and women. But something had happened to this lonely soul. Like a Sun-Dancer, he'd had his dramatic vision. He left the slave ships behind. Two hundred years ago, when he was a Methodist minister in England, John Newton had written the first four stanzas of the song.

Not one among this little group would have been recruited by a choir. But it was an honest effort . . . purest worship from the deepest place in the heart. And because of this, it was hauntingly beautiful. The sea captain's words, which had life and power, carried across the canyon.

And resonated with Charlie Moon.

*Amazing grace . . . how sweet the sound . . . that saved a wretch
 like me . . .*
once was lost . . . now am found . . .
was blind . . . but now I see . . .

Moon wondered whether Old Popeye Woman, wherever she
was . . . could see. He hoped so.

As the Ute policeman listened from his perch on Three Sisters
Mesa, the July winds would occasionally carry the song away for
a few moments. But presently the breeze would fall still. And the
sweet words would once again drift across the deep canyon. Finally, the final stanza, written by one known only to God.

It is a measure of eternity . . .

*When we've been there ten thousand years . . . bright shining as
 the sun*
*We've no less days to sing God's praise . . . Than when we
 first begun . . .*

As the last note drifted away on the promise of the wind, the
thing was finished. The priest led the little procession back to the
shiny Ford pickup and the dusty black Buick. Fond farewells were
said. Hugs and handshakes exchanged. The boy's head patted.
Doors slammed. Engines cranked. Forever blessed by what they
had done together, they departed from the canyon.

All but one. Charlie Moon did not leave. Through the long,
chilly night, the Ute policeman sat on the ledge. He watched
over the burial place of Old Popeye Woman. And thought his
lonely thoughts. When a bright dawn kissed the faces of the sandstone sisters, he got stiffly to his feet. And set his face toward
another tomb . . . not so far away.

Roy Severo was in his customary position. Leaning dangerously far back in the unpadded government-surplus swivel chair. His scuffed cowboy boots propped on the varnished desk, also a piece of government-issue furniture supplied by the Bureau of Indian Affairs. His knobby hands were folded across his oiled leather vest, his left thumb just under the gold-plated SUPD shield. He was pretending to read an old copy of *Field and Stream*.

Moon leaned against the wall. His thoughts were still in *Cañon del Espíritu*. With the tomb where his mother's whitened bones lay . . . the fine clay he'd made . . . the hours he'd spent sealing the cracks in the tomb's crumbling sandstone wall.

Roy Severo waited patiently, until Moon returned. "So what's the story, Charlie?"

The big man took a hard wooden chair, turned it backward, and straddled it. "It started at the funeral home over in Cortez. I should have guessed what Reuben had in mind. He wanted his sister's body wrapped in a blanket. Said he'd buy one and bring it back. I figure Reuben left the funeral home right after he delivered the blanket. But he talked Horace into hiding someplace inside. In the basement, or maybe a broom closet."

Severo smiled crookedly as he imagined the plot. Amateurish maybe, but effective. "So after the place was closed up that night, you figure Horace comes out of his hidey-hole. He picks up the body, already wrapped neatly in a blanket. That way he didn't have to touch the corpse. And he carries it outside."

"Yeah." Moon nodded. "Reuben would be waiting with his pickup."

"It'd be taking a big chance," Severo said, shaking his head. "Pulling a fool stunt like that."

"But you know Horace Antelope." Moon chuckled. "He'd do most anything his daddy told him."

The chief of police snorted. "Horace is dumb as a stone, Charlie."

It was Roy Severo's way to say whatever was on his mind. He was more competent than most of the politicians who served on the council. But with his lack of tact, Roy would never be elected to an office in tribal government. "Well," Moon said, "I suppose Reuben's boy is a little slow."

"Slow, my ass," Severo laughed. "If Horace's IQ went up twenty points, he might qualify as a paperweight." He shifted gears and frowned at the big policeman. "What do we do about the funeral home? Officially, they're still missing a body."

"It's taken care of, Chief. I got a paper from Spaidman & Sons, transferring custody of Stella's body—and legal responsibility for it—to her next of kin. I'll get Reuben Antelope to sign it."

"Good work," Severo said.

The Ute policeman was surprised, and mildly embarrassed, at the praise. This was the best compliment you'd ever get out of the old hard-nose.

"One last thing," the boss said casually.

Moon was instantly on his guard.

"There's talk about Hooper Antelope's death not being . . . ahhh . . . of natural causes."

"Where'd you hear that?"

"Here and there." Severo swiveled his chair and stared out the window at the parking lot. "You believe witches can kill people, Charlie?"

Moon smiled. Severo hadn't asked him if he believed in witches. Witches were a given. Roy Severo just wondered what the *uru-sawa-ci* were actually capable of. "You'd best ask my Aunt Daisy about that."

The chief of police laughed. "You know how far I'd get asking Daisy Perika questions about such stuff."

"I expect you'd do as well as I would." Moon got off his chair and pushed it against the wall.

Severo picked up the *Field and Stream* magazine and began to thumb through the tattered pages. "I want you to see to the matter of Hooper Antelope's death. It's unsettling when one of our Sun-Dancers falls down and dies—makes all us natives restless."

Moon grinned at his boss. "So you've heard from the tribal chairman?" Austin Sweetwater's nervous disposition wasn't a good thing for a politician.

"The little chump's giving me heartburn. So go saddle up. Perform some outstanding police work." The chief looked over the magazine at Moon. His pock-marked face was deadly serious. "Charlie, next week we got our own Sun Dance—I expect you to make damn sure there won't be nobody gettin' witched."

Daisy Perika sat on the steps of her creaky wooden porch, chin resting in her hands, a thoughtful expression on her wrinkled face. She could hear sounds from the FM radio drifting through the window screen. Some foreign-sounding lady who thought she could have danced all night was singing about it. Pretty voice. But the shaman was hardly listening. She was recalling the strange, frightful vision she'd had that night when thunder haunted her dreams. The old woman's mind kept coming back to the same subject. There was a job to be done. And it was hers to do.

Daisy blinked at the stark outlines of the Three Sisters who sat contentedly on the mesa. The pueblo women—safe all these centuries from that 'Pache who had pursued them to those lofty heights—were wrapped in soft garments of creamy moonlight. The Ute elder spoke to the women, as if the massive sandstone monoliths were old friends. "It ain't gonna be easy, you know."

The sisters, who'd been silent for centuries, were content to remain so.

Daisy thought some more about exactly how to get the job done. She thought very hard, until her brain fairly ached with the effort. Gradually the old woman thought she knew how to go about the task. As she rolled it around in her head, it seemed more and more like an awfully crackpot notion.

Just her cup of tea.

Charlie Moon turned the big Blazer off the paved road, steering it down the rutted lane toward the run-down sheep ranch. He topped a low piñon-studded ridge, crossed a sturdy wooden bridge over a dry creek, and found himself in Reuben Antelope's dusty front yard. He parked the SUPD police car under one of three giant cottonwoods that shaded the south side of the unpainted frame house. An old tire had been hung from one of the tree limbs. It looked like Reuben had put up a swing for little Billy.

These two might be good for each other.

The Ute policeman checked his inside coat pocket for the document. He reached for the dashboard radio, turned on KSUT, and relaxed. Until his arrival was noted, he was content to listen to a Harvard economist's analysis of mutual fund fluctuations and how such phenomena could be modeled by a subset of chaos theory. After a few minutes, Moon noticed someone pull back a yellowed curtain at a window under the long porch roof. The old man's thin face appeared briefly, then the curtain was released. The Ute policeman waited for the door to open.

It did not. So this was how it was going to be.

Moon grunted his displeasure and got out of the Blazer. He mounted the porch in one stride and banged on the door.

No response.

Moon banged hard; the door frame shuddered. "Reuben," he bellowed, "open up."

The policeman barely heard the footsteps. The porcelain knob turned slowly, the door was opened a crack. He grinned down at the boy's upturned face. "Hi, Billy. I need to talk to the nasty old man who's hiding inside."

He'd hoped for a smile, but the child's face was unsettling in its seriousness. As if Billy Antelope could see your insides . . . count your bones, one by one.

The boy stared in awe at this man-mountain topped off with a fine black cowboy hat. And a big black gun strapped on his hip. And, the boy remembered, Charlie Moon had a pretty girl-friend to talk to and go places with. And hold hands with.

Moon was trying to decide what to say next, when the old man appeared behind the child. Reuben was chewing a mouthful of tobacco; the red-brown stains were on his lips.

The old man nodded a hello. "What brings you out to my place? You want to buy a side of mutton?"

Moon thought about it. Not a bad idea, maybe. Reuben's place had run down some since his wife died, but his mutton was still as good as any. And a bargain to boot.

"That wasn't exactly what I had in mind. We need to talk." The policeman looked meaningfully at the boy.

The Ute elder stepped onto the porch, followed by the boy. Reuben spat onto a flat slab of Iron Mesa sandstone that served as a step. "Talk, then."

The Ute policeman pulled the document from inside his jacket and offered it to the old man.

Reuben accepted the sheaf of papers warily; he found his bifocals in his shirt pocket and hooked the spectacles over his nose.

Charlie Moon braced himself for the argument.

It didn't come.

Reuben's response was mild. "So if I sign this paper, I accept responsibility for my sister's remains. That funeral place over in Cortez—they're off the hook."

Moon nodded. Maybe this was going to be easy.

"Why," Reuben asked with a wry grin, "should I help 'em, the bunch of vultures that took my sister's body from the hospital without my say-so? Gimmee one good reason."

The policeman sighed. "Because you and Horace broke the law. You removed the body from the mortuary without permission."

The old man blinked at the sky and shrugged. "That's what *you* say."

"Don't bother lying to me," Moon said gently. "It's undignified for a man of your years."

The old man frowned at the policeman. "What do you know for sure?"

It was Moon's turn to grin. "Well, even though you disremembered to invite me, I attended Stella's burial service in *Cañon del Espiritu*."

The old man shrugged. "You're guessing. Lots of tribal members are buried up in Spirit Canyon."

Moon raised an eyebrow. "In the walls of the Sand Bowl?"

The old man almost swallowed the wad of tobacco, but he recovered quickly. "It ain't no big secret that some of the Antelopes are buried there."

Moon put his ace on the table. "I was surprised you talked Father Raes into blessing the burial. If the Pope ever hears about it, that poor little priest might find himself in a peck of trouble."

"Hmmph." The game was up. Reuben spat again, this time missing the sandstone porch step by inches. "You got a pencil?"

Moon offered him a ballpoint pen. "I figured you'd see it my way."

"Shit fire," the old man said. "Might as well have the damn *gishtoppo* follerin' me around."

Moon patted Billy's head. The boy reached out shyly; with the tip of one finger he touched the polished leather holster that held the policeman's .44 Magnum pistol. He guessed you had to be pretty old to be a policeman and drive one of them cars with the flashing red lights. Maybe even ten or eleven.

Reuben scribbled his name on the line and returned the document to Moon. He jammed the ballpoint into the pocket of his overall bib. The tribal elder grinned a mischievous grin, exposing gums that supported a half dozen yellowed, peglike teeth. And a wad of tobacco.

Moon looked away, toward the apple orchard. This job didn't pay nearly enough.

Reuben chuckled and slapped the policeman on the arm. "I always been a reasonable man, Charlie. You know that."

The old man spat again, aiming the tobacco juice at the sandstone step.

Nailed it dead center.

When Daisy Perika had heard the rumble of Gorman Sweetwater's old Dodge pickup truck bouncing up the rutted lane, she had known that the Great Mysterious One had answered her prayers. Her cousin was coming to the canyon to check on his precious white-faced cattle. And he always stopped to share the latest gossip from Ignacio. Now he sat at her kitchen table, barely sipping the black coffee. And not from his favorite cup.

"Where's my regular mug?"

"The one with the rabbit?"

He nodded.

"It ain't washed yet." She chuckled and her belly shook. The old man was worse than a child; he wanted his bunny-rabbit cup.

Gorman—annoyed at the old woman's laughter—gazed sullenly out the small window of her trailer home. Toward the wide mouth of *Cañon del Espiritu*. His cousin made the strongest and the worstest coffee he'd ever tried to get past his lips. "I gotta go into the canyon, have a look at my cattle. Don't have much time to waste here."

She noted that tact was not his strong point. In fact, he didn't have no strong points. "You shouldn't always be in such a hurry. Your cows'll keep."

His mind wandered to gossip. "Too bad about Hooper Antelope. Fallin' down dead at the Ute Mountain Sun Dance. And then his mother passin' on too." The old man sighed. Death was always waiting for you, eyeing the veins in your neck. Sharpening his rusty knife.

Daisy nodded. "Stella died from grief over her son." She wouldn't mention what had killed Hooper. But she had much to be thankful for. God had done His part in bringing Gorman out here. The rest was up to her. If you want to catch a hungry old catfish, first you got to bait the line. She opened the door of the chugging refrigerator. "You want something to eat?" Aside from bringing tribal gossip, it was the main reason he liked to visit. Men like Gorman just weren't able to cook decent food for themselves.

The old man stretched indolently and scratched his belly through the plaid shirt. "I had me some breakfast a little while ago." He belched. Twice.

"Oh," she said, "then I'll just make enough for me." Daisy removed a package wrapped in brown butcher paper and closed the refrigerator door.

He craned his neck as she untied the grease-spotted parcel. "What're you eatin'?"

"Nothin' much. Just some tamales."

He tried in vain to sound disinterested. "Tamales?"

She unwrapped the paper and used a butter knife to pry the delicacies apart.

He drummed his nicotine-stained fingers on the oilcloth. "Homemade?"

She nodded. "By that Rodriguez woman from up at Bayfield."

"Wrapped in corn shucks?"

"Sure." Artificially wrinkled paper that looked like corn shucks, but Gorman wouldn't know the difference.

"Made with lard?" Unconsciously, he licked his chapped lips.

Now that was a dumb question, even from Gorman. "Wouldn't buy no other kind."

He pulled a large gold-plated watch from his pocket and squinted at the white face. "Well . . . it'll be lunch time in a little while. If you don't want to eat alone, I guess I could have just a bite or two."

Mr. Whiskerfish was hooked. Daisy pretended not to hear his self-invitation.

In spite of himself, Gorman leaned forward and sniffed. "You got any of that canned red chili to put on 'em?"

"I been cookin' tamales all my life, old man, so don't you start telling me how to do my business."

"I like my chili without beans. Beans gives me gas." To demonstrate, Gorman leaned sideways in his chair and broke wind.

Daisy rolled her eyes. "Behave yourself or you'll eat outside on the porch." Of all her nice relatives, why did God send this half-wit to see her? But the answer was obvious. The Great Mysterious One had a fine sense of humor.

Her cousin got up now and was looking over her shoulder. "I like melted cheese on my chili. Cheddar's best. The sharp kind."

"Sit down, Gorman," she snapped.

He did. What a contrary old woman. No wonder all three of her husbands had died rather than live with her.

She squatted with a grunt and fumbled around under the sink, rattling pots and pans. "After we have some lunch, then you can do something for me."

Ahhh, he thought, here it comes. When a man eats himself a bite at cousin Daisy's table, he never gets somethin' for nothin'. It must be her old wooden porch needin' repairs. Damn thing was always about to fall down. It was a mystery why it didn't never hold up better; he worked on the rickety thing half a dozen times every year. "You need some carpenter work done?"

Daisy used both hands to hoist a large cast-iron skillet onto the propane stove; she leaned over to see underneath the blackened implement and adjusted a blue ring of fire. "What I need is for you to take me to see somebody."

"I'm kinda busy today . . . couldn't you wait till Charlie comes by?" There was the hint of a whine in his voice.

"It's important." Mr. Whiskerfish was wriggling, trying to spit out the hook. Daisy opened the refrigerator; where was that grated cheese?

Gorman sighed. He'd rather work on the damned porch than haul her all over creation. Drivin' a few nails into the porch would only take a few minutes. Now she'd have him out till after dark. And he wasn't no taxi driver—he was a respected local rancher with purebred Hereford cattle to check on. The old man was about to make an excuse when Daisy plopped two plastic bags on the table for his inspection.

"You can have cheddar melted on your chili. Or jack cheese."

"Oh . . . maybe a dab of both."

The delicious lunch of tamales and chili and cheese was partially digested and, except for the greasy aftertaste, forgotten. Gorman Sweetwater, whose mood was turning from grumpy to downright surly, pulled the Dodge pickup to a rattling halt under the spreading branch of a thirsty cottonwood. He cut the ignition. "I ain't got all day. I need to get back out to Spirit Canyon and see after my Herefords. So don't you stay too long."

Daisy pulled on the door handle. "This won't take long. And," she added tartly as an admonishment, "you should be glad to help a relative."

Gorman snorted. "Charlie Moon's your relative too. You could of gotten him to bring you out here in his police car."

Daisy smiled to herself. No, she couldn't. It was true that Charlie was a good nephew. And he was always willing to help an old woman. But it was best that the big policeman didn't know about this visit. Charlie might get curious. Start poking his nose around into her business. With no help from her sulking cousin, she slid cautiously out of the big pickup. After her feet touched earth, she turned toward Gorman. "I just need to check and see that Reuben's taking proper care of that little boy. You want to come inside?"

Gorman Sweetwater didn't want to agree to her suggestion. But it might be nice to talk to Reuben Antelope for a few minutes. Old bachelors understood each other. And maybe Reuben had a pint of something stashed in the cupboard. Something that'd warm the gut. He grimaced at the old woman. "Well, if you can't go inside by yourself, I guess I'll hafta go along and hold your hand." Gorman got out and slammed the pickup door.

*   *   *

Daisy sat on the porch steps with her arm around the child, who was nibbling on a candy bar she'd brought in her purse. The voices of Reuben Antelope and Gorman Sweetwater droned from inside the house like bees. Probably talking about pickup trucks or animals. Or trashy women they'd known. Known in the biblical sense. What else did old men talk about?

"Billy," she said in what she thought was a motherly tone, "d'you want to hear a story?"

The boy didn't look at her, but he nodded politely. Old people were always telling him stories. About olden times.

So the shaman told him a story. And such a wild tale it was. Billy smiled at the story. And at the funny old woman.

CHAPTER 6

Delly had pulled into the Texaco station across the high-way from the Sky Ute Lodge; she was filling the Toyota's gas tank. The young woman felt eyes watching her, but didn't turn. Men ogled her all the time, and she was used to it. Then she saw his reflection in the rear window glass. An elderly, overweight man got out of his pickup and approached her. Warily, it seemed. She glanced over her shoulder. There was a question in his wrinkled brow. "Say, aren't you that little Sands girl?"

Delly didn't particularly care for the "little girl" reference, but this old duffer was a product of another generation. "I sure am." She rewarded him with an inquisitive smile and returned the gasoline hose to the pump hook. "And you . . . you're Mr. Tall-man? My high school history teacher?"

He returned the smile, accepted her little hand in his and

patted it. "That's me. Hampton Tallman. I never forget any of my students."

"I remember you well, too." He was a kindly man, but a dull teacher.

He searched nervously in his jacket pocket, found a tattered cigar butt, and jammed it between his false teeth. "So how long you gonna be in town?"

"Don't know for sure. I need to find myself a job . . ."

He squinted through plastic-rimmed spectacles; the nose-bridge was wrapped with a narrow strip of masking tape. "I heard you been away to college. You get your degree yet?"

She dropped her gaze to his boots. "Not yet."

"So what'd you major in?"

She shrugged. "Drama. Journalism." And psychology . . . and English . . . and history . . .

"Journalism, huh? Well now that's a coincidence. Last year I took over as editor of the *Southern Ute Drum.*" He removed the cigar butt from his mouth and pointed it at her. "It's been nothin' but heartburn, kid—heartburn and ulcers—that's what I'm getting paid for. Can't find nobody who knows how to write or to sell advertisements. And last week, I lost my best reporter. Nice Ute girl, but," he grimaced, "she up and married a *matukach* plowboy. They've gone to live on a dirt farm down in East Texas. East Texas," he repeated the phrase absently, like a man uttering a familiar curse. "She says they'll make a good livin' raisin' pee-cahns." He shook his head at this idiocy, then drifted back to the present. He looked Delly up and down. Like a suspect piece of livestock. "You ever do any newspaper work, kid?"

She felt her heart thumping under her ribs. "I had a position with the *Gazette-Clarion* in north Denver . . ." Part-time job.

He raised an eyebrow. "That's a pretty fair rag. What'd you do?"

She shrugged. "Oh, you know . . . whatever came up. They

kept me pretty busy." Running errands for coffee and prune Danish.

His eyes narrowed. "You ever write any copy for the *Gazette?*"

"Sure. Local news and stuff." An occasional obit. Unless the deceased was someone important.

"Know anything about selling ads?"

"Oh yes. I worked a rotation in advertising. It was . . . very interesting." Three dull weeks taking classifieds over the telephone.

He smiled. This kid don't know beans. But she's got some spunk. And it takes spunk to do this kind of work.

Delly read his face; he wasn't buying her exaggerations. But it hardly mattered. She'd never get the position. First shot at Southern Ute jobs went to tribal members who'd stayed on the reservation. Though she was a Ute and a member of the tribe, she'd become a town Indian. An apple. Red on the outside, white on the inside. No, he'd hire a Navajo before he'd give her a job. Probably even an Apache. Don't get your hopes up.

He made a mock frown and patted her shoulder. "Tell you what, kid . . . you drop by the office sometime and talk to me."

The brush-off. "Sure, Mr. Tallman. I'll do that." Sometime.

Her expression was forlorn. A sweet-toothed little girl turned away from the candy counter. It was a look that could melt even a cold man's heart. Mr. Tallman was not a cold man. And he was a man with a mission. He glanced at his wristwatch. "Maybe you could stop by later this morning—say eleven-thirty?"

Her voice was little more than an astonished whisper. "I'll be there, sir. On the dot."

The *Drum* editor chewed on a freshly lighted cigar; he jabbed a stubby finger at the push buttons on the telephone, and waited.

The dispatcher at SUPD answered; Tallman asked for a particular officer. There was a long delay while they patched through to the squad car.

The voice Tallman heard was punctuated with static as the

radio attempted to fish the tiny signal from the sea of electromagnetic noise. He held the smoking cigar in the right side of his mouth and talked through the left. "Charlie Moon, that you?"

He listed to the confirmation.

"Well, old buddy, I found her at the Texaco station. Uh-huh. Did what you asked me to. Yeah. She's comin' over here in a few minutes."

A pause while he listed to Moon's question.

"Yeah, I made you a promise. I'll give her a job . . . but this is on your recommendation . . . this know-nothing kid messes up and you know who I'll put the blame on . . . friend or no friend . . . yeah, that's right." He chuckled and the cigar bobbled, making little waves in the stream of gray smoke. "Okay, Charlie, but don't you ask me to hire no more of your girlfriends. I got a newspaper to run." He listened to Moon's good-bye, then dropped the telephone receiver onto its cradle.

The tribal elder leaned back in his swivel chair and intertwined his fingers over his silver belt buckle. Hampton Tallman was quite satisfied with himself. For two reasons.

First, the wily old man was about to do a big favor for Charlie Moon, so the policeman would be beholden to him. It was good business practice for a newspaper to have some buddies over at the cop shop.

Second, Tallman was about to do a bigger favor for himself. He'd called the editor at the *Gazette-Clarion*. Like he'd figured, Delly Sands didn't have any significant newspaper experience. Too young for that. She'd mostly been a gopher. But the *Gazette* editor had said that the little Sands gal was a real go-getter. Not afraid of hard work. And smart, too. Yes, Tallman thought, she'll do just fine.

And the *Drum* editor had her first assignment all worked out in his mind. First, there'd be research. She'd have to do lots of digging round. Turning over rocks that some folks didn't want turned over. Maybe he'd twist Moon's arm a bit, get the big cop to help her. Under the circumstances, how could Moon refuse?

As the research progressed, the kid would write a series of stories. They'd need careful editing, of course, because this was a sensitive issue. And she was a green reporter. But by golly, this witching thing was gonna sell some newspapers!

And times being what they was, she'd be happy to get the job. Grateful. Maybe, he mused . . . maybe she'll be so grateful that she'll give me a big hug. The old man sighed a long sigh. Yessir. A hug from a pretty girl. That'd be nice.

A fringe benefit.

Charlie Moon was frying his breakfast when he thought he heard the automobile. Who'd that be? A man who lived at the end of a half-mile dirt lane didn't get many visitors. He flipped the eggs over and rolled the link sausages brown side up in the snapping grease. There was a light knock on his door. He wiped his hands on a cotton towel and went to see who tapped upon his chamber door.

The tall man peered out the slit window centered at six feet on the single slab of stained redwood. Ten yards away was a leafy cottonwood; it clung with gnarled roots to the steep bank of the river. A beat-up Toyota sedan was parked under the spreading branches of the old tree. He twisted the knob and pulled the massive door open.

He found Delly Sands standing on the brown flagstones. Looking like a little doll someone had lost. She was outfitted in a pink skirt and a white cotton blouse that stopped about three inches above the skirt. Her belly button was right there, in plain view. Looking up at him.

Moon tried not to stare back at the little eye on her bare midriff. The Ute felt a foolish grin spreading all over his face. He tried to think of an appropriate greeting. "Well," he said cleverly.

She held up one delicate hand and wiggled her fingers. "Hi."

He glanced over her head toward the Toyota sedan.

She gave him a wide-eyed look. "Charlie Moon, are you going to invite me into your house—or shall I stand out here all day?"

He backed away and she brushed past him onto the rough pine floor.

She clasped her hands and surveyed the circular room she'd heard so much about. The aura was masculine. Sturdy. Dependable. Like the man. "Oh Charlie . . . it's wonderful."

He shrugged modestly. "I don't know that it's all that great." Moon was, in fact, proud of the fact that he'd built it with his own hands. No contractor. No hired help. When he'd gotten started, there'd been no electricity out here. So he'd used hand tools. For rough-working the logs, a double-bladed axe and heavy crosscut saw. A two-handled hand knife for peeling off the bark. A five-pound hammer and a flared chisel for notching the ends. A sturdy wheelbarrow for hauling gray-blue clay from the riverbank and moving adobe bricks.

And lots of muscle and sweat.

"This place is kind of famous in La Plata County." She looked up to admire the spokelike array of hand-peeled pine vigas. They radiated from a central roof-support post that was almost three feet in diameter. The effect was like a great wagon wheel on the end of a gigantic axle emerging from the floor. "Larry says some of our people call it 'Charlie's kiva on the Pinos.' Did you know that?"

Moon grinned. He did know that. And it wasn't meant as a compliment. The Utes had once been tepee people. Kivas were viewed by the People as a peculiar invention of the Anasazi . . . an eccentricity of Pueblo Indians. Some of the Utes also called it "Moon's round mud house." Adobe structures, so popular just across the border in New Mexico, were uncommon in these parts. Uncommon and unwelcome.

Delly hugged herself, and turned to look up at him. "I just love it, Charlie." She glanced toward his massive bed. It was by a window facing the river, so the sounds of the water tumbling over the rocks would sing the big man to sleep. The Pinos, she imagined, was Charlie's lullaby river. And this was a fine bed. More than big enough for two. "That where you sleep?"

Funny question, he thought. It was the only bed in the place. Moon nodded. "You want some breakfast?"

She raised her nose like a hopeful puppy, and sniffed. "Smell's good." Icky. Pounds of animal fats and cholesterol.

He was relieved to have something to do for his guest. "I could make you some eggs and sausage. And grits if you like 'em."

She smiled a teasing smile. "Why, Charlie Moon—I didn't know real Utes ate grits."

He returned the smile, somewhat sheepishly. "When I was in the service, I had this redneck buddy from Georgia. When we visited his daddy's farm, they got me to eatin' grits and baked 'possums and sweet potatoes. I guess he got me onto all kinds of bad habits."

Delly moved closer; her head barely reached the level of his chest. "I didn't know you had *any* bad habits, Charlie. I guess there's a lot about you I've yet to find out." Unconsciously, her eyes flicked sideways toward the bed. "When I was a little girl and fell asleep, my daddy used to wrap me up in a little blanket and carry me to my bed." She offered the tall man an innocent face. "You ever put a little girl to bed, Charlie?"

Moon almost tripped over his feet getting to the woodstove.

Delly's eyes were open when a sweet vision flitted by. A tender fantasy . . . but it seemed so real. She could see herself, wrapped snugly in a pretty blanket. Only her face was showing. She was fast asleep . . . dreaming sweet dreams. And Charlie Moon was carrying her.

Moon's voice interrupted the vision. "How'd you like your eggs?"

She materialized by his side. So close he could smell her. She smelled sweet. Like spring flowers. "No eggs for me."

"Some pork sausage?"

"I don't think so."

He looked down at the top of her head. Her hair was parted

in a perfectly straight line that pointed toward the nape of her neck. Pretty little neck. "Grits and butter?"

She made a face.

He hoped she wouldn't ask for oatmeal or granola. He didn't keep such stuff in the house. "What'd you like?"

She looked him square in the eye. I'd like *you*, Charlie Moon. "Just some dry toast." Delly put her arms above her head, clasped her hands and stretched . . . pulling the blouse slightly higher above her tiny, naked waist. "Got to keep my girlish figure so's I can catch myself a man." She looked up at him, and playfully bumped his thigh with her small hip. "You know what I mean, Charlie?" She laughed; the sound was like little bells tinkling.

Moon felt his neck getting hot. In the frying pan, the sausages sizzled. "I guess I could toast you some bread in the oven."

They ate their breakfast in silence. She nibbled at a thick slice of lightly burned sourdough bread. And stared at him across the table.

Like, he thought, a cat with her paw on a mouse's tail. Wondering what she should do with him. The tension put Moon off his feed. He consumed only three eggs and a half-dozen sausage links.

She put the scorched bread aside. "I guess you're wondering why I showed up."

He didn't look up from his plate. "I imagine you heard how good my toast was."

She smiled a dreamy smile. "I've been away from home a long time, Charlie."

He downed a half cup of black coffee in one quick gulp.

Delly got up and tugged her chair around to his side of the pine table. "You remember at school—when you and my brother Larry were best buddies?"

He nodded. Those had been good days. Him and the Sandman knew it all. Had the world by the tail and their future all worked out. First, they were going to travel. See the world. Then, make a ton of money. Larry was going to run the finest hotel in Colorado Springs. Charlie Moon would have a big Hereford spread up by Gunnison. Delly had tagged along after them a lot. And hung on their every word. She'd been kinda shapeless back then. She wasn't now.

"You remember how I used to follow you around? Was I a pest?"

Sounded like trick questions, so he kept quiet.

She put her hand on his, rubbing his knuckles with the tips of her fingers. "I always liked you, Charlie. Never stopped." She waited for him to say something. Anything.

He almost choked on a forkful of sausage; his voice was raspy. "You want some more toast?"

Delly leaned lightly against his shoulder. "I've been kind of lonesome since I got back to Ignacio. Thought if I stopped by, maybe we could . . . well . . . do something together."

He was genuinely puzzled. "Like what?" She didn't look like a woman who'd want to go fishing.

She whispered. "Whatever you'd enjoy doing, Charlie."

Now what'd she mean by that? And what was she doing . . . ? She was breathing on his neck, that's what she was doing. Right under his ear. Her breath was warm. Moon was staring at the log spokes radiating from the center of the ceiling. He could've sworn that the big wooden wheel was rotating . . .

"So, Charlie—what'd you like to do?"

Moon looked longingly out the window at the swift waters of the Pinos. Water was running a bit low. Some rain in the high country would help. "I'd like to go catch some trout for lunch. But I got to go up to Granite Creek today."

"What for?"

He swiped a chunk of sourdough bread across his plate. "Police business."

She brushed a wisp of raven hair off her forehead. "Could I come along?"

He put the bread in his mouth. "I'll be kinda busy."

"I wouldn't get in the way. Honest."

"I don't know . . ."

"Of course," she rolled her eyes, "if you're afraid Myra Corn-stone wouldn't like me being with you . . ."

Moon thought about this. Afraid was the wrong word. He was a little bit *cautious*, of course. Myra was an easygoing sort of person, but she was a red-hot pistol when she got mad. "Myra's got nothing to do with it."

"Then why can't I go? You're not afraid of *me*, are you, Charlie?" She winked at him.

Moon dismissed this with a grunt, pushed his chair aside, and cleared the table. He took a stack of plates and cups to the sink.

She followed, tugging anxiously at his sleeve. "Then give me one good reason . . ."

Moon thought about this. Several good reasons came to mind. For one thing, she'd distract him from his work. For another, he wasn't supposed to haul people around in his SUPD Blazer. Except for Aunt Daisy and criminals, of course. Aunt Daisy wasn't exactly a criminal, more like a calamity waiting to happen. Someone who needed looking after by the police. Well, for that matter, Delly Sands might need some looking after. Though she hadn't mentioned it yet, Delly did work for the *Southern Ute Drum*. So most likely, she'd be on official tribal business. Sniffing around for a story about Hooper Antelope. And if she was with him, he'd be more likely to know what she was up to. What she might say about the SUPD investigation in the *Drum*. And it was a long, lonesome drive . . . she'd be good company. "Well, I guess you can come along," he said with an air of weary resignation. His stern expression made it clear that Delly had better behave herself.

She stood on tiptoe and wrapped her fingers around his neck. "Don't worry, Charlie. I'll be good." Very, very good.

On the long drive to Granite Creek, Delly Sands had little to say. She spent much of her time watching the stolid pines and fluttering aspens . . . meandering brooks fed by deep, cool springs . . . smoky blue haze slipping down narrow clefts between the mountains.

Charlie Moon wondered whether his companion really saw the mountains. Or the trees. Her brow was wrinkled into a frown that seemed out of place on her childlike face.

He interrupted the silence. "So how's the Sandman?"

She raised a dainty hand and waved the question away. "Oh . . . you know Larry."

The Ute policeman thought about this. Once, long ago, it had been true. He *had* known Larry Sands. Almost like he knew himself. But those days were a long time gone. The Sandman was someone else now. Ambition had made him hard. And he was secretive about his personal life. There were even rumors about drugs. An appalling possibility occurred to the Ute policeman. Someday, he might have to arrest Delly's brother. And turn the key in the lock. He dismissed this thought for a more pleasant one. Larry's little sister had also undergone quite a transformation. Moon allowed himself a smile. The changes in Delly . . . these were all for the better.

She put her hand on his arm. "There's something I want you to know."

He glanced at her, wondering what was coming.

"Charlie?"

"Yeah?"

"There's something I didn't tell you."

He glanced at her; she gave him the big eyes. "I did want to spend some time with you . . . but there's another reason I wanted to come along with you today."

He tried hard not to grin. Almost succeeded.

"What happened is I got myself a job."

"Oh." He assumed an innocent expression. "You running a blackjack table at the casino?"

She giggled. "It doesn't pay as good as that—but it's such a neat job. Kind of exciting." You'd better be impressed.

"Hmmm. You breakin' wild horses for rodeo stock?"

She sighed and rolled her eyes.

"Milking diamondback rattlesnakes for venom?"

"No, silly. I'm working for the *Southern Ute Drum.*"

He tried to seem surprised. "Doing what?"

"Oh, lots of stuff. But my most important assignment is to do a story on Hooper Antelope's death. You could be my first interview."

Moon wasn't surprised. When he'd talked Hampton Tallman into hiring Delly, he expected that she'd be assigned to the "witch" story. Now she'd be asking lots of questions. Wanting to know everything he knew. Which, come to think of it, wasn't all that much. "So. Your old schoolteacher gave you a job with the *Drum.* Hampton's always been nice to his students." Moon winked at her. " 'Specially if they're good-looking young ladies."

So. Charlie Moon thinks I'm good-looking. She nudged him with her elbow. "It's not what you think. And Mr. Tallman didn't hire me because I used to be his student or . . . or because I fluttered my eyes at him." She fluttered her eyes at Moon, to demonstrate.

He laughed. "Well, I can see why *that* wouldn't work." He received another nudge from her elbow. Sharp little elbow, he thought.

"Mr. Tallman gave me the job *in spite* of tribal politics." Delly flashed him a defiant look. "He picked me for the position because I'm well-qualified. Not because some pushy relative or friend called him up and talked him into it."

"Glad to hear it." Moon managed a poker face. "That's the way it should be."

🖐

The aged physician was half swallowed up by an overstuffed chair. The old monstrosity (the chair, not the physician) had the sickly hue of pond slime. The medical examiner's complexion was a healthy rose-petal pink. Walter Simpson's small slippered feet were propped on a scuffed leather stool. His eyes were almost closed. As if he napped. He did not. Through slitted lids, he observed the Granite Creek chief of police who paced like a caged panther. Dr. Walter Simpson was quite fond of Scott Parris. But in the way of such men, he exhibited his affection by dry sarcasm, cruel barbs, even insults. To those he did not care for, the old man was unfailingly polite.

Parris glanced at his wristwatch for the twentieth time. "Charlie Moon left me a voice-mail at the station; said he'd show up at your place by noon."

The white-haired man did not move; now his eyes were completely closed. His mouth was almost hidden, being sandwiched between a brushy mustache and an unclipped beard. "My appointment with Officer Moon is for noon *Indian* time. Which means sometime before dark. So settle down—your incessant treading about is beginning to annoy me."

"You don't know Charlie," Scott Parris muttered. "He's usually fairly prompt." Usually. Unless he spotted a likely looking fishing hole. And had brought along a hank of line, some long-shank hooks, and a can of red worms. Someday, he'd convince the Ute a real fisherman took his trout with a lure cunningly fashioned from tiny bits of feather. With the barb filed off the hook. Sure he would. Someday when the clouds rained pearls and rattlesnakes walked on hind legs.

Walter Simpson raised his left lid and squinted at the solemn face of a grandfather clock looming in a dark corner. Its aged ivory face looked back blankly. With every swing, the bronze pendulum clicked like a key turning in a rusty lock. "It's just ten minutes past, so relax already." He closed the eye.

"So what's he coming up here to see you about?"

Simpson sighed. Policemen weren't happy unless they were interrogating somebody with damn-fool questions. Must be something genetic that made a kid want to be a cop. "I have a BIA contract to provide my services to the Utes. The Southern clan, down at Ignacio—and the Ute Mountain bunch over at Towaoc."

"For autopsies?" The dumb question just leaped out of his mouth; Parris cringed as he waited for the sarcastic response.

"No," the medical examiner replied sweetly. "I have a contract with our Indian brethren for auto maintenance and repair. Officer Moon is bringing his police cruiser to me for an oil change. And a two hundred thousand–mile tune-up."

"You're cute today."

The M.E. opened both eyes. "There haven't been sufficient corpses coming down the pike. So, needing to make a buck one way or another, I've developed a sideline. Needless to say, I'd appreciate the business if any of Granite Creek's police cruisers should need a valve job or a set of shocks." He rubbed a finger against his thumb and winked merrily at his guest. "You send some work my way, Scotty, we'll arrange a little kickback to line your pockets."

The chief of police grunted. Doc Simpson was a smart-assed old bastard.

There was a heavy knock on the door. Heavy enough to reverberate down the hall, rattling dusty pictures hanging on the papered wall.

"That's him," Parris said. Good old Charlie Moon. *Wonder what he's up to?*

Simpson, exceedingly comfortable in his slime-green chair, grimaced and waved his liver-spotted hand in a limp gesture to indicate the direction of the front door. "Seeing that Officer Moon is your bosom buddy, perhaps you will trot down the hall, turn the knob, and open the door. And then, I suppose we must get down to my morbid business." The M.E. did not stir. *'Tis true,* he thought idly, *the practice of forensic medicine has not been all that bad a racket. But cutting up dead bodies over the decades . . . well, it is gradually beginning to lose its inherent luster and charm.* He whispered to himself: "I had it to do over . . . might go into investment banking. Seems like all of those fellows are driving Benzes and throwing money around like it was wastepaper." The medical examiner wondered where investment bankers vacationed. The Bahamas, most likely. Probably dated movie stars too. Simpson tried to imagine walking along the golden sand with a bikini-clad beauty. He tried hard. But inevitably, his mind drifted back to the grim business at hand.

Walter Simpson, though well into the last half of his eighth decade and suffering from several of the annoying ailments that older men must endure, had not lost his genuine appreciation of that mysterious sex. Plump and thin, short and tall—he appreciated them all. And this charming little girl who had arrived with Charlie Moon was so full of life . . . and such a pretty little thing. Lovely dark hair that glistened like it was oiled, huge brown eyes that seemed to perceive your innermost thoughts . . . a smile that was (he wished to think) definitely flirtatious. Not serious flirtation, of course. But intended to distract and unsettle a man. The medical examiner was distracted by this beauty. And unsettled.

Driven by Delly's presence to play the cultured host, Walter Simpson invited his guests to sit at the nineteenth-century mahogany dining table. It was covered with an antique linen cloth, whose yellowed patina matched the faded gold of the lilies on the wallpaper. The good doctor brewed an inexpensive brand of coffee for the men. He produced a long-necked bottle of homemade blackberry wine, which he offered only to Delly Sands. And he searched his ample cupboard for sweet cakes. And candied dates. And brandied pears. And other such delicacies.

To please him, she took a dainty sip from a crystal tumbler not much larger than a thimble. She insisted that it was the very best blackberry wine she'd ever tasted. This was not a lie. It was the only blackberry wine she had ever tasted. It was, truth be told, overly sweet.

But with this praise, she'd completely won Simpson's heart. He'd picked the berries with his own hands, he assured her. And mashed the fruit in an oaken tub—with his own bare feet.

Her raised eyebrows expressed the mildest doubt at this last claim.

The medical examiner insisted that he still had blackberry stains between his toes from his labors—and to prove it made as if he would gladly remove his slippers and display his feet for her inspection.

Delly clapped her hands and laughed; she assured him that it would not be necessary for him to go to such trouble. His word was more than sufficient.

So he had no need to remove his slippers; all present were relieved.

Scott Parris found the whole thing embarrassing; the old man was making an ass of himself—and over a girl who could be his granddaughter.

Charlie Moon used a cup of the so-so coffee to wash down a mouthful of candied dates and brandied pears. He cleared his throat. "Maybe we'd best get down to business."

The M.E. stared blankly at the Ute policeman, as if he'd just noticed his presence. "Business?"

Moon reached for the insulated coffee decanter and helped himself to another cupful. "I understand you've completed the autopsy on Hooper Antelope's . . . remains."

Delly, who had started to nibble on a fig, laid it on her silver plate. It was fun to be with Charlie . . . but talk about dead bodies was . . . well, that was icky.

Simpson nodded, as if the reason for Moon's visit was gradually coming back to him. "Oh yeah. Your Sun-Dancer. Maybe we'd best go along to my mor—" he glanced uncertainly at the pretty girl. "uh . . . my basement la*bor*atory." He deliberately emphasized the second syllable, giving the word a distinctive British flavor.

Parris helped himself to a sticky prune. "I've seen enough of your cadavers, Doc. I'll stay upstairs and chat with Miss Sands." He raised an eyebrow at the young woman. "Unless, of course, she has an interest in your work."

"Oh no, I'll stay where I am." Delly suppressed a shudder. Did this peculiar old man actually have Hooper Antelope's body in his *house*? Suddenly, she regretted coming on this trip with Charlie Moon. But she did have an interest in Hooper Antelope's death—and a story to write for the *Southern Ute Drum*.

Moon considered his options. The basement laboratory was the M.E.'s morgue. Where the bodies were kept in refrigerated drawers. And from what his buddy Scott Parris had told him, there was a considerable assortment of body parts on the premises. Some folks collected stamps or hanks of old barbed wire; Doc Simpson was a collector of interesting organs. The Ute policeman imagined long shelves supporting rows of carefully labeled fruit jars. In the jars was alcohol or some such preservative. Floating in the fluid were kidneys and eyeballs and gallbladders. He'd never actually had a look at a gallbladder, but the name itself was a strong disincentive to encounter such a thing. Moon told himself that he was not a superstitious man. Nevertheless, he was a Ute. And it was a part of his culture—his dear mother had taught him this—to avoid any sort of contact with dead bodies. That surely included body parts. No, Charlie Moon was a modern, well-educated man. Free of burdensome superstitions. But out of respect to his departed mother . . . "I guess all I need is your written report. And maybe an interpretation of any technical stuff."

The M.E. pulled thoughtfully at his fuzzy beard. "Well, there's not much to tell. Cause of death was myocardial infarction. Heart failure, that is. Precipitated by acute dehydration, diminished circulation, decreased pulmonary function, general stress. Subject had a history of heavy smoking that was a contributory factor. Not to mention incipient Type-Two diabetes."

Delly was inspecting her silver fork . . . turning it in her hand . . . not actually seeing it. So it wasn't . . . some kind of magic that'd killed Mr. Hooper. Thank God.

Charlie Moon also felt a sense of relief. "That's good. Death by natural causes, then." This'd help curb reservation gossip about witchcraft at the Ute Mountain Sun Dance. The tribal chairman would be happy. Chief of Police Roy Severo would also be pleased. Aunt Daisy, of course, would ignore the medical examiner's findings. The old woman saw a ghost moving in every shadow, a witch lurking behind every misfortune.

The M.E. rubbed his chin; a look of uncertainty passed over his face. "Well . . . yeah. He died by natural causes. No doubt about that." He paused, rubbing at the white stubble on his chin. "But there was . . . an anomaly."

Moon felt the muscles in his shoulders tense. *Anomaly* was a troubling word. "What was that?"

Walter Simpson seemed almost embarrassed. "Nothing much. A small contusion on his shoulder. Barely punctured the skin."

Delly felt a tingling coldness at the tips of her fingers. A puncture? But that didn't make sense . . . or did it?

The M.E. shrugged. "Looks like he fell backwards onto something."

"He did fall, in a way." Moon frowned at the memory. "Those Ute Mountain police who were moving him—they had a little accident."

The old man scowled. "Accident?"

"When they were trying to get him onto the copter, he got dumped off the gurney. I expect he landed on a sharp rock."

The medical examiner was goggle-eyed. "They dropped him? Dammit, that wasn't in the report."

Moon grinned sheepishly. "I guess they were kind of embarrassed. Didn't want it talked about."

Simpson allowed himself a long sigh. "Well . . . that would explain it. So," he asked hopefully, "when will the Utes want the remains sent back to the reservation for burial?" The M.E. needed the space. All six coolers in the basement were occupied.

Charlie Moon thought about it. "Ask your Bureau of Indian Affairs contract officer. BIA'll check with his relatives." Maybe the Antelope family would put Hooper's body in *Cañon del Espíritu.* In the Sand Bowl, sealed in a crevice close to where his mother's body lay. But if Reuben Antelope suspected that his brother had died of witchcraft, the old man might not want to get anywhere near Hooper's corpse. The Ute policeman wondered, when the time came, where should his own remains be placed? In the tribal cemetery on the banks of the Pinos? Where a man's spirit might hear the sweet sounds of fresh waters rolling across the smooth stones? Or should his body be lodged in the eternal stillness of the canyon . . . near the lonesome spot where his mother's bones were returning to dust? Being a practical man, Moon decided that this decision could wait awhile. If he put it off long enough, then after he was dead someone else would have to make the decision for him. Maybe he'd ask his best friend to tend to it. Scott Parris was a romantic. He'd put him next to his mother.

Delly reached over to touch Moon's arm. "Charlie . . ."

Poor kid looked kind of punky, he thought.

"Charlie . . . I don't feel so good. I think maybe I should go outside. Get a breath of fresh air."

The big Ute got up from his chair. "We're about done here. I'll go with you."

Scott Parris reached for a tarnished silver dispenser, helped himself to a toothpick, and focused his merry blue eyes on the M.E. "Well, Doc, looks like we'll be leaving." He stuck the wooden splinter between a pair of bicuspids. "It's sure been fun."

Walter Simpson tried to think of a snappy retort. But he couldn't. He was, he admitted to himself, a curmudgeonly old man. Arrogant and vain. Foolish about the women. But he was also a lonely man. He would miss the pretty girl and the big Ute cop. Even better to have this smart-assed Scott Parris in his three-story Victorian house than to be alone among the odd artifacts of his profession. Drifting among the heavy currents of silence. Like an old, bewhiskered jellyfish, someday to be washed up on that distant shore. Would all his silent clients be there . . . waiting expectantly for his arrival?

He hoped so. He knew them all so intimately . . . they were like dear, old friends. Almost like family.

Charlie Moon leaned on Parris' old Volvo. It was beginning to show signs of rust on the fenders.

The Granite Creek chief of police sat on the cold hood, his muscular arms folded across a broad, deep chest. Scott Parris nodded toward the Ute policeman's black, dust-streaked Blazer. Where the pretty woman waited. The toothpick jiggled between his teeth when he spoke. "So where'd you find the nice young lady?"

Moon also looked toward the Blazer, where the profile of Delly's delicate features could be seen against the dimming western light. "She's a friend. Sister of an old high school buddy."

"Well she's plenty easy on the eyes, partner. And," Parris added, "I'd say she's got her eyes on you."

The Ute policeman glanced uneasily toward the big house of six gables where Doc Simpson plied his odd trade. "Delly's just a kid."

Parris grinned mischievously. "Some kid. You better take care, Charlie."

Moon preferred another subject. "So how's your pretty red-headed gal doing?"

The *matukach* cop crunched the toothpick flat. "Anne's doing some graft-chasing story for a cable TV news outfit. In Seattle, last I heard." A long way from home.

"So when're you two going to tie the knot?"

An interesting question, Parris thought. Anne had herself a fine career. Paid a damn sight better than his. And she'd been married once too, just like him. But her dumb-assed husband had knocked her around some, so now she preferred being single. Parris preferred another subject. "When you want to do some fishin'? I hear those forest service guys who run the trout nursery just stocked the upper Piedra with a truckload of rainbows. Most of 'em ten-inchers. Some," he said hopefully, "probably bigger'n that."

"I'm busy for the next couple of weeks," the Ute policeman said. "Sun Dance coming up."

"Thought you just had one. Didn't you say this Antelope guy died at a Ute Sun Dance?"

"That was on the other reservation. Over on Sleeping Ute Mountain. The Southern Ute to-do is the last one of the summer. Not too many of our people go to watch a Sun Dance anymore, but it's still a big thing for some members of the tribe."

There was a long, comfortable silence between the two friends.

The Ute still didn't know much about this white man. Scott Parris had been a street cop on Chicago's south side, until his wife's accidental death during a trip to Canada. That had led to some heavy drinking, which led to depression. And an early departure from the force. He'd gone cold turkey on the booze and headed-West-young-man. Looking for a quiet job to carry him to retirement. Granite Creek was a small university town looking for an experienced out-of-towner to run the cop shop. With one or two particularly grim exceptions, there had not been much to give a policeman heartburn—aside from the occasional burglary or bar fight. Even the drug trade was falling off. So maybe he'd gotten a little stale. But Parris had an uncanny intuition about lots of things. Especially homicides.

"Charlie?"

"Yeah?"

"You think Doc Simpson's right about this Sun-Dancer dying of natural causes?"

Moon breathed deeply. The air was sweet. "Sure. Why not?"

"Oh, I dunno. You seem . . . kind of tense."

The Ute policeman shrugged. "There's lots of tribal talk. Half of the People think a witch killed Hooper." Moon chuckled. "The other half think so too."

"Well," Parris said. "a lot of peculiar things do happen on the reservation . . ."

Moon noticed that Scott had a peculiar glazed-eye expression.

He was in one of his funny moods. Probably because Anne was so far away. And also because Sweet Thing didn't show much interest in marrying him. Scott's sandy hair was getting a little thin on top too. That bothered some white men a lot.

"Pardner, you're starting to sound like my Aunt Daisy. I expect you need a vacation."

The *matukach* slid off the Volvo hood. "I always need a vacation, Charlie."

"Why don't you come down to Ignacio for a visit?"

"Doin' what? You're all tied up with work, said so yourself. I'd just be in the way."

It was true. "No, you wouldn't. You could help me with some things." The Ute policeman couldn't imagine *what* things.

"I can't imagine what things, Charlie." Parris sounded interested. "I don't know your reservation turf all that well."

Charlie Moon had an inspiration. "Well, maybe you could help me with this Sun Dance problem. Hooper's death's got the tribe spooked. Two or three of our regular dancers may not participate next week."

On the western horizon, the sun was kissing the rugged gray face of Capote Peak. Soon the long shadow of the mountain would slip across the town. And the temperature would drop ten degrees in as many minutes. In anticipation, Parris buttoned his jacket. "What could I do to help?"

Good question. Moon thought about it. "What any good lawman does. Hang around the Sun Dance grounds. Keep your ears open." He pushed his black Stetson back a notch. "Keep me posted on what you hear." There would be nothing worth hearing, just a lot of wild gossip. But it would keep Scott busy. Maybe keep his mind off Sweet Thing for a few days.

Parris set his battered felt hat at a jaunty angle. He reminded Moon of a hard-jawed version of Bogart. Though a bit more beefy.

"I got some vacation coming." And Anne wouldn't be home for at least a week.

"Good," Moon said. "Come on down soon's you can get away."

Delly hadn't said much on the drive home from Granite Creek. Charlie Moon wondered what she was thinking about. Probably some kind of women's stuff. Whatever that was. The policeman didn't have a clue.

Moon pulled the Blazer under the branches of the big cottonwood and cut the ignition. He rolled his window down. The cottonwood leaves rattled like dry teeth chattering. The river muttered a muted welcome to him. The sun had just slipped under a cloudless horizon. A perfect disk of amber moon was ascending through the billowing mists over Shellhammer Ridge. The face on the moon smiled at him. Or did it smirk?

They sat there. Very still. And gazed at the policeman's circular house.

And at Delly's red Toyota.

He wondered. Would she want to go back to her brother's apartment, or stay for a while? If she did, he could make some supper for the two of them.

She wondered. *Should I stay for a little while? . . . or . . .*

"Charlie?"

He turned to look at her upturned face. It was suffused with moonglow.

"I want to ask you something."

This sounded serious. "About what?"

"My assignment at the *Drum*."

"Ask away."

"Mr. Tallman . . ." she hesitated, "he said that maybe you'd help me."

"He did, huh?" Moon grinned ruefully into the darkness. That old fox. He could almost hear Tallman's gravelly voice. "Well, Charlie, you talked me into givin' her a job; least you can do is help her along a little bit."

"Charlie?"

"Yeah?"

"You will help me, won't you? I'd be so grateful." She leaned over, resting her head on his shoulder.

He looked at the top of her head. Her hair smelled good. "Maybe we could help each other."

"I'd be glad to help you, Charlie." She'd almost said "I'd do anything for you . . ."

"Well, I got something to ask you about. When old Hooper started stumbling around—right before he fell down. I was outside the corral, but you were inside. Close to the action. You see anything—or hear anything—that was . . . unusual?"

She seemed to stop breathing. Finally, she spoke. "I don't remember seeing anything unusual, except that Hooper was acting funny." Delly looked up at his profile. "But I did hear something."

"What?"

"Well, it was a kind of snapping sound. And there was something else . . ." Her voice trailed off.

"What?"

"It'll sound dumb."

He grinned. "I won't laugh."

"It sounded like . . . like a bird's wings beating." She shivered at the memory. "A large bird . . . but there wasn't any bird, Charlie."

He didn't laugh.

She shuddered.

The moon drifted slowly across the heavens. And gradually turned from amber to the flat white of bleached bone. The night was silent, except for the crystalline water rippling over smooth stones. The many voices of the river.

"Funny thing," he said. "You met my friend, today—Scott Parris."

She nodded, and snuggled closer. "The chief of police at Granite Creek. I think he's nice." Broad shoulders, too. And pretty blue eyes. "But what's funny?"

"Well, he's a policeman, like me. And his girlfriend—Anne Foster. She's writes stories for TV and newspapers. And now you work for a newspaper."

She hugged his arm and looked up. "Why Charlie Moon—that's a very suggestive statement."

He frowned down at her little face.

The moonlight sparkled in her eyes. "It almost sounded like you're saying that I'm your girlfriend."

"Hmmph," he said.

As Delly climbed the outside stairs to her brother's four-room apartment just off Goddard Avenue, many disconnected thoughts fluttered around in her mind. Above her head, dusty gray moths flitted around an electric fixture disguised as an old-fashioned gaslight. At the edge of the heavy curtains, there was a flickering blue light visible. So he was still up. Watching TV, apparently. She turned the key in the door.

Larry Sands was standing with his back to the couch, facing the oversized television screen. The olive-skinned young man was dressed only in jeans; he was methodically lifting a pair of cast-iron dumbbells. With no apparent effort, as if they were made of cork. Muscles rippled in his shoulders. The Sandman didn't look at his sister.

"I'm back," she said.

He dropped the weights on a long couch.

Mr. Personality. "Miss me?"

He did several deep knee bends. "Heard you were out with Charlie Moon today."

She took off her light jacket and hung it on a polished wooden peg by the door. "Where'd you hear that?"

Larry Sands grinned. "It's a small town, Delly."

Her eyes snapped fire. "I'm not a kid anymore. I come and go as I please."

His grin was replaced with an expression she couldn't quite read. "You oughta be careful who you run around with."

She was accustomed to his big-brother routine, but this warning caught her off guard. "Charlie Moon is one of your old friends."

"Old," he said, "is the operative word. As in 'former.' We hung out some in high school. That's all."

She raised an eyebrow. "Well, I'll see Charlie Moon whenever I want."

The Sandman frowned. "Moon's a cop."

"No kidding? So *that's* why he drives a police car and wears a badge."

Larry Sands, tired from his exercises, sat down heavily. "Don't be a smart-ass. It's always best to keep clear of the law." He gave her a sideways look. "So what's our local cop up to?"

"He keeps pretty busy. Are you interested in anything in particular?"

Larry shrugged. "There was some talk he was headed up to Granite Creek today. Somethin' about checkin' on Hooper Antelope's autopsy."

"He did see the medical examiner."

"You went along for the ride?"

"Sure. I'm doing a story for the *Drum*. On Mr. Antelope's death."

Her brother tried his charming smile. "So what'd Moon find out?"

His voice had a forced casualness that sounded little alarm bells in her head. She pretended not to have heard the question.

"So," he said again, "Moon learn anything interesting from the autopsy?"

She shrugged.

"I wouldn't want to think you'd hold out on me, Sis . . ." He reached under the couch and found a cigar box. There were no cigars in the cardboard container. There were cigarettes. Small handmade cigarettes. Twisted at the tips. Sealed with spittle. He glanced up at his sister. "Want a little hit of big brother's mystery recipe?"

She knew what it was. Mary Jane spiked with a dusting of crack. "You know I don't touch that stuff."

He did his drawling John Wayne voice. "Well suit yourself, Missy."

In spite of her annoyance, Delly admired her brother's talent. He could do a near-perfect mimic of anybody from the Duke to the tribal chairman. And he could do fantastic animal calls. Or make a noise like a steam locomotive . . . a diesel horn . . . a musical instrument . . . just about any sound you could think of. Larry was gifted, but immature. He was convinced that the drugs sharpened his wits. Made him a superman. There was no point in talking to him about it but—"Larry, I don't know how you can treat your body like that. You exercise to stay fit, then you smoke that junk—"

"Hey," he shouted, "lay off. Don't ride me about my—"

Her interruption sizzled like acid. "Your *habits?*"

He thought about this. "Yeah. My habits are my own damn business." He sneered, aiming his finger at her. Like a pistol-barrel. "Don't piss around with me, Sis. You park in my pad, you play by my rules."

Delly, hot tears blinding her eyes, spun on her heel. She headed for the spare bedroom.

Larry Sands struck a match on his jeans, lighted the twisted cigarette, and took a long, slow draw. He rested his head against the couch and closed his eyes. "Damn Goody Two-Shoes sister," he muttered absently—puffs of smoke accentuating each syllable—"what a whining little bitch she's turned into."

Delly strained to lift her heavy suitcase and pushed it onto a booth seat. She seated herself across the table, alongside her overnight case and purse. It had been, all in all, some day. A wonderful drive up to Granite Creek with Charlie Moon. Meeting Scott

Parris and Dr. Simpson, the funny little medical examiner. Eerie discussions about the condition of Hooper Antelope's corpse. She shivered. And then, the row with her brother. It was time to find her own place to live, so she'd packed her bag and moved out. The motel was expensive, but it'd have to do while she looked for her own apartment. This day was finished. Nothing more could possibly happen. A half hour in the Sky Ute Lodge restaurant while they got her room ready, then off to dreamland.

A young man with a pad materialized at her elbow. "I'm Bernard, ma'am. I'll be your server this evening." He offered her a menu.

She waved it away. "Just coffee."

The young man tugged at his starched white collar, then straightened his black tie. The waiter, who thought himself a very handsome man, was disappointed that this pretty customer didn't even look at him. On his break, he'd preened in front of the men's room mirror, brushing his hair until it was *perfecto*. Irresistible, he thought. A maiden's dream. "You want cream and sugar?"

She shook her head glumly. "Black is fine." Her back ached from lugging the suitcases.

"Certainly." He hurried away. What fantastic eyes she had . . . this was some good-looking babe. And she didn't use makeup— didn't need it. Class stuff. And from the looks of the suitcases, she was either checking in or out. In, he hoped.

Delly glanced around the motel restaurant. At this late hour, the place was nearly empty. A small party of elderly Utes, drinking coffee and eating peach pie. And laughing at one silly joke after another.

She spotted a young couple holding hands. Tourists for sure. Newlyweds maybe.

An old man came in and sat at a small table prepared for two. Indian, she thought, but not Ute. Looked vaguely familiar. But old men tended to look much alike. His eyes were focused on a menu, but Delly had the instinctive feeling that he was watching her. She was scolding herself for encouraging a neurotic imagination, when the waiter returned with a mug of steaming coffee on a brown plastic tray.

He gingerly sat the coffee on the table and made a small, though pretentious, bow. "If there's anything else you'd like ma'am . . ."

His tone was just suggestive enough to make her smile. Men never stopped hitting on her. Good for the ego, but sometimes it got tedious. She looked up. He was a pretty boy. Too pretty. Too boyish. She preferred men. Men like Charlie Moon. "There is one thing you could do."

"Yes?" He clasped his hands hopefully. Prayerfully.

She whispered in conspiratorial fashion. "Don't look now, but an old man just came in. He's sitting over there." She indicated the direction with her eyes. "I'm sure I've seen him somewhere. Do you know who he is?"

The waiter turned to straighten a cloth napkin and made a surreptitious glance at the elderly man.

The ploy was so obvious that Delly cringed in embarrassment.

The young man leaned forward and pretended to swipe at the table; he spoke in a hoarse whisper. "The gentleman is one of our guests. From Wyoming. Here for the Sun Dance next week, I expect." He paused, glancing over his shoulder at the subject of his report. "If you'd like more information, I could check with the front desk."

"Thanks. I remember him now." Of course. It was the old Shoshone man who'd been at the Ute Mountain Sun Dance. Some kind of guest of honor. And Larry had mentioned his name. It was . . . Red something or other. Red Hand? No. Red Heel. With this simple knowledge, she relaxed. The old man wasn't really watching her, of course. The Shoshone just had one of those faces that made you uneasy. And the run-in with Larry hadn't helped her nerves.

The waiter, whom she'd almost forgotten, leaned close enough for his pretty customer to smell his breath. Breath sweetened with a mint. Wintergreen, it had said on the wrapper. With a touch of fragrant cloves. But alas, there was competition. From the soup he'd had earlier, there lingered just the faintest hint of garlic. "If there's anything else you might want, I'd be happy to be . . . of service."

She arched an immaculate eyebrow and gave him a long, searching look. As if she were interested. "If there is, I'll let you know." *In your dreams, kid.*

The waiter departed, exceptionally pleased with himself. Miss Pretty Eyes was already eating out of his hand. Tomorrow . . . who could tell what tomorrow would bring? When he entered the kitchen, he was singing. He would've tap danced among the pots and pans and ladles. If he'd known how.

Delly sipped at the bitter coffee; she checked her wristwatch a half dozen times. *The room should be ready in a few minutes. I'll treat myself to a long, hot, soaking bath in the tub. Maybe read a little or watch a late movie. Then to bed. With luck, I'll put the argument with my dumb brother away in some dark closet of my mind. And sleep a sweet, dreamless sleep. Tomorrow . . . who could tell what tomorrow would bring? Maybe I'll see Charlie Moon again.*

She was feeling much better.

And then Winston Steele came into the restaurant. With the blond woman hanging on his arm. The drop-dead gorgeous blonde. Without a pound of makeup, Delly thought, what'd she look like then? Well, admit it. Still gorgeous.

Steele glanced toward the booth where Delly sat with her coffee; he noticed the young woman. And the suitcase. He looked away quickly.

As if she were a stranger!

She pretended not to notice the handsome couple. And if Steele caught her eye as he passed, she'd pretend to wonder who he was . . . some forgotten stranger perhaps? That'd be like sticking a knife in the two-timing bastard's ego.

But Steele never looked toward her. He ushered the blonde to a table that was as far away as he could get from Delly's booth. The woman, who had the curvaceous body and haughty confidence of a movie star, fumbled in her enormous purse until she found a rosewood compact. She frowned at her pale reflection in the glass disk, pursed her sensuous lips, and patted daintily at waves of golden hair.

The waiter practically sprinted to their table. Bernard could hardly believe his good fortune. Two fantastic babes in one evening. He patted his own waves of dark hair, then wiped an oily palm on his apron.

He bowed. "I am Bernard. I will be your server tonight."

He took the order. Yes . . . The lady prefers a Cobb salad? With a diet dressing. Very good, ma'am. And the gentleman? The gentleman will have the Mexican combination plate? *Rojo* . . . *Verde*? Green, yes, of course.

Delly watched the waiter fawn over the blonde as he took the order with incessant nodding and bowing. His tongue was practically hanging out. How some men behaved around such women was . . . well, it was just sickening. Delly waved at the waiter, who was making some small talk with Blondie. And grinning so widely it was a wonder the bottom of his silly face didn't fall off—trying, no doubt, to see down her low-cut black dress. Hmmpf. Mostly foam rubber. She didn't believe it for a minute.

Delly raised her cup in a forlorn gesture at the waiter.

The young man, it appeared, had forgotten she was alive. Well kiss your tip good-bye buddy.

Winston Steele had noticed Delly's fruitless summons. He said something to the waiter, who glanced toward this anxious customer.

After he'd taken Steele's order to the kitchen, Bernard appeared at her side with a coffee decanter. "Need a warm-up, ma'am?"

Delly fairly snapped at the unfortunate youth. "It's a little late for that. I need fresh coffee." Immediately, she regretted her harshness. Bernard was only a kid, trying to make a buck. Not so different from her.

He bowed and removed the offending cup. "Certainly, ma'am." He was gone in a flash. Debating with himself which of these wonderful women was the most desirable. The blond woman, of course, was astonishingly gorgeous. Like one of those women on the supermarket magazines. She was a model, maybe. But the small dark girl . . . she was so very pretty. And how her eyes flashed! Bernard had always had difficulty in making the least decision. But he decided.

It was a toss-up.

From the corner of her eye, Delly saw Winston's girlfriend get up from the table. She patted him on the shoulder, said something prissy about the ladies room and powdering her nose, and pranced away, her black spike heels clicking hollowly down the hall.

His girlfriend was barely out of sight when Steele ejected himself from the chair and marched across the restaurant—the picture of a man with a firm purpose. He was headed directly for her booth. Delly had not expected that he'd want a confrontation; she tensed.

The pale man, his hands in the pockets of his expensive tweed sports jacket, towered over her.

She looked up. Attempting to appear disinterested. But he was so handsome . . .

"Hi, Delly."

"Oh. It's you." She tried to yawn, but couldn't. So she folded a paper napkin into the shape of a triangular hat. And put it on her coffee cup.

He frowned at the paper hat. "You doing okay?"

"Great," she said brightly. Great. My pot-smoking brother just invited me out of his apartment. I've got enough money for about a week in this motel. I'm falling head over heels for a man who's already got himself a steady girl. And Myra Cornstone would cut my throat in a minute if she knew I was after her fellow. Sure. Life is great.

"Look," he said with a nervous look toward the hall where the blonde had disappeared, "I'd introduce you to my friend but—"

Delly interrupted him with a bitter laugh. "Your friend? Is that what you call 'em nowadays—your *friends*?"

His white face paled another notch. "I thought *we* were friends."

It was the wrong thing to say. Very wrong. She gave him a venomous look.

He rubbed his thumb on a platinum cuff link. "It seems you're not over the bitterness . . ."

Wrong choice again. More venom.

But now she understood why he'd come over to have this nice little chat with her. It was insurance against her coming to his table, initiating a confrontation for Blondie's benefit. Her dark eyes flashed fire at him. "Bitter isn't how I feel, *Doctor* Steele." Not unless lemons are bitter.

He swallowed hard, glanced uneasily around the restaurant. Conversations that had fluttered in the stale atmosphere were now in a holding pattern. Every ear was cocked toward them. He lowered his voice almost to a whisper. "When I participate in the Sun Dance, I don't refer to my profession."

"Fine," she said, loud enough for all the hungry ears to hear. "So you're not *Doctor* Steele while you're hanging out with the Indians." Poor Winnie. So handsome. So filthy rich. So successful. And always trying so hard to be just one of the guys.

He switched on his little-boy smile. "I'd appreciate it if you'd just call me Winston. For old time's sake."

She smiled back. For old time's sake. "I'd prefer to call you something . . . more descriptive. Maybe something with a subtitle? Let's see . . . how about 'Winston Steele: Dirty, Two-Timing, Womanizing Bastard'?"

He got the hint. And managed to look hurt. "If you'd prefer, I'll return to my table."

"I prefer. Besides, your *friend* will be back from the toilet anytime now. Bet she wouldn't want to find you chatting with another woman, would she? Too bad, though. Blondie and I could have a great talk. All about you . . . Winnie." Winston hated that corruption of his name.

"Well, maybe I'll see you later." Dr. Steele backed away slowly. Like a wary man confronted by a hungry cougar. Don't break eye contact, that was the first rule. Turn and run and sure as the sun came up, the she-cat'd have you for breakfast.

The gorgeous woman appeared, barely in time to see that her man had wandered away from their table. Shmoozing with the locals?

Steele, in an attempt to salvage the situation, immediately turned to Red Heel's table and offered the old man a hand. "It's good to see you again, sir."

The Shoshone seemed not to notice the outstretched hand, but he knew this white man . . . a dedicated Sun-Dancer. He turned his wrinkled face toward the approaching blonde. "You lead a dangerous life, young man."

Steele grinned a nervous, wolfish grin. "Yeah. Tell me about it."

Minutes later, Myra Cornstone reported to the restaurant. For her eight hours on the graveyard shift.

Delly greeted her with a smile. "I didn't know you worked here."

"I got two children to support. Chigger Bug and my grandfather."

The two young women exchanged polite pleasantries. About the weather. The quality of the restaurant's coffee. About Daisy Perika . . . such a sweet old lady, isn't she? About the church play . . . wasn't Louise-Marie's falling asleep and snoring a scream? About Myra's baby boy. Chigger Bug had a cold. But the object of their mutual affection was not mentioned. Delly wondered how long it would be before Myra would know she'd spent the day with Charlie Moon.

As it turned out, not long.

A muscular bellman showed up with the good news that Miss Sands's room was ready. He picked up the suitcase and overnight bag. Delly felt all her cares slipping away. Gone were thoughts of her foolish, selfish brother. And gone with them were bitter memories of Dr. Winston Steele, the black-hearted skirt chaser. Tonight, she'd sleep. Tomorrow, she'd show up at the *Drum* offices early. And get to work on her assignment.

It was a half hour later when Dr. Winston Steele finished his hot cherry cobbler topped with French vanilla ice cream. The lovely woman had a small portion of sugar-free fat-free frozen banana yogurt. He helped her on with a black beaded jacket and left a five-dollar tip for Bernard. As they left the restaurant, Steele had his hand on the blonde's slender waist. His fingers moved to her hip. She laughed. And whispered something into Dr. Steele's ear that made him blush.

Myra Cornstone approached the Shoshone's table. He'd nibbled away about half of his grilled cheese sandwich and left the rest to get cold. And he didn't look good; his left hand trembled. Maybe he was about to have a seizure of some kind. Only last month an old man had dropped dead in the restaurant, busted up a table when he fell. Stroke, they'd said. Myra hoped this old guy wasn't sick or something. Please Lord . . . not on my shift.

But Red Heel was sick. Sick with a terrible longing for home. His heart yearned for the Wind River country.

Myra smiled cheerfully and raised her voice, like she always did when she spoke to the elderly. As if they were all half deaf. "Can I get you anything else, sir?"

Red Heel lifted his face, wrinkled as a dried winter apple. He gazed at the young woman's face, and blinked owlishly. Like he wasn't quite sure who she was. Or where he was.

Myra placed the check facedown on the table and waited. Five to one, this old bird wouldn't leave a tip. If he did, it'd be two bits. But he looked pleasant enough. A lot like her grandfather. "If there's anything else you need . . . dessert or some coffee . . . you just let me know."

The Shoshone elder groaned as he pushed himself up from the uncomfortable chair. No. There was nothing else he needed in this place. He picked up the check and squinted at the scrawl of numbers. Four dollars and change for two pieces of burned white bread. And a piece of warm cheese. These rich Utes with their fancy restaurant, they were picking his pockets. But it was getting late.

And Red Heel was a man who settled his accounts.

CHAPTER 7

The elderly Ute woman was listening to country music on KSUT and didn't hear the sound of the automobile until it had turned off the *Cañon del Espiritu* road into the dirt driveway at her trailer home. But Daisy Perika knew who it would be before she got up to peek out the small rectangular window.

The car was, under a thin film of dust from the back road, a dull red. The young woman got out and closed the door. She hesitated for a moment, gazing off toward the dark mesas that reached down from the mountains with long, serpentine fingers. Finally, Delly Sands turned and walked toward the shaman's trailer home; she climbed the creaking pine steps to the unpainted wooden porch.

Daisy Perika opened the aluminum door before Delly had a chance to knock.

Her visitor stood there looking impossibly fresh and young.

She wore a blue cotton dress with white polka dots and shining black cowboy boots. Her black hair was done up in a single short pony tail, tied with a hank of white ribbon.

Delly nodded respectfully to the tribal elder. "Good morning, Mrs. Perika." She glanced uncertainly over her shoulder toward the giant sandstone women sitting on Three Sisters Mesa. It felt as if the Anasazi women were staring at her back. Now that was a silly thought, brought on by the strangeness of this isolated place.

The old woman simply stood there without a word, and looked at her. Up and down Daisy's eyes went, as if appraising her suitability—for what?

Delly's smile was tinged with curiosity. "Your cousin—he said you wanted to see me."

"Well I'm glad Gorman didn't forget to tell you. It's a wonder he can still find his way home."

Delly accepted Daisy's gestured invitation to come inside.

The old woman watched her visitor's enthusiastic face, her quick little steps. She seemed little more than a child. But Delly Sands wasn't a child, of course—she was a bright young lady. A good solid Ute woman. With spirit and spunk. And that was good. What Daisy had in mind wasn't for the faint of heart. If Delly would agree to help, she wouldn't have to worry so much about Charlie Moon figuring out what she was up to. And maybe she could find out what the big policeman was learning about Hooper's death. And what, if anything, her nephew intended to do about it.

"Sit," Daisy said, pointing to the visitor's chair. She didn't get that many guests, so not many folks sat there except Charlie Moon or Gorman. Sometimes Louise-Marie LaForte would stop by, pushing her line of "previously owned" cosmetics.

Delly took the chair at the kitchen table, her eyes surveying what she saw. "This is such a cute place." Not very tidy, though. "It must be—"

"Yeah," the old woman interrupted with a snort. "Cute."

"—so peaceful out here."

"It's quiet enough." And lonesome. "You want some coffee?"

Delly nodded. She'd heard about Daisy's coffee. Strong men quaked at the mere mention of the infamous brew. But this old woman was Charlie Moon's favorite aunt, and she intended to make a good impression.

"You want sugar or milk?"

Delly shook her head. "Black. And strong enough to melt the cup."

The old woman chuckled; this girl was her kind of people. She waddled toward the stove, grabbed the blackened pot, and sloshed a dollop of the dark liquid into "Gorman's cup." The liquid crystal form of a brown bunny rabbit would gradually appear as the white porcelain heated. She poured an equal dose into her own cup, and sat down across the table from the young Ute woman. She stared at the girl. Delly had certainly grown up. She'd gone off into the world of the *matukach* and done well. Learned lots of things, and developed her talents. Talents—which properly directed—might help her find out who was responsible for Hooper Antelope's death. And, indirectly, for his mother's passing. That would please poor Stella . . . help her troubled spirit rest easy.

Delly sipped at the coffee. It was . . . *unbelievable*.

Daisy raised her eyebrows. "Like it?"

"It . . . it really hits the spot." *Hit my tummy like a pound of lead.*

"Suits your taste, then?"

The guest nodded. "Remarkable flavor." *Makes my tongue want to curl up and die.*

The old woman smiled. What a nice girl.

Delly was anxious to know why the old woman had summoned her. But this wasn't like the regular world—this was the Ute elder's world. So it wouldn't do to ask. She waited.

For several minutes, not a word was said.

Something scampered across the metal roof of the trailer home.

A *squirrel*, Delly thought. Hoped.

Daisy didn't notice.

The clock on the wall, which was thirteen minutes slow, said *tick . . . tick . . . tick . . .*

Delly fancied that she could hear her heart beating.

Finally, Daisy cleared her throat. "I hear you got a job with the *Drum*."

Delly nodded. "I'm working for Mr. Tallman."

"I s'pose, workin' for the tribal newspaper, you hear about lots of things." Daisy tapped a stainless steel spoon on her coffee mug. Ping . . . ping . . . ping. "It was a bad thing . . . what happened to Hooper Antelope over at the Sleeping Ute Mountain Sun Dance. And his mamma. Poor old soul."

Delly felt a numbness in her hands. So that was it. This old woman had a reputation for messing around in such matters. "Yes. It was tragic. I guess he was too old for dancing thirsty . . . his heart must have failed."

"Hooper wasn't much over sixty, and he was strong as a buffalo." Daisy shook her head. "No. It wasn't no natural death."

"Then what do you think happened?"

The old woman spat out the words. "He was witched."

"Oh surely you don't believe . . . " Delly bit her lip.

"I don't *believe*, child. I *know*." The shaman nodded solemnly, as if to agree with herself.

Delly's hand, at some desperate signal from her subconscious, had decided to spoon sugar into the acrid coffee. The happy Bunny had appeared on the cup. He held his arms wide in a welcoming gesture, and smiled at her with his charming buck teeth. The disarming cartoon rabbit had a soothing effect. "I know that some of the older . . . some of the elders believe in witches."

Daisy's body shook with soundless chuckles. "I'm not talkin' about the ones that wear them pointy black hats and fly around on brooms at Halloween." Such things were typically foolish European superstitions. No sensible witch would fly around with his butt astraddle a hard broomstick. Not when he could take on the form of a bat or an owl. And fly with wings. "I'm talkin' about *uru-sawa-ci*."

Delly, who still remembered a smattering of the Ute tongue, knew exactly what the old woman meant. The rough translation to English was "bad witch," or *brujo* in Spanish. But you had to be Ute down to your marrow to understand the full implications of the dreaded word. She and her brother had heard it all while they were growing up. The practitioners were generally male. *Uru-sawa-ci* could cause sickness, even death. She thought of taking another sip of the black brew, then felt somewhat like Snow White confronted by the poisoned apple. She wondered if Daisy Perika had any inkling of what some of the tribal members said about her. About why she lived way out in the wilderness, all by herself. Some whispered that the old Perika woman could cast spells, cause the corn to wither, sheep and cattle to fall ill.

But why did this old woman want to talk with her? Because her father had been Sun Dance chief for much of his life? Because her brother knew all the lore there was to know about dancing thirsty? This was a delicate matter. Delly wrapped both of her small hands around the warm cup, cuddling the smiling bunny. She smiled faintly, "Do you have what the television detectives call . . . a suspect?"

Daisy frowned at her coffee mug. "I'm not ready to say who, but I think it was someone"—Daisy hesitated—"someone who knows a lot about *secret* things. Maybe it was someone who was in the Sun Dance over on Sleeping Ute Mountain."

Delly swallowed hard. *Who does she suspect? The Sioux? Winston Steele? My brother Larry? No. That's silly.*

The Ute elder stared without blinking at the young woman.

Delly shifted nervously in her chair. *What was the old busybody thinking?*

Daisy was thinking about how folks said Opportunity would sometimes come and knock right on your door. Tappity-tap. Delly Sands had gotten a worried look when she mentioned the Sun-

Dancers as possible suspects. Maybe the young woman suspected someone too. Maybe even wanted to protect him. *This might give me a place to stand . . . and a long lever to pry her with.* She leaned forward. "Would you like to help me catch a witch?"

Delly froze in place, but she felt her lips move, heard her voice answer, "How?"

The tribal elder told the young woman about her scheme. It took some telling.

Delly sat transfixed as she listened to the old woman rattle on about what she had in mind.

When Daisy had completed her pitch, she cocked her head and frowned at her guest.

The cup had grown cold in Delly's hands. The liquid crystal bunny had departed to whatever place such creatures retreat to. There was also a cold lump in the pit of her groin. She thought about what she'd heard from this old woman's lips.

This was a lunatic plot.

Had not the least chance of working.

"So," the old woman pressed, "what do you think?"

Delly stood up and took a deep breath. "I don't know . . . it is an interesting notion."

Daisy slapped her palm on the table. "Then you'll help?"

The young woman's mouth was dry. But she could not contain her natural curiosity. "What would you want me to do?"

The Ute elder's eyes turned foxy sly. "You're kind of sweet on Charlie Moon, ain't you?"

She put her hands over her eyes. "Oh my—is it that obvious?"

"You don't have to do nothing much." The old woman chuckled merrily. "Just keep close to my nephew. Maybe tell him some things I want him to hear. And from time to time, tell me what he's up to."

Any excuse for staying close to Charlie Moon was *very* interesting. Delly's thoughtful frown furrowed her smooth brow. "Well . . . he is investigating Hooper Antelope's death."

Daisy got up from the table; she rinsed her coffee mug at the sink. "I already know that. But Charlie's pretty tight-lipped about his police business—he won't tell me spit. But I expect he'll tell you whatever you ask him. If you handle him right . . . "

"I don't know . . . Charlie doesn't tell me that much either."

Daisy turned around, drying her wrinkled hands on a tattered dish towel. "Listen, young woman—I've had more than one husband, and I can tell you this: a man's brains ain't located between his *ears*, if you know what I mean." Daisy grinned at the pretty young woman—and made a suggestive gesture that shocked her guest.

There was a lengthy silence while the only sounds were the uneven humming of the worn-out refrigerator and a low, keening moan as a wind spirit pressed his heavy shoulder against the shaman's little home.

The trailer trembled.

Delly trembled.

She was tempted to assist the old woman in the scheme.

Daisy blinked at her guest. "Well. Are you out or are you in?" It was a line she'd heard once on the television. Old Chicago gangster movie.

Delly drew a deep breath before speaking. "I need to think about it, Mrs. Perika."

Daisy sighed inwardly. This young woman didn't like taking chances. She needed some incentive. "Well," the Ute elder said, "I wouldn't want you to do nothin' you didn't feel right about." The elderly woman sat down and leaned back in her chair. She folded her hands across her belly, and gazed upward at the crudely patched hole in her ceiling. Scott Parris, the police chief from Granite Creek had done that about four years ago. With a twelve-gauge shotgun.

The young woman was hardly breathing.

The Ute elder kept her eyes on the ceiling patch. Time to turn over her last card. "Well, if you don't want to help me, I guess I could ask Myra Cornstone to help me keep an eye on Charlie . . . "

Charlie Moon headed the big SUPD Blazer down the long graveled lane. Toward the home of Walks Sleeping and his granddaughter. The Ute policeman was eager to see pretty Myra
Cornstone. And the round, red face of her baby boy.

But something felt wrong inside his stomach. A persistent
warning.

He'd had this kind of premonition a couple of times before.
More than a couple.

Most recently, one midnight last March, seconds before the
left front tire blew out on the Blazer. Close call.

And a few years back, right before a Montana cowboy he'd
stopped (the white Thunderbird's taillight was on the blink) took
a potshot at him. The .22 caliber slug clipped a button off his
collar. The man, who'd been drunk, had eventually apologized to
the policeman. After the surgeon had removed all the wires from
his broken jawbone.

This time the sensation was strong. But he didn't know what
it was that nibbled at his gut. Probably just something he'd eaten
for breakfast. He recalled he'd had fried eggs. Fried potatoes.
Chicken fried steak and brown gravy. A half dozen lard biscuits.
No. It couldn't have been breakfast—that grub at Angel's always
sat well on his stomach. But maybe, he reasoned, he hadn't had
quite *enough* to eat. That must be it. So the Ute dismissed any
concern about the peculiar sensation in his gut. A good lunch
would take care of it.

Myra Cornstone had seen Moon's dusty SUPD Blazer turn in
off the highway. She'd quickly changed into a pretty dress and
put Chigger Bug to bed with a fresh bottle. She was pulling a
brush along tangled wisps of raven hair when she heard his heavy
footsteps on the plank porch.

He knocked.

Let him wait. Serve him right, the big insensitive bastard. He was probably tickled pink that Delly Sands was chasing after him! "I hate him," she muttered as she dabbed at her lips with a fresh tube of Scarlet O'Hara. "I never want to see his stupid face again."

"Myra," her grandfather called gruffly from his bedroom, "someone's at the door."

Moon knocked.

There were a half dozen men in Ignacio who knew plenty of Sun Dance lore. But if he started asking questions, they'd start wondering why he was asking. And they'd start talking. No telling where the gossip might lead. But Walks Sleeping didn't get many visitors, so he didn't generate much gossip. And there wasn't anything worth hearing about dancing thirsty that this old man didn't know.

Moon knocked again. And waited awhile.

Myra's little pickup was parked in the graveled driveway, so she had to be home.

He knocked harder.

Finally, he heard the soft pad of Myra's footsteps in the hall. Once more, he felt the warning nibbling in his gut.

But he didn't know why.

She opened the door and looked up at the tall Ute policeman.

He smiled at the pretty young woman. Waited for her to smile back.

No smile. No nothing. Disinterested. Deadpan. He noticed that both of her hands were clenched into tight little fists.

Moon lost the smile; he removed his hat. And unconsciously, held it protectively over his stomach. "Hi."

"You must be here to see Grandfather." *You damn well better say you're here to see me.*

"Yeah. I need to talk to Walks Sleeping. Police business."

Her dark eyes went flat, like a snake's.

"But I thought later, maybe you and me could . . . maybe go for a ride. We could . . . uh . . . get some lunch somewhere."

She raised one eyebrow. One millimeter. "I'm surprised you'd have the time."

He waved the hat. "Oh, I got plenty of time."

"Time for *who?*" She could have bitten her tongue, but it was too late to call the words back.

His face was a big, dumb question mark.

He really didn't understand. What a big jughead. "Forget it, Charlie."

"Look, why don't we drive up to Durango? There's a new steak place that's supposed to be . . . " He found himself talking to empty space. She'd turned and walked away. Moon stood at the door, wondering what this was all about. She was sure in a bad mood. Maybe it was one of those women things. Sure. Leave her alone, she'd be all right in a couple of days.

Myra lay on her bed, facedown, and wept bitterly. And cursed Charlie Moon. And all men. No-good stupid heartless bastards, every last one of 'em. Tall or short, fat or thin, old or young, they were all alike.

Chigger Bug raised himself on his elbows and peered through the bars of the crib at his mother. "Gababba," he protested, and shook his bottle by the nipple.

Myra got up and sat on the edge of the bed. She rubbed at her eyes. It wasn't really Charlie Moon's fault. He was what he was—a dimwitted man running on hormones—he couldn't help himself. She cursed Delly Sands. The little hotshot college girl who'd come back to town, fluttering her big eyes. *And stealing my man . . .*

Moon sat in the old man's bedroom, the wide-brimmed black Stetson balanced on his knee. It was July. It was warm. The mullioned windows were opened wide. Occasionally, a welcome breeze played with the curtains.

The aged man, who sat in a cushioned rocking chair, leaned

forward. He strained to see through milky cataracts that blocked the light from his retinas . . . to glimpse the shadow of the big Ute policeman. It was a wasted effort.

The policeman, sensing the old man's inner struggle, also leaned forward. "How are you, Grandfather?"

"Just dandy," the elder replied acidly, "for a man who's over a hunnerd years old. And blind. And can't hold his water. Seems like I got to pee every ten minutes." Which reminded him, he was thirsty. "Myra," he banged his cane on the linoleum and shouted . . . "it's warm in here. Bring us some of that lemonade." Walks Sleeping turned his head in the direction of his visitor. "I don't see much of you anymore." The blind man chuckled at his small joke.

Moon grinned. "Summertime's busy for a policeman. Come November, most of the burglars and drunks will stay inside by the fire."

The old man tapped a yellowed fingernail on the arm of his rocking chair. Myra sure needed herself a husband. He wondered if this policeman had any money in the bank. Not likely. But he knew for sure that Moon owned a nice little piece of land on the Pinos. And had built himself a sturdy house there. "You and my granddaughter . . . I understand you two been seein' each other some."

It was not a question, so Moon didn't respond.

Myra showed up with lemonade. *One* tall glass. Moon looked longingly at the cold beverage.

She took it to her grandfather, then turned on her heel and headed for the bedroom door.

"Hey," the old man called, "I expect Charlie Moon would like some lemonade too."

"Hmmph," she said. "There are people down in . . . in Haiti . . . wantin' ice-water." And slammed the door. Hard.

There was a brief silence.

The old man took a sip of his lemonade and pursed his lips. "Could be a bit sweeter."

Moon sighed. "Yeah." Boy, Myra was sure tweaked about something. Maybe he should bring her some flowers next time. Women liked to get flowers.

The old man held his glass out, and smacked his bluish lips against toothless gums. "You want a drink of mine, Charlie?"

"Thanks anyway."

"Seems like my granddaughter's in a nasty mood."

"Uh-huh. Wonder why?"

The old man grinned his toothless grin. "She was in a good mood till you showed up. You must've done something to set her off, Charlie."

"Well I didn't do nothin' to make her mad. I just said hello and asked her if she wanted to go out for some lunch after I had a talk with you."

Walks Sleeping shrugged. "Women. Who can understand their ways?"

"Not me, Grandfather."

"So what brings you out here?"

Moon leaned back in his chair. This old man had done a lot of things in his days. He'd been tribal chairman for a year or so. And a long time ago, he'd been the Southern Ute Sun Dance chief. "You heard about Hooper Antelope?"

Walks Sleeping nodded. "I did. He fell down dead over at the Ute Mountain Sun Dance. And then his mother died too." The old man cocked his head at Moon. "Why's it police business?"

Moon hesitated. "I expect you've heard the tribal gossip . . . "

The old man shook his head. "Nobody but Myra tells me anything. And mostly all she tells me is 'do this,' 'don't do that,' 'eat your green beans,' 'go to bed now.' "

"It's the usual stuff," the policeman said. "Some of the People believe he didn't die a natural death."

" 'Some of the People' you say. Anybody in partic'lar?"

Moon scowled at the linoleum. "My Aunt Daisy, for one."

The old man thought about this. Daisy Perika was a very

smart woman. Stubborn, maybe, but smart. "Why's Daisy suspicious?"

Moon shrugged. A wasted gesture on the blind man. "No good reason. Just the usual gab about witches and stuff. But it isn't just Aunt Daisy. Some of the dancers and their families are worried. Tribal chairman's getting asked a lot of hard questions, and he's nagging at the chief of police. So Roy Severo wants me to have a close look. Find out what I can."

The old man rocked in his chair, and sloshed lemonade onto his shirt. "Makes sense you'd investigate a death of one of the People. But why'd you come to see me? I haven't killed myself a man in forty years or more." He didn't smile when he said it.

The policeman wondered who Walks Sleeping had killed. "Well, I don't know everything I'd like to about the Sun Dance. Thought you could help. Tell me some things."

Walks Sleeping stopped rocking and assumed a mildly wary expression. "What kind of things, Mr. Policeman?"

It was time to tread carefully. Everything about the dance was sacred. Many things were secret. Only for the ears of the most seasoned dancers. He'd never participated in dancing thirsty. And didn't intend to. "For one thing," Moon asked, "is there any reason why someone would want to harm a Sun-Dancer?" He'd heard campfire tales, of course. But most of those were little more than speculation.

These policeman sure asked some dumb questions. "I guess," the old man said reasonably, "someone might want to harm a Sun-Dancer if they didn't like him."

"What I had in mind," Moon said patiently, "was some reason connected with the Sun Dance."

Walks Sleeping sipped at his lemonade. And tasted old memories. "You ever hear the old story about the Paiute?"

"Which Paiute?"

"The one called Three Fingers."

"He lose some fingers?"

"No. He was named after his uncle."

Moon grinned at the old man. "So his uncle was short some fingers?"

The storyteller scowled toward the policeman. "How do I know? And quit changing the subject on me. I'm way over a hunnerd years old and I have some trouble keeping my thoughts straight."

"I'm sorry, Grandfather."

The old man nodded, to indicate that the apology was accepted.

"I'd like to hear about Three Fingers." More than that, I'd like to have a cold glass of lemonade.

"Well, he was a famous Sun-Dancer—back in the 1930s. He married himself a fat woman from the White River bunch, up north. Three Fingers, he danced at every Sun Dance he could get to. He had this big medicine . . . that's what we called it back then. Many times when he danced thirsty, sick people in the Sun Dance Lodge got healings. From stomach trouble and head sickness—stuff like that. And he had him some big visions. Three Fingers—I forgot to tell you that he was a Christian—so when he had these visions, he not only saw the old Ute and Paiute people, and animal spirits. He also saw angels. And saints from them olden times. One time after he had his vision, he said he'd talked to a fellow who said his name was Francis. And this Francis told Three Fingers about how we Utes should take good care of our poor people, and those who was sick. And not be so hard on our horses and dogs. And how we should not fight all the time, or drink too much. Three Fingers said these saints talked to him a lot, and told him important things. About how a man should live." The storyteller paused for a long drink of lemonade. And swallowed a seed.

Moon wondered where this tale was going. Walks Sleeping's mind tended to drift like a log floating down a river. Maybe the old man had forgotten the question.

"Anyway, I think it was that hot summer not long before the big war started. Maybe around nineteen and forty. No. It was forty-one." He paused; his blind eyes seemed to glaze over. He was drifting in recollections. Sweet memories softened by the years that had passed.

Moon cleared his throat. "What happened in 1941, Grandfather?"

The blind man jumped, as if startled. "Who said that?"

"Me," Moon said.

"Oh. Charlie Moon—it's you. Now I remember. You asked about Three Fingers."

Not really. "What happened in 1941?"

"Three Fingers . . . that was the summer he died."

"Oh. How'd it happen?" Moon's mind was wandering now. He was wondering why Myra was acting so peculiar. Maybe she had a headache. Seemed like the women he knew were always getting headaches.

"Three Fingers died at a big Sun Dance. Up in Johnson Draw by Blue Mountain. That was where the White River bunch was camped."

Now this was getting interesting. "Anything unusual about how he died?"

The old man bowed his head. His milky eyes seemed to be looking into the lemonade glass.

"Grandfather?"

"Ummm?"

"About how Three Fingers died—was there anything unusual about it?"

"Oh. That. No . . . he just fell down on his face. And stopped living."

Moon suppressed a groan. "Grandfather, I need to know why someone might want to harm a Sun-Dancer."

"Well, after Three Fingers was buried at the *matukach* cemetery by the church . . . he came back."

"Came back . . . you mean his ghost?"

"Well of course I mean his ghost. Three Fingers came to his mother in this dream she had. That old Paiute woman still lived over in Utah, at Altonah. Three Fingers, he told his mother how he'd been witched by a young Shoshone man from up in Wyoming. Or maybe it was a Bannock. Or one of them Arapaho bunch. Anyway, he told his mother just how it was done."

Moon got up and squatted by the old man's chair. "How was it done?"

"I don't remember."

Moon groaned.

The old man laughed. "I was just foolin', Charlie. I remember like it was yesterday."

Moon rolled his eyes toward the ceiling. "Tell me."

"First, the witch sent an owl to fly in circles around his head."

Great. "An owl. And nobody at the dance noticed this?"

"I don't know. I never heard whether they did or not."

Moon pushed himself to his feet. "So that's it—his mother dreamed that an owl came and flew around his head?" This was a wasted trip.

"Owls," the Ute elder said, "are powerful creatures. Any part of an owl—if you know what to do with it—can be used to rob a dancer of his power. And when you do that, it can kill him." Walks Sleeping shook his head sadly at the memory of the tale. "And it wasn't just the owl. Three Finger's ghost told his mother there was the smell of blood in the Sun Dance Lodge . . . human blood."

"Blood. Uh-huh."

"Blood in the sacred circle is a very bad thing. That's why we don't allow women in who're having their . . . their partic'lar time of the month." The old man nodded meaningfully at his guest. "You know what I mean."

"Yeah," Moon said tiredly. "I know what you mean." Hmmm. Maybe that was what'd put Myra in such a bad mood. Moon shifted his weight.

The old man heard the floor creak. It was too soon for the policeman to go. This was a lonesome place.

"I remember another dancer that died after he was witched." He tapped his horny fingernails lightly on the arm of the rocking chair. "It was up there in the Wind River country. I recall it was one of them Bannock . . . or maybe it was a Shoshone."

"Might have been an Arapaho," Moon said with a wry smile. "Or a Crow."

The old man missed the humor. "No," he shook his head, "I don't think it was no Arapaho nor Crow."

The policeman hooked his thumbs under his cowhide gun belt. "How did this Sun-Dancer die, Grandfather?"

"The witch—they said it was a Navajo from down at Many Farms—he shot him while he was dancing."

Moon frowned. "Shot him? That should have gotten some attention."

The old man shook his head. "Not with gun, nor a bullet. He was shot with bone from a dead man's body. The witch stood outside the corral at night, and blew this piece of bone through a long tube . . . made from a hollow piece of cane. That's the kinda thing witches do, you know."

Moon used the back of his hand to wipe sweat off his brow. "So why'd he shoot the dancer with the bone?"

This young man's education was woefully lacking. "Bone from a dead man," he explained patiently, "is the worst thing you can be shot with. Kills you dead no matter where you're hit. But if a witch don't have a piece of dead man's bone, sometimes he'll use a little chunk of turquoise. They say it works almost as good, but I doubt it."

"What I meant was . . . what was the witch's *motive* in wanting to kill the Sun-Dancer?"

The old man shook his head in weary exasperation. This Charlie Moon didn't understand nothing. "It wasn't done to *kill* the Sun-Dancer."

"Then why, Grandfather?"

The aged man spoke the words slowly, as if this would help his visitor to understand. "Whether or not the dancer lives or dies—that doesn't matter none to the witch. A witch only does these things for one purpose. To steal from the Sun-Dancer."

"Steal what?" Moon knew, of course. But the Ute policeman wanted to hear exactly what the tribal elder might have to say on the matter.

The old man finally lost all his patience with this unforgivable ignorance. He banged his walking stick hard against the floor. His old voice cracked as he shouted: "To steal his *vision*, Charlie Moon—to take away his Power!"

There was a brief silence before Myra burst through the door. "Grandfather—what's wrong?"

The old man was mumbling rude remarks about how these young people didn't seem to know nothing no more. Might as well be talking to a damn blue-eyed *matukach*!

Moon smiled pleasantly at Myra Cornstone.

She didn't smile back. "Now he's upset. It'll take me all afternoon to get him settled down again." Her expression made it clear—this was all Charlie Moon's fault.

"He's running a little short on lemonade." Moon pushed the black Stetson down to his ears. "This is the kind of weather that makes a man thirsty."

Her dark eyes were hard as obsidian. You want some lemonade, Charlie Moon, you can go squeeze yourself a lemon.

He touched the brim of his hat as a gesture to the pretty young woman, said his good-bye to the old man, and politely took his leave of them. As Moon left the bedroom, Walks Sleeping was still muttering about this younger generation of Utes who didn't know nothing about the old ways . . . he was damn sorry he'd lived long enough to see such a disgrace. "Twenty more years," he was telling his granddaughter, "there won't be a real Ute left on the reservation. You wait and see."

As the policeman turned the key in the SUPD Blazer ignition, he mused about this wasted visit to the old man's home. Myra Cornstone had a measure of her grandfather's blood. Maybe she'd inherited some of his bad temper too.

Twilight had come to *Cañon del Espiritu*. The Three Sisters who resided on the sandstone mesa, clothed in swirling robes of purple mist, seemed to keep watch over the small trailer nestled far below in the piñon grove.

Inside the Ute woman's home, the atmosphere hung thick and heavy. Like a dank fog over a fresh grave. Daisy Perika was sitting at her kitchen table, staring off into space. Seeing nothing at all . . .

But this thought was on her mind: *The Southern Ute Sun Dance is only days away.*

With a grunt, Daisy pushed herself up from the chair. The old woman shuffled over to the propane stove and removed the blackened aluminum pot from the blue ring of flame. She filled her cup with brew the color of roofing tar. She sat down again at the kitchen table and stirred in a spoonful of sugar.

A heavy silence had settled over the land. Outside, she heard the cricket's legs clicking . . . inside, the wall clock's tick-ticking.

And that was all. She was alone with her troubled thoughts.

Ahhh . . . almost anything might happen at the sacred dance. If she was smart, she'd stay home. But to stay alive—really alive— a person has to take some risks. Anyway, it wasn't like she had much longer to live in Middle World. And of course, if she could expose the witch, it would show her nephew Charlie Moon a thing or two. Such a big know-it-all jughead.

And Stella Antelope would be so pleased to have her son's death avenged. The shaman was certain that Old Popeye Woman was watching. From somewhere Up There.

Billy Antelope wasn't nearly tired enough to sleep. And more than that, the balmy night of crickets and saw-whet owls was just outside. Calling to him.

The boy slid out of his enormous bed and pulled on his faded jeans. Then his brand-new blue socks with the two red stripes around the top. Reuben was snoring very loudly; he tiptoed past the sleeper's room. The old man was making funny noises as his lips fluttered. This made Billy smile; he stifled a giggle.

The boy turned the porcelain knob. He pulled on the massive front door—it squeaked on rusty hinges—and walked out onto the porch in his sock feet. The moon hanging over Shellhammer Ridge was almost perfectly round. Like a big basketball somebody had painted with shiny stuff. Maybe with aluminum paint, like Reuben used on the house roof. He wondered how far away the moon was. A long way, of course. Maybe as far as Bayfield, where Reuben took him last week to buy some socks and underwear. When these get real dirty, the old man had said, then we'll buy you some more. Reuben didn't much like to wash clothes.

He sat down on the unpainted pine planks and let his thin legs dangle over the ground. An aged bluetick hound roused itself from a dusty bed underneath the house. Braving the stinging pain in arthritic joints, the weary animal climbed the porch steps. Reclining with a whuffing sound, the beast laid its massive head in the child's lap.

Billy rubbed the old dog's bristly neck.

A tail flopped gratefully on the porch.

He scratched the animal behind a floppy ear.

The hound responded by raising its head and licking the child's chin.

The boy was barely aware of the dog. He was staring at the moon. And thinking his thoughts. Mainly, he was recalling Mrs. Perika's visit. And all the neat stuff she'd told him.

And then he thought about Grandma Stella—she was always telling him now you be careful Billy. It's a hard and dangerous world out there. You look both ways before you cross the road, you hear me? And when they'd come out to Reuben's farm, she'd say don't run with a sharp stick in your hand—you could fall and poke your eye out. Now be a good boy and don't shoot your BB gun out there by the chicken coop. Or at God's little birds. You might hit one and then wouldn't you feel bad?

The child knew he shouldn't shoot at a bird with his BB gun. But sometimes it was hard to know what was the right thing to do. Grandma always told him if you don't know whether you should do something or not, you come and ask me. I'll tell you what's right.

Sometimes at night—when he was in bed—he used to talk to Daddy and Momma. And sometimes they talked back to him. And told him to behave himself and be a good boy and always ask Grandma Stella before you do anything that might be dangerous and all that sort of stuff grown-ups are always saying. Billy Antelope stared wide-eyed at the night sky. Maybe that's where Grandma had gone to live . . . up there with the stars. He wondered what Grandma would think about what old Mrs. Perika had told him. He thought maybe he should ask her.

So he did.

Angel's Cafe

Every year, three or four days before the dance was to commence, the participants congregated for a meal at dawn. Willie Blacksnow, the amiable chief of the Southern Ute Sun Dance, called it his "sunrise powwow." All of the prospective dancers were expected to be there and it was considered bad form not to show up. There would also be a smattering of singers and drummers—and Sun Dance chiefs, both retired Utes and distinguished visitors from other tribes. The breakfast was a friendly, communal affair. Aside from the social purpose, the meal also served a utilitarian function. Although the fundamental rules of the dance did not vary, there might be minor changes made by the chief of a particular dance. It was necessary that participants were informed of any variations in procedures. This avoided embarrassment.

For the past dozen years, the breakfast had been provided by the owner of Angel's Cafe, who always opened an hour early to prepare the meal. Angel kept the doors locked to other customers until 7 A.M. It was, the Hispanic man told his guests, a great honor to serve them—and he meant it. The proprietor, eager to accommodate this auspicious gathering, had placed six tables end to end. These were covered with spotless white cotton tablecloths. Insulated decanters of steaming coffee were distributed along the length of the makeshift table. And Angel brought out his finest steel flatware—the set with polished black phenolic handles.

Willie Blacksnow sat at one end, presiding over the congregation. He frequently looked up from his plate of eggs and frijoles, smiling and nodding at those along the table. He conversed quietly with the men who were near enough to hear his soft voice. As he chewed, he commented upon the weather. Thin clouds drifting in from Utah. There might be some rain.

On Blacksnow's right hand was Red Heel. The old Shoshone was characteristically silent, responding to the Ute chief's comments with faint nods. His spirit seemed to be far away.

On the Sun Dance chief's left was the Ute Mountain Sun Dance chief. Poker Martinez sipped at a cup of coffee; he occasionally glanced down the table toward the gathering of dancers. Most of the faces were familiar.

The surly Sioux was there. Except to place his order, he had not spoken one word. Stone Pipe was spooning oatmeal between his thin lips. Because he avoided caffeine, he did not partake of the coffee.

Across the table from the Sioux was the *matukach*, who seemed unaware of the occasional cold glares from Stone Pipe. Winston Steele was busy with a plate of scrambled eggs and pancakes.

Larry Sands sat next to the white man. The Sandman, who yawned and rubbed at bloodshot eyes, was stirring a spoon in a tall glass of tomato juice.

A scattering of young Ute dancers from the Southern and Ute Mountain tribes completed the gathering.

Charlie Moon sat at the far end of the table. The Ute policeman's attention was on his plate. Three fried eggs. A mound of crispy home fries. Chicken-fried steak soaked in brown gravy. And a covered pan of Angel's made-from-scratch biscuits. A fresh jar of orange marmalade. The ostensible reason for the presence of this representative of the Southern Ute Police Department was as always. Traffic control. Keeping the crowd orderly. Finding parents of lost children. Spiriting away the occasional drunk who had little enough sense to sip his whisky on the sacred Sun Dance grounds.

But this year, there was an additional tension among the participants at the sunrise powwow. A quiet expectation. An unspoken question. What was Charlie Moon going to do about the potential threat to them all?

For several weeks, these men had been preparing for the ordeal. Most had been training by taking long walks in the sun. Some jogged along the rocky deer paths on Shellhammer Ridge. Most had—on the Sun Dance chief's advice—altered their diets. They were advised to eat plenty of fruits and vegetables, but to minimize the consumption of meat. It was a time for drinking water; beer could wait. The dancers talked among themselves. Also about the weather. About how they felt good—ready to dance until their tongues hung out! Secretly, most felt some level of inner fear.

The grumpy Sioux, the silent *matukach*, and the groggy Sandman did not participate in this conversation.

Willie Blacksnow had decided that it was about time to get the group's attention. He'd give his annual lecture about the sacred nature of dancing thirsty. Of the goals. Healings. Visions. It was a fine speech, perfected by many orations. Hardly a word changed from one year to the next. Though he was not a vain man, he did relish this chance to preside. To be seen as a worthy leader, and respected by all present. He raised his coffee spoon above his cup; when he tapped the porcelain, the men would fall silent.

But the Sun Dance chief did not have the opportunity to tap his meeting to order. There came another tapping. At the locked door of Angel's Cafe.

Charlie Moon looked over his right shoulder toward the door. "Well I'll be darned . . . " Delly Sands saw the Ute policeman, and rapped her knuckles on the door harder than ever.

The Sandman took one glance at his sister's face in the doorway and turned back to his tomato juice.

Angel, his face twisted with anxiety, hurried to the door. He shook his head at her entreaties. "No, the restaurant is reserved," he shouted, pointing at the hand-lettered sign that announced this fact. "Come back at seven."

She held up a card.

Angel leaned close to the glass and squinted. The card said *Southern Ute Drum*. Her name was written on the card in violet ink.

Delly held the press card by a corner, pointing toward the long table. "I'm working for the *Drum*. I'm here to cover the Sun Dance breakfast."

The proprietor of Angel's Cafe backed away from the door. Now this was a knotty problem. It was understood that no one came to the sunrise powwow except by invitation of the Sun Dance chief. And from the strained expression on Willie Blacksnow's face, he hadn't invited this woman. But on the other hand, she had been sent by the Southern Ute's tribal newspaper. If he let her in, Willie would get all bent out of shape. If he didn't let her in, then he'd have the editor of the *Southern Ute Drum* yelling at him about freedom of the press and all that bullshit. Either way, he'd have the Utes mad at him. What could he do?

Pass the buck, of course.

Angel turned to look toward the table of men. "It's a young lady," Angel said innocently. "From the newspaper."

Willie Blacksnow grunted his displeasure. "What newspaper?"

"The *Drum*." There was a trace of satisfaction in Angel's

voice. Now this was Willie's problem. "She says she's supposed to do a story about your breakfast powwow."

The Sun Dance chief paused to consider this. They'd never had a woman at a Sun Dance breakfast. On the other hand, this was the tribal newspaper. And the woman was a Ute. Ute women were getting involved in all sorts of tribal affairs nowadays. If he didn't let her in, his wife would gripe at him. But if he did invite her in, some of the dancers—especially the Sioux—would see it as a sign of weakness. Giving in to the new ways . . .

Delly waited.

Angel waited.

The men at the table waited.

All looked to the Sun Dance chief for a decision. The indecision in Willie Blacksnow's face was plain to see.

Moon got up and pushed his chair aside. "She's with me."

The Sun Dance chief felt a surge of relief. Now he could put up a show of resistance to demonstrate his orthodoxy, then give in to the wishes of the police department. "I dunno, Charlie. We never had any . . . uh . . . outsiders at our Sun Dance breakfasts." He looked to the out-of-town Sun Dance chiefs on his left and right for support. " 'Specially not any women."

Moon grinned. "Then leave her standing outside. That'll make a good story."

Willie frowned. "Story?"

"Sure. She'll write it up. They'll print it in the *Drum*. What'll they call it? Hmmm. Maybe: 'Ute Reporter Denied Entry to Angel's Cafe. Sun Dance Chief Responsible.' "

Angel wrung his hands. "What should I do?"

Willie Blacksnow had ambitions to run for the tribal council next year. Southern Ute women outvoted men by almost two to one. "It's up to you, Charlie."

Stone Pipe grunted his displeasure. These Utes were a bunch of pissant apples.

Poker Martinez's face was without expression. The visiting

Sun Dance chief was a guest. This decision was a matter for the local chief.

Winston Steele grinned. He'd made a quiet bet with Delly's brother that she'd get in. The Sandman—who was not amused—was already searching his wallet for a fiver.

Moon walked past Angel and twisted the lock.

Delly Sands beamed at him. "Good morning, Charlie. I'd about decided I wasn't welcome here."

He smiled. "Wasn't that way at all. We were all so happy to see you, there was a big fuss about who'd get the honor of opening the door. I won."

Delly squeezed his big hand with both of hers. She'd heard every word through the door.

Some of the younger dancers—who didn't really mind the presence of a pretty young lady at the table—were moving their chairs to make room for the attractive visitor.

"Where'd you like to sit?" Moon asked.

She motioned for him to lean close.

He did.

She stood on tiptoes and whispered into his ear. "In your lap?"

Moon straightened his back quickly and cleared his throat. "Hmmm," he said.

Angel relocked the door. He crossed himself, and prayed that there would be no more unwanted visitors.

Delly seated herself by Charlie Moon; she ordered toast and orange juice.

The breakfast continued for some minutes, in complete silence. For every person present except Moon, the tension was like a bent branch about to snap. The Ute policeman was enjoying Willie's amusing predicament.

Finally, Willie Blacksnow cleared his throat. And, as if it were necessary, the Sun Dance chief tapped his spoon on the coffee cup. All eyes looked to him.

He stood up and gave his customary oration. It was a fine speech. Not loud or showy. His voice was even and well-modulated, his insights thoughtful and to the point. As in other years, it took precisely twenty minutes to summarize the history and sacred nature of dancing thirsty. Sacred duty. Manly endurance. A possibility of wonderful healings . . . and marvelous visions.

Delly penciled notes on a small pad.

When the Sun Dance chief had said his say, he sat down. There was a murmur of grateful appreciation from his audience. There were solemn nods from the visiting Sun Dance chiefs, the singers, the drummers. Most of the dancers, even Larry Sands, had been duly attentive. The sullen Sioux spooned up the last of his oatmeal.

Willie Blacksnow waited. "Are there any questions?"

Delly opened her mouth, then shut it.

Blacksnow, sensing some advantage over the newspaper reporter, smiled benignly at the pretty girl. "Miss Sands, I hear that you're writing a story about dancing thirsty."

She nodded. But that wasn't *exactly* what she was writing about.

Blacksnow cocked his head quizzically. "What aspects of the ceremony most interest you?"

Delly, normally so bubbly, seemed smaller than usual. She cleared her throat, glancing quickly at Moon and then toward the Sun Dance chief. "My boss at the *Drum* . . . Mr. Tallman . . . has asked me to investigate . . . " She paused and looked at her coffee cup. ". . . To do a piece about Mr. Hooper Antelope's death."

The visiting chief from the Ute Mountain tribe was appalled. Poker Martinez's thin face hardened. Bringing up a tragedy that had happened at his dance . . . this was very bad manners. And she'd even spoken the dead man's name. But what could you expect from a young woman who'd gone away to get educated at a white man's school?

The tension that had been relieved by Blacksnow's fine oration returned to hover over the congregation. Like a bad smell.

The Sun Dance chief sighed inwardly. "From what I heard . . ." Willie Blacksnow would not say Hooper Antelope's name aloud. "Our dancer died . . . of natural causes." He shot a questioning look at Charlie Moon.

The Ute policeman ignored him.

Willie Blacksnow was not to be ignored. "Well, Charlie? Ain't that the way it was?"

For the barest moment, Moon hesitated. "That's what the medical examiner said." He stared back at the Sun Dance chief until Willie looked at his plate.

The Sandman surprised the gathering by giving voice to the silent question on everyone's lips. "We all heard about the M.E.'s report. What do *you* think, Charlie?"

Moon felt the eyes of twenty souls focused on his face. He tapped a steel fork on his plate. The sound was like a metronome. Tic. Tic. Tic. And the seconds were eaten up.

The policeman finally looked up. "Unless some new evidence turns up to change my mind, I'll have to go along with the official version."

The Sandman grinned at his little sister. "So what's the *Drum's* editorial view on the old man's death?"

Delly shrugged. "I don't know anything about an editorial view. We're . . . I'm just looking for facts."

Willie Blacksnow pursued this. "The tribal newspaper could be very helpful."

She knew what he meant. "What do you mean?"

He gestured with a grand wave of his spoon. "There are lots of rumors floating around. Gets tribal members upset. Some are already sayin' that the same thing could happen at our own Sun Dance. The *Drum* could calm people down."

Delly smiled sweetly. "And what would you have the *Drum* tell our people, Mr. Blacksnow?"

Well, that should be obvious enough. Maybe this college kid wasn't so smart as people said. "Why tell em what *really* happened over at the Ute Mountain dance."

Delly felt them all watching her. One gaze was especially intense—challenging. Her own dark eyes flashed fire. "Maybe I will." If it came to that . . .

Later that day, long after the sunrise powwow had ended, several customers took their lunch at Angel's cafe. And gossiped:

YOUTH: *I hear that Sands girl got herself a good job over at* the Drum.

ELDER: *Uh-huh. Looks like Larry's little sister's got some connections.*

YOUTH: *They say she's goin' to write about what happened at the Sun Dance over on Ute Mountain. You know, about ol' Hooper fallin' down dead and all that.*

ELDER: *I wouldn't say his name out loud . . . you might call up his ghost.*

YOUTH: *(With a smirk.) Sure.*

ELDER: *It's true. Speak the name of the dead, and sometimes they'll come up and tap you right on the shoulder.*

YOUTH: *(With an apprehensive glance over his left shoulder.) Some of the People are saying that Hoop—that the old man was killed by . . . by a witch.*

ELDER: *I'd keep my voice down when I mention* brujos— *you never know when one of 'em might be listening.*

YOUTH: *And I heard that Delly Sands knows plenty. She's gonna write a big story for the* Drum. *They say she might even name* the one who did the witchin'.

ELDER: *Maybe. If the* brujo *don't get her first.*

A Dream

The shaded lamp cast a yellowish glow on his hands. He squinted, but not because of the glare from the sixty-watt bulb. The object of his attention was quite small. And it must be shaped just so. Initially, he had used the blade of his pocket knife. Then, a fine-grained file with a triangular cross section. A task of such importance must not be done without attention to craftsmanship. Now he polished the tiny cylinder with an emery cloth until the light reflected off its surface.

Finally, holding his breath, he used a pair of stainless steel tweezers to raise the object. To turn it this way and that. And inspect it for flaws. Ahhh . . . it looked just fine. But would it fit properly? He slid the thing partway into the black metal cylinder. A smile crossed his face. Yes. It wasn't too tight. Just snug. Perfect. He felt a measure of honest pride.

The craftsman left the work on the table, fumbled in a worn leather briefcase, then returned to his cushioned chair. He opened a small plastic bag, held it carefully over the table, and allowed a few grains of yellow corn pollen to fall upon the dark instrument. And upon the tiny object he'd fashioned with such care. Now he switched off the lamp, and welcomed the cool darkness. He lay back on the bed, clasping his fingers behind his neck.

His lips moved to form silent words. In the words were the distorted remembrance of things past. In the words were the seeds of madness . . . and destruction.

In the stillness, he heard things. Guttural voices . . . mutterings of the dead. Broad wings cutting the wind . . . the shrill call of whistles fashioned from bone.

He closed his eyes . . . and saw darkness. But in this darkness were flitting visions. Colors dancing like flames . . . gaunt forms of men who were no more . . . eagle plumes hung on deerskin cords . . . and the sacred tree. And a cloud with whiskers like an old man . . .

Finally, he slept. And dreamed a feverish dream. A pretentious dream. Of touching that great Power that moves worlds.

Another Dream

Daisy Perika knelt by her cot and said her prayers. Soon, she settled herself into bed and slipped off into slumber. The shaman's mind drifted toward the dreamtime. And melded with it.

In her dream, Daisy floated above a Sun Dance Lodge. But though sun had set, the dancers were not resting from their exertions. They were all approaching the tree at once. In their mouths were whistles made not of eagle bone, but of dry reeds. Their hands were painted black, their faces white. This was wrong—a bad thing.

And then the shaman was at another place. A place that had been bright with light, but was now dark as the bottom of a deep well. Someone was there in the blackness . . . a young woman. Not a *matukach*—this was a woman of the People. It was the Sands girl . . . Delly was walking among the shadows. Toward some uncertain fate. The shaman could taste the presence of evil . . . she tried to call out to the young woman, but her voice was mute.

Delly walked toward some type of shelter . . . a means of escape. Once there, the shaman thought, she will be safe. Daisy whispered urgently: "Hurry, child . . . hurry."

But out of the depths of the shadows a form came forth. Not an animal. Something that moved upright . . . on two legs. A human being . . . or something much worse?

"Hurry now, Delly," the shaman whispered, "Run—run."

But the young woman seemed unaware of the danger. Delly Sands walked slowly, as if entranced by the sweetness of the night.

The dark form moved behind her . . . the shadow creature, though somewhat amorphous, had the shape of a man. An arm was raised . . .

And the shaman heard a sharp snapping sound . . . like a small bone breaking.

The dreamer sat up suddenly in her bed. Her fingers clasped the covers, her hands trembled. "Delly," she called impotently . . . "Delly Sands . . . run away . . . hurry . . . "

When the elderly woman was fully awake, she swung her aching legs over the side of the small bed. She sat alone in the stillness. Listening to the small sounds that emphasized the heavy silence.

The old refrigerator hummed for a moment, sputtered, hiccuped, then stopped.

A pine-scented breath was exhaled from the mouth of the Canyon of the Spirits. It pushed against the trailer; the oxidized aluminum panels creaked in mild protest.

A small cliff owl, perched among the folds of the skirt of Three Sisters Mesa, called to her mate.

What shall I do? Daisy held her breath; she waited for the answer.

A quarter-mile away, the owl cocked her head, blinked round yellow eyes . . . and waited.

There was no answer.

Daisy shuddered. This was a lonely place. Though the air of the July night was mild, the elderly woman pulled a thin cotton blanket around her shoulders. The shaman had no doubt that Delly Sands stood in harm's way. But what should she do? What *could* she do—tell Delly to watch out for shadows?

She puzzled about it.

The dark form that followed the young woman . . . this was a dream symbol. It represented someone. The witch who'd killed Hooper Antelope, of course. And indirectly, caused the death of his mother. Sad to say, there was no law in Colorado against witching. Charlie Moon, even if he could understand the danger—even if he knew who the witch was—the policeman couldn't make an arrest. She nodded, agreeing with herself. Yes. Charlie couldn't do anything. All the more reason to do something herself. The shaman made a solemn promise to the troubled soul of Old Popeye Woman.

There was, however, a more immediate problem. Delly Sands must be warned of the shadow that followed her . . . of the hand that would surely be raised against her.

The old shaman stared into the outer darkness.

Once more, the owl called to her mate.

CHAPTER 8

Delly Sands paused, the easier to admire the thing. Her name, engraved in two-inch-high white letters on a laminated plastic panel, was mounted on the office door. Just like Hampton Tallman had promised. Her own little office. She smiled as she closed the door behind her. The curmudgeonly editor of the *Drum* was an old sweetheart.

She dropped her purse on the rickety "visitor's" chair and sat down at her desk. On the desk, left behind by the previous tenant, was a translucent green vase—holding a single red tulip. A dusty, plastic tulip. *In another week or so—when the place really feels like it's mine—that'll have to go.* To her right, pushed up against the plastered wall, was a neat row of well-used books, also inherited from the departed journalist. A worn copy of *Webster's Seventh Collegiate Dictionary. The World Almanac*—last year's edition. *The*

228

New York Public Library Desk Reference. Delaney's *The Southern Utes, A Tribal History.*

Delly sorted through a sheaf of news releases from local organizations, and some almost illegible notes in Tallman's handwriting. He had given her an old IBM Selectric typewriter he'd inherited from the previous editor of the *Southern Ute Drum*, because he was afraid of the machine. "Just lay your little finger on one of them keys," he'd said with a doleful nod, "and the consarned thing'll take off rat-tat-tat like a German machine gun." Computers and word processors were in another category altogether. Too contemptible to mention in polite conversation. But when Tallman had swallowed a couple of shots of rye whisky, he'd vent his anger, cursing these unnerving products of misguided modern technology. It was all a plot, he'd say. All of those religious sects out there—like them Rosicrucians and that Microsoft bunch—they're plotting to take over the whole damn planet by snagging the rest of us in the World Wide Web! But, he would assure anyone who'd listen, these infernal machines will soon pass away. "Mark my word," he'd add with a crafty, knowing look, "in fifteen, maybe twenty years at the outside, people will wake up. They'll throw all this electronic trash in the ash can. Computers for writing a letter . . . computers wired to your car's engine . . . automatic fuel injectors . . . all history. Yessir, folks'll go back to using number two lead pencils and lined paper tablets. And there'll be good ol' carburetors in your pickup truck. The old-fashioned kind of carburetor," he'd add with a nostalgic sigh, "and a manual choke right on the dashboard."

Delly squinted at the editor's scribbled notes. Squinting didn't help. Something about an AA meeting at Peaceful Spirit Center—was she to cover it? A note about health insurance—did she want dental coverage? A reminder—she should see the secretary and fill out some social security forms.

She sighed, and pushed Tallman's notes aside. She'd take them to his secretary. Betty could read the *Drum* editor's obscure scribbles better than Tallman could. Under the stack, Delly found a single sheet of paper folded neatly into thirds. It was stationery from the Sky Ute Lodge. On it, printed in ballpoint ink, were these words:

> THEY SAY YOU ARE WRITING A NEWSPAPER STORY ABOUT THE SUN DANCE WITCHING. I KNOW WHO IS BEHIND IT. YOU WANT TO TALK? I WILL BE AT THE SKY UTE LODGE FOR SUPPER. TONIGHT.

There was, of course, no signature. The *Drum* newspaper offices were open nine hours every day—anybody or his sister could have dropped the note on her desk. It might be nothing more than a dumb practical joke from somebody on the *Drum* staff. Like that pimply-faced boy who'd been making calf eyes at her. No. Pimple Face didn't have that much imagination. More likely, the invitation was from some local weirdo who didn't know squat about what'd happened at the Ute Mountain Sun Dance. This was probably his idea of how to make a hot date with the new girl in town. But not all weirdos, Delly reminded herself, are harmless. Somehow . . . this didn't feel right. Creepy crawlies wiggled along her spine. Maybe I should call Charlie Moon. Such a sweet man. She smiled. And then maybe not. This is my job. The weirdo might actually know something—and I'd like to find out exactly *what* he knows. The sight of the big Southern Ute policeman might scare him speechless. Anyway, she told herself, the Sky Ute Lodge restaurant is a very public place. Busy every evening. Safe as being in mamma's arms.

Daisy Perika was off her feed. The elderly Ute woman had barely been able to finish a breakfast of lumpy pancakes and maple-flavored syrup. She had, for the first time since last winter—when she'd been down with the flu—not eaten a bite of lunch. All day, she had worried about Delly Sands. She had to talk to the young woman . . . warn her. But without a telephone, no neighbors within miles, and no more than a couple of visitors a week, how could she get word to the Sands girl?

Father Raes always said that when you needed something and couldn't work it out on your own—ask God for help. Daisy had mixed feelings about the efficacy of prayer. Once, almost a dozen years ago, she'd prayed for a telephone. Still didn't have one. But sometimes she prayed for something and got what she needed in nothing flat.

She pushed the trailer door open and made her way carefully onto the creaky pine porch. Bracing herself on the flimsy railing, she sat down, resting her feet on the steps. The old shaman looked up at the serene figures of the Pueblo women on Three Sisters Mesa who, since they'd been chased up there by the 'Paches five or six hundred years ago, had presided over the entrance to *Cañon del Espiritu*. According to a smart-alecky *matukach* geologist the tribe had hired to search for natural gas deposits, the sandstone figures had been formed slowly by the winds over several million years. Daisy sighed. It just showed how them colleges was turning out educated fools.

The old woman closed her eyes tightly, so she could see only darkness speckled with little flashes of light. She took in a deep breath, and began to speak to the Great Mysterious One. "Well, I hope you're doing okay. I'm all right except for this hurtin' in my back and I didn't sleep so good last night. But I know you're busy as all getout and got lots of things on your mind. So enough about me. Thing is, I'm worried about little Delly Sands. I think she's likely to get hurt." She also had other urgent business in town, but it'd probably be best not to bring that up. Daisy barely opened her left eye and peeked at the sky. "I need to talk to her. About that dream I had. You know the one. And you know I still ain't got no telephone out here." It was on the tip of her tongue to remind God that she had asked him for a phone years ago, but she thought better of it. She had an important favor to ask so there was no need in irritating the Great Mysterious One. "Thing is, I need a ride into town. If you could send someone out—but please, not Louise-Marie LaForte 'cause she'd likely get me killed in that old car. And not my cousin Gorman Sweetwater; he wasn't all that nice the last time I needed him to take me to see somebody. God, I think you ought to have a stern talk with Gorman about his manners. A man should treat his family lots better than my cousin does." She paused, like a diner studying a menu, and thought about what she required in the way of a chauffeur. "What I want," she finally said, "is someone who's *reliable*."

Immediately, she heard the distant sound of an engine.

Benny Thurman's freckled face was twisted into an uncharacteristic scowl. It was dumb to come all the way out here into this wilderness. And unprofitable. But somebody in this desolate place had a parcel addressed to them. And it was company policy—God knows why—to deliver it. The big brown van creaked as he maneuvered his way along the rutted gravel road. The man back at the apple orchard had said her place was on the right, just before you got to the mouth of Spirit Canyon. Just follow the electric poles till they stop at her trailer house, the farmer had said, and grinned as he bit a big chunk out of a green apple and chewed it. Like he knew some private joke. Maybe this woman had a really bad dog.

Benny's stomach was feeling all weak and fluttery, like it always got when he was worried that he might get dog-bit. Or get the big van stuck somewhere out in the boonies. He shifted into Low; the diesel growled like a chained bulldog. He topped a small ridge. There was a glint of sunlight reflecting off metal. Right where the electric poles stopped. Yeah. This had to be the old woman's trailer house. No sign of a dog. And it looked like there was just enough room to get the truck turned around and outta here . . . back to paved roads and civilization. His stomach began to settle down.

He turned into the narrow dirt lane, fingers of dry juniper branches scraped the side of the van. There was an old shriveled-up woman sitting on a porch that looked like it might fall down any minute. She got up and was hobbling toward the van. Probably the poor old soul was lonesome for some company and would want to talk about the weather and stuff. But he had a lot of other packages to deliver. Be nice to all our customers, but don't hang around and gab—that was also company policy. Benny set the parking brake. He stepped behind the seat to get her parcel. He didn't hear the woman's grunt as she climbed into the van. He did feel her shadow on his back.

He turned. The old woman was staring at him with those little black eyes. Benny put on his smiling business face. "Sorry, ma'am, we don't allow anyone except employees in the van."

The woman continued to stare. Looked old as Moses; maybe she was deaf.

He stood up, pointed to the door, and shouted in her face. "Lady, you'll have to get out of the van. It's company policy."

She scowled at him. "Don't raise your voice at your elders, young man."

Benny opened his mouth to speak. Didn't have anything to say.

Daisy glared at the steering wheel. "There's only one seat."

"Yes ma'am," he muttered, "that's for me. See, we don't have another seat because we don't carry any passengers." He motioned to the stack of boxes in the rear of the van. "We just deliver parcels. So if you'll please—"

Daisy pushed past him. "I'll just sit back here."

She must be crazy. Benny's freckles danced on his nose; his ruddy skin turned a bright pink. "Now ma'am, you'll have to get out of the truck! I got to finish my route and you can't—"

She sat down on a large box marked FRAGILE—HANDLE WITH CARE. There was a sound of glass breaking. "What brings you out here, young man?"

Benny stood, openmouthed. He closed his eyes and counted. Toward ten. He stopped at seven. And opened his eyes. His voice had an edge to it. "I came out here to deliver a parcel to you."

Daisy looked around her. "Where is it?" It was always nice to get something unexpected.

He shook his head wearily and reread the computer printout for the third time. "It should be here, but I can't find it."

"Well," she smirked at the hapless delivery man, "losing people's packages, that's no way to run a railroad."

He swallowed hard. "Ma'am . . . why are you sitting in my van?"

"Because you're going to deliver me to Ignacio."

"And why, pray tell, would I do that?"

"So I can talk to Delly Sands." This white boy was a little slow on the pickup. "When we get there, I'll give you a dollar."

Benny sat down in the driver's seat. He took a long, deep breath. "Ma'am, I can't take you to Ignacio."

"Why not? It's on your route, isn't it?"

Benny bit his lower lip. His voice was now monotone. Almost robotic. "Yes, it is. But-you-can-not-ride-in-this-van."

"Why not?"

He turned to face his stubborn adversary. "Read my lips, Granny: Because-It-Is-Against-Company-Policy!"

Daisy waved her hand impatiently. "Well then, sonny, we'll just have to change company policy—'cause I ain't movin' a inch till we get to Ignacio." She knew that United Parcel Service was a reputable company. No way was this fine young man going to throw a poor old woman out of his truck. Doin' somethin' like that would cause talk. But he was sure excitable, even for a *matukach*. His face had turned red as a sugar beet. And he had a funny little twitch jerking there right by his eye. She chuckled. He was kind of cute.

Benny, at the edge of tears, gripped the steering wheel with white knuckles. He rested his forehead on the center button. The horn bleated like a sick sheep. "God help me," he muttered.

"Prayer," the old woman said approvingly, "is a good thing. In fact, that's what brought you out here today." Daisy thought this pious observation would make him feel better.

It did not.

Delly left work at five sharp. She enjoyed a hot shower in her new apartment, rubbed vitamin-E cream on her face, pulled on a pair of nylons, and slipped into a pretty white summer dress. The writer of the note hadn't said what time he'd show up at the Sky Ute Lodge restaurant. So she'd best be there early. She was at the restaurant at six-thirty.

Myra Cornstone was on the afternoon shift. She offered Delly a plastic smile. "One for dinner?"

Delly nodded. "Yes. I'm eating alone tonight." She looked toward a dim corner. "Can I have a table over there?" That way, she'd have her back to the wall. And it would be easy to see who came into the restaurant.

With a brisk stride, Myra led the way to the secluded corner. She flipped a plastic menu on the table. "You want to hear about our specials tonight?"

Delly shrugged. "I suppose. Is there anything you'd recommend?"

"The lamb stew is usually pretty good." *How about a dose of rat poison you man-stealing little bitch?*

Delly seated herself. *Myra's being pleasant enough. Maybe she's gotten over Charlie Moon. Probably already found herself a new cowboy.* "I'm in no hurry for dinner. Right now, I'll just have a cup of tea." *Might be here a long time, waiting for the guy to show. No need to rush things.*

The UPS driver pulled the ungainly vehicle to the side of the road. This was like a nightmare he couldn't wake up from, and his mind was telling him threatening tales. The peculiar Indian woman might not get out now, like she'd promised. She might change her mind at the last second, and insist on riding forever in his van. Like a wrinkled old shotgun on a stagecoach. He turned to watch her get up off the crushed box and hobble stiffly to the front of the van. Benny, his ordeal almost over, sighed with relief. Silently, he thanked God for his deliverance from this stubborn old woman.

She waved a small parcel at him. "I found it behind some boxes. It's from my niece up at Granite Creek. Prob'ly somethin' else I can't use." Daisy paused by the van door. "That's a big step down." She glared meaningfully at him.

He got out, walked around the van, and steadied her as she descended. When Daisy Perika had her feet firmly planted on the earth, she fumbled in her apron pocket, found a quarter and pressed it into his hand. "I know I said I'd give you a dollar, but I forgot I didn't have my purse with me."

Absently, the driver pocketed the coin.

"So next time you make a delivery out to my place, I'll give you the six bits. And that," she patted his arm in motherly fashion, "is a promise."

"Yes ma'am." He grinned weakly and tipped his hat. "Guess I'll have to trust you for it."

Delly Sands sipped at her tea, and thought about how quickly things had changed in Ignacio during the time she'd been away. Not that many people in the restaurant looked familiar. Except for an old fellow who got up slowly from a booth. The lame man, who leaned on a bamboo walking stick, paid his bill and left. She thought she recognized him. Of course . . . the old Paiute man who'd sung his song at the Ute Mountain Sun Dance.

Myra Cornstone brought hot water and another tea bag, but didn't ask whether her customer was ready for dinner. Delly was grateful for this. She sat at her table in the dim corner, watching customers come and go. And waited for the oddball who'd left the hand-printed note on her desk over at the *Drum*.

It was almost eight when her brother showed up. Larry Sands glanced her way with a sulky expression, but didn't speak. He slid into a booth and was hidden from Delly's view. Good for you, she thought. Don't even speak to your sister. Sit there and sulk, like a little boy.

Winston Steele arrived a few minutes later, with the gorgeous blonde hanging on his arm. They didn't notice Delly, but they did wave at her brother. Dr. Steele parked his girlfriend at a table, then went over to chat with the Sandman. Larry apparently said something about his sister. Dr. Steele glanced briefly at Delly's corner table, then looked uneasily toward his date. Delly entertained a fantasy. She would go over to Steele's table and introduce herself to the blonde. And tell her a thing or two about the good doctor. But she didn't.

She waited. Steele and his date ordered their dinner. Others came and went. A Ute family with two tiny girls. Weary tourists clutching road maps. Blank-eyed gamblers taking a few minutes off from the casino for a sandwich and black coffee. She tensed when an elderly man approached her table. He was dressed in baggy khaki trousers and a faded denim jacket. And had a hopeful look in his eyes. Yes. This could be the guy who claimed he knew who was "witching" Sun-Dancers. He looked like a man who would carry such tales.

He leaned close; Delly smelled the stale odor of beer on his breath. The old man produced a handful of necklaces from some hidden cache under his jacket. "You want to buy some genuine Indian jewelry . . . real turquoise?"

Delly felt her face flush; the old man had taken her for a tourist! The young Ute woman shook her head. It was nice stuff, she told him, but she couldn't afford it.

Accustomed to such rejections, he nodded politely and departed to visit Steele's table. Delly watched as Blondie oohed and ahhed at strings of turquoise and jet and coral. And old pawn made from coin silver. It was all "so scrumptious"—she couldn't make up her mind. So her boyfriend, the chump with his brains between his legs, bought a half dozen pieces. She cooed at him, reached under the table, and tickled his knee. Or something. Delly felt nauseous. And denied that there was a pang of jealousy.

Dr. Winston Steele was history. Charlie Moon . . . now there was a man to settle down with.

It was at this moment Myra Cornstone showed up with her order pad. "You ready for dinner?"

"Sure. The lamb stew, I guess. And a green salad."

Myra scribbled on the pad. LS. GS.

Delly looked up. "So how've you been?"

Myra shrugged. "Okay." *Like you care.*

"And Chigger Bug?"

Despite herself, Myra warmed to the question. "He's fine. Growing like a turnip."

"It must be nice . . . having a child."

"It is." Myra offered her customer a crooked, bitter smile.

"I'd like to have a kid of my own someday," Delly said. "And a husband, of course."

"Yeah," Myra said wistfully. "A husband would be nice."

It was well past dark and the night air was cool. Almost chilly. Daisy Perika tried hard not to think about her aching legs, the fat blisters forming on her heels. She could walk half a day on the sandy floor of *Cañon del Espiritu* without a problem. But this concrete sidewalk was hard on an old woman's feet. When she'd caught the ride to Ignacio with the nice UPS man, she hadn't planned to do this much walking. When she stopped for a ham sandwich at Angel's diner, she'd learned that Delly'd had a falling-out with her brother and moved out of his place. Not surprising. Larry Sands was a peculiar young man. Delly was supposed to be staying at the Sky Ute Lodge. But the man at the desk said Miss Sands had already moved out. Now that Delly had herself a job, she'd gotten herself a place of her own.

Finally here she was, at the North Village Apartments. Fancy. A fine two-story brick building. Real gaslights in the front yard. The windows had white shutters and flower boxes with clumps of red geraniums. Daisy limped up to the door marked MANAGER and pressed her thumb on the rectangular black button. Inside, the bell played a few bars of "Home on the Range." A stooped, gray-haired man opened the door and blinked suspiciously through thick spectacles at the small Ute woman. "Yes?"

"Which one is Delly Sands' apartment?"

He hesitated, then jerked his thumb upward. "Two-eleven."

Daisy groaned. "Upstairs?"

He nodded.

She groaned again.

"But Miss Sands isn't in just now. I saw her drive away," he glanced at his wristwatch, "maybe a couple of hours ago. During *Wheel of Fortune.*"

The old woman looked toward an aluminum lawn chair. "Then I'll wait."

He looked doubtful. "Might be a long wait."

"I'm older'n sin. All I got left is time."

It was late, and Delly had not returned to her apartment. Time to go somewhere and find a bed. Daisy Perika could have knocked on any of a hundred doors in Ignacio, and she'd have been welcomed in for the night. She could have telephoned the Southern Ute police station and the dispatcher would have immediately summoned Charlie Moon. The elderly woman hadn't even considered this possibility.

Louise-Marie LaForte could not sleep. So she sat in her bed with a small leather-bound volume. She read of "The Walrus and the Carpenter."

The old house was dark, the porch floor creaked under her feet. Daisy Perika rapped on the door, and winced from the pain in her arthritic knuckles.

Silence.

She kicked at the door. Twice. "Hey—wake up in there!"

There was a groan of bedsprings. A patter of bare feet on varnished wood.

The voice was flinty with threat, like a rasp on steel. "Who is it? I got my Smith and Western in my hand, so don't try anything funny."

"Put that old horse-pistol away, Louise-Marie, before you shoot your foot off. And it's a Smith and *Wesson*."

The voice softened. "Daisy—is that you?"

"Last time I looked in the mirror, it was. Now open the door."

The porch light came on. A rusty latch turned. Louise-Marie, her hair done up in tight little gray curls, peered through the screened door. "I was about to go to sleep. What're you doing out so late at night?"

"I'm goin' door-to-door, takin' up a collection."

She waved the pistol in Daisy's face. "Collection? For what, dearie?"

"It's for the Southern Ute navy, Louise-Marie. We're going to buy us one o' them old World War Two battleships. And float it down on Navajo Lake."

"Oh, you're funnin' me." The French-Canadian woman opened the screened door and stepped back as the night visitor hobbled past her. She followed Daisy into the parlor. Without waiting for an invitation, the aged Ute woman sat down.

Louise-Marie's stomach began to feel queasy. You never knew what strange things this old woman was up to. "You were funnin' me, weren't you, Daisy?" Well, sure she was. Those Navajos would never let the Utes put a big old battleship in their precious lake.

Daisy Perika sat on a worn couch in the French-Canadian woman's cozy parlor, a cup of lukewarm tea in her hands. Why people would drink this stuff instead of good coffee was beyond all reckoning. But Louise-Marie was practically a foreigner, and it was probably all in the way she was brought up. The Ute woman looked around. This was an awfully big old house, with at least a couple of unused bedrooms. Good place to stay for the night.

The host sat with her small hands folded, and gazed sweetly upon her unexpected guest.

Daisy stirred the tea with an antique silver-plated spoon. Maybe she shouldn't ask any favors of Louise-Marie. The old woman would eventually want something in return. But fair was fair. And what was it those Ute sailors said: any port in a storm? She chuckled to herself.

Louise-Marie, who had pulled a rocking chair close to her guest, peeped over the top of silver-rimmed bifocals. "How's the tea? Sweet enough?"

Daisy pretended to take a sip. "It's fine." *Sooner have alkali water.*

The white woman glanced through the curtains at the darkness. "You're out kind of late."

The visitor nodded, and looked around the spacious parlor at the scattering of spindly looking furniture. On every flat space, there were armies of dainty little porcelain figurines arranged in their battalions. All kinds of fuzzy-looking pictures hung on the wall. And plastic flowers were jammed into plastic vases. "Well, you sure have lots of nice things." *Never saw so much old junk in one place.*

The old woman beamed. "Why thank you, Daisy." This was an opportunity to bring up a subject she'd been hesitant to broach. "To make this room just *perfect* . . . what I'd really like to have"— she drew a deep breath—"is a nice little Indian blanket to hang on the wall over my bed."

The Ute woman barely smiled. She knew exactly where this was going. Ever since last Christmas, when Gorman had given her that ugly little gray blanket, Louise-Marie had coveted it. "Well you ought to go out and buy yourself one then."

Louise-Marie sighed. "Well, I'd really like to have one just like that little thing you use for a throw rug by your bed. *Oui*— it'd match the colors in here so well. I wonder if you'd ever consider parting with it?"

"Wouldn't be right to sell it," Daisy said in a self-righteous tone. "It was a gift from a member of my family." *A worthless piece of rag from my beer-soaked cousin.*

Her host's face dropped. "Oh, well of course I'd never want to—"

"Of course," the Ute woman added quickly, "we might work out a trade of some sort."

"Well, if you think of anything you'd like in exchange, just let me know." She pushed a lacquered wooden tray across the polished table. "Would you like to have a cookie with your tea? They're my favorites—Pecan Sandies."

"Sure." The Ute woman grabbed a handful, dropping several into her coat pocket. Daisy looked slyly at her host. "I thought you did a good job at the church play. Layin' up there on that little bed, you looked sure enough dead."

The old lady blushed to her ears. "Oh, it's too embarrassing to talk about. I actually went to sleep. And"—her voice dropped to a mortified whisper—"they say I *snored.*"

"Whoever said that was teasin' you, Louise-Marie. I didn't hear anything that sounded like a snore." *Sounded more like a stuck pig's final death-rattle.*

"Really? You didn't hear me snore at *all?*"

"Nope. And I was right there on the front row." It wasn't an actual lie, Daisy assured herself. Sure, she was twisting the tail of Truth till it squealed, but it was a pure, unselfish act. Done only to make a friend feel better.

Much relieved, Louise-Marie rocked back and forth. "I'm glad you came by. I feel like talking to somebody."

Daisy nibbled at a cookie. "What you wanta talk about?"

Louise-Marie made a grand flourish with her tiny pink hand. "We shall talk . . . of many things. Of shoes—and ships—and sealing wax. Of cabbages and kings. And why the sea is boiling hot—and whether pigs have wings."

Daisy rolled her eyes. The older Louise-Marie got, the less sense she made. "I ain't much interested in wax or cabbages."

Louise-Marie lowered her voice to a whisper. "Everybody's

talking about Hooper Antelope. How he died over there on Sleeping Ute Mountain. And then his mother, poor soul."

Daisy nodded. "I was right there when it happened."

Little lights sparkled like fireflies in Louise-Marie's pale blue eyes. She leaned forward expectantly.

The Ute woman also leaned forward; they were eye-to-eye. "It was awful. Hooper floppin' and jerkin' there on the ground. Suckin' for air like a fish somebody threw on the bank. And then Charlie and this *matukach* dancer, they tried to save him. I could of told them it wasn't no use."

Louise-Marie nodded eagerly, her little gray head bobbing.

"They'll say he died of natural causes." The Ute woman shook her head defiantly. "But he didn't."

A china cup trembled in Louise-Marie's quivering hand. "No? Then how . . ."

The shaman's eyes were like flat black stones. "Hooper was witched."

Louise-Marie shuddered with a delicious fear. "Witched? How dreadful." *How marvelous.*

Daisy nodded grimly. "Witched. And when Stella knew her son was dead, it broke her heart. That's what killed her." Absent-mindedly, she took a gulp of tea, and immediately regretted this rash action. She munched on a Pecan Sandie. These cookies were a bit dry, but they were free.

"Poor Old Popeye . . . Poor Stella," Louise-Marie sighed. "She was such a good soul. And suffered so many . . . infirmities."

Daisy made a hateful face at the teacup. "Uh-huh. Stella was born with a clubfoot. And after she got that sugar diabetes, she went blind as a mole."

Louise-Marie was shocked at this blunt language. There were much kinder ways of describing a person's physical limitations. Like "locomotionally impaired." And "visually challenged."

The Ute shaman got a faraway look in her eyes. "But I think Old Popeye Woman could see some things that other folks couldn't."

Like a magnet, this provocative statement pulled Louise-Marie to the very edge of her chair. "Like what—what things?"

Daisy allowed herself a dramatic pause. "Her eyes was blind as stones, but there's more'n one way to see." The old shaman tapped at her temple. "I'm sure Stella saw who witched her son."

The French-Canadian woman nodded wisely. "Stranger things have happened."

"You know my nephew, Charlie Moon."

"I certainly do." Louise-Marie smiled sweetly. "A fine young man. He's always been very kind to me."

"Hmmpf. He's a big jughead. Charlie don't say so, but I can see it in his face. He thinks I've slipped off the saddle."

Louise-Marie blinked. "Done what?" This woman was far too old to be riding a horse.

"Gone soft in the head. Charlie thinks I ain't as smart as I used to be when I was younger." She stuffed half a Pecan Sandie into her mouth.

"Now that's simply not true. Why you're every bit as clever as I am."

Daisy choked on the cookie.

The evening dragged on. Delly ate the greasy lamb stew slowly; her meal was cold before she finished. She nibbled on the remains of the salad. She'd had all the tea she could hold.

Delly watched diners come and go. She hadn't noticed the old Shoshone man's arrival; he was sitting at a table in a far corner. He must be staying in the motel. Red Heel munched absentmindedly at a sandwich, drank two cups of coffee, then paid his bill and meandered away as if he wasn't sure where he was.

Larry Sands finished his meal. Her brother left a pile of greenbacks on his table, said his goodnights to Steele and the flashy blonde, and left. Without a backward glance at his sister.

Steele and his golden-haired nymph enjoyed a fine meal of grilled almond trout and new potatoes. And dessert. And left arm-in-arm. Blondie whispering and wriggling and giggling; him blushing and grinning and tugging at his collar. Like a couple of overheated teenagers. As the couple departed, Blondie glanced over her shoulder. At Delly. What was in that look? Self-satisfaction . . . even smugness?

Well, you can have him. And no, I am certainly not jealous. How absurd that such a thought should even come into my head.

Still, the writer of the note did not show. A dozen times, Delly thought about leaving. But maybe her contact was waiting until the restaurant was less crowded to make his appearance. She checked her wristwatch ten times in fifteen minutes.

At eleven-thirty, Myra Cornstone went off duty. Aside from a small band of noisy teenagers and the graveyard crew, there was no one left in the restaurant. Feeling like a fool, Delly finally gave it up. It'd been dumb to pay any attention to a silly note some bozo had left on her desk. A growing suspicion that it had been a prank by someone on the *Drum* staff haunted her. They'd probably already called the restaurant to see if she'd taken the bait. Sure. Tomorrow, they'd have a good laugh at her expense. But she'd learned her lesson. Never again would she pay the least attention to an anonymous message. She left a dollar tip for Myra, and paid her bill at the cash register.

Delly left the Sky Ute Lodge, glanced toward the bright lights inside the casino, and headed toward her car. Somewhere in the deep recesses of her mind there was a whispered question: Why was the parking lot so dark? She was within ten paces of the old Toyota when two things happened. Though separated in time by less than one-tenth of one second, these events seemed simultaneous to the young woman.

A sharp report, like a dry twig snapping . . . a sharp sting in her flesh.

Charlie Moon was enjoying a midnight snack of apple pie surrounded by French vanilla ice cream when he got the call. The SUPD night dispatcher was somewhat uncertain. Someone

injured at the Sky Ute Lodge parking lot, he said. Daniel Bignight
was already on the scene.

Moon abandoned his dessert, sprinted to the SUPD Blazer
and roared north along Goddard Avenue. When he turned in to
the motel-casino parking lot, he saw two black-and-whites with
pulsating red-and-blue lights. One squad car belonged to the
Ignacio town police, the other was SUPD. Five people were
clustered around a small woman in a white dress. A pair of very
well-dressed women were patting her shoulder, apparently muttering comforting words. Three middle-aged men, decked out in
thousand-dollar suits, stood by uncertainly. Full house.

He wondered who the victim was. Gambler, most likely. Or
maybe somebody who worked at the motel. Or in the motel
restaurant . . . the possibility that it might be Myra Cornstone
drew a tight knot in his stomach. And then, in the beams from
the Blazer headlights, Moon saw her face. He skidded the blunt-
nosed automobile to a halt behind Bignight's low-slung Chevrolet
squad car; the V-8 engine had barely died when Moon's boots hit
the ground.

He brushed past Bignight.

Delly saw the tall Ute policeman and broke away from the
sympathetic covey of gamblers. Suddenly, she was in Charlie
Moon's arms.

"What happened?"

"I don't know, Charlie. It was awfully dark and I was having
a hard time finding my car. Then I felt this sting and—"

He pushed her away for a better look. "You hurt?"

She reached over her left shoulder and rubbed the sore spot.
"I'm not bleeding or anything—and it doesn't hurt so much now."

Daniel Bignight ambled up. He touched his hat and smiled
shyly at Delly, then addressed his words to Moon. "Somebody
shot out a bunch of the streetlights on the north end of the
parking lot. Most likely some dumb kid with a slingshot. I figure
when he saw Miss Sands, he must've aimed a chunk of gravel
at her."

Delly returned Bignight's smile.

Moon's eyes surveyed the parking lot. There were rows of expensive automobiles. "Was any car glass shot up?"

The Taos Pueblo man shook his head. "Don't look like it."

Moon left Delly in Officer Bignight's care and headed for her Toyota. He switched on a pocket flashlight and moved the beam over the surface of Delly's car. He tried the door. The old bucket was locked up tight. No broken window glass. The policeman made a circle around the automobile. Headlights and taillights unbroken. No signs of vandalism. So Bignight must be right. Some half-wit kid with a slingshot had been using the streetlights for target practice. Saw Delly and launched a stone at her. Damn! If she'd turned her head, it could've put her eye out.

One of SUPD's younger officers showed up quietly at Moon's side. She was swinging a five-cell flashlight like a club. "Charlie, I found something."

"What've you got, Elena?"

"Whoever it was didn't use no slingshot, Charlie." She put something into his hand. "I found this under a busted streetlight. Not the bag," she added quickly, "what's in it."

Moon focused the flashlight beam on the object she'd dropped into a plastic sandwich bag. It was a misshapen lead pellet. Smaller than a .22, he thought. Looked like a .17 caliber. Kind of thing you shoot from an air rifle.

"That's impressive police work." He smiled at the young woman. "You got a pretty good pair of eyes."

Elena smiled back. Sooner or later, maybe he'd notice that she had a pretty pair of eyes.

But Moon didn't notice. His mind was occupied with other matters. So Delly Sands hadn't been hit by a rock from some dumb kid's slingshot. Whoever it was had shot out the parking lot lights with an air rifle. But not all of the lights. Just those on the north end of the lot. Where Delly's car was parked. Then, it looked like he'd waited in the dark. For Delly to show up. And taken a potshot at her. But that didn't make much sense. Why go to all that trouble, just to shoot someone with an air rifle? You couldn't cause serious injury with one of those things. Not unless you hit your target in the eyeball with the lead pellet. And Delly had been shot from behind.

And then he remembered what Walks Sleeping had said. Something the old man had told him about how witches killed their victims. The old man's words bounced around inside Charlie Moon's head like loaded dice rattling in a cup.

And they came up snake eyes.

Maybe this wasn't an ordinary someone. He'd shot lead pellets to knock out the lights over the parking lot. But what if this shooter imagined he was a witch? Then he might just—

No. That was a crazy notion.

But these were crazy times. And if his hunch was right, he had to find out.

Before Delly did.

Delly Sands was, despite everything, quite pleased with how this wretched evening was turning out. True, she'd been suckered into a meeting with a supposed informant who hadn't shown. Also true, some kid had taken a shot at her. Maybe it wasn't a slingshot, Moon had told her. Could have been an air rifle. So there might be a small lead pellet under the skin on her shoulder. No big deal really, but infection could be a problem if it wasn't taken out right away.

The tribal clinic was closed at this late hour, so she had planned to drive herself to the emergency room in Durango. But the Ute policeman had hustled her into his SUPD squad car. Now they were heading north on Route 172. Severely breaking the speed limit. Dancing on the Blazer's black hood were dull reflections of red-and-blue lights that pulsed in synchrony with her heartbeat. To her left, behind the wheel, was the grim-faced silhouette of Charlie Moon. Such a sweet man . . . he was so worried about her. That was a good sign. But it had been a long day and she was terribly weary. She yawned.

He reached over to touch her forehead. No sign of fever. "Sleepy?"

"A little." Briefly, she held his large hand against her cheek.

Soon, she was asleep. Charlie Moon keyed the radio transmitter to Scramble mode. He reached for the dashboard microphone, keyed the switch, and spoke softly. "Moon to dispatch."

The graveyard dispatcher responded almost immediately. "Hi, Charlie. How's the young lady?"

"Fine. Patch me through to Doc Amundsen."

"Say again?"

Slowly, enunciating each syllable, Moon repeated the request. "And don't make a record of the call."

"Yes, sir," he said. Charlie Moon was a nice guy, but when he used that tone you did exactly what you were told and kept your mouth shut. The dispatcher looked up the number in the telephone directory. He dialed, and waited for an answer. After seven rings, Amundsen answered. The old man sounded sleepy and irritable.

The graveyard dispatcher used his professional voice. "Dr. Amundsen, this is SUPD in Ignacio. Please hold for Officer Moon." He threw a toggle switch to connect the radio console to the telephone receiver. The dispatcher watched the VU meter jiggle. "I'd give a day's pay to listen in," he muttered under his breath.

Delly had dozed for a few minutes. A sharp twinge of pain in her shoulder awakened her suddenly. Charlie Moon must've been talking on the radio; he was hanging the microphone on its hook. She rubbed at the small wound, then leaned forward and frowned at the crisscross pattern of headlights on the highway. It was awfully dark out there. No sign yet of the lights of Durango. "Charlie, are we almost there?"

"Almost." Moon smiled. She sounded like a little kid going on a picnic.

He slowed near a mailbox, jammed the brake pedal, and turned the wheel hard.

She held on to the shoulder strap and glanced uncertainly at the policeman. "I thought you were taking me to the emergency room. At Mercy Hospital."

"No need to go all the way to Durango. We got a good surgeon close by. He's a friend of mine." *And he owes me a couple of favors.*

The Blazer bounced down a long, graveled lane between two perfectly straight rows of lodgepole pine. In the moonlight she saw a two-story house huddled in a grove of large trees. A farmhouse? Must be a country doctor. There were lights on downstairs. "Is he expecting us?"

The Ute policeman nodded.

The porch lights went on. A paunchy, sandy-haired man opened the front door while the SUPD Blazer was sliding to a stop under an enormous maple.

Dr. Amundsen led the policeman and the patient to a room that he referred to with an air of pride as "my surgery." At the doctor's instruction, Delly sat on a small couch. Exhausted, she tried hard to fight off sleep. But she was conscious of every breath she took. She counted . . . one breath . . . two . . . three . . . I'm so awfully tired.

The men had withdrawn to a dim hallway; she could hear the sonorous drone of their voices. But not the words. She leaned back on the couch. And surrendered to sleep.

Dr. Amundsen's face was a shade paler than usual. "On the phone, you said you had a police emergency but you sure as hell didn't tell me—"

Moon leaned against the wall, his arms folded across his chest. "It is an emergency. She's been shot."

Amundsen went bug-eyed with rage. "Well what'n hell you

doing, bringing her *here?* If she's been shot, she should be at the E.R. in Durango."

"It wasn't a regular shooting. Just an air rifle." Moon glanced through the surgery doorway. Delly seemed to be asleep. "It's a superficial wound. But I don't want to take her to a . . . uh . . . to the hospital."

The older man cocked his head and squinted at the tall policeman. Trying to read the Ute's face. Blank page. "What'n blazes is going on here, Charlie?"

Moon ignored the heart of the question. "She's got something in her shoulder. You got to dig it out."

"Hmmph." This big Ute was, as usual, up to something that was decidedly unkosher. "Why do you want *me* to extract a damn BB from this young lady's shoulder? You know I don't—"

"She wasn't shot with a BB gun. We're talking seventeen-caliber air rifle, or maybe an air pistol. After you've got it out, she'll want to see it." Moon placed a plastic bag in Amundsen's hand. "This is what you'll show her."

Amundsen opened the sandwich bag. He held the little piece of lead between his thumb and finger, rolling it like a marble. He scowled at Moon. "But why don't I just show her the pellet I extract?"

"Because," Moon said slowly, "it may not be a chunk of lead."

He dropped the pellet into his pocket. "Then what'n hell may it be?"

Moon told him.

My goodness. This was getting curiouser and curiouser. Dr. Amundsen glanced into the surgery at his patient and shook his head in weary astonishment. "Well now, that's about the damnedest thing I ever heard of. I don't know if I should do this, Charlie. I could get in some trouble. You know it's not really in my line to—"

"This is important to me, Doc. I'd consider it a favor."

"But it's very irregular. I'm practically retired nowadays and anyway—"

The policeman put a comforting hand on the worried man's shoulder. "If it ever comes up you can say I talked you into doing it. Medical emergency, police business, and all that kinda stuff. I'll back you up one hundred percent."

Amundsen thought about it. Despite the Ute cop's assurances, there were definite professional risks. But Charlie Moon was a friend who'd done him some good turns. And the Ute's word was good as gold. And maybe this would even be a little bit of fun— doing something out of the ordinary. He needed some fun in his life.

Her sleep was deep almost to unconsciousness, like that of a small child. Delly barely responded when Charlie Moon gently lifted her from the couch. He sat her on the surgeon's table; the cold stainless steel startled her back to consciousness.

The doctor approached, his left hand behind his back. He smiled nervously, exposing nicotine-stained teeth.

Delly was startled when he used his thumb to push her upper lip up. "Ahhh . . . hold still, now . . . that's a good girl. Easy now . . . gums look nice and pink." Now he pushed her eyelid up. "Hmmm," he said sagely, but did not comment on what he saw. Amundsen backed away from his patient. He looked over Delly's head. Now . . . I'll . . . uh . . . have to ask you to unbutton your dress." The old man blushed a dull crimson. "But you don't have to take it all the way off. Just push the top part over your shoulder so's—so's I can see the . . . the wound."

Delly repressed an urge to giggle. She'd undressed for doctors before, and they'd never minded asking. This old man was a peculiar fellow. He'd poked his thumb under her lip, rolled her eyelid up like a scroll, yet he was embarrassed to suggest that she undress just enough to bare her shoulder. She noticed that Moon had his back to her. The policeman's attention was apparently absorbed by a framed photograph of a tall woman standing by an Irish setter. This was all so unreal—like a bizarre dream. She unfastened the top three buttons of her dress and exposed the wounded shoulder.

Dr. Amundsen walked around the table, waving the small hypodermic he'd been hiding. "Charlie, injecting this anesthetic will sting a little bit. Might make her jump around some. You better hold onto her." He swabbed the puncture wound with a brownish-yellow disinfectant.

Delly smiled dreamily at the policeman. *You want to hold me Charlie?*

Moon frowned over his shoulder at the old man. "She'll be still for you, Doc; it's not like she's . . . " His voice trailed off.

The old man's blue eyes flashed fire. "Lissen, cop, who's the doctor around here?"

Moon swallowed a snappy comeback. He took Delly gently by the arms. "Doc's gotta give you a shot. For the pain. Then he'll take the pellet out."

She nodded absently. His hands felt warm on her skin. She barely flinched when the needle was pressed into her shoulder.

It was a trivial piece of surgery, requiring his smallest scalpel blade. The foreign object was barely a millimeter under the skin. Amundsen grasped it with a small forceps and pulled it like a loose tooth. He held the thing close to the lower lens of his bifocals. Hmmm. Just like the cop'd said . . . peculiar. But you never knew what to expect from these Indians.

The surgeon raised an eyebrow at Moon, then wrapped the thing into a small wad of sterile cotton. He reached into his pocket and found the .17 caliber lead pellet the Ute policeman had given him; he dropped this into an enameled tray. Delly flinched when she heard the sound of the pellet striking metal. She took a deep breath. "I want to see it."

Doc Amundsen swabbed the one-centimeter incision with an extra helping of the antiseptic fluid. "See what, young lady?" He was enjoying this small conspiracy.

This old fellow was a little slow. "The . . . thing you took out of me."

The surgeon picked the lead pellet up with his rubber-gloved fingers. He held it over her shoulder, dropping it into Delly's open palm. "Make a great conversation piece. You could put it on a charm bracelet." He winked over her head at the Ute policeman. *Yep. Charlie Moon is gonna owe me bigtime for this little piece of work.*

Delly stared. "It's so . . . so small."

"It's only a seventeen-caliber air gun pellet," Moon said with a grin. "What'd you expect, a forty-four Magnum?" He wondered what she'd expected. Delly, like her brother Larry, had grown up hearing their father's grim tales. She and the Sandman knew all the Ute witchcraft lore. But tonight, what she *didn't* know would help this minor wound heal. Maybe even save her life.

She turned the dull gray lump with her little finger. "But why's it so . . . so distorted?"

The policeman explained: "It's a soft lead pellet, so it gets all bent out of shape when it hits something." *Especially something hard. Like a streetlight.*

Amundsen reached into a sterile tray; he grasped a curved suture needle in the jaws of the forceps. "Now hold onto her again, Charlie. We'll need some sutures to close the incision."

Delly smiled at the big Ute, who held her shoulders with such a gentle touch.

He returned the smile. *She was going to be just fine.*

Dr. Amundsen led the pair to the door; he turned and patted Delly's head. "Now you keep the wound clean and it'll do just fine."

Delly nodded sleepily.

Moon shook Amundsen's outstretched hand, and expertly palmed a wad of cotton. "Thanks, Doc. I appreciate what you did."

The old man's belly shook as he chuckled. "Don't mention it, Charlie. And," he added in a raspy whisper, "I really mean that."

Granite Creek, Colorado

The policemen stood as far away from the medical examiner as was possible in the dank basement laboratory.

The Ute squinted at the checkerboard of acoustic ceiling tiles. He'd already counted them twice. Twenty by seventeen. Three hundred and forty. One visit to the M.E. in a year was plenty, Moon thought. Two times in the same month was altogether too many. But if this hunch pays off . . .

Scott Parris had his old hat in his hands. He was examining the dirty sweatband, the crumpled felt. His thoughts were in disconnected bits and pieces like a jigsaw puzzle scattered on the floor. *Anne's still in Seattle. Maybe I need to buy me a new hat. Maybe I need a new life. Where a man doesn't have to deal with small-town politicians and drunk drivers and battered wives who won't sign complaints and . . . dead bodies.*

The policemen were well aware that the body on the table was not the remains of Hooper Antelope.

Dr. Simpson hummed happily as he worked over the blackened, half-frozen corpse. This piece of meat had, only three days before, been a living human being. A successful insurance salesman who'd been playing golf in a summer thunderstorm. The long finger of electric fire had, an awed witness said, ". . . Caught old Sammy right on the backswing." Lightning, the medical examiner mused, loves a hoisted seven iron . . . enough to reach out and touch it. Dr. Simpson sneaked a sideways glance in the general direction of the lawmen. "I suppose you coppers got a good reason for interrupting my work?"

Moon nodded. "Maybe."

The M.E. sniffed. "Go ahead, be mysterious about it. See if I give a damn." He pulled a wrinkled sheet over the corpse and grinned at the tough pair of lawmen. Couple of big sissies who were scared of dead bodies, that's what they were. "Maybe you fellows would like to go upstairs."

Both men nodded.

The M.E. poured three cups of weak coffee. "So what brings such distinguished representatives of the constabulary back to my home and official place of business?"

"That little puncture you found on Hooper Antelope's back," Moon said. "I think it's a gunshot wound."

Simpson raised an eyebrow. "You must surely be joking."

"It wasn't an ordinary lead bullet. You have a closer look, you'll find a small pellet under the skin."

This earned a second lofted eyebrow from the M.E. *Closer look* indeed. Who did this bumpkin copper think he was talking to? "What kind of pellet?"

Moon lowered his gaze. "It's made from . . . bone."

The M.E. frowned suspiciously. "Bone?"

The Ute shuffled his big boots under the table.

Dr. Simpson chortled. "You kidding me?"

Moon shook his head.

"Read my lips, Officer Moon—the impression in Mr. Antelope's back was not caused by any kind of gunshot wound. Not from lead or bone . . . or tooth of lizard. What I found was a minor contusion, consistent with the body of the deceased being dropped off the gurney onto a rock by those Ute Mountain cops. Just like you told me before. It was certainly not sufficient to cause death."

The Ute policeman frowned stubbornly at the coffee cup.

The old man rubbed his eyes and sighed. "Do tell me—from whence cometh this hypothetical fragment of bone?"

Charlie Moon shrugged. "It'll be human bone. From a dead man. Or dead woman, maybe. I dunno."

"Anything else you want to tell me, Sherlock?"

"Well, it'll be shaped like a cylinder. And I can tell you its diameter."

"I wait with bated breath," Simpson said serenely.

Maybe he should just show the old man the thing Doc Amundsen took out of Delly's shoulder. Maybe not. "Point one-seven inches. More or less."

The old man gawked at the Ute. "How in thunderation d'you figure that?"

"It was shot from a seventeen-caliber air gun."

The M.E. shook his head in pretended awe. "Well, that's just amazing. I guess you could teach me a thing or two about my business."

Moon, who appreciated the compliment, smiled. "I'm sure it's there. Right under the skin on Hooper's back."

Simpson ground his teeth. This was insufferable. Not to be tolerated. The medical examiner glared at the Ute policeman. He tried to think of a snappy reply. This was the best he could do: "Wanna bet?"

The magic words. The Ute swallowed his smile. "Well, maybe."

The M.E. grinned wolfishly through his scraggly beard. "How much can you afford to lose, copper?"

Moon managed an uneasy expression. Like *he* was the fish about to be hooked. "Oh . . . I dunno. A coupla dollars maybe?" That'd be just the right bait.

Simpson sneered at this. "Let's make it a twenty." Teach the overgrown yokel a lesson.

"I don't know . . . twenty? . . . well, maybe," the Ute said. It'd be nice to raise the ante, but that might scare the old man off.

"I want a piece of the action," Parris said. "Let's make it fifty."

The M.E. snorted. "Whose side you bettin' on?"

Parris flipped a quarter, caught it, and pretended to check which side was up. "Guess I'll hafta go with Charlie."

"Well," Moon said cautiously, "if you're in for fifty, pardner—I guess I'll have to back you up."

The medical examiner squinted suspiciously over his bifocals. "Let's get this straight. If I am able to find this . . . bone pellet in the remains of the deceased, I lose the bet. Otherwise, I win."

Moon nodded.

"As long as you do your best to find it," Parris said quickly. This old guy was slippery as boiled okra.

"Gentlemen," the M.E. said solemnly, "put your *dinero* on the table."

The lawmen produced wallets and counted out greenbacks. The cash was placed on the table. Simpson covered the pile with five crisp twenties.

Parris grinned. "Now you can get the body out of the refrigerator and get to work."

Simpson grinned back. He slapped his hand over the cash and snatched it off the table. "No can do."

Parris was on his feet. "What?"

"You will recall the precise terms of the bet, coppers. If I am able to find Officer Moon's hypothetical bone pellet in the remains of the deceased, I lose the bet. Otherwise, I win."

Both lawmen watched him stuff the greenbacks in his shirt pocket, where it made an obscene bulge.

"I cannot *possibly* find said hypothetical bone pellet," the M.E. said calmly. "Therefore, the pot is mine."

"Why can't you find it?" Moon asked softly.

"Oh. Simpson put his fingertips to his lips. "Dear me—I must be getting old and silly—did I forget to mention it?"

Parris felt his stomach turn. "Mention what, you old fraud?"

"No need to get testy." The M.E. sipped daintily at his coffee. "Several days ago, a minor bureaucrat with the Bureau of Indian Affairs—through which bureaucracy I have my contract with the Southern Ute Tribe—directed that the remains of said Mr. Hooper Antelope be immediately transferred to a mortuary in Durango."

Scott Parris glowered at the M.E. "Then the bet's still on. All you have to do is get the body back and—"

"In light of the fact that the survivors of the deceased have refused to accept the remains—at the direction of the BIA and with the concurrence of tribal authorities—the body has been cremated."

Moon closed his eyes and groaned. This was a bad piece of luck. But he wasn't surprised that Reuben Antelope didn't want to go near his nephew's body. For a traditional Ute, dealing with any corpse was bad enough. It was far worse if the man had died of witchcraft.

Dr. Walter Simpson patted the wad of greenbacks stashed in his pocket. Upon occasion, life was so *very* sweet.

It was a sultry July midafternoon. The Sugar Bowl Cafe was empty except for the lawmen and a bored waiter. A solitary bottlefly buzzed in lazy circles, occasionally banging his segmented head against the plate glass window.

The policemen were finishing a late lunch. Parris savored the last bite of his sandwich. A grilled cheese garnished with sliced bread and butter pickles. He downed a swallow of cold milk.

Moon was working on his second bacon-cheeseburger. And thinking about pie. With ice cream. "Pardner, I sure feel bad about how that bet turned out. Sorry you got sucked into it."

Parris shrugged. "It's only money." *Only money I needed to buy groceries with.* He wiped his mouth with a paper napkin. "Charlie, would you have felt bad if we'd taken that old man's hundred dollars?"

Moon looked up from his burger. "Nope."

"Me neither. He's a nasty old miser who'd be glad to beat us out of our last dime."

The Ute thought about this. "I guess that's why I like him."

"Me too." Parris felt a twinge of nostalgia. "Doc Simpson reminds me of my old man."

The sleepy-looking waiter approached the table. Would the gentlemen care for dessert?

Moon scanned the menu and ordered rhubarb pie. And lemon ice cream. Three scoops.

The waiter made a sickly face and puckered his mouth.

Looks like a 'possum sucking on a green persimmon, Parris thought. The *matukach* policeman briefly considered a slab of carrot cake, but his belt felt tight around the gut. He passed.

The waiter departed.

"Charlie, I understand that Miss Sands was shot with a piece of bone. And you figure somebody shot that Sun-Dancer with the same thing. But I don't quite get the connection."

Moon peeled the thin paper skin from a toothpick. "Right about the time Hooper fell down, Delly heard something . . . a cracking sound. I didn't think much about it when she told me. But it could've been somebody outside the brush corral with an air rifle." He paused thoughtfully. "Or if the shooter was inside the Sun Dance lodge, it was probably an air pistol . . . that'd be fairly easy to conceal."

The Ute policeman rolled this over in his mind. Whoever pulled the trigger had probably tried to hide the sound under the drumbeat. Hooper was in poor health and the old man had apparently pushed himself too far in dancing thirsty. He was also a traditional Ute, so if he realized what had happened, it might very well have been enough to push him over the edge. Belief in witches is a powerful thing. Moon sighed, imagining Aunt Daisy's smug, self-satisfied expression if she ever found out about this. "I figure the same guy who shot the bone at Hooper, later on he took a pop at Delly Sands."

The waiter showed up with a tray. He sniffed his disapproval as he placed the rhubarb pie and lemon ice cream in front of the big Ute, then departed.

Parris eyed the thick slab of pie and licked his lips. "But why shoot the girl?"

Moon speared the pie with a fork, and sawed off a chunk with a dull knife. "Because she's gonna write a newspaper article about Hooper's death. There's even gossip around Ignacio that she'll name the witch." The Ute policeman removed a small plastic box from his jacket pocket. He slid the exhibit across the table.

Parris squinted at the tiny object in the box. "This is what she was shot with?"

Moon nodded as he munched on the pie. "Dead man's bone. Or at least that's what she was supposed to believe it was."

Parris shook his head in wonder. "But such a little piece of bone . . ."   `

"It doesn't take much." The Ute allowed himself a thin smile. "A raven's egg dropped in your pocket . . . an owl's wing placed where you'll step on it . . . a little piece of grave bone shot under your skin. O' course, it don't work unless you know it's been done to you." He dipped a tarnished spoon into the lemon ice cream. Doc Amundsen had done Delly a big favor. Now that she thought she'd been shot with an ordinary pellet of lead, she'd be just fine.

Moon folded his long frame into the SUPD Blazer. The Ute policeman stared through the windshield at a buffalo-shaped cloud drifting southward, its fat underbelly tickled by the fingerlike projections of Longhand Mountain. Farther south, several such clouds were coalescing into a menacing gray herd. Tossing their shaggy heads, their hard black hooves striking fire off the flinty mountains. A storm was gathering over the reservation. Moon looked at his friend. "Aunt Daisy's up to something." He could feel it.

Parris, who leaned on the Blazer door, chuckled. "Like what?"

The Ute had been asking himself this same question. "I don't know exactly. But I'm sure she wants to find out who the 'witch' is. Before I can settle the issue, of course. And then rub my nose in it."

The white man, who knew the old woman well, grinned. "Nothing like a little family rivalry to make life interesting."

"Aunt Daisy makes my life plenty interesting," the Ute said grimly, "and I'm afraid she's going to get herself into a whole pot of trouble. Whoever shot the dead man's bone into Hooper Antelope and Delly Sands isn't somebody to be messed with." He looked up at his friend. "You gonna accept my invitation to come down to Ignacio?" His earlier invitation had been intended as a favor to his "pardner." Now he could really use some help.

Parris shrugged. "I don't know. I'd probably just get in your way."

The Ute stuffed the key into the ignition switch. "I could use someone to keep an eye on the Sun Dance when I'm not around. Somebody who'll pass for a tourist. If you could find some time, I could sure use your help, pardner. You very busy for the next few days?"

Parris thought about it. Was he busy?

Not much.

Not unless you counted twelve hours a day dedicated to the Granite Creek Police Department. Planning the budget for the next fiscal year. Endless meetings with representatives of county government to beg for new squad cars to replace the old buckets with over 300,000 miles on the odometers. And a few extra dollars so his officers could have a two percent raise this year.

But this was Charlie Moon asking.

"Sure, Charlie. Things are pretty quiet. I could spare some time."

Ignacio

Delly sat across from her elderly visitor, who was seated on the couch.

Daisy Perika seemed relaxed. The very picture of contentment. The elderly Ute woman looked around at the polished furniture, the wide-screen television, the two-inch-deep rug. "Nice place you got here."

Delly nodded. "Thanks. Now that I've got a job, I can afford a decent apartment."

"I heard about you gettin' shot at."

The young woman touched her bandaged shoulder. "It wasn't serious."

The shaman scowled. "Not serious?"

Delly passed a crystal ashtray across the coffee table to her guest.

Daisy accepted the dish, and eyed the contents. "What's this?"

"A lead pellet," Delly said. "That's what the doctor removed from my shoulder."

The old woman held the dull gray object close to her nose and squinted over the top of her spectacles. A shadow passed over her wrinkled face. "I'd come into town to see you. I had this dream . . . about someone going to hurt you."

The young woman suppressed a smile. These spooky old people were much alike. After something bad happened, they'd always tell you they'd had some kind of premonition. But they never managed to tell you *before* the bad thing happened. "Well, thanks, Mrs. Perika. But I'm okay."

"Hmmph," the shaman said. She gave the pellet one final glare, then dropped it into the ashtray. "I heard my nephew took you up to the hospital in Durango."

"Not exactly. Charlie was in a hurry to get me some medical attention. He stopped at a country doctor's house somewhere north of Ignacio—near Oxford, I think. Nice old fellow." She smiled at the memory of the man's inspection of her gums. And his embarrassment when he asked her to unbutton her dress. Funny old guy. For a doctor.

"I never heard of no doctor who lived at Oxford." Daisy squinted one eye at the young woman. "What was his name?"

"Now that you mention it," Delly said, "I don't remember." Had Charlie not bothered to introduce her? Or had she simply forgotten the man's name? Not that it really mattered.

The old Ute woman frowned thoughtfully. "What'd he look like?"

Delly tried to remember. "Well . . . he was fairly old. Chubby.

About medium height. Kind of pale-looking . . . had some freckles. And he had a reddish beard."

A crooked grin settled on Daisy Perika's face. That Charlie Moon, he was some piece of work. Stubborn, sometimes. But, all in all, a fine nephew.

Delly noticed the grin, and wondered what it meant.

The Ute shaman leaned toward Delly Sands, her dark eyes glinting. Daisy Perika was hunched forward. Like a toad about to snap up an unwary fly. "You'll still be able to help me . . . keep an eye on Charlie Moon?"

Delly swallowed hard, and nodded.

Daisy got up. "Well, I got to get back to my place." She was hoping Delly Sands might offer her a ride home. But the hint was not taken.

It was an hour past dark as the aged Oldsmobile hummed eastward along Route 151 toward Arboles. The French-Canadian woman couldn't stop talking about one thing and another. And, it seemed, could not speak to her passenger without glancing sideways at her.

Daisy Perika elbowed her elderly chauffeur, "You keep your eyes on the road. I'd like to get home alive."

Louise-Marie, hurt by this lack of confidence in her skills, sniffed. "Me, I never worry." Her tone turned pious. "But whenever I'm driving anywhere, I always pray to God for my safe arrival." She glanced at her passenger. "You should pray some too."

"Don't you start preaching at me," Daisy snapped. The Ute woman raised her hand to shield her eyes from the blinding headlights of an approaching truck. "I don't know how you can see the road when them lights hit the windshield. It blinds me so's I can't see nothing."

"Just do what I do, Dearie."

"And what do *you* do?" Daisy grumped.

"Close my eyes."

Immediately, the shaman began to pray.

Delly Sands, bothered by the memory of Daisy Perika's knowing smile, tried to recall that night when Charlie Moon had taken her to see the doctor. She barely remembered seeing something painted on a mailbox just as the Ute policeman had turned off the paved highway into the lane that led to the surgeon's house. But she couldn't quite recall the name . . . except that it sounded like one of those explorers who'd walked to the South Pole. It was just on the tip of her tongue. If she could find the name, she'd recognize it.

Delly spent twenty minutes with the Durango telephone directory, which also listed numbers for Ignacio, Oxford, Bayfield, and a half dozen other outlying communities. Most particularly, she studied the yellow pages. Reading and rereading the entries under Physicians & Surgeons. Osteopathic. Podiatric. M.D. There were pages and pages of physicians. They were listed alphabetically, by their specialties—Allergy to Urology. And by name, Albertson to Zukoff. But none of the names sounded right. She had finally given up, and was flipping through the pages. She was near the end of the yellow section when she saw the heading.

And immediately recognized the name . . .

Charlie Moon knocked lightly on the apartment door.

He didn't hear her bare feet on the carpet. Delly opened the door a crack; it caught on the brass chain. Her dark hair was glistening wet from the shower. The slender young woman wore but a single garment. And had a peculiar look in her eye.

Somewhere in his subconscious, a little bell rang a warning. The Ute policeman ignored it. He interpreted her sly half smile as being mildly seductive. Cute, that's what she was. "You doin' okay?"

She unhooked the chain. "I'm great. Perfect." Her eyes flashed. "And I owe it all to my good friend, Charlie Moon, who—when I was shot in the back—took me to a competent physician."

"Well, it wasn't nothin'. Just doin' my job." Moon smiled, because he was pleased to see her looking so well. And just plain pleased to see her.

Delly recoiled inwardly at the silly grin on the big cop's face. So. Charlie Moon was pleased with himself. Probably bragging down at the police station about the little prank he'd played on the Town Indian who'd come back to the reservation. She stepped aside and pulled the door wide. "You want to come in?"

The policeman took one step inside and paused. He shuffled his boots on the carpet. He removed his hat. "Thought maybe I should take you over to the tribal clinic. Get somebody to take out the stitches."

"Why not take me back to the doctor who removed the pellet?" Her face was a wide-eyed picture of innocence. "He was very nice."

Moon looked over her head, at nothing in particular. "Well I don't mind callin' on him for an emergency. But I'd hate to bother him about a little thing like takin' out stitches."

"But he *is* a competent surgeon. Isn't he?"

"Oh sure." He waved his hat in a dismissive gesture. "How's your shoulder doin'?"

"It's healing wonderfully." She turned sideways, and started to unbutton her bathrobe. "You want to see?"

"We . . . well," he stammered, ". . . I don't know if . . . you want me to close the door first?"

"No," she whispered provocatively, "just close your *eyes*, Charlie. And don't open them till I tell you."

He did.

Delly Sands doubled up her little hand into a tight fist. She drew it back. And rammed it into Charlie Moon. Hard. Just below his silver belt buckle.

"Oooooofff!" He doubled over, staggered backward, stumbled over the door sill and across the porch until his butt rammed against the steel porch railing. He stood there for several seconds with his hands on his knees, trying hard to get his breath.

"Del . . . Delly?"

Her voice was little-girl sweet. "Yes, Charlie?"

"Can I open my eyes now?"

"Yes, you may."

"Delly . . . why'd you hit me?"

She told him. And slammed the door. Hard.

Charlie Moon thought himself a reasonable man. He always tried to see things from the other fellow's perspective. Now he tried to see the issue from Delly Sands' point of view. Well, sure. He could have taken her all the way to Durango after she'd been shot with the air gun. But he wasn't acquainted with those doctors who worked in the emergency room at Mercy Hospital. It was unlikely they'd have agreed to tell their patient they'd removed an ordinary lead pellet from her shoulder. That'd be a bald-faced lie and those M.D.s at Mercy had their standards. No. He'd needed someone a man could count on in a pinch. Like Doc Amundsen.

The policeman pointed the Blazer toward the Southern Ute Police Department. He rubbed his aching gut. *Oh boy . . . feels like Delly Sands drove a two-by-four straight into my belly.* Don't see why she was so sore. Doc Amundsen did a fine job on her shoulder wound. And, Moon recalled with some appreciation of the irony, Amundsen was a practitioner with a specialty that'd earned him considerable distinction. And made him well-suited to doctor the likes of Delly Sands. The old veterinarian specialized in the treatment of all sorts of wild animals. Like coyotes and foxes and weasels. And little sidewinder rattlesnakes that struck a man when he wasn't looking.

Banner Hardware & General Merchandise

The clerk was stocking shelves with glue and epoxy when he noticed the little old lady. There were a couple of small cans of paint in her shopping cart and a one-inch brush. She was grunting and stretching . . . reaching for a permanent marker mounted on a pegboard display. She was short, maybe a couple of inches under five feet. The plastic packet containing the black felt-tipped pen was well out of her reach.

Frustrated, she muttered to herself.

He smiled, removed the package for her, and nodded politely. "Good morning, ma'am."

She nodded—with a somewhat blank look—and dropped the marker pen into her shopping cart.

He hoped she wasn't another of these folks who'd wandered away from the nursing home. Only last week a befuddled old man had drifted into the store and insisted on purchasing a bus ticket to Denver. He had ignored the clerk's repeated assurances that this was not and never had been the Greyhound station. More-over, the daffy old geezer intended to pay for the ticket with crumpled pieces of notebook paper.

"Anything else I can help you with?" She was almost cute. In a wrinkled-apple-face sort of way. Reminded him of his maternal grandmother.

She took in a deep breath, like a swimmer about to make a deep dive. "Yes, young man. I need to buy me a saw."

"Well, ma'am, you're in the right place. You want a regular carpenter's saw?"

She frowned thoughtfully. "I don't think so."

"A hacksaw then?"

She muttered something that he didn't hear.

Many of his customers were bumbling do-it-yourselfers who needed his professional guidance. The clerk was an accomplished carpenter and eager to contribute his knowledge for the edification of the unenlightened. But it was necessary to keep it simple. "Will you be sawing wood . . . or metal?"

She shook her head. "No, I don't think so."

The young man grinned. Balmy or not, she was still a cus-tomer. And Banner Hardware treated all its customers with due respect. "Let's go have a look at what's in stock." He escorted his hopeful patron to the Handee-Man Tools aisle. There was quite a selection of gleaming instruments. Sinister claw hammers, cast-iron crowbars, blunt-nose punches, gleaming electric drill motors, delicate spirit levels, angular carpenter's squares, plastic-handled screwdrivers, rubber-grip pliers, heavy-duty bolt cutters, and pointy-toothed saws of every variety.

He waited patiently, his hands in the pockets of his blue Banner Hardware blazer.

The elderly woman stared at the selection of instruments for a full minute. Eventually, she reached for a coping saw. This looked like just the thing for such a . . . delicate task. And there was a fine assortment of blades. She selected a very thin sliver of steel, with triangular teeth so small she could hardly see them. But she could feel them against her sensitive fingertips. My, they were *ever* so sharp. Yes, she shook her head, this should do nicely.

The helpful young man showed her how to insert a replacement blade in the frame, how to tighten the pawl.

"Now then," the clerk said, "will there be anything else today?"

Indeed, there would be. She told him.

"Certainly," he said. "That'll be in Sporting Goods. Aisle three."

With the coping saw stashed in her shopping cart, she followed him.

From another shelf, also too high for her reach, he produced a cardboard tube for her inspection.

She turned the container in her hand. The box was much like the ones those tasteless potato chips came in.

"Just two dollars and ninety-eight cents a dozen," he said, anxious to close the sale. Business was business, but this was getting tedious. She was so damned deliberate about everything.

She frowned. "I don't need a whole boxful—just one will do."

His reply was gentle, but firm. "I'm sorry ma'am, but we can't break a package. How would we sell the remaining eleven?"

The customer was about to say "One at a time, I suppose," but didn't. She sighed and accepted the entire dozen. Anyway, maybe it wouldn't hurt to have some extras, just in case things didn't go quite right with the first one.

The clerk guessed that this little old lady was buying the saw for her own use. Some oddball household project. But the second purchase must be for someone much younger. Someone more athletic.

He was wrong. On both counts.

Her purchase was not for a household project.

All the items were for her own use.

But the carpenter-clerk had hit one bent nail right on the head.

Oddball.

Canyon of the Spirits

Father Raes, though Daisy had much fun at his expense, was a favorite of the old shaman's. Such an innocent man. And unlike some priests, he respected the old ways of the People. Though most *matukach* thought the notion of the "Ute leprechaun" to be comical, the Catholic priest did not smile at a mention of the *pitukupf*. Father Raes had traveled to a variety of primitive, exotic places, and experienced many strange things.

The scholarly Jesuit—who was also an anthropologist—had studied the subject of the dwarf with some care. He'd pored over such old accounts as could be found in the excellent anthropology library at Fort Lewis College. He'd had lengthy conversations with tribal elders—some of whom claimed to have actually seen the "little men." The *pitukupf*, according to these experts, were spirits who made their homes in remote places, usually in abandoned badger holes. Early on cool autumn mornings, you could see the smoke of the dwarf's fire coming from the entrance to his underground dwelling. If the Ute people moved—as they had several times at the U.S. government's bidding—the mysterious dwarves always followed them. The little men were often helpful to the

People, though they expected gifts for their services. A *pitukupf*, if annoyed, was also quite capable of making serious mischief. For one thing, they would kill horses if these animals strayed too close to their underground homes. Everyone knew that Gorman Sweetwater had lost a fine mare when he'd left the animal within spitting distance of the entrance to the home of the *pitukupf* who lived in *Cañon del Espíritu*. The Utes—who were great lovers of horses—found this eccentricity of the little men to be puzzling. But they didn't blame the dwarf; a *pitukupf* was what he was and could not be expected to change his nature. The death of the mare was Gorman's fault; he should have known better than to leave it so close to the home of the little man.

The priest, after much thoughtful consideration, had arrived at a private conclusion. The dwarf was probably no more than the product of tribal folklore and excited imaginations. But on the other hand, he remembered his experiences as a student researcher in the steaming jungles of Brazil and Venezuela—where the demons feared by the natives had proved to be all too real. Yes, even though many of the tales of the dwarf's exploits were certainly fanciful, there was some possibility that the *pitukupf* represented singular spiritual entities who had—at some distant time in the forgotten past—attached themselves to the Utes. But whether imaginary or real, no good could come of associations between humans and such—whatever they were. So it was prudent to advise his flock to avoid contact with these . . . these creatures. He had, with some gentleness, offered his advice to Daisy Perika, urging the old woman to resist any temptation to visit the "little man." A Christian lady, after all, had no need to commune with a solitary spirit who lived in a badger hole. There was a definite risk in such an association. Furthermore, as an elder of the Southern Utes, she was setting a bad example to the youth of her tribe.

Daisy had nodded sagely with the learned cleric's assessment, as if she recognized the wisdom in it.

But the shaman had made no promises.

*   *   *

Daisy Perika was returning from a long walk. She'd been almost a mile into *Cañon del Espiritu*. A small basket was looped over her left elbow; she carried the stout oak digging stick in her right hand. Early July was the time for purple bottlereed and orange foxtail, for miner's floss and Apache flute. Some of these plants would provide tubers for treatment of headaches, indigestion, and nosebleeds. The tribal elder would boil the leaves of others; such teas were effective against failing eyesight, dizzy spells, and miscarriage. The basket—after much stooping and digging—was filled with these herbal treasures. She was pleased with her morning's work. It was a good and honorable thing, to make medicines for the People. Not to mention that she could also make a little money by providing this service.

And, she told herself, her sole purpose in coming into the canyon was to gather these medicinal plants. It was not as if there was another reason for her to wander into this place.

Had not Father Raes warned her about "communing" with the little man who lived in the badger hole? Yes, he had. And was she not a good Christian? Yes, she was. So Daisy had no intention of doing anything that would offend the kindly priest, or the church. It was, she told herself, a mere coincidence that her walk out of the canyon was taking her very near the entrance to the little man's home—it just happened that a fine deer path passed within a yard of the abandoned badger hole. And she was not pausing because she was close enough to flip a nickel into the hole, but because there was such a fine juniper tree in this place—the shade would be a good place to rest her legs for a few minutes. Her left hand slipped into her apron pocket. Now what was this? Why, it was a little two-blade pocketknife with iridescent blue plastic handles. She dug deeper in the pocket, and found a white cotton sack filled with tobacco. She smiled. It was not as if she had brought these things for the *pitukupf*, but as long as she was passing by on her way home, would it not be neighborly to leave a small gift? Yes. You should love your neighbor as yourself. Leaving a little present for someone who had so little in the way of worldly belongings—was this not an act of Christian charity? Of course it was. Father Raes would be proud of her if he knew that she was taking pity on someone poorer than herself. But she wouldn't mention this act of kindness to the priest. No, a charitable act—as Father Raes often reminded his flock—was best kept secret. What'd the priest say? Yes . . . "don't let your left hand know what your right hand is doing." A clever saying. Using the oak digging stick to brace herself, Daisy leaned over and laid the knife and tobacco at the entrance to the badger hole. It wasn't like she expected anything in return. Of course, if the dwarf decided to do her a favor of some sort . . . could she refuse? Of course not. That would be impolite.

She hobbled stiffly to the shade of the aged juniper. Daisy hung the herb basket on a stubby branch, and grunted as she sat down. The old woman leaned her tired back against the gnarled trunk. On a branch above her head, a mountain bluebird warbled its sweet song. The midday sun drifted behind a thin cloud. A light breeze rustled the dry limbs of the tree. The breath of the canyon smelled of sage and other fragrant plants. Ahhh . . . this was a good thing. To rest after one's labors. Gradually, the old woman's aching limbs relaxed. Her eyes closed. Daisy breathed in shallow, regular gasps. Within a minute, her lower jaw fell, her mouth gaped open.

The shaman slept. And dreamed her dreams. She floated far above the earth. Below her was a land that she had never seen. There was a broad, deep river that meandered through the dark forest like a great serpent. The mossy bank was lined with trees whose leaves were green and gold and blue. Some of the trees had blossoms. These flowers were pink and white—their fragrance was like the sweetest roses. And then she felt herself drifting away from this dream . . . leaving this forested place. Moving with the sun's path across the sky.

Within three heartbeats, she was in the sky over *Cañon del Espiritu*. To the northeast, the finger of Chimney Rock pointed toward the drifting clouds. At the mouth of the Canyon of the Spirits, she saw her little trailer home. And she could see the Three Sisters squatting eternally on the mesa above the canyon. There, just below in the canyon was her tired body. Sleeping under a juniper tree.

Yet *here* she was . . . among the clouds. Curious.

Now she was falling, or was the earth coming up to smite her? It mattered not . . . death seemed very close. She closed her eyes, and asked for God's protection.

But the shaman did not strike the ground. She fell *into* the earth, as if it were a great molten sea. Daisy drifted downward ever so slowly, like a lump of rock falling through molasses. She reached out to touch this and that . . . moldering glacial stone . . . crumbling mammoth bone . . . sinewy root of piñon tree . . . chalky shell of forgotten sea . . .

And then she was in the underground home of the little man.

There were no corners, no sharp places in the subterranean abode of the *pitukupf*. It was, except for a few comforts provided by the dwarf, much like the lair of a badger. Or what Daisy imagined a badger's lair to be. Hairlike roots hung from the ceiling, which had a rough skin of cracked sandstone and veins of blue clay. The walls were layers of slate, limestone, and compressed debris from an ancient riverbed. The floor was sandstone of a pale gray hue, and this was swept clean by the little man's grass broom. In one wall (she imagined that it was the north wall, but how could one really tell?), there was a fireplace hewn into the earth. There was no proper chimney; the smoke from his small fire hung on the ceiling, and drifted upward through the badger hole.

The dwarf—who pretended to be unaware of her presence—was dressed in crudely fashioned buckskin moccasins, tattered breeches decorated with porcupine quills, a long-sleeved shirt of cotton (dyed green as aspen leaves), and a vest of some dark, coarse weave. He sat on a three-legged stool, his thin face illumined by glowing embers of piñon in the small fireplace.

The *pitukupf* had already found her gifts. The sack of tobacco was stuffed into his vest pocket. He pared his horny, yellow fingernails with the smaller blade in the blue-handled pocketknife.

Still, he ignored his guest. The shaman cleared her throat. "Ahhh-hmmm."

He spat into the fireplace, folded the blade into the knife, and placed the implement on the hearth. He reached into the vest pocket for the tobacco.

Daisy spoke. "You heard about Hooper Antelope? How he died at the Sun Dance over at Sleeping Ute Mountain?" She knew he had, of course. This was merely a way to start a conversation with the dwarf.

He nodded, and pulled at the cotton sack with his yellowed teeth.

"You remember his mamma—Stella Antelope—the one folks call Old Popeye Woman 'cause of the way her bad eye's all pooched out?"

Another nod. The dwarf was pouring a small measure of fragrant tobacco into the bowl of a clay pipe.

"Well, I guess you know that Stella died too."

He held a dried piñon splinter to the fire until it grew a shivering tongue of yellow flame, then touched this to the bowl of the pipe.

Daisy leaned forward. "They're saying Hooper died from natural causes . . . but I believe a *witch* is responsible."

The dwarf winced at the mention of such a person; he turned and looked over the pipe at his visitor. A perfectly straight wisp of smoke drifted upward, spread out like a flat mushroom on the ceiling, and hung on the hairlike roots.

Daisy withered under his stare. "The police can't do nothing about it, but I got a plan . . . to catch the witch."

This brought a twinkle to his dark eyes.

So Daisy told him what she'd accomplished so far.

The *pitukupf* listened with considerable attention, occasionally nodding, and this pleased the teller of the tale.

And then she told him exactly what she had in mind to do.

The dwarf's eyes widened in astonishment. He shook his head, making sinuous waves in the stream of pipe smoke. He began to speak to the shaman. He spoke in a very old version of the Ute tongue, so it was necessary for Daisy to listen very closely.

She agreed with what she heard. Yes, of course, witches were dangerous. And unpredictable. A person did have to be awfully careful. My, he sounded like her mother when Daisy was a child, warning her little daughter about all the dangers and difficulties she'd encounter in this hard life. But Mamma had warned her about ordinary hazards. Like rattlesnakes and owls. Lying men and alcohol. Electricity and motor cars.

But the dwarf, now waving his clay pipe in his hand, was speaking in strange riddles. Some of the oldest Ute words, she could not understand. But Daisy caught this much: he said peculiar things about . . . tiny bones . . . tumbled stones . . . an empty tomb. They were vague phrases, yet filled with sinister warning. This path she had set out on was a crooked one. It would be best if she repented of this daring plan to catch a witch. It would be the wise thing to do.

Daisy thanked him with exaggerated praise. The *pitukupf* who lived in *Cañon del Espiritu*, she said, was known among all the People for his wisdom. It was a wise person who took his advice.

But the shaman made no promises.

When Daisy Perika awakened, her aged limbs were stiff. Her bones felt brittle, like branches on a tree long dead. The sun was low in the sky, resting on the broad shoulder of the largest of the Three Sisters. The old woman stretched, yawned, and rubbed her hands together to encourage circulation. She braced her back on the piñon, and used the digging stick to push herself erect. Daisy removed the herb basket from the branch and hung it over her elbow. This visit with the *pitukupf* had been very strange. But then, they usually were. The little man generally told her something, but she often didn't understand exactly what he'd meant until much later. When it was too late for his information to be of any help. But this time, he'd been fairly direct in his warning. What it boiled down to was "Don't mess with witches." Good advice, she had to admit.

She limped away toward home, feeling dreadfully old and weary. The dwarf, peculiar little fellow, might be a thousand years old. Or maybe the *pitukupf* was as old as creation itself. Nowadays, most of the People had taken up the thinking of the *matukach*—they didn't believe the little man existed. But hadn't she seen him with her own eyes? And didn't the *pitukupf* already have the gifts she'd left at the entrance to his underground home? Of course he did. So he was as genuine as the three pueblo sisters sitting up there on the sandstone mesa, as real as the warm earth under her feet. Of course, Charlie Moon—that overgrown smart-aleck—he would believe it was all just an old woman's dream. She could imagine what the tribal policeman would say if she told him the tale of this visit with the little man. "Go back where you were, Aunt Daisy, and you'll see that the pocketknife and the tobacco are still there on the ground by the badger hole—right where you left them."

For just a moment, she thought about looking back. She even paused in her stride.

To know the answer all she need do was glance over her shoulder.

So straightforward a task it was.

So convoluted in its implications.

But to look back and verify that the gifts had been removed by the *pitukupf*, she knew, would show disrespect to the little man—even question his very existence.

Anyhow, there wasn't any need to do it. *The little folding knife and the tobacco sack can't still be where I left 'em. I've been inside the home of the dwarf. I've seen what I've seen, and I know what I know.* The *pitukupf* had the tobacco sack right there in his shirt pocket, the folding-knife in his hand. She boiled with fury at Charlie Moon. *That big jughead is always butting into my business, making trouble for me, even when he ain't here!*

The Ute elder clenched her jaw in stubborn determination. She set her face toward the mouth of *Cañon del Espiritu*, and home.

And never looked back.

She had better things to do . . .

The elderly woman had almost everything she needed, but there was one last item. She'd searched high and low for such a long time. Finally, here it was, in a shoe box with a bunch of other odds and ends. A heavy rubber band.

She stretched it . . . it did not break.

CHAPTER 9

Charlie Moon was at his desk. He used a ballpoint pen to fill out an arrest form on Jackknife. This was not the old Ute's real name. He had been given the moniker after a spectacular accident back in those days when he worked for a trucking firm out of Albuquerque. He was no longer employed as a driver of semis. But Jackknife had his own GMC flatbed truck, on which he hauled such things as bales of hay and stacks of lumber which he did not bother to tie down. On this particular day, he had been driving exceedingly fast in a thirty-five-mile-an-hour zone. Worse still, he'd been taking his half of the road directly out of the middle. The double yellow line he'd been straddling had been painted on the blacktop because of the blind curve. Jackknife had met an Ignacio school bus on this hairpin—and angrily shook his fist at the terrified driver—who'd opted for the ditch. Except for a few scratches and some bruises, the kids and driver were unharmed.

279

Moon had been called to the scene by a passing motorist who had a cellular telephone in her Audi. It hadn't been hard to make the arrest. The furious driver of the school bus was the old man's niece. Her statement to the policeman was delivered through gritted teeth: "If you want him alive, Charlie Moon, you better find him before I do."

Moon had assured her that he would.

The Ute policeman had found Jackknife's pickup parked at Tillie's Navajo Bar and Grille. The inebriated man was arguing with Tillie. The thickset *matukach* woman had refused to serve him a beer, and was relieved to see the Ute policeman's tall form fill her doorway. Would Moon please remove this Jackknife person from the premises before she felt compelled to hit the foulmouthed old fool right between his beady eyes with a long-necked beer bottle?

Moon had assured her that he would.

The old Ute, confronted by the lawman, claimed the damn school bus had practically run him off the road. But Jackknife, who was a forgiving and magnanimous soul, was willing to live and let live. He'd offered to buy Moon a beer. Moon had politely declined, and raised the charge of reckless driving. Jackknife, straddling a bar stool, swore he hadn't even seen the school bus coming around the curve. Why? "Because I'm blind in one eye and can't hardly see outta the other."

Moon had asked the old man to leave the bar and accompany him to SUPD headquarters where he would be provided with bed and breakfast while this thing was sorted out.

Jackknife politely declined the offer. Would Charlie like to hear a good joke?

Moon had shaken his head. The policeman explained that while he generally appreciated a joke, he wasn't in quite the mood for humor.

Jackknife was quite unmoved by the policeman's remarks. What, the besotted old man had asked the policeman, is yellow, has black rubber tires, and lays on its back in a ditch? From

Moon's bemused expression, the drunk assumed that the cop had no idea. Why a dead school bus, Jackknife said. He laughed until interrupted by a fit of wheezing and coughing.

Under the circumstances, Moon had not appreciated the punch line. And Tillie, who had fire in her eye, was wielding a long-neck bottle like a club.

Jackknife, whom the big Ute carried to the Blazer by the seat of his britches, was now curled up on a bunk in the SUPD jug. Snoring like thunder and slobbering on his chin. It wasn't the first time he'd been hauled in on similar charges. They couldn't pull his drivers' license. He had none. As soon as the old man woke up, a junior SUPD officer would drive him home. The Southern Ute Tribe was tired of providing room and board for this man who was an embarrassment to the People.

Word had been quietly passed from the tribal chairman to Chief of Police Roy Severo. "The issue of Jackknife must be settled, once and for all."

Roy Severo had grinned at the chairman . . . did the tribal leaders want him killed?

The response was solemn and hesitant. Well . . . no. Not just yet, anyway. But if Jackknife caused any more mischief on the public highways, the council might be looking for a new chief of police.

The current chief of police had passed the word to Charlie Moon. Loudly. "I want that dumb horse's ass off the road before he kills somebody. You understand what I mean?"

Charlie Moon had understood. Jackknife would not be hauling hay on his old GMC flatbed for quite some time. If ever.

Before he had left the parking lot in front of Tillie's Navajo Bar and Grille, the Ute policeman had removed several essential items from under the hood of Jackknife's truck.

The carburetor.

The distributor.

The high voltage coil.

Most of the ignition wiring . . . and a few other odds and ends.

Already, he'd passed the word around to the local repair shops. Anyone who repaired the old man's disabled truck would be asked to personally explain to Officer Moon why such action was deemed to be in the best interests of the community. It was a polite request that was certain to be understood. Jackknife would have to get his old truck towed a long way from La Plata County to find a mechanic who'd replace all the parts Moon had thrown into the landfill. Because Jackknife could not afford a tow truck— or the mechanical repairs—he would be using his feet for transportation. But he'd have to be careful about walking along the highway. His niece swore that first chance she got she'd run him down with the school bus. The small children she transported were both pleased and excited by the prospect.

But now, there was a report to file on Jackknife's latest offense. Moon, who did not have a happy relationship with the department's sullen computer, scrawled on a yellow pad. Thus occupied, the policeman did not see his visitor enter his office, nor hear her footsteps. She wore no fragrance.

He felt her presence.

Moon looked up.

Delly attempted a smile. "Hi, Charlie."

Warily, he scooted backward in the chair.

She looked meekly at the floor. "I hope you're not mad at me . . ."

"Hmmph," he said.

"I came to apologize."

He leaned back in his swivel chair; it creaked. "I guess you didn't much like my choice in doctors."

"Well, Charlie, it wasn't nice of you to take me to a veterinarian. It's not like I'm an *animal* or something."

It was too easy; he let it pass. "Amundsen was close by. Besides, he's a pretty good surgeon."

She frowned at the battered top of his government surplus

desk, and ran her finger across the uneven pine grain. "I was upset, 'cause I thought you'd done it as some kind of a dumb joke . . . making me think he was a real doctor. You shouldn't have treated me that way, Charlie. I'd never lie to you."

"It wasn't a joke, " he said wearily, "and I didn't lie. I never told you Amundsen was anything he wasn't."

"Well," Delly said brightly, "let's put it all behind us."

"Oh, I don't know." Moon rubbed the place where she'd slammed her sharp little fist into his gut. Below the belt, he reminded himself. "As a sworn officer of the law, I don't generally condone violence."

She stamped her foot. "But you've *got* to forgive me, Charlie Moon."

He managed a hurt expression. "It ain't that easy. Not when a girl's told you to close your eyes so's she can undress a little bit . . . and then when you're not lookin' she hits you . . . well . . ."

She was close to tears. "But, Charlie, I *said* I was sorry—what more do you want?"

He furrowed his brow and stared at the ceiling. "Well . . . I guess there is one thing you could do."

"Tell me."

"You could buy me something."

She rolled her eyes. "Buy you what?"

He told her.

She offered him her hand across the desk. "It's a deal."

Moon, inordinately pleased with himself, got up. He took her small hand in his and flashed a wide grin. Who said there was no free lunch?

It was an unhappy coincidence that on this particular morning, Myra Cornstone had also decided to make amends with Charlie Moon.

It was partly because she'd heard some gossip about him and Delly Sands having some kind of a falling-out. But mostly because she missed him so bad that it hurt. Myra had already called the SUPD dispatcher, and Nancy Beyal had assured her that this was Moon's day to spend at the station. He'd jailed old Jackknife again, and had a ton of paperwork to do. On the short drive from her grandfather's house to Ignacio, Myra had rehearsed just what she'd do and say when she got to the police station. She'd pretend that nothing bad had happened. Charlie, who couldn't possibly have understood the reasons for her hurt feelings, would buy it. The big buffalo would figure she'd just had one of those mysterious "female problems" and was all better now. He was *so* dumb about women.

After they talked a bit, she'd invite him to lunch—her treat. No matter how busy Charlie was, an invitation to a free meal always managed to break him loose. They'd drop by Angel's Cafe and have some laughs. Maybe he'd tell her something about his investigation of Hooper Antelope's death. Sure. Before long, things would be like they used to be. Before Delly Sands came back to the reservation and started wagging her little butt around Charlie. Like a bitch in heat.

Myra was a hundred yards from the SUPD building when she saw Charlie Moon leaving the police station. With someone hanging on his arm like Virginia creeper on a fence post. The young woman's fingers went numb on the steering wheel . . . her thoughts began to drift into the fantasy world of denial. Maybe this wasn't real . . . maybe this was someone else.

No.

There was not another Ute policeman nearly as tall as Charlie Moon. But who was that woman? Maybe only one of his cousins come to visit . . . Myra slowed the Japanese pickup and leaned forward to peer through the sandblasted windshield. The Virginia creeper was Delly Sands. She was laughing gaily at something the policeman was saying. They looked so happy together.

Well damn the both of you!

She spat the words through clenched teeth: "I hope you *die*."

Tears blinded Myra's eyes. She stomped her little foot onto the accelerator pedal.

Dr. Amundsen sat in the darkening room. It was late afternoon. A mild breeze played with lace-edged curtains at the parlor windows. Furthermore, he could hear the trilling serenade of a mockingbird in the enormous maple that shaded his front porch. But did either the whimsical breeze or the twilight serenade bring pleasure to him? They did not. Creeping doubts about the professional risk he'd taken gnawed at the veterinarian's vitals. He reached for a crystal decanter and spilled inexpensive port into a thin-stemmed glass. The decanter was almost empty. It had been full only an hour earlier. He took a long sip, licked his lips, and contemplated the errors of his ways. Professional and otherwise.

He did not immediately hear the rapping on his front door. Presently, the persistent knocking became loud enough to penetrate his dark reverie. He grunted his displeasure, got up from the leather easy chair, and ambled down the dim hallway.

He opened the door. There on his porch, stood the embodiment of his recent nightmares. He gaped at this apparition for a moment, then opened his mouth. No words came out.

"Hello—Dr. Amundsen?" Delly Sands thought he looked different in the daylight. Older. And tired. And he smelled like he'd been tipping the bottle.

He stared at her blankly, then closed his eyes. Maybe this was a bad dream. Maybe she would go away. He opened one eye to take a peek. Damn. She was still there.

"It's me. Your patient." She smiled prettily, showing a set of perfect teeth. "You surely haven't forgotten what you did for me?"

The smile looked like a sneer to the veterinarian. And the little teeth looked sharp . . . like a Gila monster's. He gulped. And wished he had the decanter of wine in his mitt. He'd down what was left in one swallow.

She rubbed at her shoulder. "I came back to—"

"Thing you gotta understand," he interrupted with a dismissive wave of his hand, "it was all Charlie Moon's damnfool idea . . . he claimed it was an emergency. I didn't want nothing to do with any such goings-on, and I told him so. Surgery on humans is something I'm not licensed to do. But no, he had to have his way."

"Look," she said, "I know all about it and you don't—"

He wiped his hand over his eyes. "Charlie Moon made me do it."

"Charlie was in a hurry to have the pellet removed. He didn't want to drive me all the way to Durango, so he stopped off here instead." She reached out to pat his hand reassuringly. "I came back to see what I owe you. And so you could take the stitches out. I know you're not a real doctor and it's okay." She'd thought this would please him.

He glared at her. *Not a real doctor?* Indeed. He leaned close to her face. "Listen, my misinformed young lady, as a skilled veterinarian my training is extensive beyond your wildest dreams. I am required to have expertise in the treatment of dozens of animal species. Not just dogs and cats and horses and cattle. I am called upon to mend the wings of hawk and eagle, to tend the broken bones of weasel and raccoon, to repair the spine of snake and lizard, and furthermore . . ." words temporarily failed him. "Whereas," he wagged one stubby finger before her face, "your so-called *real doctors* need study only one member of the family of anthropoids. And at that, most of them specialize. Hmmpff. Skin doctors, foot doctors, eye doctors," he waved his hands in disdain, "my word, what an easy life *they* have."

"I'm sorry, I didn't mean to—"

"I would have much preferred that Charlie Moon take you to see one of your *real doctors*. In fact, I tried very hard to persuade him to take you to the E.R. at Mercy Hospital." Amundsen sighed. "But Moon was afraid that you'd find out that . . ." Even through the alcoholic fog, he managed to catch his tongue. But not quite in time.

She frowned suspiciously at the flustered man. "Just what was Charlie Moon afraid I'd find out?"

He backed into the doorway, palms outward as if to protect himself. "I can't say, young lady. Now really, Charlie would have my . . ."

Delly doubled up her hands into tiny fists; she took a threatening step forward.

Her eyes were like little black beads. Lizard's eyes, he thought.

"Dr. Amundsen—you don't need to be concerned about what Charlie Moon might do."

His stuttered reply was hopeful. "N—no?"

"No. It's *me* you should be afraid of." Delly tapped her little fist on his broad chest. "Now talk to me. Before I start to make some serious trouble."

For a moment, he hesitated. Charlie Moon wouldn't like it if he spilled his guts to this pint-sized woman. But those little lizard eyes burned a hole in his soul.

So he talked.

About how the Ute policeman had brought him a little chunk of lead to show the patient. About a piece of something he'd removed from her shoulder. No. Not a lead pellet. A small cylinder. Sort of yellowish-white. Looked like it might have been fashioned of ivory. Or maybe bone.

"Bone?" she whispered.

Yes. Quite possibly bone. And no, he couldn't show it to her. He'd given that peculiar object to Officer Moon.

When he finished talking, Amundsen felt an enormous sense of relief. Surely she understood. He'd only tried to help in an emergency. A police emergency.

As she turned and walked away from the porch, Delly Sands could barely feel her feet touching the earth. But she finally understood why Charlie Moon hadn't taken her to the emergency room at Mercy Hospital . . . why he'd brought her to this veterinary surgeon. The policeman and this silly old man had both taken a big risk. All for her sake . . . so that she might be safe from certain knowledge. Knowledge which has the power to kill. She fumbled with the Toyota door, slid inside, and sat there, staring through the bug-spotted windshield at the lovely pastoral scene surrounding Amundsen's home. Seeing nothing. It took a few minutes for the young woman to come to grips with the dreadful implications of what she'd learned. Her shoulder, which hadn't hurt for days, began to throb as if she'd been stung by a black wasp. She knew what the pain was, of course.

The presence of evil.

The Sandman was playing the host. Dinner was in the oven. Now, the wine. Larry Sands was both pleased and flattered to have a visit from Winston Steele—a smart fellow, who knew how to wring success out of this dreary world. Steele was a world-class Sun-Dancer. A successful physician, raking in the big bucks. And that blond fox—now wasn't she something to look at? Face like one of those gals on *Baywatch*. And what a pair of legs. And that wasn't all.

Larry Sands was carrying a lacquered Japanese tray from his small kitchen to the parlor when the telephone warbled. "Now who'n hell can that be," he glanced apologetically at Steele and the blond nymph. "This'll just take a minute."

He jammed the receiver against his ear. "Yeah?" It was his sister. The Sandman groaned. "If you forgot some of your stuff, I'll bring it by your place tomorrow."

"We've got to talk, Larry."

"Look, Sis, I got some important people here and—"

"This is important."

The Sandman grinned at his guests. Imitating an amiable brother who was in the habit of humoring his lunatic sister, he balanced the phone on his shoulder. "So what's up?"

Delly took a deep breath. "Larry . . . I'm going to publish a story in next week's *Drum*."

"Great," he said, "I hope you get a Pulitzer." He hesitated. "What's your story about?"

"It's about . . . about the witch who killed Hooper Antelope."

Her brother managed a dry chuckle. "Hell, Sis, that's just tribal gossip. Anyway, what do you know about that bullshit that Charlie Moon don't already know?"

"In my story," Delly said with grim deliberation, "I'll name the person responsible for Hooper Antelope's death."

The silence that followed was heavy. Like being underwater.

Charlie Moon was cruising through the narrow side streets of Ignacio, paying particular attention to those neighborhoods where the Utes lived. Of all the aspects of police work on the checkerboard reservation, he found night patrols to be the most desirable. For one thing, it was generally a quiet, uneventful duty. Gave a man time away from the artificial busy-ness of the daytime. Gave him time to think. And these days, the Ute policeman was thinking about the upcoming Sun Dance. And about somebody who imagined he was a witch. And was convinced he could steal a dancer's power by some kind of hocus-pocus. Like shooting his victim with a pellet fashioned of dead man's bone. It was a crazy notion. But if the dancer believed in such stuff—and every dancer was a mystic of sorts—then the witch had the power to destroy. If Hooper Antelope had been free of the fear of witches, he'd be alive today. Even Delly Sands, though she was intelligent and well-educated, was a potential victim of this *brujo*.

Charlie Moon realized that he had to do something.

But how did you catch a witch? And even if you caught him, how could you prosecute? It was different in the old days. When the land was ruled by the Native Americans, there had been brutal and effective ways of dealing with those who cast spells. The Spaniards had been kindred spirits with the People, and their legal system had specific means for dealing with those who practiced the dark crafts. Both systems had, quite naturally, led to excesses. If you had an enemy, declare him a practitioner of witchcraft. A fearful, unjust society would do the rest. Many innocents had died or suffered permanent exile as a result.

Everything changed when the English-speaking Americans had moved westward. The whites were marked forever by their tragic Salem experience. The American legal code did not recognize the existence of witchcraft. But the *matukach* were quite prepared to deal with those who punished "witches." It had, in Charlie Moon's considered opinion, been a great step forward. The only solution was to stamp out the superstition. Laugh at the "witches," they'll go away.

This is what he'd thought.

Moon slowed as he passed by a small apartment complex. This was where Delly Sands lived. And then he noticed the Cadillac in the parking lot. Two men were in the front seat. Talking excitedly. One waving his hands. The other nervously patting the steering wheel. Probably didn't mean a thing . . . a couple of guys arguing about sports or politics . . . but it didn't smell right. Moon cut his headlights and coasted to a stop behind a cluster of lilac bushes. He unscrewed the lamp from the dome light and dropped it into the ashtray. The Ute lawman got out of the SUPD Blazer and walked along a picket fence that bordered the parking lot. When he had a clear view of the Caddy, he paused. Moon removed a portable radio transceiver from the canvas holster on his belt. He pressed the transmit button.

"Nancy, you there?"

The dispatcher answered immediately. "Sure, Charlie. What's up?"

"Run this plate for me." He gave her the license number. "Yellow Cadillac. Looks brand-new."

"Ten-four. Give me a couple of minutes."

Moon waited patiently.

Two minutes passed.

Then three.

The squelch sizzled on the transceiver. "Dispatcher calling Officer Moon."

"Yeah?"

"You got a Cadillac Seville. Sold by a dealer in Denver to a

Dr. Winston Steele just this spring. No wants, no warrants on the Cadillac. Except for a couple of speeding violations, Steele has a clean record. You need anything else, Charlie?"

"Nope."

The Ute policeman stuffed the transceiver into its holster. Interesting. Dr. Steele was scheduled to participate in next week's Southern Ute Sun Dance. Moon already knew that the man was registered at the Sky Ute Lodge. His blond girlfriend was stashed in an adjoining room. So why was Steele sitting here in the parking lot by Delly Sands' apartment building? And who was that fellow in the Caddy with him?

The last question was answered almost immediately. The dome light on the Cadillac flashed on. Larry Sands pushed the passenger-side door open; he slammed it and looked up toward his sister's second-floor apartment. Winston Steele got out of the driver's side.

Moon watched them climb the outside stairs to the second level. There was a brief discussion, then the Sandman pressed the doorbell.

Delly opened the door. A few words were exchanged. The two men stepped inside. She shut the door. And that was that.

The Ute policeman relaxed. So Larry Sands had brought his Sun-Dancer buddy on a visit to see his sister. And neither the Sandman or the *matukach* doctor were doing anything suspicious. So it would be appropriate for a responsible police officer to move on. And keep his nose out of Delly's family business. That's what a sensible lawman would do. Charlie Moon found himself a comfortable spot under a Russian olive, and sat down. He leaned against the trunk and watched the apartment. This might take a long time. He watched the shadows of someone in Delly's apartment—it was one of the men—moving back and forth. Arms waving. He thought he could hear voices raised, but the muffled sounds might have come from any of a dozen apartments. Might be a good idea to "drop in" on Delly. Just to make sure everything was all right.

Moon was getting to his feet when the apartment door opened. Steele exited first, followed by Larry Sands, who turned to shout at his sister. Moon caught some of the words: ". . . You'll be damn sorry . . . Don't say I didn't warn . . ."

Within seconds, the pair of men slammed the Caddy's heavy doors. Steele kicked up gravel as he left the parking lot.

Moon thought about following the Cadillac. But that wasn't necessary. He could pick them up if the need arose. He stood under the Russian olive and watched Delly Sands's apartment. It was late. Sooner or later, she'd turn out the lights. And go to bed. Then, he'd leave.

He waited almost an hour.

Finally, she turned out the lights. But Delly Sands did not go to bed. She opened the apartment door, hurried down the stairs, and almost ran to her little Toyota.

Moon hurried to his Blazer and started the engine.

Father Raes Delfino was reading, for the tenth time, *The Wind in the Willows*. The Catholic priest loved these tales of Badger and Rat and Toad. As he read them late into the evenings, he fantasized that he had been assigned to a quiet country church in a rural English village. Life would be so simple . . . so sweet. This is what the good priest was thinking when someone rapped on his door. He quickly placed the children's book under a magazine and hurried to see who had come to visit so long after dark. Probably the parent of a sick child, requesting prayer. Or a poor woman attempting to escape a husband who had come home drunk and abusive. Or maybe a member of the altar guild with a question about the budget for flowers. Certainly it would not be Daisy Perika with one of her theological questions meant to stump him. That pesky old woman tended to stay home after dark. Thank God for such blessings.

The priest opened the door.

A young woman was on the rectory porch.

He adjusted his spectacles. "Yes?"

"It's me, Father Raes. Delly Sands."

"Oh, my," he beamed upon his guest, ". . . our little angel. You were quite a smash at the church play." He stepped aside. "Do come in. I'll fix you a cup of tea."

"Don't have time. Please—I just want to leave something with you." She fumbled in her purse, produced a manila envelope and pressed it into his hand.

"My dear young lady, I don't quite understand—"

"Please," she said, "just take it."

He nodded graciously. It would be a donation. Members of his flock—even total strangers—stopped by at the oddest times to offer their gifts. To cover guilt for some secret sin. Or to offer thanks for unexpected good fortune. The priest was well aware that Miss Sands had recently landed a good job with the *Southern Ute Drum*.

"Are you quite certain you don't have time to come in and—"

"Not right now . . . I'm in kind of a hurry, Father." She turned and he heard the clatter of her shoes on the porch steps.

And then she was gone. Into the darkness.

"Well," he said. But there was nothing to do but close the door.

He absentmindedly tossed the envelope onto his desk. Whatever it was, it could wait until the morrow. The priest plopped into his comfortable chair, grabbed the novel about animals who walked and talked like men, and immediately realized that he'd forgotten to use a bookmark. He'd lost his place in the tale of the terrible Toad's misadventures. He began to fret.

"Blast," he growled.

A good mouth-filling oath was an effective release for the passions.

Eventually, Father Raes found the page. He settled back to enjoy the tale. Within a minute, the priest was lost in another world.

There was a knock on the door. The priest tossed *Wind in the Willows* aside and ground his teeth. "Blast," he said again. "Double blast." She must be back again. Probably wanted her blasted envelope. Well, she could have it!

He fairly flung the door open. A very tall man, dressed in black, was standing on the porch, hat in hand. Only his face was easily visible. "Charlie Moon?"

The Ute policeman nodded. "That's what they call me."

"I didn't expect to see you. I thought it was someone else returning . . ."

"Delly Sands maybe?"

The Jesuit's tone was mildly sarcastic. "You're prescient."

The face smiled, showing a brief flash of white. "If you say so."

"Forgive me for being somewhat snide, but I am not at all pleased to have the police keeping an account of my visitors."

"It's nothing official, Father. I'm a friend of Delly's. Kind of looking out for her interests."

"If you say so."

Moon chuckled. Father Raes was a good egg.

The good egg sighed. "Do come in, Charlie. I'll brew you a cup of tea."

"Thanks anyway, Father. I really don't have the time."

"It seems that everyone is in a hurry on this evening."

"About Delly—I just wondered whether—"

"You wish to know the nature of Miss Sands' business in visiting the rectory."

"Ahhh . . . Yeah." The priest had a way of cutting right to the bone.

"Forget it."

"Well . . . I . . . uh . . ."

"Charlie, you know quite well that my business with members of this parish is strictly confidential. Now either come in so I can close the door, or leave me in peace."

The Ute policeman jammed his black Stetson down to his ears. "Well, I guess I'll be movin' along."

The weary priest settled himself into the chair. He counted to ten, to relax his nerves. He reached for the wonderful book. And realized that, once more, he'd been in such a hurry to answer the door that he'd forgotten to mark his place. He clenched his hands into fists. "Double and triple blast!"

It didn't help.

He got up and paced the floor. He removed a rosary from his jacket pocket. He counted the black wooden beads and recited a long series of prayers. This, thank God, always brought peace to his soul. Within minutes, the priest had calmed down. Perhaps a glass of milk, then to bed. Yes, that was just the ticket. And then he remembered the thing Miss Sands had left in his care. And the policeman's interest in said young lady. Father Raes found it on his desk. He turned it over and stared in no little astonishment. Nine words were written on the manila envelope.

TO BE OPENED IN THE EVENT OF MY DEATH

As Charlie Moon pulled out of the graveled parking lot and drove away from the rectory, his thoughts were completely occupied with Delly Sands. Why, an hour after the visit from Dr. Winston Steele and her brother, had she hurried off to visit the parish priest? And what was in the envelope she'd left with Father Raes Delfino? If the policeman's thoughts had not been thus occupied, Moon might have noticed that another person had taken an interest in Delly Sands. And in Charlie Moon.

The solitary observer is immersed in the inky shadows of a blue spruce. He watches the Ute policeman depart from the rectory. The one who watches is in no hurry to leave. He does nothing in haste. To purchase success, one must spend time.

Patience is one of his chief virtues.

And thus cloaked by darkness, he lingers. And thinks his meandering thoughts. His fingers are cold . . . his mouth dry. He rubs his hands together. Ahhh . . . should have brought some coffee. But a cigarette would be just the thing. He presses the chrome-plated cigar lighter into the dashboard receptacle. A current of electrons moves through the nichrome ribbon coiled inside the lighter . . . tiny streams of ions ebb and flow through the synapses in his brain. Electrons agitate and heat the metallic molecules . . . ionic particles beneath his skull perturb and warm the imagination . . .

And the temperature rises.

Still, he waits. Delaying an action until the appropriate moment is the kernel of wisdom. And his lifelong habit.

At the appropriate moment, the cigar lighter—its business end glowing red—pops halfway out of the dashboard receptacle. Unhurriedly, he presses the searing metal against the tip of an unfiltered cigarette. He inhales deeply and sighs, exhaling a lungful of smoke to billow against the windshield. He ponders the rumors he's heard floating around the cafes of Ignacio . . . and the imponderable mysteries that lie before him. But unlike Charlie Moon, he harbors no doubts about what this budding journalist is up to. And his interest in the young woman is not driven by a concern for her safety.

Quite the contrary.

The pellet of dead man's bone did not kill her, and that is baffling. But when one method fails . . . there is always another. On the seat beside him, rolled up in an oily cloth, is a .17-caliber air pistol. At this moment, it is loaded with a conventional lead pellet.

Tonight, he will not go to his bed. It would be impossible to sleep. Instead, he will sit on the bank of the Pinos. There are many trees there. And in one of these trees, there is sure to be an owl. He will sit underneath such a tree . . . and listen to the mournful call of that feathered messenger of death. And make his preparations for this season's final Sun Dance.

CHAPTER 10

The Dance

In the choppy Uto-Aztecan tongue of the *Nuuci*, it is called *Tãgu—Wuñ*, which means Thirsty Stand. This annual ceremonial is a most solemn occasion; a time of fasting, sacrifice, and prayer. The invocation for this particular time of dancing thirsty—given in a dream to Lila Blacksnow, youngest daughter of the Sun Dance chief—is this:

Great Spirit of Our Grandfathers—Creator of Worlds—Be With Us

The site of the Southern Ute Sun Dance lies a few miles north of Ignacio. It is situated in a broad, flat valley dotted with piñon, juniper, and tumbleweed. During the winter months, the earth at this place is covered with a heavy blanket of ice-encrusted snow. Shrill winds roar off the mountains and torture the twisted trees. In February, this is a field of bone-chilling cold. It is said that even the spirits avoid this frigid plain.

In July, this is a place of gritty dust and humming whirlwinds . . . and insatiable thirst. And perhaps—for one or two souls—a place to taste the Power. And the glory.

For the convenience of those who come to witness the sacred event, the earth has been partially cleared of brush and weeds. And many will come. This site is much easier to get to than the remote site on Sleeping Ute Mountain. They will come in groups of two or three, and as families. A few will come alone. They will arrive in shiny new automobiles, in creaky pickup trucks with leaky mufflers, in expensive chrome-plated campers outfitted with air conditioners and color television.

In the approximate center of the Sun Dance grounds is the circular corral. The single opening to the brush structure faces—as tradition demands—toward the east. Where the sun comes from. The seasoned dancers have taken up honored positions on the west side of the Sun Dance Lodge . . . to greet the sun at each rising.

The drummers and the singer sit just inside the corral on the south side of the entrance; here they will have a little shade from the porous wall of willow branches. There will also be a place for spectators to sit inside the corral near the entrance, but on the north side—with the sun in their faces. These curious souls, their eyes protected behind tinted glass, will generally not endure more than a few hours of the ordeal. But as they depart, their places will be quickly taken by others anxious to witness this peculiar spectacle of suffering.

A large proportion of those who come to watch the dance will not be Native Americans. Most of these will be of those pale-skinned people the Ute call the *matukach*.

Why do they come to this place—these folk who live in small towns, in quiet suburbs, in busy cities? What brings the professors of psychology, the plumbers of pipes, the practitioners of poetry to this archaic ceremony? Why is it, that behind their bland expressions of polite interest in this event, this dance makes them shiver inside, and savor an unsettling but delicious sense of both fear and longing?

It is this. To even the most sophisticated, the most civilized, Dancing Thirsty is a ritual that clenches at the very gut. It whispers to the elemental essence of the animal and awakens shadowy half-memories of forgotten ancestors . . . unnamed tribes . . . roaming dark Celtic forests . . . braving bone-chilling winds on barren Asian Steppes . . . spilling captives' blood on altars of graven stone . . . crossing rolling seas in boats of birch and mammoth skin . . . of lands and people nevermore. These urbane citizens witness the dance in the sun to hear the shrill call of the bone whistle . . . to look upon the tree decorated with mysterious ribbons and painted stripes. All hint of dark connections to a time and people that history never knew. Ages barely hinted at in relics of flaked stone and chiseled bone . . . and blood-red handprints on walls of stone.

Most of the Utes know how to behave at a Sun Dance. For those few who do not—and for the benefit of visitors to the reservation—the "rules of good manners and decorum" are published in the *Southern Ute Drum*.

Drugs and alcohol are prohibited on the Sun Dance grounds.

No cameras, tape recorders, metal chairs, food, or water are allowed in the Medicine Lodge area.

Do not stand in the entrance to the corral; a clear passage to the Medicine Lodge must remain open. Do not enter or exit the corral while the drum is going.

No dogs or motorcycles allowed. They distract the dancers.

Children are not allowed to play near the corral at any time.

Dress should reflect reverence for the dance. No halters, swim suits, perfumes, or shiny objects that may distract the dancers.

Men who have become fathers within the past two months cannot dance.

Women who are menstruating, pregnant, or who have had a child within the past two months must not enter the corral.

Except for a very few, those who come will abide by the rules set down by the chief of the dance. It is true that a few noisy children will play outside the corral. Some young men will bring six-packs of cold beer, but they will stay well away from the Medicine Lodge and out of sight of the Southern Ute Police. One elderly Ute woman will break several rules with brazen unconcern. She will bring her folding metal chair. And sit in the entrance to the sacred corral.

And these are the least of the infractions that Daisy Perika will commit.

Because this is the high country—where even July mornings are frigid—the fiery trial will begin with a chill that causes men to shiver and relish that last cup of steaming coffee.

Darkness covers the Sun Dance Lodge; blankets cover the dancers. There are fewer participants this summer than most. Those Utes who stayed away had many reasons. And excuses.

"A muscle spasm in my back . . . can't walk more'n a few steps."

"A sick wife who needs watching after. Got the flu, I guess."

"A bad head cold. Head feels big as a basketball."

Not one of them, of course, mention Hooper Antelope's death. Or a fear of witchcraft. These are modern Americans.

The hard-faced Sioux is here, of course—at the west side of the corral where the experienced dancers gather. Wasn't he afraid he'd end up like poor old Hooper Antelope? This man from the Dakotas fears neither man nor beast . . . perhaps not even those supposed practitioners of the dark arts. But Stone Pipe firmly refuses to discuss the subject of witchcraft. Bad luck, he says.

Winston Steele is sitting at the left hand of Stone Pipe. The *matukach* dancer—perhaps to make a point—has taken his place beside this stony-faced Sioux who does not bother to conceal his distaste for all white men. And especially for this blue-eyed devil who has the effrontery to participate in a sacred ritual that should be reserved for Native Americans. But Winston Steele will not acknowledge the presence of the Sioux. Except in this manner: he is determined to pace him step-for-step at dancing thirsty. And, if possible, to outlast him.

On the opposite side of the *matukach* dancer from the Sioux is Delly Sands' brother. The Sandman's face has a hollow-eyed, haunted expression. There is much speculation that he is ill . . . or hung over from a bout with drugs and alcohol . . . or frightened that he may suffer the same fate that ended the life of Hooper Antelope. But like the Sioux, Larry Sands does not care to speak of witches.

The Kiowa drummers—accustomed to the lesser altitudes— mutter among themselves about this accursed high country where even summer nights can freeze a man's . . . extremities. They rub their hands together briskly.

The old Paiute singer has arrived at the corral after a hearty breakfast of scrambled eggs, fried bread, and sweetened black coffee. In his mind, he goes over the list of songs he will sing. He hopes the drummers can keep the rhythm . . . but you know the Kiowa.

The Sun Dance chief stands in the entrance to the brush corral. At this moment, Willy Blacksnow has two duties.

He waits for the morning.

He is guardian of the sacred tree.

The Utes have stripped the cottonwood of bark. Tied in a fork of the tree is a thick sheaf of willow branches. The fork is also crowned with four satin ribbons. The colors of the ribbons represent the four cardinal directions—and the four races of the world. The colors are red . . . white . . . yellow . . . and blue. At the waist of the tree are three belts of paint. The upper ring is white for Day. In the center is a black ring; this represents Night. Supporting Night and Day is a circle of deep red. This is the color of Earth.

The Sun Dance chief bows his head and closes his eyes. He mutters a brief prayer and crosses himself. To this Christian, the cottonwood post is a symbol of that Tree of Life which blossoms forever . . . and of that grim tree between the thieves where the Redeemer of the world was nailed. He mutters a prayer of thanks for the ultimate sacrifice made by the Great Mysterious One— whose Word became flesh and walked among us.

Now, he turns to face the east. He can see that first sign of the hills awakening from slumber . . . the sweet promise of a new day. It grows slowly, this diffuse radiance. The warmth of dawn spreads across the horizon . . . resting like a downy shawl upon the massive shoulders of the mountains named for the beloved disciple. Presently, over the stark profile of the San Juans, the source of the light appears. For the briefest of moments this silver scythe explodes into fire on the crown of a pine-studded ridge called Black Mule. Above the broad valley of the Pinos, the misty substance of a long sliver of drifting cloud is illuminated . . . and becomes a feather of glistening gold.

The chief of the Southern Ute Sun Dance, who has been eagerly anticipating this first moment of day, stands at the entrance of the brush enclosure and faces his warm friend . . . his cruel adversary. His is a long shadow; it slithers like a black lizard's ghost across the bare earth . . . to touch the pale flesh of the cottonwood planted in the center of the sacred circle.

As the earth turns, he waits. Squinting at the dawn. Watching the disk of fire rise so slowly from behind the bowed spine of the dark mountain. For just a moment, he feels himself to be another man . . . in another century. Now the sun, in preparation for its long journey across the sky, rests momentarily on the sturdy shoulder of Black Mule. It is time. The Sun Dance chief raises his arms.

The dancers—who have been seated—rise to offer greetings to this nearby star, this thermonuclear furnace whose radiations will scorch their bodies and cause their tongues to swell with a terrible thirst. But on this first morning, these are strong, confident men . . . happy to see the sun. Eager to be about this serious business.

The Sun Dance chief lowers his arms.

At this moment, it begins.

The trio of Kiowas begin their drumming. Somewhat asynchronous at first . . . then together as one.

The lame Paiute singer, who leans on his bamboo staff, begins to sing. Hoarsely at first . . . then with a mellow fluidity.

Each dancer has an eagle leg-bone whistle suspended on a cord from his neck. Some of the whistles are undecorated; others are adorned with a puffy eagle plume or a small hank of scarlet ribbon. The dancers, singly or in pairs, put these sacred instruments to their lips and blow shrill, eerie notes as they advance toward the center of the corral—where the symbolic tree stands. Each of these seekers of visions hopes that he may have the will and physical endurance to stay the course. So that he may—if only for a fleeting moment—catch a glimpse of that ineffable presence . . . approach the incomprehensible . . . transcend the boundary to the transcendent. And perhaps . . . just perhaps . . . be touched by that eternal flame that flickers in that world to come.

And gain a portion of the Power. To heal. To be healed.

Among those who have come to move among these dancers, these curious spectators, this solemn gathering of tribes, there is another soul . . . and yet another. They have come with different motives.

One is afraid.

One is not.

*   *   *

It was late morning when the Sun Dance chief glanced over his shoulder and breathed the sigh of the beaten man. Despite his many complaints to the Council of Elders, she's done it again. Daisy Perika has showed up with that accursed aluminum lawn chair. She knows well enough—that because the frame is made of metal—it is not allowed inside the brush corral. She has, he grudgingly admits, not brought the chair inside the sacred circle where men dance. But the infernal thing should not be partially blocking the entrance, where she sits like a toad with her handful of fresh willow branches, waving them to encourage the dancers. Willie Blacksnow, though annoyed, would not dare confront this distinguished tribal elder with a direct order to remove the offending chair. For one thing, as long as any of the *Nuuci* can remember, Daisy Perika has attended the dance, waving her willows to revitalize those men who dance thirsty. As did her mother before her . . . and her mother before her. For another, he has no doubt that the stubborn old woman would simply refuse to obey any order of his—and then what would he do? Look the fool, of course. So the beleaguered chief of the Sun Dance—who has sufficient troubles to occupy his mind—pretends to be unaware of the impudent woman's presence. And the brazen impropriety of her metal contraption.

Daisy is aware of the fussy old man's attitude. Every summer, old weasel-face uses the same strategy. Acts like he hasn't noticed her. Or her metal chair. Indeed, the Sun Dance chief's pretended ignorance of her presence is something the shaman is pleased about. This will work in her favor. Yes . . . if all goes well, before another sunrise lights up the sky, she'll know for sure who the witch is. And once she knows . . . well there are ways to deal with a witch. Ways that her nephew Charlie Moon could not imagine.

It was two hours before noon. Charlie Moon sat in his Blazer, watching Officer Daniel Bignight, who was parked at the entrance to the Sun Dance grounds. Bignight was directing traffic and handing out leaflets that documented the protocol. It was a reprint of the admonitions that had been published in the *Drum*.

Bignight's job was not a busy one. On the first day of a Sun Dance, there wasn't all that much traffic to direct. Only a few tourists showed up this early. There would also be a couple of anthropologists and a half dozen Indian groupies who attended all of the dances. The interest of the local folk grew on the third day, when fatigue and thirst were taking their toll on the dancers. Then, the people from Ignacio came in droves to watch the suffering.

Charlie Moon spotted a familiar-looking pickup with a battered aluminum shell. The driver accepted one of Bignight's leaflets and headed for a grove of trees. Moon twisted the Blazer's ignition key. The Ute policeman followed the truck to a shady spot under the dry branches of a leaning juniper.

Scott Parris got out of his old pickup. He pushed his felt hat back and squinted at his Ute friend. "Hiya, Charlie."

Moon grinned. "This your first Sun Dance?"

Parris nodded. "Yeah." He looked around and tugged at his collar. "Jeepers, it's hot here. Like standing in a frying pan."

The Ute slammed the Blazer door; he accepted Parris' outstretched hand. "Shoot, pardner, this is the cool of the morning. Wait till about four o'clock, then it'll have warmed up a bit."

The white man grimaced, making little wrinkles around his blue eyes. "And to think I let you talk me into this foolishness."

Moon chuckled. "This'll be like a vacation."

"I thought you had some work for me to do." Parris' eyes twinkled merrily. "Preventing skullduggery and mischief. Keeping my eyeballs peeled for witches and such."

It was as if a cloud passed over Moon's face. "I don't expect anything to happen for at least a day or so . . . if then." The Ute policeman nodded toward the brush corral. "But my aunt Daisy's already showed up. Normally, she wouldn't get here until the second day of the dance."

Parris followed Moon's gaze. "You still think Mrs. Perika's up to something?"

The Ute policeman removed his hat and rubbed his hand through a thick shock of black hair. "Yeah. And I'd give a week's salary to know what. She's got that funny look on her face—like a kid who's about to steal the cookies."

Parris swatted his hand at a horsefly. Missed. "Maybe she's gonna catch the witch for you, Charlie." The insolent fly buzzed circles around his head.

Moon snorted. But his friend's barb had hit home.

The *matukach* opened the shell door, then lowered the tailgate. He climbed into the truck bed on his knees and began to sort out his gear. Bedroll. Groceries. A plastic cooler filled with ice and soft drinks. A new Coleman stove. An old Coleman lantern. His voice echoed hollowly under the aluminum shell. "I guess I'd best stay out of her sight."

"Yeah. Aside from me and Delly Sands—and Myra Cornstone if she shows up—Aunt Daisy's probably the only person here who'd recognize you. It might be best if you stayed away from the corral till after dark. Then you can work your way over there amongst the tourists. And kinda keep a watch on things for me. I've got to go into Ignacio later this evening. Me and the chief of police have a meeting with the tribal chairman about this 'witch' business. He'll want to know just what we're doing to make sure none of our dancers keels over like old Hooper Antelope did. But come tomorrow morning, I'll be here twenty-four hours a day."

"You gonna use some of your Ute cops to help keep a lookout for this witch?"

Charlie Moon smiled thinly at the white man's innocent question. "Every last one of 'em believes in witches," he said evenly. "I've got a half dozen men who'd grit their teeth and face off a whole squad of Hell's Angels if it came right down to it. But not a mother's son of 'em would so much as look a little boy in the eye, if they thought he was *uru-sawa-ci.*"

"Witches," Parris said over his shoulder, "kind of scare me
too. But not the Indian kind. When I was a kid, I had awful
nightmares about that old green-faced witch in *The Wizard of Oz*."

"She *was* kind of scary," Moon said thoughtfully. "Had that
funny laugh, too." He attempted to imitate the witch's evil cackle.
'Heh-heh-heh."

"In my bad dreams," Parris said with a scowl, "she was always
stealing my dog. And she'd make her getaway on my bicycle."

The Ute leaned on the pickup and grinned. "And I bet your
dog was named Lassie. Or Spot."

"Well you'd lose the bet."

"Hmmm." Moon frowned with concentration. "Must've been
Rover then."

The *matukach*, by way of a smirk, dismissed the suggestion as
absurd. Anyways, Rover had been a good old dog. Parris seated
himself on the tailgate. He reached into the camper and dragged
out a large cardboard box. In the container were tins of assorted
soup. A box of low-salt crackers. A plastic bag of trail mix, also
low-salt. A couple of Granola bars. Five bags of dehydrated fruit.
Figs, apricots, pears, prunes, raisins. Shelled walnuts. A bunch of
fresh carrots. A half dozen apples in a paper bag. It was the usual
fare of a sensible man who—unlike the big Ute—was cautious
about the kind of food he put into his body.

Moon, who saw only the soup and crackers, felt his stomach
rumble. "Looks like you brought enough grub for the both of us."

"Yeah. I always bring plenty." Parris poked his hand into the
bag of apples.

Moon leaned forward and sniffed expectantly. "What've you
got there, partner?"

"You like Twinkies?"

"Sure." Moon salivated. "How many you got?"

"Hmmm. Lemmee see." Parris peeked into the paper bag at
the winesaps. "Eight or nine, I guess."

"That'll take care of *my* midmorning snack, partner. But
what'll you eat?"

*   *   *

For hours, as she had attempted to encourage the weary dancers, the sun had been in Daisy Perika's eyes. Now, the red disk
was about to slip behind Bridge Timber Mountain. The shaman
allowed her gaze to drift around the sacred circle. The strongest
dancers were against the west wall of the brush corral. Stone Pipe,
the sullen Sioux, was seated beside the slender *matukach*. On the
other side of the white man was Larry Sands. On the south side
were a few novice dancers; they were sitting on dusty blankets.
Some rubbed at the soles of their feet and frowned at blisters. All
dreamed of cold water. Or iced beer. Or ice cream. Immediately
to Daisy's left were the drummers. And the lame Paiute man who
sang through his nose. Like most other old men, he had great
tufts of hair growing out of his ears. And such large, leathery ears
they were—with great purple lobes that hung like ripe plums.
Poor old fellow also had a mouth big enough to swallow a grape-
fruit whole. And maybe three yellowed teeth in his head. After
a thoughtful comparison to several other unfortunates she remembered, Daisy decided that this was most likely the ugliest man she
had ever seen.

To her right, on the north side of the Sun Dance Lodge, were
a few spectators. A paunchy, bearded professor from Fort Lewis
College, who was writing in a little notebook. The blond woman
who traveled with the white Sun-Dancer was sitting cross-legged
on a new blanket. Delly Sands sat next to the yellow-haired
woman. Delly was, Daisy assumed, here to gather information for
her Sun Dance story that'd be printed next week in the *Southern
Ute Drum*. Delly might have plenty to write about.

Already, the shaman's game had begun. Early this morning,
the old woman had stopped by to visit with the tribal chairman.
To warn him about what would happen to his already slim
chances for reelection if another dancer died. It was bad enough
when a Southern Ute died over there on the Ute Mountain reservation. But what if one of our dancers got witched right here
on the Southern Ute lands—where he, as tribal chairman, was

esponsible for the health and welfare of all of the Southern Utes? The police, she pointed out, didn't seem to be all that interested n catching the witch. What they needed was some firm leader-hip. From the tribal chairman, of course. The wily politician had istened patiently, and—when it appeared that she had no inten-ion of leaving his office—finally agreed to her "suggestion." To nave a serious talk with Charlie Moon and chief of police Roy Severo. Daisy had further suggested that tomorrow might be too ate. The chairman should see the policemen this very day. At a ime, she added reasonably, when Charlie wouldn't be needed at he Sun Dance grounds.

Exactly when was that, he'd asked wearily.

"Sometime after dark," she'd said. "When the first day's danc-ng is finished. Then, it'll be all quiet and peaceful . . ."

He parked his pickup near the young woman's aged Toyota. It vas hours before dark, but few people were around. Most were nuddled in groups near the Sun Dance Lodge. They exchanged tories about past dances, gossiped about neighbors, observed how peculiar the weather had been this year, argued about baseball eams and their prospects.

He made his way toward the rusty automobile, attempting to ook casual. He paused, kicked at a pebble, and glanced casually over his shoulder. Someone might be watching, but it seemed unlikely. Anyway, when you wanted to accomplish something mportant, there was always some level of risk that must be accepted.

He approached the car boldly, as if it were his own. If it was ocked, he'd have to break some glass. But the driver's door was not locked. Good luck.

He got to work.

The old car had vinyl seat covers. They were tight, but he nanaged to work a corner loose. This would only take another ew seconds. And then he'd be out of here.

The old man heard a slight sound. Coming from behind him. Boots crunching on gravel. Getting closer. He looked up at th window on the passenger side of the Toyota and saw the reflectio of a man. Big man, broad shoulders, stiff-legged walk. This wasn' no Ute cop, but you could tell by the determined way he wa coming—the scowl on his face—he was a cop for sure. If caugh in the act, he'd just brazen it out. He hadn't broken any laws. A least not any written in the white man's law books. As the Sho shone turned, he was hurriedly stuffing the remaining feathers int the pocket of his denim jacket.

Misfortune and mistake coupled to begat calamity.

The Shoshone's misfortune was that he had left the air pisto in the pocket where he was now attempting to hide th feathers . . . and that the pistol handle was in plain view.

The mistake was made by Scott Parris, who believed the sus pect was reaching for a potentially lethal weapon . . .

Calamity fell upon the Shoshone. It came the form of a heav fist on his chin.

And then all was blackness . . . and silence.

Consciousness ambled back slowly, like an overtired hors finding its way home. Vision came in little white spots, then bi patches. But it was wavy, like looking through water. Then, h heard the mutter of voices. Faraway voices. But they weren't reall so far away.

Two men stood above him.

The broad-shouldered white man. His memory came back i fractured bits . . . this must be the mean bastard who'd hit him And there was the tall Ute. Charlie Moon. And they were talkin about him like he was a sack of potatoes lying here on the dirt.

"I saw him heading toward Miss Sands' car, Charlie. All was gonna do was ask him what he was up to, then he saw m and put his hand into his pocket to grab the weapon. This i what he was packing." Scott Parris gave the pistol to Charli Moon. "So I had to bop him one." Parris felt bad about hittin such an old man. But when a suspect looked like he was pulling a gun, you lowered the boom.

Moon squatted by the dazed man; the big Ute grinned down at the Shoshone elder. "How're you feeling?"

Red Heel grunted, and rubbed at his chin. It felt big as a baseball. And it was sore, like a boil that needed lancing. He glared his hatred at the white man with the brick-hard fists.

Moon waved a handful of feathers in front of his face. "This is what you were stuffing under the young lady's seat cover. Owl feathers, is my guess." The Ute policeman touched the tip of the old man's nose with a feather. "You want 'em back?" Red Heel recoiled. Almost as if he were afraid of the feathers, Moon thought. Interesting.

The Shoshone elder, with some help from Scott Parris, got to his feet. His legs wanted to buckle at the knees, but the *matukach* policeman caught him before he fell again.

Red Heel heard Moon reading something off a card. Something about how anything he said might be held against him in a court of law. And if he couldn't afford a lawyer . . . the court would appoint one to defend him. And so on . . .

The Shoshone elder stared blankly off toward the rounded forms of the San Juans. His mouth was a tight slit in a wrinkled, weatherworn mask of a face.

"Well," Moon said to Parris, "this old hard case ain't gonna talk to us. But it don't matter. We know what he's been up to." The Ute policeman gestured grandly toward the dust-streaked SUPD Blazer. "Sir, the Southern Ute Tribe is pleased to offer you a complimentary ride back to Ignacio. And free room and board in our modern correctional facilities."

Nancy Beyal was happy to hear from Charlie Moon. The dispatcher hadn't had an interesting call on the radio all day. Moon was always interesting.

"What's up, Charlie?"

There was a sizzling of static, then the big man's voice boomed over the speaker. "You know about that meeting Roy Severo and I have with the Chairman?"

She pressed the button on her microphone. "Sure. What about it?"

"Tell the chief I can't make it."

Nancy made a face. Charlie Moon was always thinking of reasons to avoid meetings. Especially with the chief of police or the tribal chairman. And he always left it to her to do the explaining. "The chief'll want to know why, Charlie."

"Tell Severo . . . tell him it's urgent police business."

Roy Severo had heard Moon's voice on the speaker, and bolted from his office. Now the chief of police was leaning over the dispatcher's shoulder, his black eyes fairly burning. He whispered in her ear. "Ask him to describe the nature of the business."

Nancy grinned up at the chief. "What kind of police business, Charlie?"

Moon tapped the microphone switch with his thumb; this is what the dispatcher heard. "Signal . . . –reaking up, —ancy. Can't hear———, –alk to you later."

Severo rubbed his stomach, which growled in response. "Damn," he muttered darkly, "Charlie Moon's the cause of my peptic ulcers. I don't know why I don't fire that big clown."

Nancy averted her eyes and smiled. She knew why. And so did Roy Severo. Moon was a man who got the job done. And on top of that, Roy Severo liked him very much.

Daisy Perika saw Moon's Blazer leave the Sun Dance grounds. She squinted, and watched until the SUPD vehicle was a tiny black speck in the distance. The old Ute woman assumed that her nephew was off to the meeting with the tribal chairman.

Charlie Moon leaned against the south wall of the SUPD building. It was a balmy afternoon, and the world was at peace. He watched a lazy trustee pretend to cut weeds at the edge of the parking lot.

Across the street, on the lawn near a tribal office building, a family picnic was in progress. A little boy chased after a rambunctious pet duck that had broken a twine leash. The creature waddled importantly into the street, squawking and flapping its wings in an authoritative manner. This commotion distracted a pretty girl passing by on a bicycle, who skidded to a sideways stop. She had long, well-tanned legs. Moon scooped up the fat duck for the anxious child and tipped his Stetson at the young lady. Was she okay?

She assured him that she certainly was and flashed a half-mocking smile at the tall policeman with the disgruntled duck tucked under his arm. Were these his normal duties?

His response was deadpan. Yes ma'am. Officer Moon. On temporary assignment to Duck Patrol. At your service.

Pretending displeasure with his manner, she straightened out the ten-speed and brushed a wisp of brown hair away from her gray eyes.

Moon returned the child and his highly agitated pet to the family picnic, then turned to watch the long-legged girl cycle away.

She glanced at him over her shoulder. And winked!

Well now . . . it'd been a good day. And things were looking up. Later this evening, he'd head back to the Sun Dance grounds and find Scott Parris. The two of them would pay a visit to Aunt Daisy, who'd most likely be sitting at the entrance to the corral. Waving her willow branches to encourage the dancers. Squeaking the metal chair just often enough to annoy the Sun Dance chief. Moon imagined how he'd tell his aunt about catching the old Shoshone *uru-suwa-ci* with a handful of owl feathers. It had required nothing more than the application of standard police method. No magic needed, thank you ma'am. It was true there'd been some luck involved—what with Scott spotting Red Heel messing around in Delly Sands's car. But Aunt Daisy didn't need to know about that.

And there were other small blessings.

Chief of Police Roy Severo, who had no idea of what Moon had accomplished, was off to a dismal meeting with the tribal chairman. Without him.

But it wasn't like everything was perfect. Even though they'd caught Red Heel red-handed—and that had a nice ring to it— they couldn't very well charge the old Shoshone with putting owl feathers in Delly Sands' car. So the thing wasn't quite finished.

Once again, the contrary pet escaped from the little boy's clutches. And made a beeline for the policeman. In an attempt to bite the big Ute on the leg, the duck got a beakful of cotton trousers. The child gave up his pursuit; he pointed at the entertainment and laughed. Moon frowned down at the duck. The duck—who had not the least respect for sworn officers of the law—scowled back at the policeman. And believing the cloth to be the man's skin, twisted it this way and that.

Red Heel, who'd spent a few nights in jails before, was not particularly worried. There was no law on the books against putting owl feathers under someone's seat cover. And there wasn't no law against carrying an air pistol. He was certain of that. This big Ute cop was just trying to scare him. But all he had to do was keep his mouth shut and in a day or two, they'd tire of the game and let him go. If they didn't, he'd insist on calling the Shoshone Tribal Council's lawyer up in Riverton. That'd put some pressure on these smart-assed Utes. In the meantime, he'd just rest. And wait. Patience was something he had plenty of. And it looked like he was the only prisoner in the Ute jail. It was clean, too. And quiet. And they'd feed him three squares a day. Kind of like having a little hotel all to yourself. With room service.

A smirk appeared on the old man's face. He stretched out on the cot, folded his hands across his chest, and closed his eyes.

He was drifting off to sleep when he heard the door open in the partition that separated the cells from the squad room. Red Heel rolled over on his bunk. A skinny little man walked up to his cell. Looked like a Navajo. Red Heel didn't much care for Navajos, so he didn't speak to this one. But the Shoshone watched the Navajo like a snake watches a hawk.

The odd visitor did not speak to Red Heel. Nor look at him. He went about his business. He removed something from his shirt. A rolled up piece of cloth. He unrolled the cloth and produced . . . a feather. A white feather!

The Shoshone elder sat up on his bunk.

With enormous care, as if this were the beginning of an elaborate sand painting, the Navajo used the tip of the feather to draw an invisible figure on the floor. He muttered something in the guttural Navajo dialect. To the Shoshone's ears, it sounded like a solemn incantation. Then, he placed the feather on the floor. With the hollow shaft pointing directly at the prisoner in the cell.

Red Heel got to his feet. He grasped the iron bars with both hands. "What are you doing, old man?"

The Navajo did not answer. Indeed, he seemed not to hear. He raised both hands in a gesture to the heavens. In the Navajo dialect, he sang a monotonic song. Red Heel, being a Shoshone, was not conversant in this strange tongue.

Having sung his song, his business was finished. The peculiar visitor turned, and departed.

For some fifteen minutes, the Shoshone sat on his bunk. And stared at the feather. He had no doubt—this plume had been taken from a rare white owl. And the albino owl had great power. What kind of terrible curse had the damned old Navajo put on him? Finally, he leaped to his feet and began to call for someone to come . . . anyone.

Nancy Beyal opened the door and glared at the loud-mouthed Shoshone. "What's the matter with you!"

Red Heel's eyes rolled, he was gasping for breath. "That damn ugly Navajo . . . ahhhh . . . he put . . ."

"*What* Navajo?"

The Shoshone pointed at the floor. "Take it away."

She looked blankly at the floor. "Take what away?"

"The feather . . . take it away. Please."

Nancy rolled her eyes. "There ain't no feathers here, old man. You're either drunk or you had a bad dream." She pointed at his bunk. "Now go back to sleep and don't you do any more yelling. I'm the dispatcher and I got to stay by the radio. You bother me again, you don't get no supper, you hear?"

She turned and slammed the metal door behind her.

Charlie Moon was waiting. "How's our prisoner doin', Nancy?"

"Not too good." The dispatcher cut her eyes toward the cell block with a worried expression. She didn't like being a part of this kind of stunt. "He's all spooked about that old Navajo trustee you sent in there to scare him. I think he'll be crawlin' up the walls if we don't take that feather away pretty soon."

Moon raised his eyebrows and made an innocent face. "What Navajo . . . what feather?"

The Navajo, who was on a southbound bus with a dozen other passengers, was mightily pleased with himself. It had been a good deal the big Ute policeman had offered him. Do a little favor for the Southern Ute Tribe, and be cut loose six days early. No more jail time for the charge of public drunkenness. No more cutting of noxious Ute weeds. He felt very good. Good enough to sing aloud. And so he did. He bellowed out the same extemporaneous composition he'd sung when he'd placed the white feather by the Shoshone's jail cell. And like the Shoshone prisoner, the other passengers on the bus did not understand the Navajo dialect.

What the Navajo sang was this:

> Tonight, I go home to Dennehotso . . .
> Tonight, I go home to Dennehotso . . .
> And never again will I drink any more whiskey . . .

But first I must leave a white duck feather . . .
A duck feather for this accursed Shoshone witch.

Father Raes Delfino sat in his parlor. And stared at the envelope Delly Sands had left in his care. It was—because she was
presumed to be still alive—unopened. The Jesuit priest had spent
half the day in prayer. The other half in agony. He knew it. In
the very marrow of his bones, he knew it. Something dreadful
was about to happen. And he might be the only person who
could prevent a calamity. He knew where she'd be, of course. But
as her priest, did he have the right . . . ?

This *thinking* was getting him nowhere. Action was called for.
The Jesuit pulled on his jacket, jammed his black felt hat down
on his head, and fairly burst out the rectory door.

On this first day of the Southern Ute Sun Dance the broad plain
north of Ignacio had been blessed by a sky that was almost clear
of cloud. Now, as the old shaman sat in her chair by the entrance
to the brush corral, the somber cloth of evening was drawn to
that invisible seam between twilight and true night. It was dark
enough overhead for a few stars to show, and on the western
horizon was the teasing farewell of a day passing by . . . a slow
blush of rouge . . . a flirting wink of crimson eye.

None of the Sun-Dancers was standing. Some lay on their
blankets, others rested their backs against the brush enclosure.
Their faces were illuminated by the amber flicker of a small campfire built near the sacred tree. The time for dancing on this day
was finished. The drummers and the singer would perform for
another hour, then depart to their camps among the juniper
and piñon.

At that time, the few visitors who remained would also be
asked to leave. When no one remained except the dancers, the
Sun Dance chief would hang a white cotton sheet across the

entrance to the corral. And then, the bone-weary chasers of visions would sleep like exhausted children who had played too hard. This is what everyone expected to happen on this night.

Almost everyone.

Daisy Perika sat in her chair at the entrance to the Sun Dance Lodge.

The drummers drummed. Listlessly, she thought.

Five more minutes passed into history.

The old Paiute singer sang one of his droning songs. For at least the fourth time, she thought. Some foolishness about a Flathead woman who took a bear for a husband. Them Flathead women, Daisy mused, must be hard up for men. Thankfully, the Paiute singer completed his hymn. Leaning heavily on his bamboo walking stick, he limped past the shaman and left the corral. Just like an old man, she thought. Has to go take a pee every half hour.

Still, she sat, the willow wands limp in her grasp. Though the July evening was balmy with the leftover heat of day, her hands felt oddly cold.

The elderly shaman suffered mixed emotions. One part of Daisy's mind told her that this would be a night like all other nights. Another portion of her brain, that ancient reptilian segment nestled at the base of her skull, knew that something *would* happen. It whispered inside her head: "Oh yes . . . they'll come . . . wait and see."

So the Ute shaman set her face toward the sacred tree at the center of the circle. And waited.

When it began, Daisy Perika *felt* rather than heard the approach. Her old heart thumped rapidly under her breastbone; her feet wanted to run away with her body. But it was too late for a retreat. Whatever happened, she'd have to see it through. Very deliberately, she turned to look.

Something was there. A small form moving through the darkness. Coming closer. The old woman's hands trembled; she pulled the shawl tightly around her shoulders.

Yes. It was the child. And with him . . .

Now, twilight was a memory . . . the cold hand of true night was upon the land. Muttering clouds were gathering over the San Juans. One by one, the stars were blotted out.

Willie Blacksnow had made a valiant attempt to ignore the presence of Daisy Perika. Now he turned to see if the troublesome old woman was still there, hunched up in that damned metal lawn chair. She was. But she was staring into the darkness beyond the Sun Dance Lodge.

And he saw what had drawn Daisy Perika's attention.

It was nothing much. A little boy approaching the brush corral. Looked like Billy Antelope. Strange. The unfortunate child still wore that hank of clothesline rope around his waist. And stranger still . . . someone was following behind the child. Someone very short . . . hunched over. Looked like an old woman. And she was holding on to the rope . . . tapping along with a cane. Just like— But Old Popeye Woman was dead and buried!

The peculiar couple approached the entrance of the Sun Dance Lodge.

The boy paused, and glanced at Daisy Perika. The old woman behind him was dressed in a dark cloak. She was about the size of Old Popeye Woman. She limped like Old Popeye Woman. And in her hand, she carried a striped walking cane.

Willie Blacksnow scowled. What kind of farce was this? The Sun Dance chief stalked toward the unwelcome visitors. He was within a few steps of the corral entrance when the child looked up. Willie Blacksnow, who intended to get to the bottom of this funny business, was about to ask some harsh questions. But he did not. The Sun Dance chief hesitated . . . he felt a shiver ripple along his spine. As the boy came toward him, Willie Blacksnow stepped aside.

The child passed by the Sun Dance chief as if he did not

recognize that this was a man of considerable importance. As did the old woman who held the taut rope with one gnarled hand and carried the striped cane in the other. And dragged one foot along the dusty ground inside the corral.

There was, at first, a whispering from the seated dancers.

"Who's that . . . that old woman with the boy?"

The whispering was raised to a muttering.

"It looks like . . . but it can't be . . . Old Popeye Woman is *dead*."

Uneasiness was blossoming into a fear that made grown men shudder.

Daisy Perika sat in the chair and trembled. And prayed . . .

Delly Sands watched this drama as one might observe a dream sequence. Daisy had told her that she'd flush out the witch. It had seemed silly at the time. But here, in the flickering light of the campfire, watching the boy lead the old woman by the rope—it was downright eerie . . . there was something terribly wrong about this . . .

Larry Sands could not believe his eyes . . . such things simply did not happen . . . this was a nightmare.

The blond anthropologist gawked. What on earth was going on?

The child approached the drummers. These folk were out-of-towners; they knew nothing of Little Rope Boy or Old Popeye Woman. They stared with open curiosity at the child and the little figure shrouded in black. They also heard the mutterings from the seated Sun-Dancers, and felt the tension that was growing like noxious weeds. The old woman raised the striped cane above their heads. She waved it back and forth, like a wand. The drummers grinned self-consciously at each other and shrugged; were they being blessed . . . or cursed?

The child and the woman moved on.

One by one, the shrouded figure paused by the seated dancers and peered out from under the hood. The ritual was the same.

The old woman would raise her cane, and pass it over the head of the man.

Some men trembled.

Others raised their arms in defensive gestures.

One giggled nervously.

The Catholics, some who had not attended church since confirmation, crossed themselves and tried desperately to remember a prayer.

One young dancer lost control of his bladder. He got to his feet and bolted from the sacred corral. No one laughed.

The boy and the woman stopped near the Sioux. Stone Pipe had heard the anxious mutterings of the Utes. And he knew about Old Popeye Woman. He'd seen her at the Ute Mountain Dance, where her son had died. He also knew that this woman was supposed to be dead. And buried somewhere out there in the canyon country. This appearance was incomprehensible. He had never experienced such mind-numbing fear. Very deliberately, he got to his feet. More than anything he had ever desired, the Sioux wanted to run. But Stone Pipe played the man. To keep his hands from trembling in the sight of all—particularly the accursed white dancer—he folded his arms across his broad chest and clenched his big hands into white-knuckled fists. Stone Pipe thought he heard someone else speaking. And was astonished to realize that this quavering voice was his own. "Old woman . . . what do you want from me?"

The hooded specter stood like a post in front of the Sioux warrior. Her face, hidden in the darkness under the hood, looked him up and down. Weighed his soul. Tested his mettle.

The child, roped to his charge, took no notice of Stone Pipe. His interest lay elsewhere.

The lame woman tapped the child's shoulder with her cane. They moved on. To the white man.

Larry Sands, who had sat at the left hand of Winston Steele, had slipped away in the semidarkness. Daisy Perika had not missed this. The old woman watched as the young Ute dancer paused briefly by his sister. The Sandman pointed toward the hooded woman and muttered something to Delly. Something with a sense of urgency. Delly Sands shook her head at her brother. He spat out a parting remark, turned away, and hurried from the corral.

The hooded woman repeated her performance with the white man.

Dr. Winston Steele was of two minds. As a man of science, he was fascinated. And determined to make good observations. But some elemental part of his being was frightened to the point where it seemed his knees would knock together. Despite the dread that threatened to smother him, Steele leaned close to the old woman. Peering into the place where a face should be. There was, it seemed . . . no face to be seen. Only an empty void of darkness under the hood. His observation was faulty.

She turned away from the white dancer, and seemed about to pass on. But the hooded figure hesitated, then paused. She stared at the empty place at Steele's left hand. At the rumpled yellow blanket the Sandman had left behind. Very slowly, she passed her striped cane over the emptiness . . . as if in an attempt to conjure up the missing dancer. It seemed that the enigmatic visitor conjured up nothing . . . except a low grumble of thunder from the storm hovering over the mountains.

The angry clouds were spreading long fingerlike tendrils over the desolate valley. Over the Sun Dance Lodge.

Now, the boy and the old woman moved toward the few spectators who remained. Much to the learned man's dismay, they passed by the professor from Fort Lewis College without so much as a glance his way.

Delly Sands was next in line, and she was greatly distracted by the apparition of Old Popeye Woman. She had not a thought for the recurrent pains in her shoulder . . . where the dead man's bone had been lodged. She could not imagine how Daisy Perika had managed this appearance . . . but it would make a fantastic story for the *Drum*.

Now, the boy and the hooded figure were within a few steps . . .

As she had before the others, the hooded woman paused. The child stared at Delly, but his small face was blank. Unreadable.

A few fat drops of rain fell from the heavens, making moist pockmarks in the dust.

For a long moment, the apparition stood before the young Ute woman. Then, she did a peculiar thing. She raised the striped cane . . . reached out with it . . . and touched Delly lightly on the shoulder. The young woman—who was privy to the shaman's game—did not flinch.

Still grasping the rope and the cane, the apparition raised both arms. Her hands were small, delicate, and very dark. Her wrists thin and spindly. The hood that had covered her face slipped back a little. It was at this moment that three long snakes of blue-white fire slithered across the eastern sky. In this brief illumination from the lightning, Delly Sands glimpsed a portion of the face that had been hidden in darkness. There was a great bulging eye. White like an eggshell. With a coal-black iris in the center.

Now there was a deep rumble of thunder that echoed off the mountains; the very earth shuddered.

Delly wasn't the only one who had seen the horrible eye.

Salina Timms, sitting at Delly Sands's left hand, had been transfixed until this moment. Now, the anthropologist grabbed her throat and whimpered. The blonde crawled for a yard or so, managed to get to her feet, and stumbled from the corral—almost tripping on her folded parasol. In her haste to leave, Salina brushed past a lame man who had paused just outside the entrance to the brush corral. It was the elderly Paiute singer, who had returned from his trip to the latrine. Hardly noticing the panicked blond woman, he stood with open mouth, staring in awe at the spectacle of the aged crone led by the child. The singer knew who this was—Old Popeye Woman and Little Rope Boy. His limbs began to quake. One step at a time, with little assistance from his bamboo staff, he retreated into the darkness. But the singer could not take his eyes off the hooded figure of the woman.

The thing was finished. The child and the hooded figure turned away from Delly Sands. As if he were in a trance, Billy Antelope moved toward the opening in the brush corral. The clubfooted woman was close behind . . . grasping at the hank of rope . . . tap-tapping the dust with her gaudy candy-stripe cane.

And then they were gone.

For a moment Delly felt a heavy mass sitting on her chest. It was difficult to breathe, though she did not hear the sounds of her raspy gasps for air. Presently the young woman felt no weight at all, but an incredible lightness. And once again, she experienced the sweet, fleeting vision. It was a little different this time. When it had happened in Charlie Moon's house, she'd seen herself as a young woman. Now she saw a chubby little girl with long hair . . . fast asleep . . . wrapped snugly in a blanket. And a strong man was carrying her . . . to a place where she would rest. But the man was not her father.

As in the first vision, the man was Charlie Moon.

Daisy Perika hadn't noticed that Delly was struggling for each breath. The shaman's metal chair was empty.

A half dozen men were gathered around the young woman. Dr. Winston Steele kneeled and touched her forehead. "Delly . . . say something. C'mon kid . . . talk to me!"

Her eyes were rolled back, showing only white. She did not answer. She did not breathe. The physician placed his thumb under her jawbone. Pulse was weak. And getting weaker. Immediately, he started mouth-to-mouth resuscitation.

Father Raes Delfino seemed to materialize at his side. "Is there anything I can do . . . to help?"

The physician removed his lips from Delly's and glanced at the small man's collar. "No, Father. Nothing."

The priest folded his hands. And prayed. It was never too late.

Charlie Moon eased the Blazer out of the SUPD parking lot, eager to get back to the Sun Dance grounds. First order of business was to find Scott Parris, and then Aunt Daisy. And tell her about how his *matukach* pardner had caught the so-called witch in Delly Sands' Toyota, stuffing owl feathers under her seat cover. And about how he'd locked up the old goat. And was, even as they spoke, turning the Shoshone's "magic" against him.

Moon headed north.

The Ute policeman made a left into the Sun Dance grounds. Daniel Bignight's white Chevy cruiser was parked near the entrance, but the Taos Pueblo man was not at his post. The place seemed unnaturally still. Moon pointed the blunt nose of the Blazer toward the Sun Dance Lodge. Before he got to the brush corral, the Ute policeman noticed something moving in the shadows. Looked like an elderly woman. Moon slowed the Blazer and turned to sweep the headlights over the prowler.

It was Aunt Daisy.

She was wandering around this way and that. Stopping to poke around at parked cars . . . like she was looking for something—or somebody . . . then passing on. She was up to something. But what?

Daisy Perika wished that her eyes would become accustomed to the darkness. But it didn't matter all that much, long as she didn't trip over a rock. And fall down and break a hip bone. She'd thought she knew just where to find them, but in the dark it was hard to know where you were.

She almost bumped into the old automobile. Daisy felt her way along the fender, toward the door. "It's me," she whispered, "you in there?"

"Yes," came the feeble reply. "I'm here."

"Well," Daisy said, "you better get moving. I just saw my nephew's police car. Charlie's back." Congratulations, though richly deserved, could wait until tomorrow.

Louise-Marie LaForte was wringing her little hands. "I got my costume all tangled up in the gearshift, Daisy. I can't drive this car till I get myself sorted out. Dear me . . . Oh dear me."

"Well hurry, now, and get yourself untangled. You got to be outta here. Charlie might turn up any minute now."

The Ute woman felt a tap on her shoulder and heard a deep voice immediately behind her. "You called?"

Simultaneously, the elderly woman did three things, any one of which is stressful for one of so many years. Daisy lurched forward like a frightened rabbit, bounced off the automobile like a basketball—and screamed. Very loud. "Aiiieeeeeeeee!"

She turned, her hand clutching at her neck. Even in the darkness, the tall form of her nephew was unmistakable. It took her a long moment to regain her breath. "Charlie Moon . . . you big jughead . . . you coulda scared me to death!"

Moon pressed the button on a long flashlight. Daisy raised her hands to shield her eyes. He swept the beam over the black automobile. He grinned at the driver and tipped his hat. "Good evening, ma'am. Fancy meeting you here."

Louise-Marie nodded nervously; her chins quivered.

The policeman leaned forward, and peered inside the old automobile. "Why that's a nice outfit you're wearing, Louise-Marie. Black dress. Black cape. And you've even got yourself a fine walking stick. Painted with pretty red and white stripes, too." He noticed a thin line encircling her head, and something over her ear. A heavy rubber band . . . a white hemisphere. Looked like she'd sawed a Ping-Pong ball in half. It had a round black spot in the center. He pulled it out half an inch and let go.

Pop.

Louise-Marie reacted with a twitch of her shoulders.

The big plastic eye glared back at the Ute policeman.

"I can't quite put my finger on it . . . but there's something awfully familiar about this outfit." He turned and frowned thoughtfully at his aunt. "Who does she remind you of in that getup?"

Daisy jutted her chin out stubbornly, but said not a word. She hoped Louise-Marie would—just this once—keep her mouth shut.

Miracle of all miracles, the French-Canadian woman did just that.

Faced with this silence, Charlie Moon managed a stern frown. He delivered an equally stern lecture about the folly of messing around in business that was best left to the established authorities. In light of the fact that neither Louise-Marie nor her disreputable automobile were licensed to travel on Colorado's public highways, the policeman also insisted that the ladies accept a ride to their respective homes—with the compliments of the Southern Ute Police Department. He would direct an officer to take them home. But Moon promised them that he would not forget them. Indeed, he would come calling. And quite soon. He reached a long arm into the old automobile and removed the keys from the ignition switch. "You two stay put."

Daisy started to mouth a protest.

But he was gone.

They were waiting for Charlie Moon at the entrance to the brush corral. His friend Scott Parris. Daniel Bignight. Dr. Winston Steele. And . . . the priest.

This didn't look good. Moon slowed his pace. "What is it?"

Parris removed his battered felt hat; he looked at the earth under his feet. It seemed barely able to support his weight.

Bignight's voice was a mournful croak. "I called for an ambulance, Charlie. But it was already . . . too late."

The physician opened his mouth, but could find no words.

"Charlie," Father Raes said as he touched the big man's arm, "Delly Sands. She's gone."

Moon stood very still. Like one of those lonely, towering pines that dot the Sun Dance grounds. It was seconds before he spoke. It seemed like minutes. "Tell me."

The physician cleared his throat. "I'm not absolutely sure . . . but Delly . . . Miss Sands had a history of asthma. It appears to have been . . . an unusually strong attack. It happens." He raised his hands in a gesture of utter despair.

Father Raes reached into an inside coat pocket. He removed an envelope. "She left this with me . . . I think you'll remember when, Charlie. I opened it immediately after she . . . expired. There was a brief note to me. Regarding her burial. And another message for you." He handed a folded sheaf of papers to the Ute policeman.

A letter from a dead woman. Moon stuffed the papers into his pocket.

"Charlie," the priest said, "Delly requested that . . . if something happened to her . . . you take her remains to Cañon del Espiritu. For a traditional burial. I thought that perhaps we could take her to the church tonight . . . some of the women could prepare the body."

Remains. A hollow word. It meant . . . that which was left behind. Moon nodded. Somehow, the big Ute managed to find his voice. "I'll take her to the canyon . . . tomorrow." He already knew where she would rest. It was a very special place. A sacred place.

The Taos Pueblo man had driven his Chevrolet cruiser to the spot where Louise-Marie's dilapidated old car was parked in a sparse grove of piñon. The SUPD officer had his instructions from Charlie Moon. Send Daisy Perika back to the Sun Dance Lodge. Take the French-Canadian woman home. He was under strict orders not to mention the death of the Sands woman. That was a family matter that Moon would tend to.

The elderly Ute woman leaned into the rear window of Daniel Bignight's cruiser. Louise-Marie LaForte, perched on the big seat, seemed smaller than ever. With one eye, Daisy warily watched the policeman, who was tapping his thumbs on the steering wheel.

Louise-Marie LaForte, who had not spoken since Charlie Moon had confronted her, was still dressed up in her meticulously fashioned Old Popeye Woman costume. She had secreted the absurd Ping-Pong eyeball inside her velvet purse.

Daisy Perika leaned close to the shorter woman and whispered in her ear. "Don't let Charlie Moon scare you, Louise-Marie. My nephew likes to act tough, but he won't cause us any real trouble. If he tries, I'll twist both his ears right off his head."

Unexpectedly, the aging actress began to weep. Her little shoulders shook under the black cape. She found a tissue in her pocket and began to dab at her eyes. Between sobs, she managed a few words. "Oh . . . I'm so sorry, Daisy." Now she had an attack of hiccups.

"Pinch your nose and hold your breath," the shaman said. That was a sure cure.

"For . . . *eeech* . . . how long?" Louise-Marie gasped.

"Ten minutes," the Ute woman replied dryly. "Or till you go blind. Whichever comes first." Daisy chuckled. She was, despite Moon's discovery of her plot, in a rare good mood.

"I don't want . . . *eeech* . . . to go blind," her companion blurted. "And I'm so sorry that . . . *eeech* . . ."

"Shush up now," the Ute woman said, "it wasn't your fault you got your outfit all tangled up in that gearshift." It was entirely her fault, of course. If Louise-Marie had driven away from the Sun Dance grounds right after she'd left the brush corral, Charlie Moon might have suspected that his aunt was behind all this, but he wouldn't have been able to prove a thing.

The little boy had been perfect, though. Billy had managed to slip away to Reuben Antelope's camp before Moon showed up. He was a good little fellow. A crackerjack.

It was a shame she hadn't gotten someone else for the part of Old Popeye Woman. But Louise-Marie was exactly the right size . . . and she had some experience in play-acting. A combination of timidity and greed had also played a part. Louise-Marie had, as she'd expected, been afraid to take such a risk. She had refused to play the role until Daisy offered to pay for her services. And a few dollars wouldn't do it. Louise-Marie insisted on having the Indian blanket that served as a throw-rug by Daisy's small bed. The *valuable* blanket. Daisy smiled.

Officer Bignight revved the Chevy V-8. He glanced at his wristwatch, then turned to look at the old woman leaning on his cruiser. "Mrs. Perika, I think I should be taking Mrs. LaForte on home—"

"Shush," Daisy snapped. "If you need to do some thinkin', I'll let you know." These Pueblo people were such worriers.

Daniel Bignight turned away and sighed. This cranky old Ute woman reminded him of his ill-tempered grandmother.

Louise-Marie didn't let go of her nose, but she gulped a quick breath through her mouth. "Ahhhh . . . I thig my higgups are cured . . . *eeech* . . . oh dear . . ."

"It was just bad luck," Daisy Perika added soothingly. Yes. That was it. Bad luck. The Ute woman sighed. No matter how hard you planned, some little thing you could never have predicted would happen, and things would go wrong. Louise-Marie and little Billy Antelope had done a fine job. Scared the pee out of everybody but the drummers, and they were too ignorant to know when to be scared. There were, unfortunately, several suspects who might be the witch. Two dancers—including that smart-mouthed Larry Sands—had actually hotfooted it from the corral! Even the yellow-haired woman had panicked and fled.

And a time or two, Daisy reflected with grim admiration, Louise-Marie almost had *me* convinced.

However you looked at it, this night would be one to remember. For years to come, the People would talk about that night when Old Popeye Woman had come back from the grave . . . to walk with her grandson through the Sun Dance Lodge. Daisy thought there was a good chance that her part in this drama would not become public knowledge. For all his faults, Charlie

Moon was tight-lipped about family business. And the little Antelope boy knew how to keep his mouth shut. Delly Sands certainly had no reason to tell what she knew. No, her secret was safe. Unless . . . unless Louise-Marie lost her nerve. And started blubbering and blabbing. But there were other ways to keep this old woman quiet.

Almost on cue, the elderly actress stopped sobbing. She raised her head to squint at the Ute woman who leaned on the squad car.

"Daisy, cad I led go ob my nose now?"

"Sure."

Louise-Marie was much relieved. Her hiccups had departed. "Daisy?"

"Hmmph," the shaman grunted.

"I'm so sorry . . ."

"Don't start up with that again. Didn't I already tell you it was all right?"

"You mean I . . . I'll still get the . . ." Louise-Marie bit her tongue. She'd almost said "the Two Grey Hills blanket." Daisy Perika had no idea that she had such a rare treasure in her home—worth maybe a thousand dollars! She drew a deep breath, and started over. "Will I still get that little Indian blanket you promised me if I helped?"

"Sure," Daisy said gruffly. She'd known all along what Louise-Marie thought. But it wasn't actually a Two Grey Hills, of course. It was a cheap knock-off Gorman had bought down in Juarez and given her for a Christmas present. She'd be glad to be rid of it.

"Well," the French-Canadian woman said with a sniff, "I thought maybe you were peeved at me."

The Ute woman turned on her companion with a scowl. "Why should I be?"

Louise-Marie told her why. In a mere dozen words.

Daisy Perika opened her mouth and tried to speak . . . but the words were frozen in her throat.

Daniel Bignight stuck his round, burr-cut head outside the

cruiser window. "I'm sorry, Mrs. Perika, but I *got* to take Mrs. LaForte home. You're supposed to go back to the Sun Dance Lodge. And see Charlie Moon." Abruptly, he dropped the gear into Drive and pressed his boot against the accelerator.

Daisy Perika watched the big car slip away through the piñons, the slitted red eyes of the taillights squinting back at her through a hazy billow of dust. The Ute woman turned toward the brush corral and starting walking. Louise-Marie's words buzzed in her head like a bumblebee trapped in a jar. This was foolishness. Didn't make any sense at all. Unless . . . no. That would be like the sun coming up in the west. Impossible. Louise-Marie must be confused. Maybe, to boost her courage, she'd had a drink of her homemade plum wine. A big drink. A quart maybe.

Daisy stumbled over a juniper root. It was awfully dark .

Moon met his aunt halfway.

She stopped and waited for him to speak first.

"Tomorrow afternoon," he said softly, "I'll come by your place."

This was an old man's voice . . . weary of the world. But it came out of the young man's mouth.

"For what?" she snapped. She wasn't going to sit still for one of his sanctimonious lectures about obeying the law and being a responsible citizen and how she wasn't as young as she used to be. And how she might end up in real trouble someday if she didn't mend her ways. And so on and so on.

There was a long silence. And then the shaman sensed something. Something like a ghost walking by . . . her feet were suddenly cold and numb, like she'd been wading the Piedra in December.

The Ute policeman raised his face to the moonless sky. As if to view those faraway candles someone had set in the midst of eternal darkness. But he closed his eyes. "We have someone to bury."

With sighs and groans, the Sun Dance chief announced the termination of this year's dance.

Though this decision had been expected, there was a stunned hush. One by one, those who had come to seek visions rolled up their blankets and departed. They did not speak to one another. There was nothing left to say.

Willie Blacksnow strung a few yards of yellow nylon rope across the entrance to the Sun Dance Lodge. The campfire was little more than a pile of lukewarm ashes. He'd come back tomorrow and take the sacred tree down. And next week, he'd make an announcement to the Council of Elders.

Never again would he serve as chief of the Sun Dance.

Horace Antelope watched his father, who kneeled beside the suitcase. Reuben Antelope was stuffing in kid's underwear, shirts, even a couple of small toys. He'd never seen Daddy pack a suitcase before. He'd never seen Daddy afraid before, either. Horace wasn't one bit afraid. But he was jealous of what Billy had done. And he was furious that he had not been a witness to the spectacle. He wanted to get the kid to tell him all about it, but Billy wasn't much for talking. Anyway, if he asked, Horace figured Daddy might give him the back of his hand. Daddy seemed awfully nervous, and he was taking Billy away somewheres.

As he jammed things into the boy's grip, Reuben Antelope avoided looking at little Billy. The elderly Ute hadn't seen what'd happened at the Sun Dance Lodge tonight, but he'd heard the same hair-raising story from a half dozen witnesses. He hadn't asked Billy to tell his version of the tale. And he damn sure wasn't going to. The old man didn't want to hear any more about it. He was—and he hated to admit this—almost afraid of this strange child. But by tomorrow, this trouble would be far behind him. By late morning, they'd be in northern Utah. There were some relatives on the Uintah reservation who would look after the boy until a more permanent arrangement could be made. And because Reuben wasn't looking forward to answering any questions about something he didn't understand, he'd take his own good time coming back to La Plata County. Maybe it'd do Horace good to have to shift for himself for a while. Might help make a man out of him.

Billy Antelope sat on his bed, swinging his thin legs. He watched the old man fumble with the cardboard suitcase. The boy's small body was still humming with excitement. What a night this had been! And the child knew that Daisy Perika's promise would be fulfilled. Someday—at all the dances—they would sing songs about what he had done on this night.

He should have been in his bedroll at this hour, but the old Paiute singer was driving west on Route 160. Any sensible man of his years should have been sleeping, that's what his wife would say. He imagined a conversation with her.

"You're way too old to be up this late. You need your rest."

"Tell me," he asked his absent wife, "how can a man sleep on a night such as this . . . when the dead walk in the Sun Dance Lodge?"

"I don't want to hear no silly talk. And you'd better keep your mind on your driving, you foolish old man. First thing you know, you'll get yourself lost and I'll have to come find you."

His reply was a snort. But realizing that his mind was indeed wandering, he blinked at the yellow puddles his misaligned headlights spilled on the gray strip of asphalt. And reminded himself that he'd have to take Route 666 at Cortez, and head toward

Hovenweep country and the Utah border. And then a right turn and just a hop and a jump to Ucolo . . . and hearth and home.

But as he drove his pickup westward, he was perfectly happy. Because he had played a part in this tale. And because he had important work to do . . . the beginnings of a fine song. The Paiute man was more than a singer. He was also a composer of deathless songs. And by this means, a teller of amazing tales. So as he slipped along the shining ribbon of Route 160, he began to compose his next work. Lacking the helpful rhythm of the drum, he patted his hand on the gearshift. He would try a few words . . . work them into a proper phrase . . . discard something clunky here . . . add something nifty over there . . . and then sing a line or two in his high, nasal, voice. And listen to the sound of it.

He sang as he entered Cortez, and made the connection to Route 666.

He sang even louder as he threaded his way through the rustic fabric of Hovenweep country.

By the time he had crossed the Utah border—and passed by the turnoff to Ucolo—the Paiute had completed his composition. In the weeks to come, he would fix a bit here and there, but this was a fine song. So his work was done except for one thing. A song must have a name. Descriptive, but not too long. "Hmmm," he said aloud, "how about 'Ute Boy Who Leads Ghost-Woman on a Rope'?" Yes. That would do quite well. And he would sing this song at every Bear Dance, Sun Dance, Prairie Chicken Dance, and Gourd Dance. From the Dakotas to New Mexico. And for select audiences, he would tell the astounding tale behind the song—the unbelievable things he had seen with his own eyes. Soon, other singers would begin to sing his wonderful song. They would add verses, of course. And tell their own versions of the tale about the Ute boy and the dead woman who walked among us. Because he was old, and would not sing at dances for many more years, this prospect pleased the Paiute composer.

He blinked at the oncoming headlights of a large truck, then squinted into the inky darkness. Funny. *I should of come to the Ucolo turnoff by now . . .*

Though the hour was late, word of the young woman's death passed quickly among those camped at the Sun Dance grounds, and from there filtered out to the byways of Ignacio. At Father Raes' urgent call, a few women hurried to the church to prepare the body.

Though she had not been summoned by the priest, it was inevitable that Saralyn Gomez would make her appearance. This gaunt elder of the Hispanic community—who seemed little more than a corpse herself—arrived with the customary yellow basket hung over the crook of her arm. In the small hamper were stubs of lime-green candles, a pair of rubber gloves, an enameled incense burner, a brown paper bag of cedar shavings, bits of waxed string, and an assortment of sealed containers. Among the latter was a quart-sized Mason canning jar, filled with Mrs. Gomez's special mortuary preparation. There were a variety of common and exotic herbs in the concoction, but the key ingredient was a pungent chemical she'd purchased at the local hardware store. Though labeled as paint thinner, it had a remarkable ability to penetrate human skin.

Those who had just washed Delly Sands's corpse stood aside for the small but formidable woman.

Saralyn wasted no time getting down to business. She pulled on thin rubber gloves to protect her hands and scooped up a daub of ointment from the jar. With admirable deftness, the old woman's bony fingers massaged the stiffening flesh with the amber gel. She paid special attention to the joints, first kneading and flexing the knees, hips, and ankles—then the shoulders, elbows and wrists. Finally, she worked the ointment into the neck and facial tissue.

Some among her audience knew from past experience that

Saralyn's ministrations would make the corpse soft and supple . . . as if the young woman was not dead, but merely slept.

Her first task completed, Saralyn discarded the rubber gloves. She removed a long-necked blue bottle from her basket, uncorked it, and began to apply a pale aromatic oil to Delly's olive skin.

The onlookers leaned forward, and sniffed with approval. The light fragrance hinted of crushed rose petals. And perhaps . . . violets. Surely, they thought, this was made from a secret recipe passed down through the old crone's family. It was—truth be told—a product once widely used by barbers as a post-haircut scalp tonic. Her audience watched her work with varying mixtures of awe, admiration . . . and internal shudders.

Her task completed, Saralyn Gomez packed her basket. And left as silently as she had come. With neither parting word nor passing nod to the other women.

Some breathed more easily now; all were relieved to see the back of her. Their activities commenced once more. In their own tongue, the Ute women sang old songs about birth and life and death—the great circle. The Anglo and Hispanic women clothed the corpse in a simple white cotton dress. On her bare feet, they slipped doeskin moccasins. A beautician arranged Delly's short black hair into a style that framed her oval face.

Immediately following the preparation of the body, solemn rites of the church were performed at St. Ignatius. Delly had few relatives in the area. A shy cousin showed up and seated herself in a dark corner; a weeping aunt placed a small bouquet of wildflowers in the folded hands of the corpse. Scott Parris was among the congregation, as were Dr. Winston Steele, Willie Blacksnow, and Daniel Bignight. Even Stone Pipe was there. These men sat silently in the church, their eyes reflecting the flickering light from tall candles placed at the head and feet of the body.

Larry Sands was not among the mourners. It was rumored that Delly's brother had left Ignacio. Never to return, some whispered.

As the holy service began, Charlie Moon appeared and sat by

his best friend's side. Not a word passed between the Ute and Scott Parris.

The priest, though pleased to see the Ute policeman, would have understood his absence. In the hours to come, Moon's burden would be sufficient.

When the service had ended, the silent company filed out into the pine-scented chill of the July night.

Three aged Ute women stayed behind. Until sunrise, these elders watched over the earthly remains of Delly Sands. The solemn trio sang hymns . . . and chanted prayers . . . they sighed deep sighs and wiped away many tears. And—taking care not to touch the corpse—they sewed the frail body into a fine woolen blanket. So that only her waxen face was exposed, and a few tufts of raven hair . . .

In a hopeful attempt to catch a few hours sleep, Scott Parris crawled into the back of his pickup, pulled off his boots, and rolled up in a blanket. He stared at the darkness. And listened to the harmonious chirping of a thousand mindless insects. And thought his thoughts. For countless millennia before the planet had witnessed the first murmurings of human beings, the voice of the cricket would have been heard.

Finally, Parris dozed. And dreamed a dream. He was at a gay carnival with Charlie Moon and Daisy Perika, who was munching on cotton candy. They had boarded a gaudy roller coaster . . . were moving slowly upward . . . toward the apex of an enormous height. Now they were at the zenith of the spindly structure— miles above the milling crowds and tents—and the rails ended in front of them! But they sped ahead into the abyss . . . falling . . . falling . . .

For a while after he parked the Blazer in the SUPD lot, Charlie Moon sat behind the wheel. Staring off into the darkness.

Trying not to think . . . about anything. Trying not to *feel* anything.

It was not possible.

Not until he'd confronted the Shoshone elder. Maybe the old man would talk. Maybe he wouldn't. At this point, Moon didn't much care. But one way or another, the thing had to be finished.

Red Heel had not slept. He was sitting on his bunk when the door opened in the partition that segregated the row of cells from the main body of the police station. The prisoner took little notice of this intrusion.

Charlie Moon seated himself on an uncomfortable folding chair. He propped his boot heels on the sill of a small window covered with rusted steel grating. He didn't look at the old man who sat in the cell.

The single white feather was still on the floor outside the bars. The Shoshone elder could not takes his eyes off the dreaded object. Red Heel's hands were folded. As if he prayed for deliverance. The Shoshone would not ask the policeman to remove the feather. After considering his experience through the small hours, Red Heel was firmly convinced that the old Navajo had been an evil spirit . . . a witch sent by an enemy. The white owl feather, though it looked real, was not. It was a spirit feather. Invisible except to the intended victim of the curse.

The Ute policeman waited ten minutes.

Fifteen.

Twenty.

Finally, the prisoner nibbled at his lower lip. "I ain't broke no law. You oughta let me outta here."

Moon sat in a heavy silence; his eyes were closed. The Shoshone elder was right. Come morning, he'd have to tell Roy Severo about the arrest. All he had on the old man was that he'd put some feathers in an automobile. And he was carrying an air pistol. The chief of police would ask what the hell is the charge and then he'd spring the old geezer.

"Please," the Shoshone said.

The policeman let the prisoner stew for another minute before he spoke. "I might be able to do something for you—if you do something for me."

The Shoshone's heart began to race. "Name it."

Moon opened his eyes. "I want the truth."

The Shoshone elder shrank into the cot where he sat. "Truth about what?"

"About you, old man. You come down from Wyoming, to the Ute Mountain Sun Dance, and one of our dancers dies." The policeman turned. But he didn't look directly at Red Heel. He stared at a bare sixty-watt bulb hanging from the ceiling on a twisted cord of insulated copper. It was swinging back and forth. Like a pendulum connected to some cosmic clock. "I already know you shot him with dead man's bone." With the body cremated, it was impossible to prove that such a thing had happened to Hooper Antelope. But this old Shoshone wouldn't know that Hooper had been reduced to a peck of ashes.

The prisoner had barely heard the policeman's words. It seemed to him that the dreadful white feather had moved . . . ever so slightly . . . closer to his cell.

Moon continued in a soft monotone. "Then you found out Delly Sands was going to write a story in our tribal newspaper. About who'd witched old Hooper. So . . . that night in the Sky Ute Lodge parking lot . . . you shot *her* with the bone."

And like Hooper and his mother, Delly was dead now. And Red Heel would be going back to the Wind River reservation. Still, the old buzzard should at least admit what he'd been up to. And then, Moon thought, it'll be over. And maybe I'll be able to get a couple of hours sleep. It's going to be a long day.

Now the policeman looked at the prisoner. "But the bone didn't kill her. So last night, you stuffed owl feathers under her seat cover. So she'd sit on 'em."

The lightbulb was still moving. But the pendulum swung not

so far now. It was as if some great hidden timepiece were weary, like the policeman . . . gradually winding down.

Red Heel's face was like stone. He stared without blinking at the white feather on the floor. The Shoshone elder took a deep breath and licked his lips. *I'd give a five dollar bill for a cigarette.* "You want to know . . . everything?"

"Everything," the Ute policeman echoed.

"And if I tell you . . . you promise to turn me loose?"

Moon nodded. "You have my word." Come sunup, he'd have to let him go anyway.

The Shoshone elder thought about this. Tales about this big Ute policeman were told up in the Wind River country. A lot of things were bound to be exaggerations, but everybody agreed on one thing. If Charlie Moon gave you his word, that was good as money in the bank. Maybe better.

"Okay," Red Heel said. "We got a deal. Can I have a cigarette?"

Moon seemed not to hear this request.

The Shoshone elder began to talk. Slowly, at first. Then the words spilled out of his mouth.

It wasn't a long story, and Charlie Moon was grateful. It was, from the Ute policeman's perspective, a tale filled with bitterness, superstition, hatred, anger, self-delusion, terrible errors . . . and outright lies.

His tale finished, the old Shoshone leaned back, closed his eyes, and sighed. As if he'd laid down a great burden. Down by the riverside. He glanced at the white feather on the floor. "Will you turn me loose now?"

Moon had no choice, even though he believed less than half of what this twisted old soul had told him. He'd given his word. The Ute policeman unlocked the cell door. It opened with a whining creak of hinges.

With an old man's groan, Red Heel pushed himself off the cot. He exited the cell in a crablike sideways gait, taking care not to place his feet anywhere near the white spirit feather. Moon led the old man across the darkened SUPD offices, past the lighted desk where they got barely a glance from the graveyard-shift dispatcher. Moon unlocked the heavy door that opened onto the graveled parking lot.

The Shoshone paused at the threshold. "My pickup is still way out there at the Sun Dance grounds. I thought maybe you could give me a ride . . ."

"You thought wrong," Moon said softly. "And there's one more thing."

"Yeah?"

"Don't ever come back."

The policeman's words had been spoken . . . so gently. The Shoshone elder felt like his face had been slapped.

The thin shadow of a man slipped away through the open door. And like a swallow in the twilight, he was gone. Moon didn't watch him go.

For almost an hour, the Ute policeman sat at his desk, his face resting in his large hands. Completely alone. He thought his lonely thoughts. Delly was gone. He hadn't even had a chance to say good-bye.

But this infinitely sad realization reminded the weary policeman of something. So much had happened on this night, he'd almost forgotten about it. He put his hand into his pocket and found the folded papers Father Raes had given him only hours ago. Years ago. Moon unfolded the blue-tinted stationery and began to read Delly's last words to him. The paper was wrinkled, the ink stained with her tears. It was hard reading.

Very hard.

CHAPTER 11

The Burial

Scott Parris was no longer dreaming, though the setting was as unreal as the truncated roller coaster. He sat behind the steering wheel of his pickup truck. He felt lightheaded . . . giddy. Like a small boy in church who has thought of something terribly funny . . . and is terrified that he may laugh out loud during the grown-up congregation's most solemn prayers. And be humiliated.

This was, after all, a dark comedy.

While Daisy Perika followed as a passenger in the priest's black automobile, the *matukach* lawman drove his groaning pickup truck over ruts and ridges . . . into the yawning mouth of *Cañon del Espiritu*. And was swallowed up.

Charlie Moon sat beside him, his face chiseled from dusky granite. Looking centuries older than his years. The Ute cradled the blanket-shrouded body of Delly Sands in his arms . . . like a loving father might hold his sleeping infant.

343

Her face was so childlike . . . so divinely serene . . . as she slept that endless sleep.

There was a certain kind of bittersweet madness about this . . . an insanity bordering on wisdom. Crazy notions flitted like butterflies through Scott Parris' mind. *Nobody's wearing a seat belt . . . what if I hit a big bump . . . and bounce the truck too hard . . . and the doors come open. And we all fall out . . . me . . . and Charlie Moon . . . and the dead girl in the blanket. What then? Must get hold of myself.* "God help me," the white man muttered, gripping the wheel all the more tightly. "God help us all."

Father Raes Delfino followed the twin billows of dust kicked up by the tires of Scott Parris' pickup truck. He wanted to say something to comfort the old Ute woman who sat beside him, but could think of nothing.

It was Daisy who spoke. "Bein' a priest and all—I expect you know God pretty well."

Father Raes felt his stomach knot. He knew what was coming. One of Daisy Perika's annoying, unanswerable theological questions. Designed to make the parish priest look foolish. She entertained herself in this manner. The old woman was worse than a Pharisee. But there was no escape. The driver resigned himself to suffer yet another outrage; he smiled thinly. "We're on speaking terms."

Daisy took a deep breath. "If a person does something that was meant to be helpful . . . but then it turns out bad . . . does God make allowances?"

The Jesuit was astonished. But Daisy Perika was always capable of surprising him. He would not have suspected that this sly old Ute woman would ask such a meaningful question. Or that she was capable of feeling guilt. A scholar at heart, he considered his response carefully. "Daisy, God always understands our motives. And our Father in Heaven never ceases to love us. If you confess your sins honestly and—"

"You mean I got to come to Confession? And tell you everything I've done?"

"God forbid," he muttered to himself. He shifted to Low and heard the worn engine growl a clattering complaint. It occurred to the priest that this desolate place was a long way from the Vatican. "It is not absolutely necessary for you to participate in a formal Confession unless you feel . . . compelled to do so." The Catholic priest felt himself blush. "I feel sure that your personal confession and prayer will suffice." When there was no response, he glanced at his passenger.

The shaman's head was bowed, her lips moved silently.

Scott Parris marveled at his ability to adapt. But he had not done it alone. His urgent prayer had been answered. The answer was in this place . . . *was* this place. Inside this silent, ageless canyon, bathed in the cool shadows of these towering walls, there was a sense that the most fantastic things were permissible . . . even mandatory. After he had driven less than a mile along the sinuous lane, it seemed the most natural thing in the world that this old pickup truck was a rusty hearse, and that Charlie Moon—that singular pallbearer—held the shrouded corpse in his arms.

Moon grunted and nodded when they had reached the place. Parris braked the truck to a gentle stop and cut the ignition. He glanced in the rearview mirror and saw the priest's car not far behind.

Father Raes slowed, and stopped in the rutted lane. The priest hurried around his dust-caked automobile to open the door for Daisy. The Ute woman groaned as she got out, and pulled her knitted woolen shawl tightly around her shoulders. Though it was late afternoon, the air was cool. The towering sandstone walls were steep, and the canyon was narrow. At midday, the July sun had but a few hours to warm this place. Already, they were in deep shadows.

The Ute policeman, cradling the small burden in his arms,

moved away without a word. The small procession followed Charlie Moon into a side canyon that meandered for less than five hundred yards before it became a steep, boulder-strewn ascent to the top of the dry mesa. There was a place where sunlight illuminated a patch of buffalo grass. Moon laid the corpse here. He kneeled for a moment, and smoothed a tuft of Delly's black hair.

The trio of mourners stood back at a respectful distance.

Scott Parris knew not what to do. He folded his hands behind his back and waited for the slightest summons from Moon.

Daisy Perika blinked at the walls of the canyon . . . at the sky where a great boat-shaped cloud sailed eastward like a canoe on an invisible lake. Despite her mumbled confession to the Great Mysterious One, the numbing guilt remained. It went to the very marrow of her bones. Had her mad scheme to expose the witch led to this calamity? And who was the witch? Larry Sands, the priest had told her, had left the reservation. There were rumors floating around that Charlie Moon had arrested an old Shoshone man . . . and then turned him loose. And there was that blond woman who'd hurried out of the Sun Dance Lodge.

The priest bowed his head and offered a silent prayer to the Everlasting. But the church had finished its task. This final moment belonged to the Utes.

Moon stood over the blanket-wrapped corpse. He closed his eyes. It seemed that his lips moved, but they heard no words.

The mourners waited patiently.

Presently, the Ute sighed the deepest of sighs. He nodded toward his *matukach* friend. Scott Parris followed the tall man to a place that was a dozen steps up the small canyon.

There was already a tomb here. A long hollow had been filled with stones. It was not a recent burial. But there was fresh clay between the stones.

The priest glanced at Daisy Perika.

She read the question in his eyes. "It's the place where they put Charlie's mother."

Near the existing tomb, there was a deep cleft in the sandstone wall. The eternal winds had carved it into the shape of a crescent moon. It had the appearance of a cradle that might rock a child to sleep . . . when mortals were not watching. Moon began to gather slabs of reddish-brown sandstone. Parris did the same.

The priest, who had not been invited to partake in the communion of these intimate labors, understood. He kept his place by Daisy Perika, ready to comfort her. No tear found its way down the wrinkles of the old woman's face. So it seemed to Father Raes that she needed no solace from her priest.

He was mistaken.

Once a large pile of stones were deposited near the new tomb, Moon returned to Delly's body. The spot of sunshine was gradually disappearing . . . evaporating as life itself vanished into the mists. He lifted the body as if it weighed less than nothing and carried it to the cleft in the rock. He placed it gently there . . . as if slipping a sleeping child into her crib. There you are . . . sweet dreams now.

And then the task began.

Moon accepted stones offered by his friend, and placed them expertly into the wind-carved crescent. He did this work with loving care, but he did not tarry, for night was not so far away. Soon, the tomb was closed so that not the smallest rodent could enter therein. Tomorrow, he would return with clay and water from the Piedra, and seal the most minute crack. No living creature must disturb her sleep.

When the thing was accomplished, Moon walked slowly down the slope toward the priest and the old woman. Scott Parris, for reasons that he did not quite understand, remained near the crypt.

Moon nodded at the priest.

Father Raes felt insignificant in this Canyon of the Spirits . . . this great cathedral hewn by the hand of the Creator . . . Yahweh . . . The Great Mysterious One. Father Raes Delfino raised his face to the heavens. The small priest's voice was filled with power—his words boomed off the walls of stone.

"Before the mountains were brought forth,
or the land and the earth were born,
from age to age you are God.

Who can ascend the mountain of the Lord?
or may stand in his holy place?
Father, your love never fails . . .

Hear our call . . . keep us from danger.
O look upon us and be merciful, for we are wretched and alone.
See our hardship and poverty, and pardon all our sins.

Grant this through our Lord Jesus Christ, your only begotten Son,
who lives and reigns through you and the Holy Spirit,
One God, now and forever. Amen."

There was another amen—a distant rumble of summer thunder. A brisk wind moved down the canyon. It was a sweet breeze, smelling of fresh rain. It hummed its hymns among the stones. The trees lifted their arms. The little Jesuit bowed his head and prayed silently. Then, he looked toward the small congregation. "It is finished," he said simply. "Unless someone has words to say . . ."

Moon had no words.

Daisy dropped her gaze to the sandy soil under her feet.

Scott Parris remembered an odd thing. From the days of his youth. Some mischievous boys had created a small disturbance during a revival meeting at the Oak Grove Methodist Church. They had been lined up in a row. And asked by the gentle pastor to recite a verse from the Gospel. This was, of course, a task much too hard for them. Until one youth remembered the shortest verse in all of the New Testament. And perhaps, the most poignant— the words most rich with meaning. The deep sorrow of Jesus as he stood before the tomb of his friend Lazarus.

Once again, he remembered the words.

Parris stood before the tomb. He bowed his head.

"Jesus wept," he said softly.

Daisy wept.

When the thing was done, Father Raes offered the Ute woman a ride back to her trailer home near the mouth of *Cañon del Espiritu.* She declined.

Daisy Perika had unfinished business with her nephew. She stood between the solemn lawmen as Father Raes' automobile disappeared around a distant bend in the canyon. She watched until all the dust had settled. And gathered up all her courage.

She turned to her nephew and looked him square in the face.

"I'm sorry . . ." she said.

Scott Parris twisted the battered felt hat in his hands. This was family business. He took himself several steps away.

Moon had never heard his aunt admit to being sorry about anything. He put his big hand on the small woman's shoulder. "It's okay." Delly's time had come, that's all. Like the last aspen leaf of October would flutter to earth.

"I know," Daisy continued doggedly, "that you think it's all my fault . . . if I hadn't of gotten Louise-Marie to pretend she was Stella Antelope and talked Billy into leading her into the Sun Dance Lodge . . ."

Moon did not answer.

"But it isn't my fault. Louise-Marie told me herself that—" She bit her lip.

For the first time on this day, the policeman's instinct surfaced in the Ute. "What'd Louise-Marie tell you?"

The aged woman leaned on her walking stick and gazed off into the gathering mists. Should she tell Charlie Moon something he wouldn't believe? "Louise-Marie said . . . that she never went into the Sun Dance Lodge. She wasn't able to, because when she first got to the grounds—that was when she got her clothes all hung up in the gearshift. When I showed up at her car, she hadn't been there five minutes. So it couldn't of been Louise-Marie that Billy brought to the corral. It had to be . . . Stella Antelope herself." She shuddered convulsively. "What happened was . . . Old Popeye Woman . . . she got out of her grave yesterday. And came to the dance."

The Ute policeman shook his head wearily. This was just like Aunt Daisy and Louise-Marie LaForte. Rather than accept responsibility for their daft actions, they told each other impossible tales. It had not really been *they* who were responsible . . . it was some dead woman who'd climbed out of her tomb. And a little child had led his dead grandmother around the sacred circle, so that she might identify the witch who'd killed her son. But Moon could not be angry. These elderly ladies were not really liars—not in the usual sense. This was self-deception. Somehow, they managed to *believe* these impossible things. And though his aunt did not know this, Moon did not hold them responsible for the tragedy. Delly was an asthmatic. Most likely, she'd been alarmed by the appearance of Louise-Marie in her role as Old Popeye Woman. But it might have been anything that set the attack off. Despite the pain that ached in him, Moon almost smiled.

Daisy Perika noticed this almost smile. And was filled with a cold fury. She stamped her oaken walking stick into the sand. "Don't you laugh at me, Charlie Moon! Stella Antelope *did* get out of her grave," she snapped, "and she'll go back to it."

"Back where? You mean to the Sand Bowl?"

Daisy's face showed her surprise that he knew of the secret burial spot. "She has to come back," the shaman muttered doggedly. "And before it's good dark."

Moon rubbed his chin thoughtfully, "Well, she'd have headed across national forest land . . . waded Ute Creek and then Beaver Creek . . . that's about twenty miles of hard walking. And another twenty coming back." He assumed a concerned expression. "Maybe we ought to drive on up the canyon to meet her. Poor old body's gonna be plenty tired—I expect she'd appreciate a ride in Scott's pickup."

Daisy swung her walking stick and smacked her nephew sharply on the shins.

Scott Parris, who was out of earshot, darted a startled glance at them. And then turned away. This was none of his business.

Moon laughed out loud. *This* pain was a good thing. It would go away.

Daisy made a face at him.

The policeman backed out of the range of her sturdy stick. "Come to think of it," he said slyly, "we're not far from Stella's grave. I guess we better go and check on it."

The old Ute shaman shook her head. "No. That wouldn't be a good thing to do."

Moon headed toward the pickup.

"I'm not going," she said flatly.

He turned and eyed his aunt. "Afraid we'll find her grave undisturbed? All the stones in place? Just like her brother left them?"

She waved the walking stick at her nephew. "You got no business going up there." The dead had their own business to attend to. The living must not mess with it.

She seemed near panic. Moon relented. He went to speak to his friend.

Parris greeted him with a nod.

"I'm going to stay here awhile," the Ute said. "Would you take my aunt home?"

"Sure. I'll come back and get you," he glanced at the graying sky, "about dark?"

"No need, pardner. I'll walk out."

Moon waited until he could no longer hear the sounds of the departing pickup echoing off the sandstone walls. Now, except for the ghosts that were supposed to inhabit this solitary place, he was quite alone. And the heavy quiet was much more than the mere absence of sound. In this place of silent echoes, the very solitude had a substance that ebbed and flowed with the shifting winds. For a moment, he felt lost in the hollow belly of *Cañon del Espiritu* . . . suspended in time.

But there was still work to be done. Private work. The Ute policeman turned, and trudged back into the small side canyon where Delly Sands' corpse rested. Near her crypt, he made a small fire of dry piñon twigs. He seated himself on an oblong boulder of sandstone. While the yellow tongues licked at the resinous branches, Moon removed Delly's note from the pocket of his worn denim jacket.

Moon knew that the Sandman knew a bit of Delly's story . . . and Dr. Winston Steele. And Red Heel, of course. But aside from himself . . . and Delly's spirit . . . perhaps only the priest knew the whole tale. Two years earlier, she'd learned that she had a disease. A malignancy that grew in the depths of her body . . . in the very marrow of her bones. Dr. Winston Steele—the *matukach* Sun-Dancer and her brother's friend—had been her physician. And more. She'd had radiation therapy. For a while—along with the mind-numbing fear of imminent death—the pain had gone away. But after a time . . . the dark pain had returned. Then, she had submitted to several sessions of chemotherapy. There had been another remission of symptoms, but her hair had fallen out. And she'd lost twenty pounds. This was why she was so thin, and why her hair was short. Moon recalled Myra Cornstone's observation at the church play . . . she'd said Delly Sands looked too thin . . . like she'd been sick. But he'd dismissed the remark.

The chemotherapy had barely held the disease in check. Delly, desperate for relief from this assault, had turned away from conventional medicine. The young woman had remembered the stories of healings she'd heard from her father, who had firmly believed in the power of the Sun Dance. Spectators, more often than the dancers themselves, were healed. She began to attend Sun Dances with her brother and Dr. Steele. She had shared her secret hope with no one. The first two or three dances had been disappointments. It was at the Shoshone dance last year—when she'd had so little hair left that she'd worn a wig—that opportunity had, quite literally, fallen from the sky. Wandering away from the Sun Dance Lodge, she had found a small owl. Freshly dead. It was at this moment that she remembered an obscure piece of Sun Dance lore from her father's mouth. There were ways . . . insidious ways to steal the power of the dancer. Delly had wavered. This was a terrible thing even to consider—her father would have considered it to be the worst sort of witchcraft. But she was without hope . . . terribly desperate. For a moment, she seemed to float above her own body . . . it was as if she watched herself kneel by the corpse of the owl . . . and remove a single feather from its wing.

Delly had walked back to the sacred circle. With the small feather in her hand. She had stared at it, turning it between her fingers. Such a small, inconsequential thing . . . how could there be any power in it? An old-fashioned superstition. She practically heard the voice of Father Raes Delfino whisper in her ear. It was almost amusing, she had thought, how her conscience seemed to take on the form and voice of the Jesuit priest. This is what the voice had said: *"There are powers that heal and those which destroy . . . there are powers that should not be invoked."*

Delly had ignored the small voice.

She turned, instead, to reason.

And this was her reasoning: This world is a hard place, and cruel. When circumstances become desperate, when conventional solutions fail, you do what you must to take care of yourself. This was *natural* law.

The whispering voice had persisted. It protested: *"This is unlawful . . ."*

"Shut up," she'd said aloud.

The voice was stilled.

When you were in great need, she'd told herself, you had a *right* to take that which would preserve your life. Yes. She would reach out and *take* it. If a Sun-Dancer had his vision, it couldn't hurt to try. A strong man could surely spare a little of his Power to one in such great need. So she'd placed the small feather in the band of her straw hat. And searched among the pebbles until she found a razor-sharp sliver of gray flint. Almost immediately, she had felt a surge of strength course through her frail body. She'd set her face toward the sacred place where men volunteered to suffer . . . all for a taste of the Power.

It was a dangerous act. But so simple. She entered the brush corral and waited patiently. Almost as if it was foreordained, a dancer fell into a trancelike state. She closed her eyes and gritted her teeth . . . and made the painful wound in her flesh.

The blue-armed dancer had immediately smelled the fresh blood.

His eyes had searched the Sun Dance Lodge for the source of this offending odor. Though Delly's heart pounded under her ribs, her courage did not fail. When he faced her, she had simply taken off her straw hat. And rubbed the gray owl feather. And repeated the cryptic Ute words she'd heard from her father's lips. Calling the owl from his nest in Lower World. And she'd felt the Power flow through her bones like liquid fire!

Even before the blue-armed warrior staggered and fell, she had hurried away from the corral—exultant in her renewed health. As she waited in Steele's Cadillac, Delly had felt a flood of strength and confidence welling up inside. That night, the long ride back to Denver with her brother and the physician had been odd. Usually, they talked about nothing except the dance. But on this evening they talked about baseball. About investing in real estate. About the Sandman's plans for medical school. Hardly a word about the dance. The physician, because of her delicate state of health, had thought it best that she not hear of the tragedy. Winston Steele, who firmly believed in the mind-body connection to healing, preferred to keep death far from her thoughts. The Sandman, who saw no point in dwelling on the death of the

Shoshone dancer, had agreed to shield his sister from this corrosive knowledge.

And for months, she prospered.

But upon a gray morning in late November, Doubt and Fear returned. Now inseparable companions, they walked hand-in-hand. These grim twins were her silent company at breakfast, the numbing coldness in her groin—they composed the somber orchestras of her dreams. They accompanied her to University Hospital, where lymph nodes were removed and analyzed. The pain increased. Dr. Steele prescribed a new course of chemotherapy. Again, tufts of hair came loose from her scalp. The nausea was terrible. Symptoms of the disease retreated, but the Twins stayed on. They gathered their strength at night, as she lay in her small bed, desiring untroubled sleep above all things. Doubt sat heavily on her chest . . . Fear muttered in her ear and said this:

The malignant cells are not defeated . . . they hide in the marrow of your bones . . . waiting for a sign of weakness . . . biding their time for that final assault on your frail body.

But the young woman was not weak. She was a fighter . . . determined to live. In the bright light of noonday, in the shadows of midnight, she resisted.

When Fear and Doubt whispered to her, she shouted back.

"Get away from me, you stinking bastards. You're wrong . . . I am going to live."

The Twins answered:

"You will surely die."

"Watch me . . . and see."

This is how she survived the long, cruel months of winter. Holding on until summer would warm her bones. She came to Ignacio not to visit her brother but to draw sustenance from among the strongest of her people. She came to steal strength from those who danced thirsty on Sleeping Ute Mountain. There had been no need to alter the simple method that had worked so well at the Shoshone dance. How had she done it?

Charlie Moon remembered the bitter words in her letter.

By the pricking of my thumbs.

She had pierced her flesh with the pointed tip of a nail file.

Hooper Antelope—like the blue-armed Shoshone Sun-Dancer—had immediately smelled the odor of fresh human blood. When the old man had faced her, she'd looked him straight in the eye. Brazen as brass, she'd rubbed the owl feather she kept in her hat band . . . and said the secret words . . . and seen the expression of horror creep over his face.

And then she'd heard it.

The beating of the owl's wings. Delly had recognized the certain omen of death . . . *her* death, she thought. Just recompense for her sins . . .

But it was Hooper Antelope who had died.

She'd been stunned . . . horrified at the deadly consequences of her actions. Delly had meant to divert only a portion of the power he'd encountered in his vision.

But the owl had come for the old man who danced.

When Winston Steele had attempted to revive the fallen man, she'd hoped . . . prayed . . . that he would succeed.

But it was too late.

At first, she'd had no doubt that Hooper was dead because of the blood pricked from her thumb . . . and the owl feather. But Dr. Steele had pronounced the death to be of natural causes. Heat stroke. And he was a competent physician, wasn't he? He ought to know why the old man was dead. And the medical examiner had found nothing to challenge Steele's diagnosis. So for a while, she'd been able to dismiss responsibility for this unfortunate outcome.

Once again, Delly had felt new strength in her limbs. She

was certain that the malignant cells in her marrow were perishing. The sweetness of life was returning to her body.

But in spite of this, a dark uncertainty haunted her.

The old Shoshone man, the one called Red Heel, had been at the Ute Mountain dance. Pretending not to notice her . . . and watching her every move through his little snakelike eyes. He looked so familiar. She'd seen him somewhere . . .

Later, Delly had realized that the snapping sound she'd heard had been his air gun . . . the launching of the dead man's bone. It had missed her face by inches. That might have been the end of it, but the Shoshone elder was a persistent man. On the second occasion, in the darkened parking lot, his aim had been true. If the fragment of bone had not been removed within the hour, she would surely have died.

Delly had called a Shoshone friend in Wyoming. It was a small community . . . the man called Red Heel was well known. The tribal elder was a former Sun Dance chief. And the devoted uncle of the blue-armed dancer. The man she'd stolen the Power from in last year's Sun Dance. She'd learned her victim's name. The blue-armed dancer was Joseph Sparrow. But the news that galvanized the young woman was this: Red Heel's nephew had died at that Sun Dance. Like Hooper Antelope, he was . . . no more.

The Shoshone elder must have seen her rub the owl feather . . . steal the Power from his nephew. Maybe he'd guessed she would be at the Ute Mountain Lodge, where her brother and the white man were dancing. Or maybe the old man was attending all of the Sun Dances this year, searching for the woman with the owl feather in her hat band. But whatever had driven him south, Red Heel had come. If the Shoshone elder had harbored any doubt of her guilt, this would have been cast aside when he'd seen her rubbing the owl feather . . . stealing the Power from Hooper Antelope.

In her soul, Delly Sands was certain. She was responsible for the death of two men, and Old Popeye Woman. It had become impossible to dismiss the responsibility for what she'd done. On the brightest day, guilt hung over her like a fog. In the far reaches of that mist, Death waited until the appointed time. She knew not how the end would come. But it was over. The beating of the owl's wings had not been for Hooper Antelope alone.

She was weary of the struggle. The end, when it came, would be welcome.

The disease that slept within her bones could awaken . . . and end her life.

So be it.

The Shoshone elder might yet destroy her.

Let him come.

But first must come confession.

And, God willing . . . a cleansing.

On that night while Moon watched her apartment, Delly had called her brother. Larry Sands had hurried to visit his sister. And brought the *matukach* physician with him. The young woman had revealed her attempts at vision theft. And her intent to publish a story in the *Drum*. A full confession, before all the People. This would erase at least some of her guilt.

The Sandman had been stunned. At first, he sat and stared unbelievingly at his little sister. This must be some kind of sick joke.

Winston Steele seemed less surprised at the revelation; perhaps he had suspected her all along. The physician had counseled prudence. Let's think about this for a while. It was not clear to what extent—if any—that she was actually responsible for the deaths of the Sun-Dancers. Perhaps it would be best to let the secret rest. Don't do anything hasty.

She had not relented.

Her brother had finally found his voice. Sensing the gravity of the situation, he managed to make his point with a measure of calmness. Delly would be a fool to tell such a crazy tale—she would be ruined in Ignacio.

She was, Delly had replied calmly, already ruined.

Larry Sands played the family card. What of *his* place in this community? How could he ever dance thirsty again, if people learned that his little sister had played at witchcraft like some silly schoolgirl? No good would come of making admissions, he promised.

Her response was a stubborn silence.

His pleading useless, he screamed. And threatened. She had asked him to leave, and Dr. Steele had taken the Sandman away.

Delly Sands had penned her final testament after the men had left her apartment. One epistle to the priest. Another for Charlie Moon.

Red Heel's bitter tale about Delly Sands had been—as far as it went—a true account.

The Shoshone elder's tale had begun at the Wind River Sun Dance the previous summer. He had seen his nephew—interrupted from his vision—pause and stare in the general direction of the young woman who had the large straw hat in her lap. Red Heel had not actually seen her do anything provocative. But after his nephew's death, he had asked around. Quietly. And learned who she was—the sister of the young Ute dancer who was called Sandman. And then he had remembered something that seemed insignificant at the time . . . the small feather in her hat band. It might be merely an ornament, of course. But what if it was not? Red Heel was almost certain of her guilt. As the final act of his life on this earth, he would make sure that this Ute woman—if she was indeed a witch—would never again harm a Sun-Dancer. To this end, he had taken a great personal risk. The Shoshone elder had made a long trek into the desert. To a secret place known to him since his youth. Against all his instincts, he had opened an ancient burial. Not to rob it of artifacts . . . but to obtain the most powerful kind of dead man's bone.

January had come upon winds that screamed for revenge. Wading snowdrifts up to his knees, the old man had visited his nephew's grave on the barren prairie. He'd stood by the river called Popo Agie—a snake of blue ice—and made his promise. In March, he fashioned his first cylindrical pellets of bone. And polished them to fit snugly in the breech of his air pistol.

Through the frigid Wyoming springtime, he had waited and made his plans. In May, the snows finally melted and the earth softened. His heart did not.

She had not returned to the Shoshone Sun Dance this summer. He'd made the journey to other dances. Up to the rolling hills of the Dakotas. Over to the deserts of Utah. Neither had he seen her in these places. The old man grew weary of his travels. But the dances at the two Ute reservations in Colorado were yet to come. So he'd made a telephone call to Towaoc and gossiped with Poker Martinez, chief of the dance. How was the Ute Mountain Sun Dance coming along? Did they have many good dancers this summer? Among other things, he'd learned that Delly's brother would dance on Sleeping Ute Mountain and also on the Southern Ute reservation. So perhaps the young Ute woman would also be there. Red Heel had driven hundreds of miles south to attend the dance on the great mountain. As he'd hoped, the young woman showed up.

With the same straw hat . . . and the small feather was still in the band.

In fact, there were *two* feathers now. The old Shoshone had watched her every move, breathed every breath she breathed. And then that weary old Ute dancer had stood so long before the sacred tree . . . and approached the lands where visions were. All eyes except Red Heel's were on the dancer. The Shoshone had watched in horror as the young woman drew blood from her thumbs. Blood for the dancer to smell. And when she took off her hat, he was certain. No, there could be no doubt about who'd killed his nephew. His trembling hand had found the air pistol hidden under a blanket in his lap. He'd aimed. As her finger moved to rub the warm owl feather, his finger tightened on the cold steel of the trigger. There was a snapping sound as he shot the bone at her. But the witch did not flinch.

May his soul be forgiven—he had missed!

Because his old hand was not so steady anymore, another dancer had fallen under the spell of this witch who wore the innocent face of a child.

But this was only a setback. Red Heel's determination to destroy the witch was only increased by his failure—and his certain knowledge of her guilt.

The Shoshone elder had left a message on Delly Sands' desk at the *Drum* offices. To lure her to the Sky Ute Lodge restaurant. That night in the motel parking lot, the old Shoshone had used lead pellets to shatter the electric lamps in the streetlights. He had hidden in the darkness and waited. Red Heel had shot at Delly again . . . and this time he had not missed. But, to his amazement, she had not died. This witch, he concluded, had accumulated great powers. For whatever dark reason, the dead man's bone was useless against her. The old man had turned to other means. In a final act of desperation, he'd killed an owl with his air pistol and was stuffing the feathers in Delly's old car at the Sun Dance grounds when Scott Parris had interrupted him. Red Heel had thought he knew the whole story. But the Shoshone elder—though he'd taken on the job of preventing a witch from destroying other Sun-Dancers—was like other men. He'd known only a portion of the truth.

The Ute policeman took one final look at Delly Sands' note. Among her words, was this farewell . . .

GOODBYE CHARLIE MOON.
I'LL MISS YOU MOST OF ALL

Moon closed his eyes; he crumpled the papers in his hand. And made an offering to the flames of the small fire. Now, her dark secret . . . her bright spirit . . . drifted upward with the sparks . . . toward the heavens.

Charlie Moon, hollow and cold to the core, trudged down a rocky incline toward the dirt lane in the floor of *Cañon del Espiritu*. It was the Ute's intention to turn toward the mouth of the canyon. After an easy hour's walk, he'd be at Aunt Daisy's home. And have some supper. Visit with his aunt . . . talk with his friend Scott Parris, who waited there. And in this modest way, take up his life again.

But when he reached the little road at the bottom of *Cañon del Espiritu* . . . such a queer thing happened

Quite without consciously willing it, Charlie Moon turned away from the mouth of the canyon. Away from the path that led to the bright, open spaces. He set his face toward the gathering darkness between the steep walls. It was as if some deep part of his mind—that place where dreams and nightmares are born—had taken control of his legs. The Ute policeman was at first surprised, then somewhat bemused by this phenomenon . . . but he thought he knew where his legs were taking him.

And decided to go along for the ride.

And so he walked. Between towering walls of sandstone stained with rusty streaks from rainwater that spilled over from the mesas. Among the thickets of piñon and juniper. Upon dusty deer paths that meandered through fragrant sage and scarlet tufts of Apache plume. Along the rocky bed of a small stream that was almost dry.

Deeper into the Canyon of the Spirits, where gray twilight was entwined with swirling blue mists.

As Charlie Moon approached that wind-sculpted formation called the Sand Bowl, he walked upon soft gray limestone—the very bedrock of the land. At the edge of the oval depression, he took a step onto the sand . . . and paused.

One foot on the solid rock, another on the shifting grains.

The tall man's long shadow pointed like a dark finger across the expanse of sand. Toward that distant pockmarked wall. Honeycombed by the winds of eons into a multitude of fantastic catacombs. Toward the very spot where Reuben Antelope had placed his sister's body in a small cavern. And sealed Old Popeye Woman behind the sturdy wall of stones and clay.

The story, written clearly, was a simple one for the Ute to read.

The stones that Reuben Antelope had placed so carefully had been removed. They were scattered before the tomb . . . strewn across the sands. Even at this distance, it was obvious that the crypt was empty. Had some artifact hunter, mistaking Stella Antelope's resting place for a Stone Age burial, broken into the crypt in search of artifacts? The policeman's immediate instinct was overwhelming—it was his duty to arrest the vandal who'd committed this sacrilege. The empty tomb must be examined for any hint of the identity of the intruder. There might still be footprints in the sand . . .

But he did not move. The long legs that had so blithely brought him to this mysterious place . . . now these strong limbs of sinew and muscle and bone were planted like posts. He could have willed them to move, but he did not. Moon stood there, staring at the distant crypt.

There were reasons for his hesitation.

First, there *were* prints in the sand. A single set of footprints. Leading in a very straight, purposeful line. Across the sands they came, ending on a cluster of black pebbles near the jutting shelf of limestone. Not two yards from the spot where the policeman stood. This, in itself, was not queer. *This* was queer: there were no footprints heading *toward* the crypt.

Now Charlie Moon was not a man easily diverted from the path of common sense. There must, he reasoned, be a commonplace explanation for this phenomenon. His mind raced, searching for answers. Almost immediately, he had a solution to the dilemma. Since the tumult in the Sun Dance Lodge last night, Reuben Antelope and the little boy had disappeared. Horace claimed he didn't know where his father had taken Billy. Or when they would return. But because of the scandalous events at the dance, Reuben must have removed his sister's body from the tomb. Of course. By now, Stella was safely buried in another place. Some truly secret place.

But why was there only one set of prints . . . leading *away* from the disturbed burial chamber? Nature, the Ute knew, created its own sly illusions. Most likely, a strong wind had come up while Reuben was prying the stones from his sister's tomb. The footprints he'd made when approaching the grave site would have been swept away. But the winds had died before he departed with his burden . . . and they had been still since then. A simple explanation for the single set of footprints that left the tomb. No magic was required.

This should have been the end of it.

But to his left, not five yards away, he saw it. Neatly folded, hanging in the crotch of a dead piñon.

It was a blanket.

Dark blue.

With broad red zigzags.

Lightning in a midnight sky.

Moon's mouth was suddenly dry as the sands. Reuben Antelope might well have taken his sister's body away for reburial. But it was unthinkable that the old Ute would have removed the blanket from her corpse.

The policeman moved closer to the prints in the sand, and kneeled. And felt a chill ripple along his spine. There had been some wind since even these footprints were made. The edges were softened . . . blurred. But these were not the marks of Reuben Antelope's big boots. They were small prints. Of bare feet. And one foot was terribly misshapen . . . there was a barely visible mark in the sand behind it. The lame foot had been dragged.

The Ute policeman got to his feet, and backed away . . . off these sands. He placed both boots upon the solid foundation of stone. But it seemed that even the bedrock was shifting under him . . .

Now his very thoughts zigzaged, like the symbolic lightning on Stella's burial blanket.

This proposition drummed in his head: *Dead bodies do not get up and walk away*. He was very nearly certain of this. Somewhere, in a great volume, was there not a Law written down to prohibit such things?

But he'd seen the peculiar prints plainly enough. These were real.

They could have been faked, of course. But why . . . and by whom? Could this be a part of Daisy's zany scheme? Maybe, all along, she'd hoped he'd come to this place. By her mumblings about Stella's body returning before dark, she'd practically suggested it. The policeman wanted to believe this. But he knew his Aunt Daisy well. Her mind did take some strange twists, but they were always characteristic of her. She would never be involved in moving a corpse. No . . . this was not her doing.

He stood there until the darkness began to flow like brackish water into the depths of the canyon. Now it was difficult to see the prints. The discarded blanket was a dark, funereal pennant hanging in the crotch of the tree. The empty tomb was a black, slitted eye in the pockmarked face of the canyon. Staring at the policeman.

Winking at him?

As if on some cosmic cue, the orchestra of night began to tune its discordant instruments. The Mormon crickets scraped their black, sawtooth legs together . . . the dry breeze rattled the leathery leaves of scrub oak . . . a swift bat flitted by, beaming its ultrasound radar at the unwary yucca moth . . . tiny nocturnal rodents squeaked and scampered among the grasses as they began their anxious search for food.

These were not the only sounds that disturbed the vast stillness of the Canyon of the Spirits.

The Ute's hearing was keen.

His skin prickled.

Some distance away, crunching in the dry grass, moving among the loose stones . . . footsteps. Soft footsteps . . . a short and a long . . . one foot dragging? The searching, pecking sound of . . . a wooden cane clicking on the stones?

No, the rational part of his mind said. *This cannot be.*

But another voice whispered to his soul: *Take your leave from the Canyon of the Spirits. On such a night as this . . . you do not belong here.*

But such a rare opportunity this was. To know the truth, all he had to do was . . . to be still. Charlie Moon could wait . . . and see . . . if in this vast, unfathomable universe there were such singular things as old women whose corpses walked upon the earth. This was what Aunt Daisy believed. If it was true, Stella Antelope would soon be here. Old Popeye Woman would once again take up her blanket. Leaning her dead weight against the striped cane, she would drag her malformed foot across the sands. And she would return to the tomb her brother had prepared for her.

And there drift off to sleep that final sleep?

To know the answer . . . all he need do was abide here for a moment . . . among the gathering shadows.

So straightforward a task it was.

So convoluted in its implications.

But a decision must be made.

And soon.

For it—whatever *it* was—was drawing nearer. The footsteps were more distinct now. That patient pecking . . . that rhythmic tapping . . . that rapping, snapping . . . echoing off the canyon walls. The blind woman's striped cane?

Charlie Moon confronted his fears directly. And honestly. Did the very thought of Old Popeye Woman's dead body . . . the possibility of its purposeful locomotion along the floor of *Cañon del Espíritu* . . . did this notion cause him to shiver . . . just a little? Well, he admitted . . . yes, it did. Hidden within the heart of every man is that small boy who shudders at those dread things who shuffle among the shadows.

But Moon was not—in the ordinary sense—afraid. He was afraid in the extraordinary sense. The man was filled with unanswered questions. And approaching now—though unbidden—might be the answer to a fundamental question. Perhaps all his questions. And though he did not understand why, this he did fear—an encounter with the unequivocal Answer.

Soon he would have a visitor. Perhaps nothing more than a lame hiker with a freshly cut walking stick.

Or perhaps . . . not.

Should he remain in this place . . . and see who would come? Charlie Moon filled his lungs with the scented breath of the canyon. For an eternal moment, he hesitated. On this night, in this place, he was an intruder. An outsider. Despite his wish to be deaf to this sinister approach, he listened intently. It was as if the ordinary creatures of night also paused and cocked their ears. Now all was silent—except for . . .

> A soft pad-padding . . . bare feet treading
> encoded footsteps . . . one short . . . one long
> a hollow rapping . . . a tap-tapping
> someone who had awakened . . . and departed
> was returning . . . to sleep once more?

To know . . . to know. All he need do was tarry here . . .

But his flesh crawled as if he had worms under his skin.

Maybe a man could know too much . . .

Charlie Moon turned his back upon it all. Upon the one who approached . . . upon the oval basin of dry, shifting sands . . . the pitted walls of empty tomb. He set his face toward the mouth of the canyon.

The Ute took the first step . . . of his long walk home.

Hours ago, soft shadows had swept across the broad valley of the Pinos, preparing the way for night. Now, pine-scented breezes drifted down from the slopes of the San Juans to sweep away the latent warmth from the parched earth.

It was, for most, a summer night much like any other.

Some folk enjoyed their wholesome suppers of pinto beans and chili and corn bread. More than a few watched the flickering television screen, the window of the box wherein the beautiful people lived their glamorous lives.

A few—the very old and very young—were already in their beds.

In the modest rectory at St. Ignatius Catholic Church, this was not at all a night like other nights. Father Raes Delfino had forgotten to take his evening meal. His hands folded behind the small of his back, he treaded back and forth across the worn carpet. An old panther, he mused self-consciously. Longing for that ultimate freedom, searching out the boundaries of his cage? He paused his pacing, and attempted to stare through the rectory window.

Into the outer darkness.

Father Raes saw only his reflection in the glazing. A short, wiry man with a strong jaw. Deep-set eyes nestled under bushy brows, a square head crowned with thick iron-gray hair. Altogether, he admitted, a rather severe-looking fellow. Did his appearance intimidate the timid among his flock? Father Raes Delfino—who was not at all severe—smiled wanly and sighed deeply. So often, he mused, we are not quite as we appear to others.

The priest sat down once more at his desk, drumming his fingers on the varnished oak. He stared at the oval halo of light under the gooseneck lamp. The Jesuit had read and reread each word on the few scraps of paper he'd found in the file cabinet— that musty archive inherited from his predecessor. He touched each document . . . odd . . . now that she was dead, they felt . . . hallowed by her passing. Each surface, it seemed, had assumed the yellowed patina of a respectable age. From the church's point of view, these were the defining events of her life. The records dealt with birth . . . baptism . . . confirmation . . . and death. Sad, the celibate man thought, that the sacrament of marriage was missing from the chain. Nevertheless, the circle of her life on earth was now closed.

The meticulous cleric had searched the files to confirm a curious hunch. It was as he had suspected. "Delly" was merely a nickname. Hung on the hapless child, no doubt, for the usual reason. The three-syllable name with which she had been christened did not flow trippingly off the tongue. The priest, in the course of conducting his business, had encountered a host of superstitions nourished by those among his flock. Though some were corrosive, most were fairly harmless. Among the latter was the relatively common belief in the power of a name. This was probably why so many parents gave their children the names of saints. Certainly not a practice to be discouraged. But sometimes it went much further. Horace Antelope was infected by the notion that a person's name could even control their destiny. Like all believers in such foolishness, Horace had managed to find a few examples to prove his point. Mr. Piper was a plumber, Mr. Ashe a fireman. The priest smiled and shook his head.

But out of the mouths of babes . . . one never knew from whence may come some obscure truth.

Father Raes Delfino was cursed in this manner: he was open to all ideas—and intellectually honest to a fault. This thoughtful man was also plagued by his ability to see some merit in the most oddball viewpoint . . . of issues both lofty and mundane. And so this imaginative dreamer, this tough-minded scholar, often debated with himself.

Characteristically, it was the lonely visionary—craving the comfort of conversation—who initiated these discourses. So he began with this provocative statement:

"Is it not written:
   'A good name is to be chosen above riches'?"
   The scholar groaned. "Spare me your musty proverbs.

And more than that, do not burden me with flawed interpretations. This dictum speaks to the issue of reputation, not of the influence of a specific name. The notion of a name itself having power over the individual—like all superstitions—is nonsense. Relatively harmless nonsense," the scholar added gently, *"but nonsense all the same."*

The dreamer was silenced, but only for a moment. "Still . . . might not there be a grain of psychological truth in such beliefs?"

"No. There might not be."

The dreamer pressed the point: "Would a sensible father name his daughter Jezebel . . . would any sane mother christen her son Judas?"

"No, but these are extreme examples," the scholar parried. "In our society, such infamous names would be intolerable burdens to the child. This exaggeration proves nothing."

"I did overstate my case," the dreamer admitted, "but is it not possible that a certain name might confer subtle suggestions? Drive a person—even if unconsciously—to emulate . . . by association . . . some archetypal behavior?"

"You reach rather beyond your grasp."

"Might you not at least admit to the possibility?"

"I might," the scholar said, "but I will not. It would only encourage you in this foolishness."

The whole man, wearied of this fractured pair, dismissed scholar and dreamer alike. The priest pushed himself up from the chair. Once again, he took up his pacing.

But the question crept stealthily back into his mind—what's in a name?

This lovely young Ute woman who had attempted—perhaps even succeeded—in stealing strength from the strongest of men.

Her name was . . . Delilah.